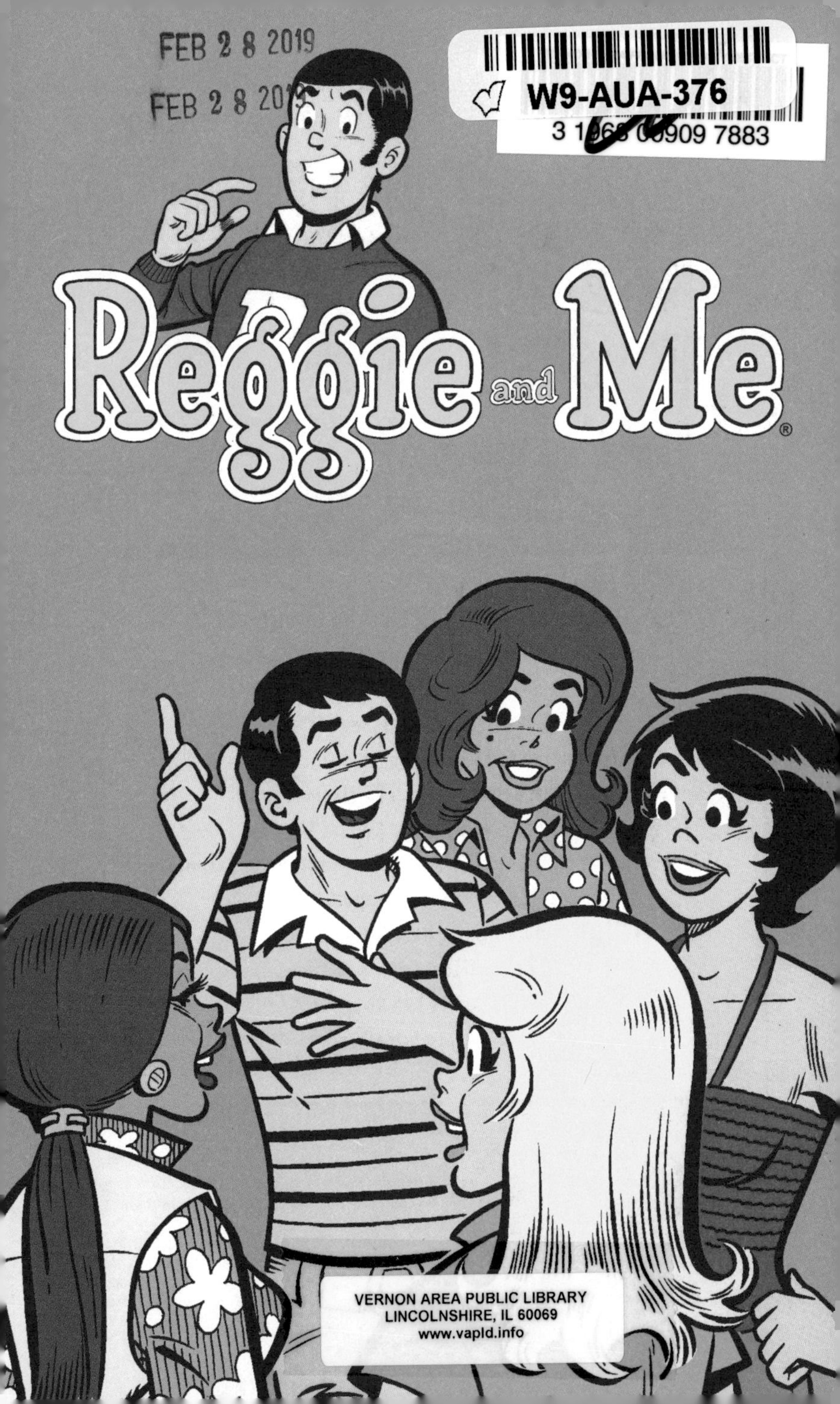
Reggie and Me®

Reggie and Me

Publisher / Co-CEO: Jon Goldwater
Co-President / Editor-In-Chief: Victor Gorelick
Co-President: Mike Pellerito
Co-President: Alex Segura
Chief Creative Officer: Roberto Aguirre-Sacasa
Chief Operating Officer: William Mooar
Chief Financial Officer: Robert Wintle
Director of Book Sales & Operations: Jonathan Betancourt
Production Manager: Stephen Oswald
Lead Designer: Kari McLachlan
Associate Editor: Carlos Antunes
Editor: Jamie Lee Rotante
Co-CEO: Nancy Silberkleit

Reggie And Me Vol. 1 © 2019 Archie Comic Publications, Inc. Archie characters
created by John L. Goldwater; the likenesses of the original Archie characters were
created by Bob Montana. The individual characters' names and likenesses are the
exclusive trademarks of Archie Comic Publications, Inc. All rights reserved. Nothing
may be reprinted in whole or part without written permission from Archie Comic
Publications, Inc. All stories previously published and copyrighted by Archie Comic
Publications, Inc. (or its predecessors) in magazine form 1966-1974.

Printed in USA. First Printing. January, 2019. ISBN: 978-1-68255-835-5

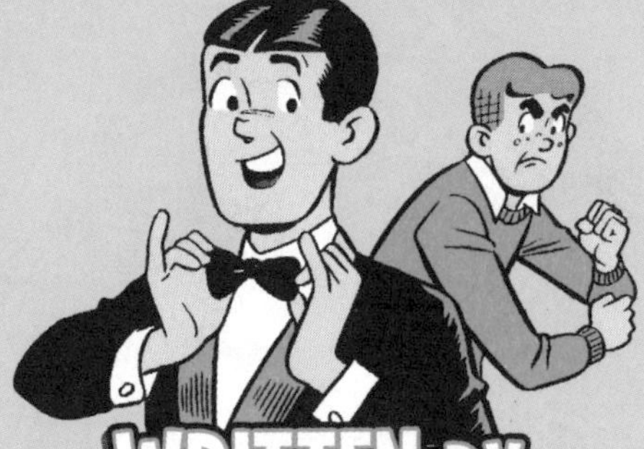

WRITTEN BY

George Gladir, Al Hartley, Frank Doyle,
Bob Bolling & Dick Malmgren

ART BY

Bill Vigoda, Al Hartley, Bob White, Bob Bolling,
Harry Lucey, Samm Schwartz, Stan Goldberg, Dick Malmgren,
Mario Acquaviva, Jon D'Agostino, Marty Epp, Henry Scarpelli,
Rudy Lapick, Bob Smith, Bill Yoshida & Barry Grossman

This book contains some material that was originally created in a less socially sensitive time in our society and reflects attitudes that may be interpreted as being unacceptable today. The stories are reprinted here without alteration for historical reference.

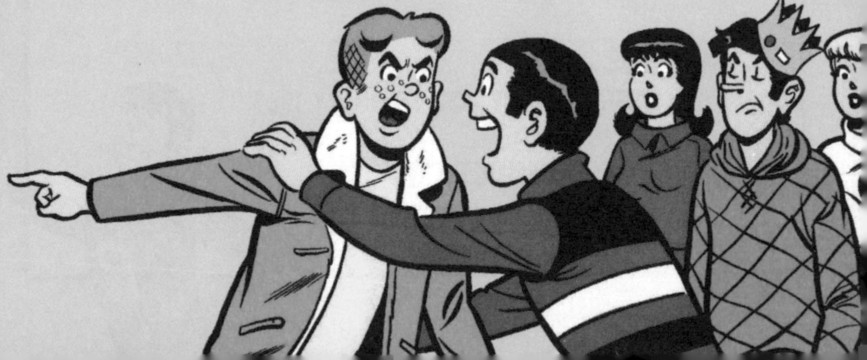

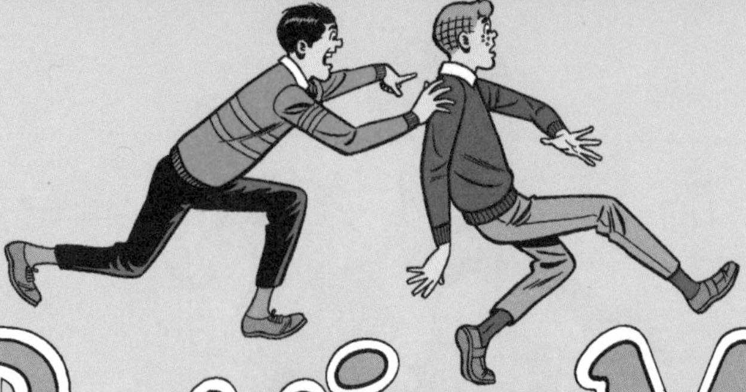

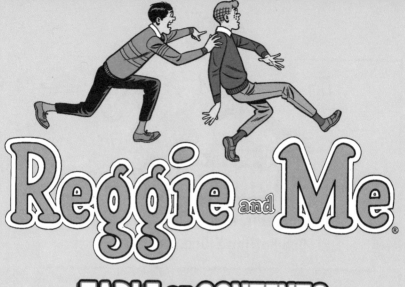

Reggie and Me®

TABLE OF CONTENTS

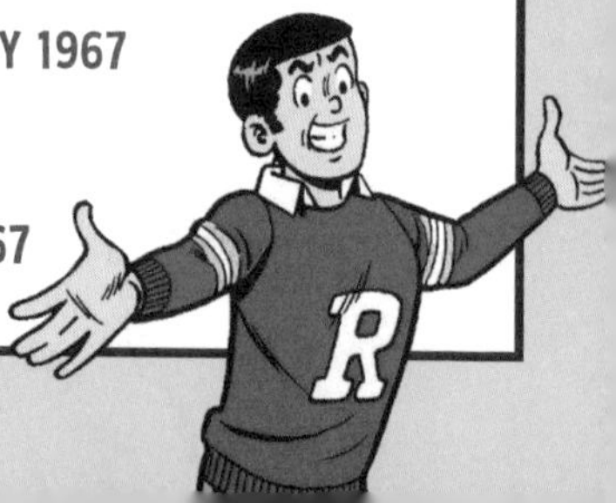

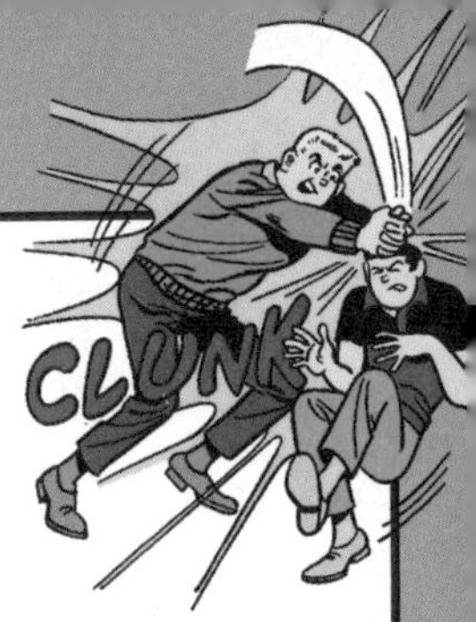
CLUNK

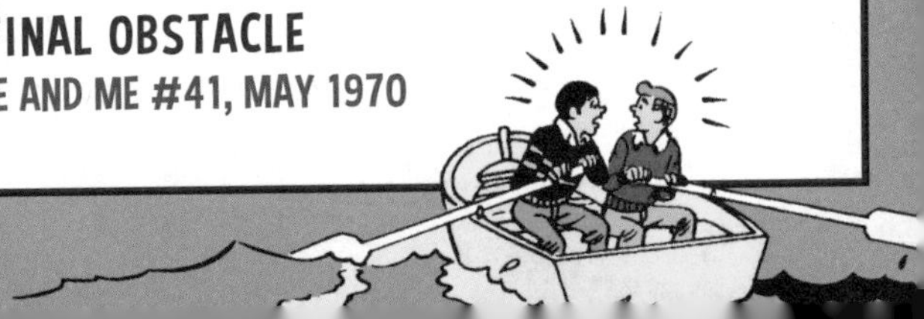

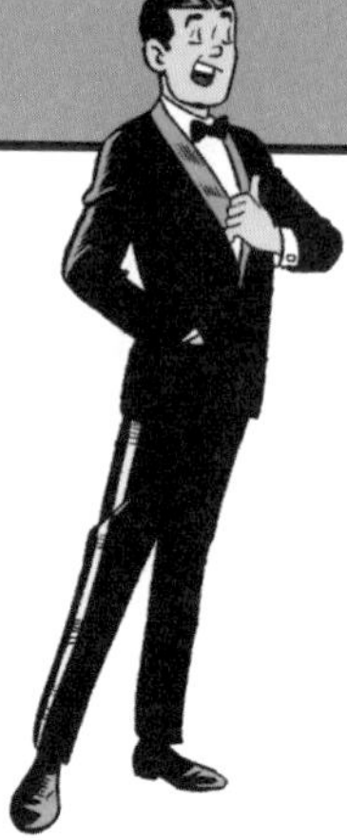

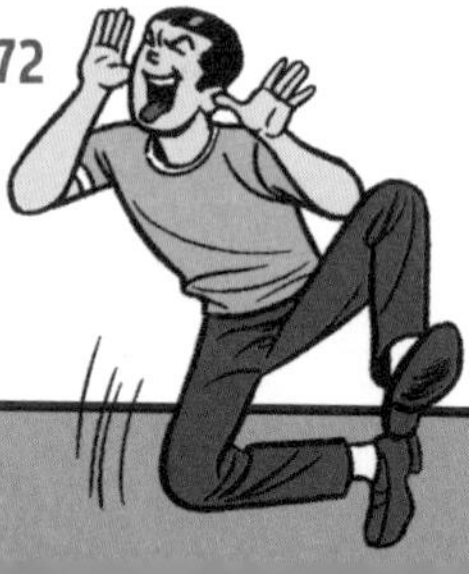

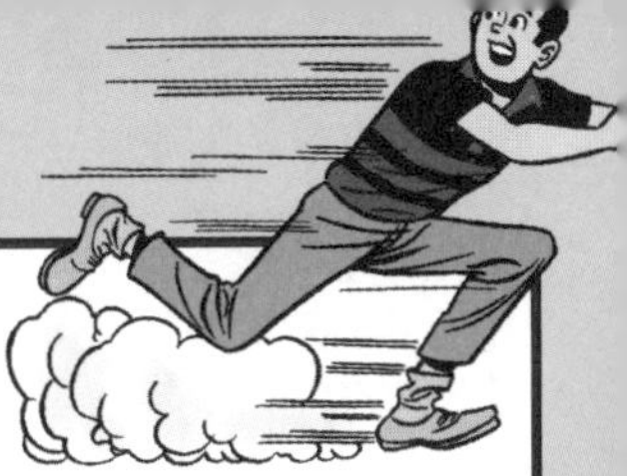

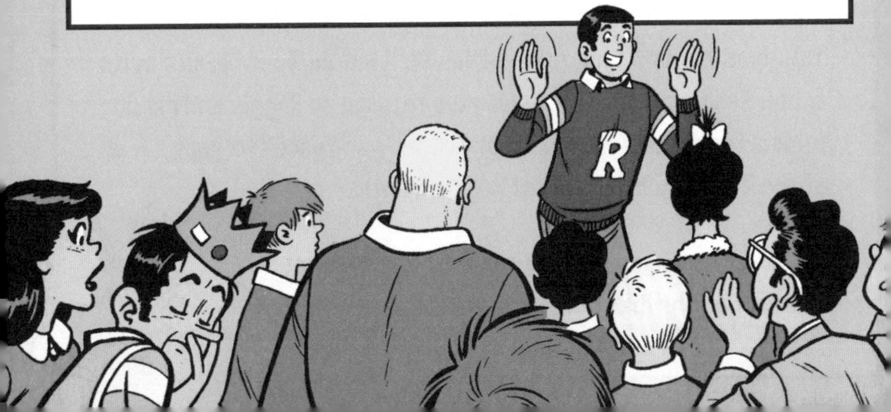

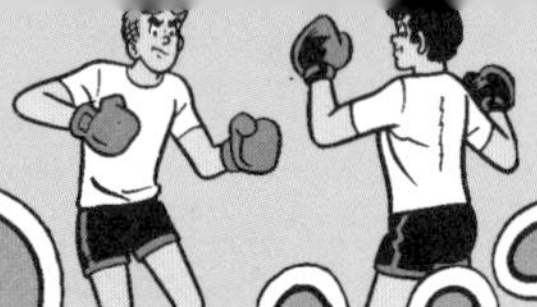

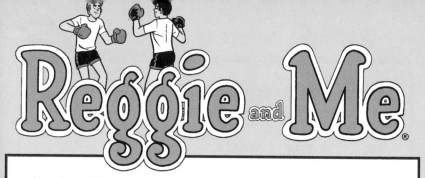

Reggie and Me

Reggie and Me was an ongoing comic book series that ran from 1966 to 1980. Reggie Mantle first appeared briefly in *Jackpot Comics* #5 (published in Spring 1942) before making a full appearance in issue #6. Reggie proved that he was a perfect foil for our red-headed hero, Archie Andrews, and was given his own series in 1950 titled *Archie's Rival, Reggie*. This series ran for fourteen issues and was later revived with the same number in 1963, but with a new name: *Reggie*. It was then changed to *Reggie and Me* beginning with issue #19 and kept that title until its end in September 1980 at issue 126—that's thirty years of everyone's favorite rival taking center-stage!

And that wasn't the end of Reggie's time in the spotlight! The *Reggie and Me* title would return two more times over the years—first as a digital-only exclusive comic written by Bill Golliher with art by Bill Galvan that featured Reggie and the "me" being his new pal: a dachshund named Runty! Then, in 2016 a reboot of *Reggie and Me* was published as part of Archie Comics' New Riverdale lineup. This was a five-issue mini-series written by Tom DeFalco with art by Sandy Jarrell. The series also focused on Reggie and his dog (now with the cool new name of "Vader") and gave everyone a look at the kinder, gentler side of Reggie Mantle.

But now it's time to enjoy some of the earliest mischief and hijinks in the original *Reggie and Me*!

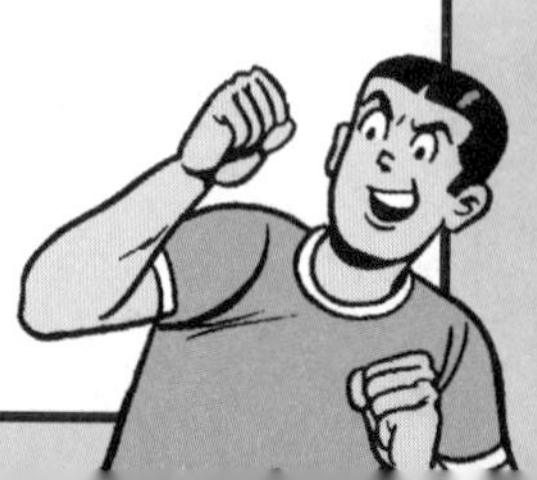

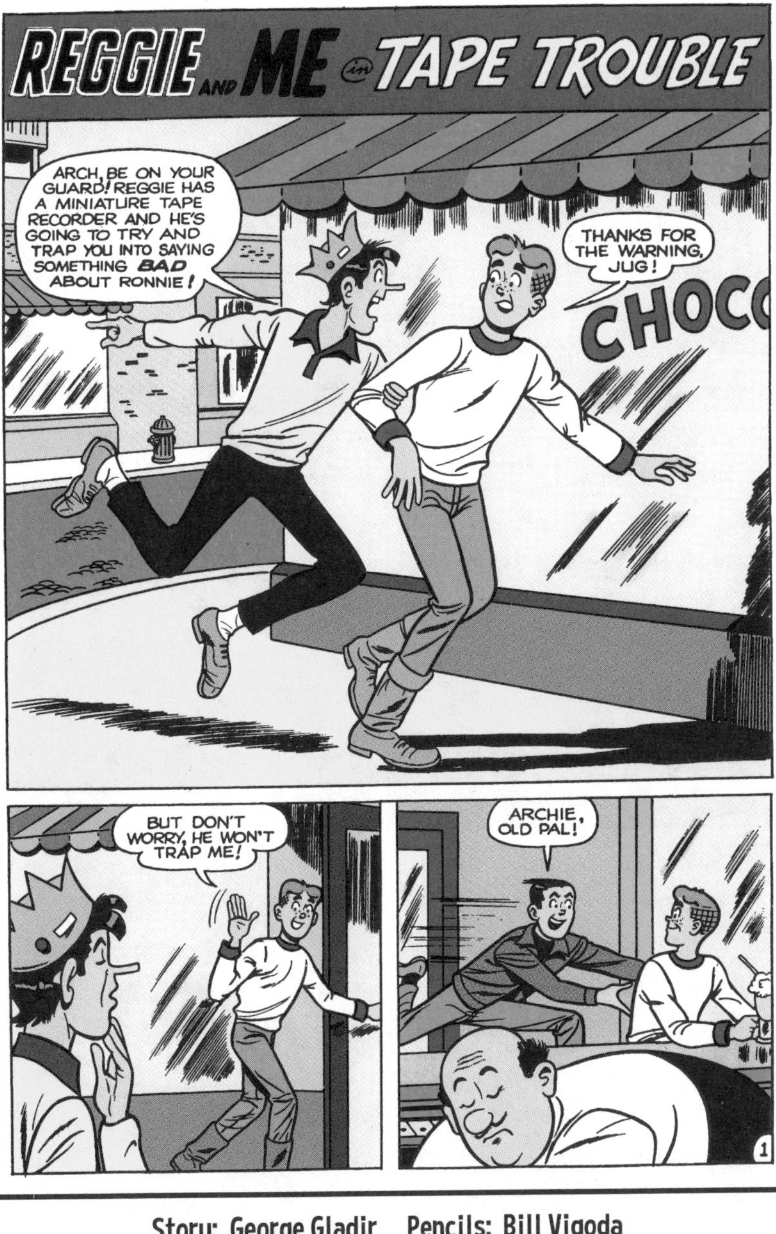
REGGIE AND ME in TAPE TROUBLE
ARCH, BE ON YOUR GUARD! REGGIE HAS A MINIATURE TAPE RECORDER AND HE'S GOING TO TRY AND TRAP YOU INTO SAYING SOMETHING BAD ABOUT RONNIE!
THANKS FOR THE WARNING, JUG!
CHOCO
BUT DON'T WORRY, HE WON'T TRAP ME!
ARCHIE, OLD PAL!
1

Story: George Gladir Pencils: Bill Vigoda
Inks & Letters: Mario Acquaviva

Originally printed in REGGIE AND ME #20, OCTOBER 1966

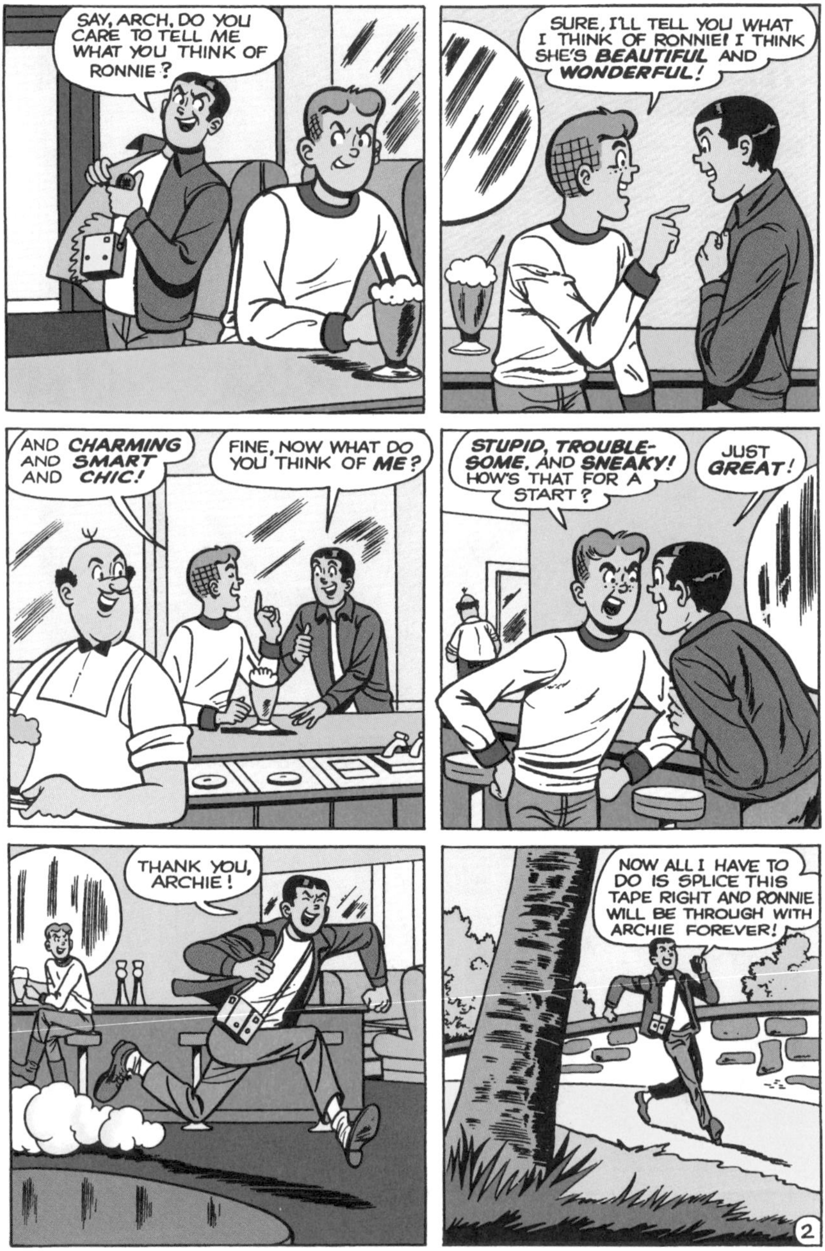
SAY, ARCH, DO YOU CARE TO TELL ME WHAT YOU THINK OF RONNIE?
SURE, I'LL TELL YOU WHAT I THINK OF RONNIE! I THINK SHE'S BEAUTIFUL AND WONDERFUL!
AND CHARMING AND SMART AND CHIC!
FINE, NOW WHAT DO YOU THINK OF ME?
STUPID, TROUBLE-SOME, AND SNEAKY! HOW'S THAT FOR A START?
JUST GREAT!
THANK YOU, ARCHIE!
NOW ALL I HAVE TO DO IS SPLICE THIS TAPE RIGHT AND RONNIE WILL BE THROUGH WITH ARCHIE FOREVER!
2

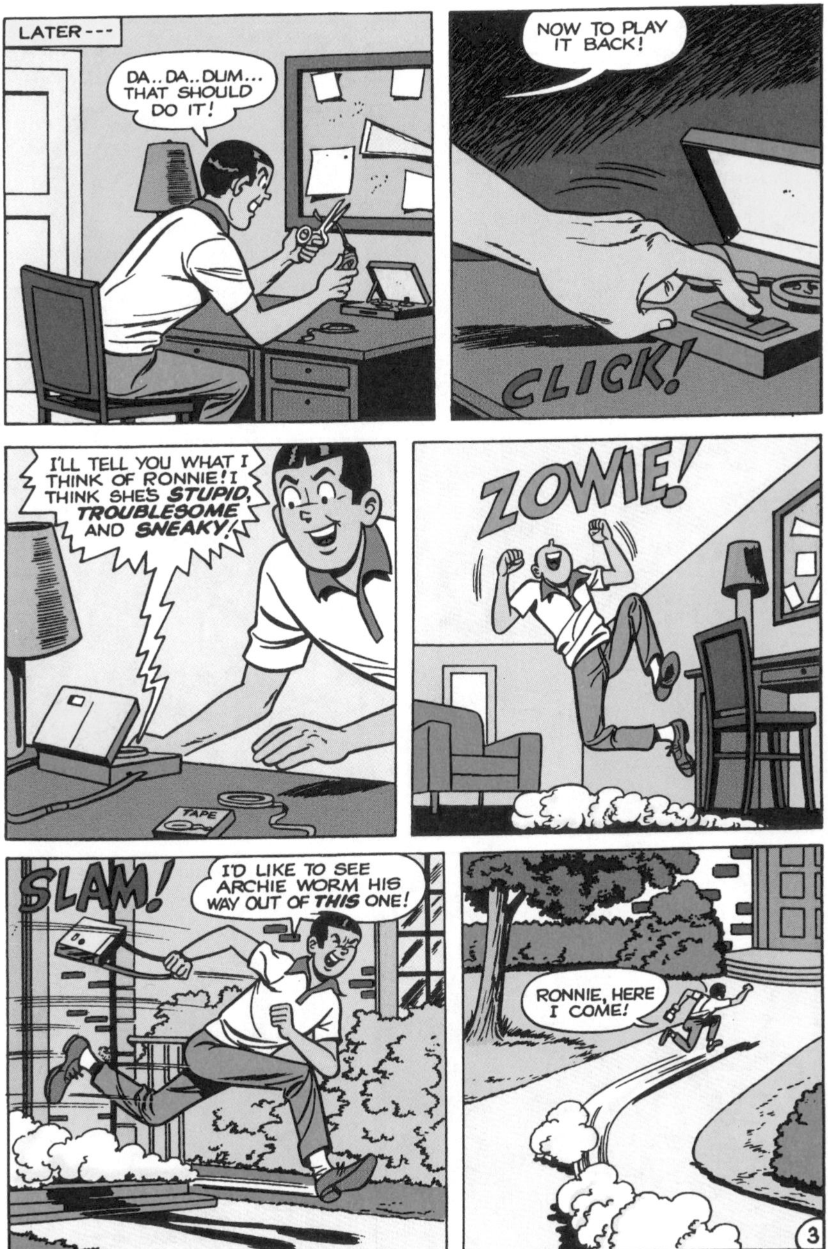
LATER---
DA..DA..DUM... THAT SHOULD DO IT!
NOW TO PLAY IT BACK!
CLICK!
I'LL TELL YOU WHAT I THINK OF RONNIE! I THINK SHE'S **STUPID, TROUBLESOME** AND **SNEAKY**!
TAPE
ZOWIE!
SLAM!
I'D LIKE TO SEE ARCHIE WORM HIS WAY OUT OF **THIS** ONE!
RONNIE, HERE I COME!
3

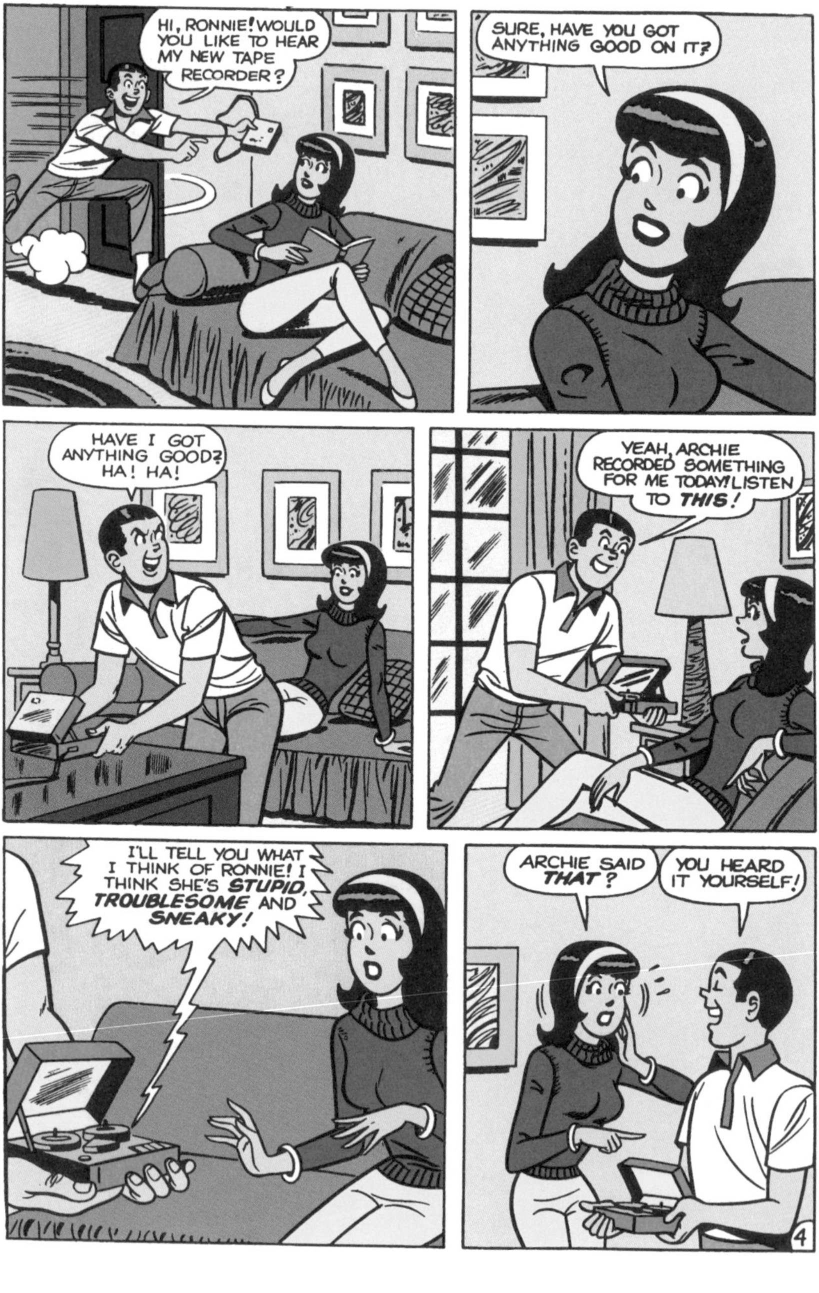
HI, RONNIE! WOULD YOU LIKE TO HEAR MY NEW TAPE RECORDER?
SURE, HAVE YOU GOT ANYTHING GOOD ON IT?
HAVE I GOT ANYTHING GOOD? HA! HA!
YEAH, ARCHIE RECORDED SOMETHING FOR ME TODAY! LISTEN TO THIS!
I'LL TELL YOU WHAT I THINK OF RONNIE! I THINK SHE'S STUPID, TROUBLESOME AND SNEAKY!
ARCHIE SAID THAT?
YOU HEARD IT YOURSELF!
4

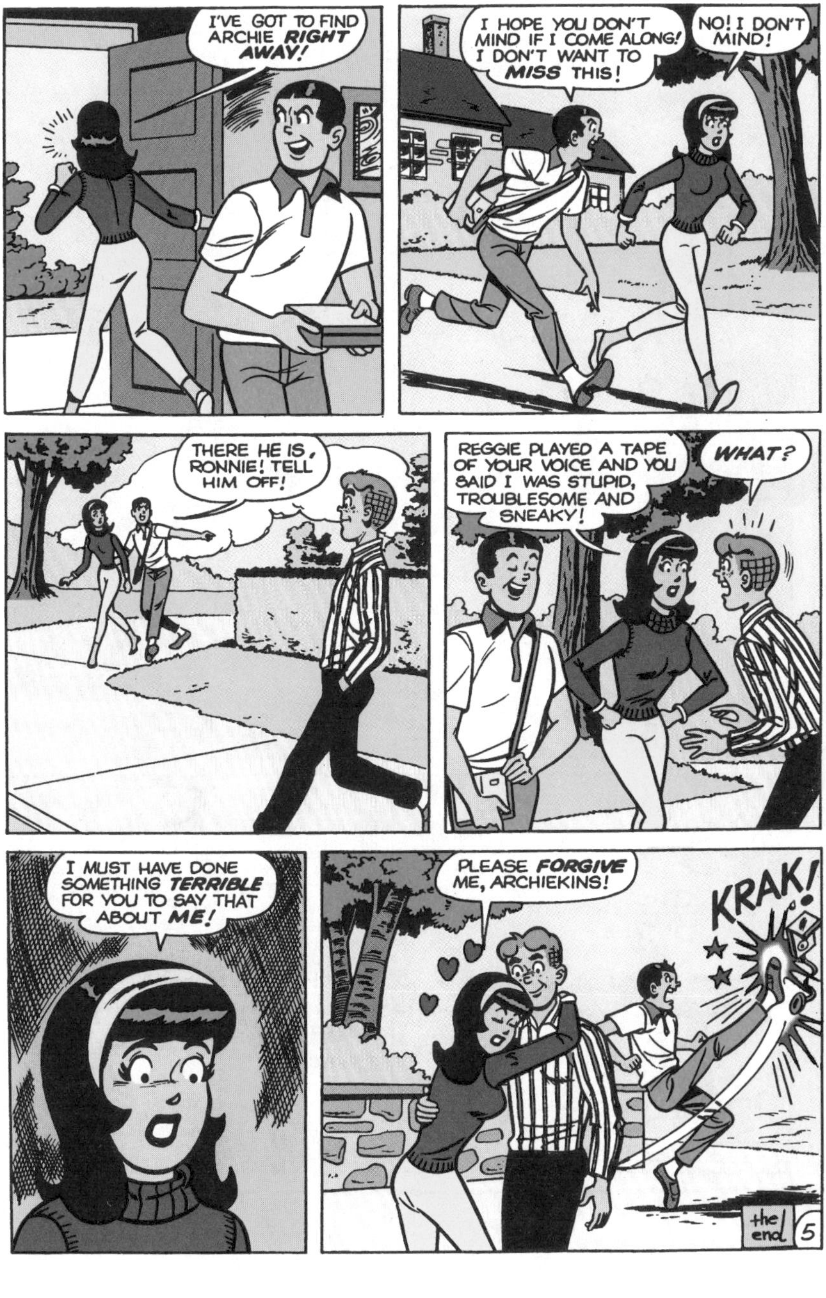
I'VE GOT TO FIND ARCHIE RIGHT AWAY!
I HOPE YOU DON'T MIND IF I COME ALONG! I DON'T WANT TO MISS THIS!
NO! I DON'T MIND!
THERE HE IS, RONNIE! TELL HIM OFF!
REGGIE PLAYED A TAPE OF YOUR VOICE AND YOU SAID I WAS STUPID, TROUBLESOME AND SNEAKY!
WHAT?
I MUST HAVE DONE SOMETHING TERRIBLE FOR YOU TO SAY THAT ABOUT ME!
PLEASE FORGIVE ME, ARCHIEKINS!
KRAK!
the end
5

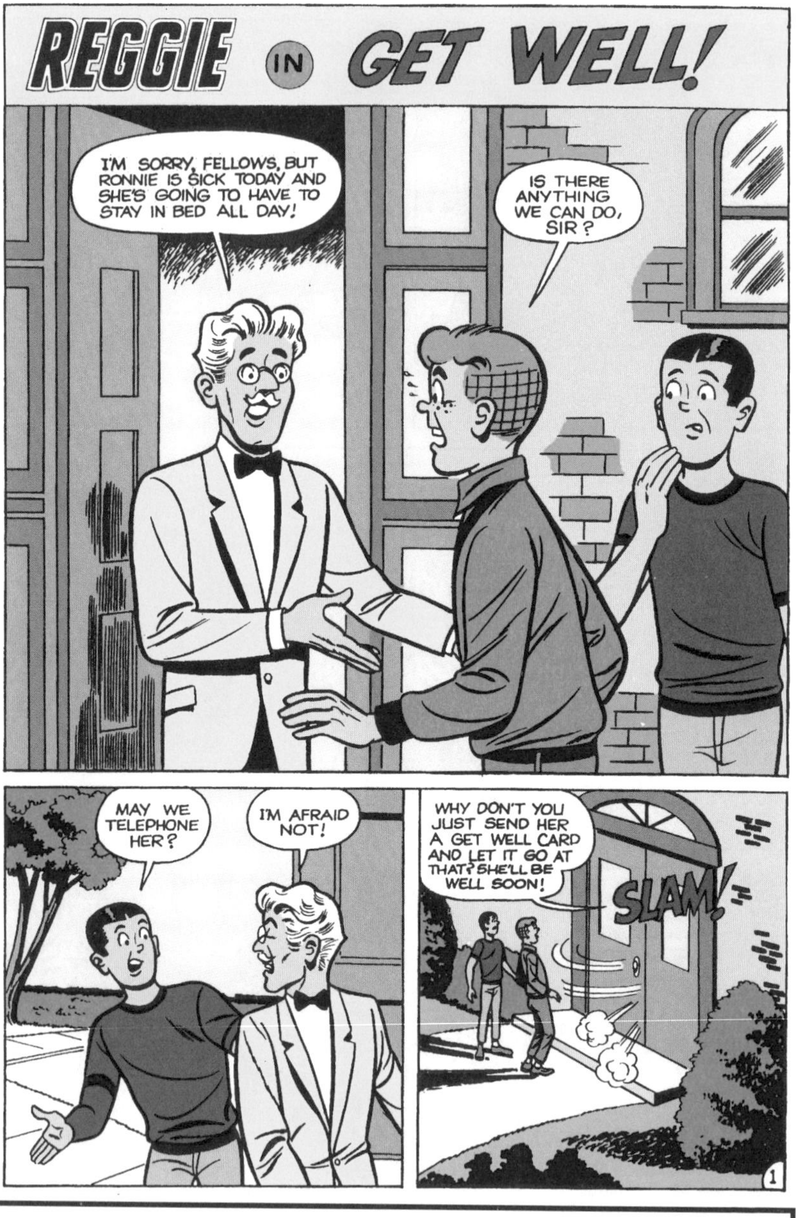
REGGIE IN GET WELL!
I'M SORRY, FELLOWS, BUT RONNIE IS SICK TODAY AND SHE'S GOING TO HAVE TO STAY IN BED ALL DAY!
IS THERE ANYTHING WE CAN DO, SIR?
MAY WE TELEPHONE HER?
I'M AFRAID NOT!
WHY DON'T YOU JUST SEND HER A GET WELL CARD AND LET IT GO AT THAT? SHE'LL BE WELL SOON!
SLAM!
1

Pencils: Bill Vigoda

Inks & Letters: Mario Acquaviva Colors: Barry Grossman

Originally printed in REGGIE AND ME #21, DECEMBER 1966

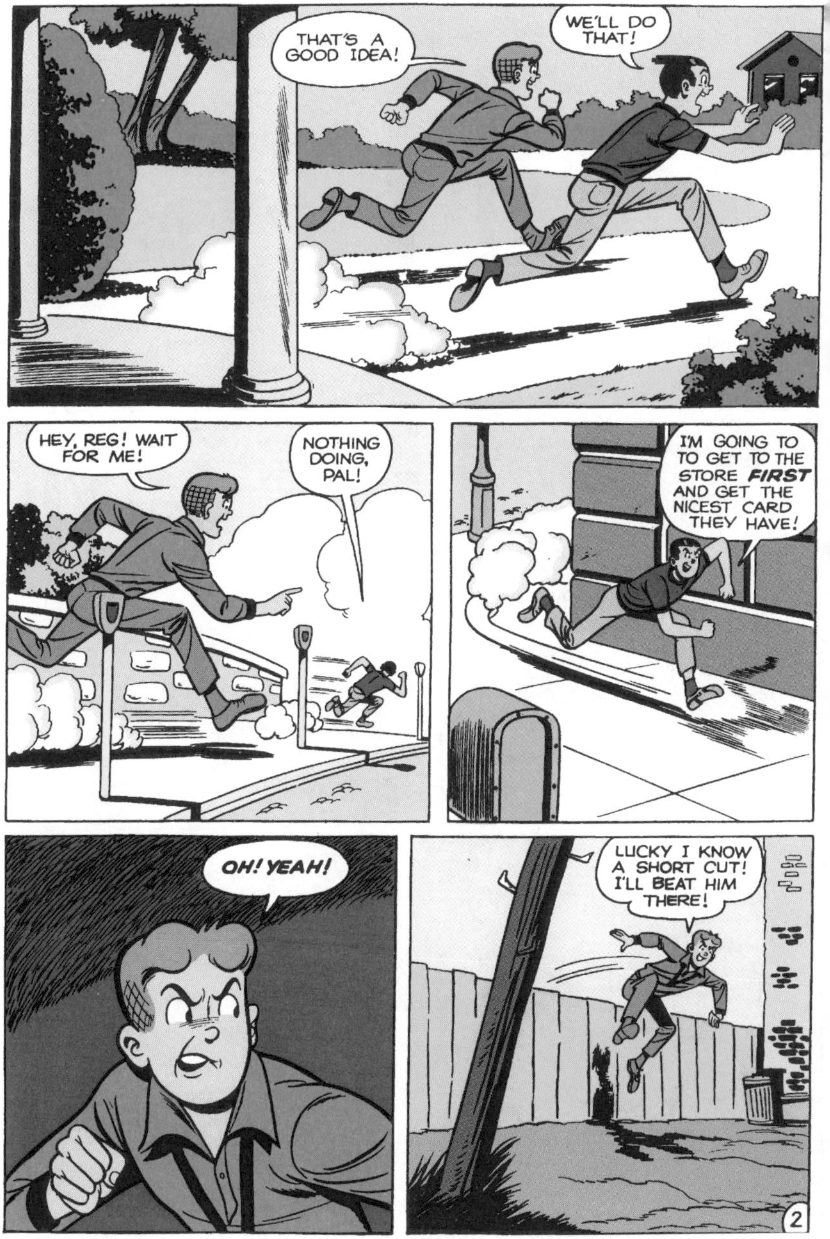
THAT'S A GOOD IDEA!
WE'LL DO THAT!
HEY, REG! WAIT FOR ME!
NOTHING DOING, PAL!
I'M GOING TO TO GET TO THE STORE FIRST AND GET THE NICEST CARD THEY HAVE!
OH! YEAH!
LUCKY I KNOW A SHORT CUT! I'LL BEAT HIM THERE!
2

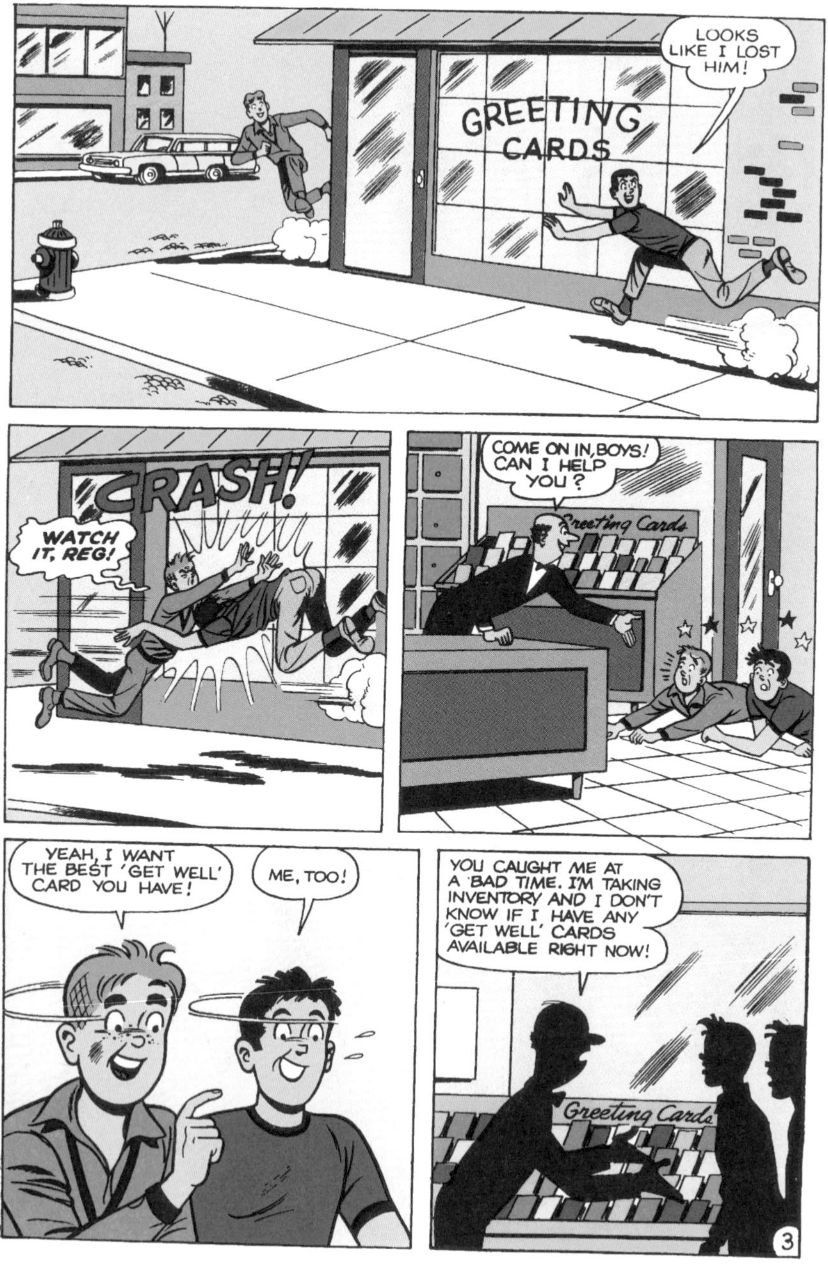
LOOKS LIKE I LOST HIM!
GREETING CARDS
CRASH!
WATCH IT, REG!
COME ON IN, BOYS! CAN I HELP YOU?
Greeting Cards
YEAH, I WANT THE BEST 'GET WELL' CARD YOU HAVE!
ME, TOO!
YOU CAUGHT ME AT A BAD TIME. I'M TAKING INVENTORY AND I DON'T KNOW IF I HAVE ANY 'GET WELL' CARDS AVAILABLE RIGHT NOW!
Greeting Cards
3

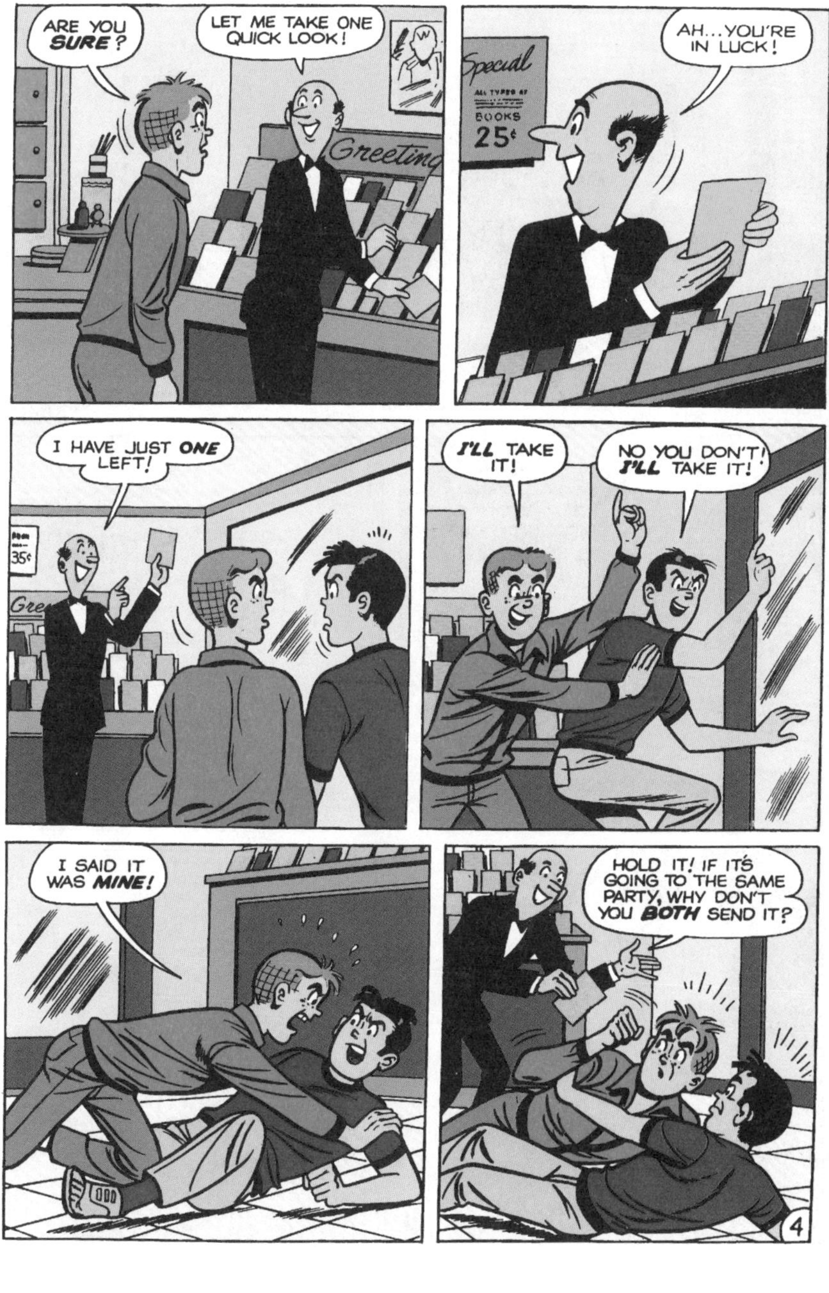
ARE YOU SURE?
LET ME TAKE ONE QUICK LOOK!
Greeting
Special
BOOKS 25¢
AH...YOU'RE IN LUCK!
I HAVE JUST ONE LEFT!
35¢
I'LL TAKE IT!
NO YOU DON'T! I'LL TAKE IT!
I SAID IT WAS MINE!
HOLD IT! IF IT'S GOING TO THE SAME PARTY, WHY DON'T YOU BOTH SEND IT?
4

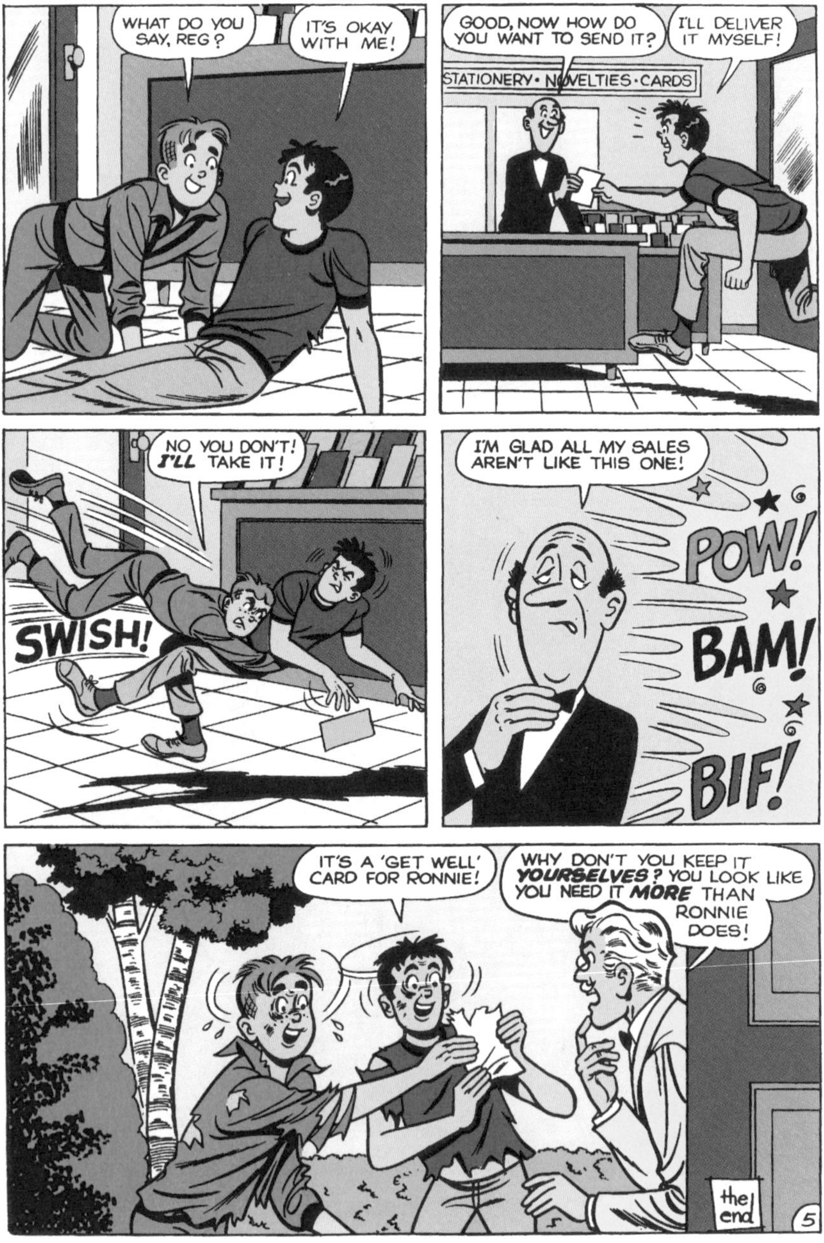
WHAT DO YOU SAY, REG?
IT'S OKAY WITH ME!
GOOD, NOW HOW DO YOU WANT TO SEND IT?
I'LL DELIVER IT MYSELF!
STATIONERY • NOVELTIES • CARDS
NO YOU DON'T! I'LL TAKE IT!
SWISH!
I'M GLAD ALL MY SALES AREN'T LIKE THIS ONE!
POW!
BAM!
BIF!
IT'S A 'GET WELL' CARD FOR RONNIE!
WHY DON'T YOU KEEP IT YOURSELVES? YOU LOOK LIKE YOU NEED IT MORE THAN RONNIE DOES!
the end
5

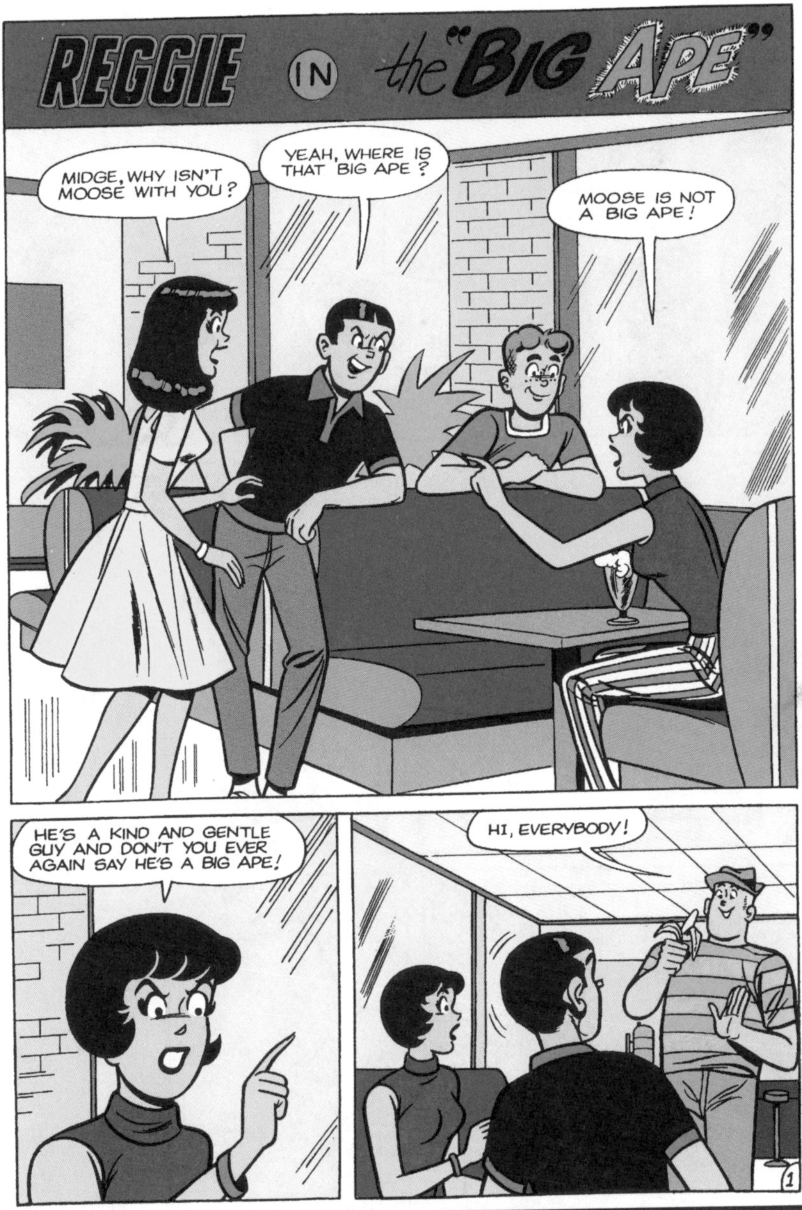
REGGIE IN the "BIG APE"
MIDGE, WHY ISN'T MOOSE WITH YOU?
YEAH, WHERE IS THAT BIG APE?
MOOSE IS NOT A BIG APE!
HE'S A KIND AND GENTLE GUY AND DON'T YOU EVER AGAIN SAY HE'S A BIG APE!
HI, EVERYBODY!
1

Story: Frank Doyle Pencils: Bill Vigoda
Inks & Letters: Mario Acquaviva

Originally printed in REGGIE AND ME #21, DECEMBER 1966

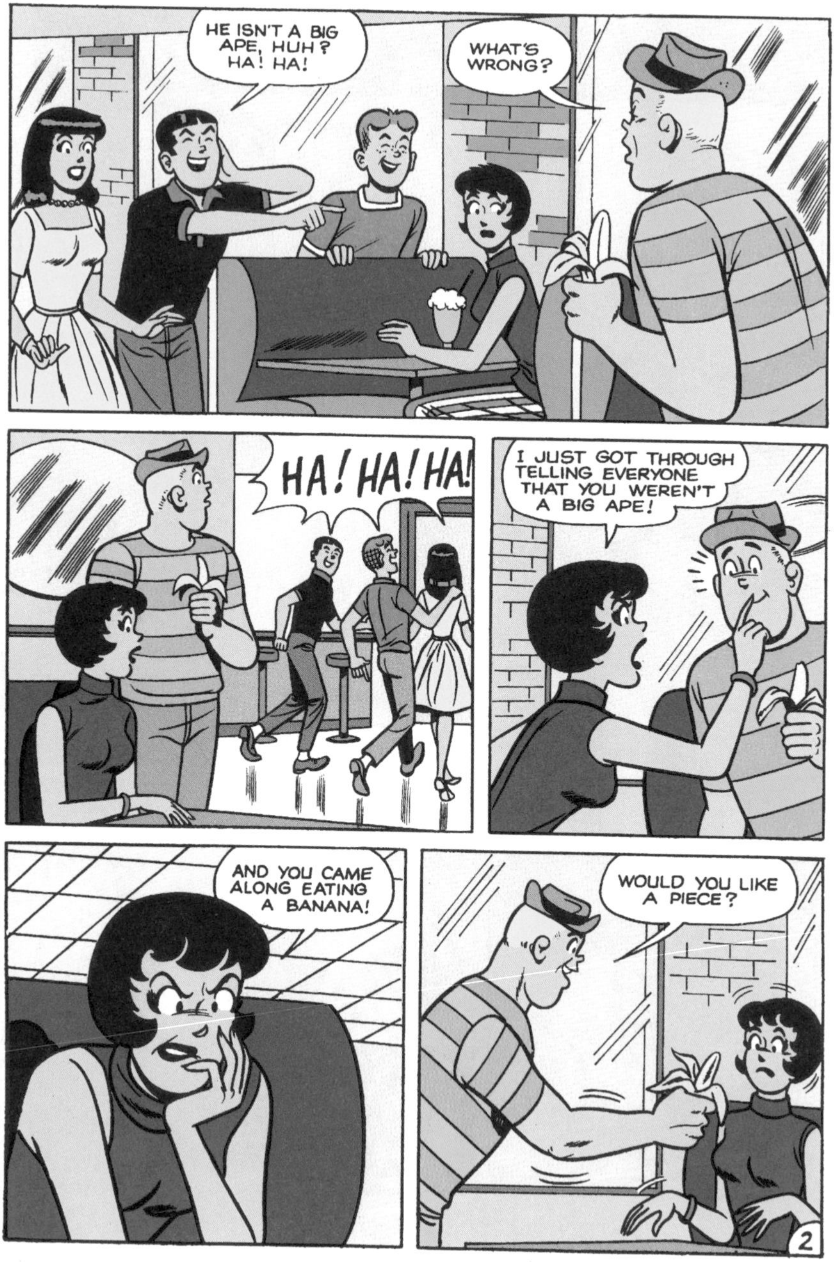
HE ISN'T A BIG APE, HUH? HA! HA!
WHAT'S WRONG?
HA! HA! HA!
I JUST GOT THROUGH TELLING EVERYONE THAT YOU WEREN'T A BIG APE!
AND YOU CAME ALONG EATING A BANANA!
WOULD YOU LIKE A PIECE?
2

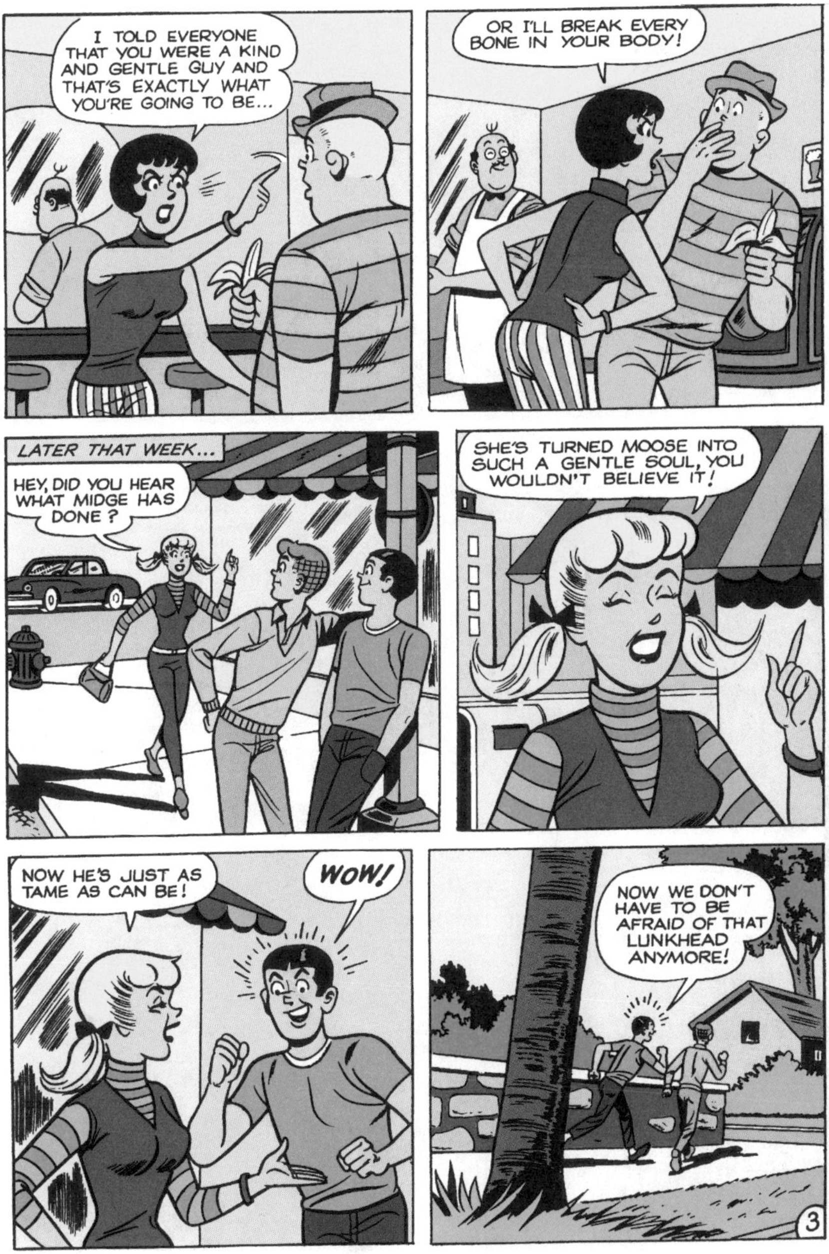
I TOLD EVERYONE THAT YOU WERE A KIND AND GENTLE GUY AND THAT'S EXACTLY WHAT YOU'RE GOING TO BE...
OR I'LL BREAK EVERY BONE IN YOUR BODY!
LATER THAT WEEK...
HEY, DID YOU HEAR WHAT MIDGE HAS DONE?
SHE'S TURNED MOOSE INTO SUCH A GENTLE SOUL, YOU WOULDN'T BELIEVE IT!
NOW HE'S JUST AS TAME AS CAN BE!
WOW!
NOW WE DON'T HAVE TO BE AFRAID OF THAT LUNKHEAD ANYMORE!
3

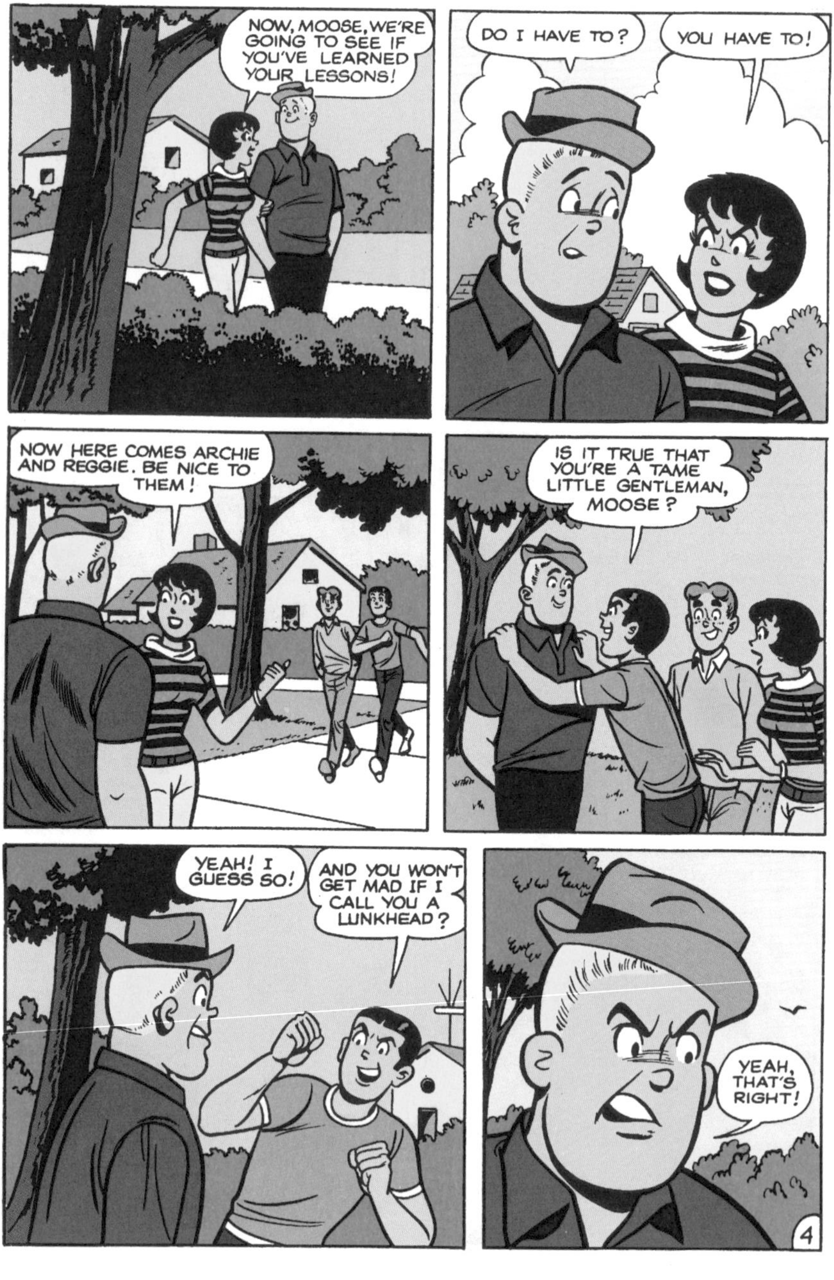
NOW, MOOSE, WE'RE GOING TO SEE IF YOU'VE LEARNED YOUR LESSONS!
DO I HAVE TO?
YOU HAVE TO!
NOW HERE COMES ARCHIE AND REGGIE. BE NICE TO THEM!
IS IT TRUE THAT YOU'RE A TAME LITTLE GENTLEMAN, MOOSE?
YEAH! I GUESS SO!
AND YOU WON'T GET MAD IF I CALL YOU A LUNKHEAD?
YEAH, THAT'S RIGHT!
4

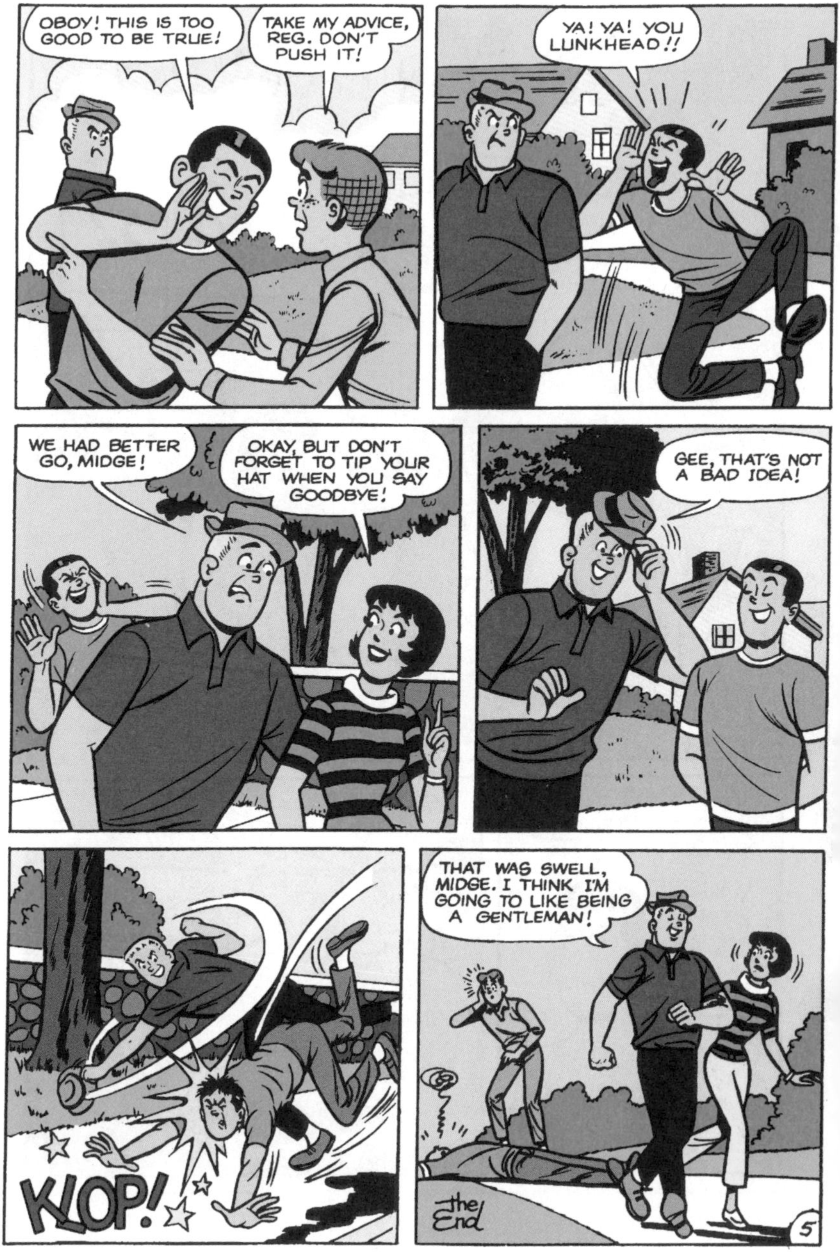
OBOY! THIS IS TOO GOOD TO BE TRUE!
TAKE MY ADVICE, REG. DON'T PUSH IT!
YA! YA! YOU LUNKHEAD!!
WE HAD BETTER GO, MIDGE!
OKAY, BUT DON'T FORGET TO TIP YOUR HAT WHEN YOU SAY GOODBYE!
GEE, THAT'S NOT A BAD IDEA!
KLOP!
THAT WAS SWELL, MIDGE. I THINK I'M GOING TO LIKE BEING A GENTLEMAN!
the End
5

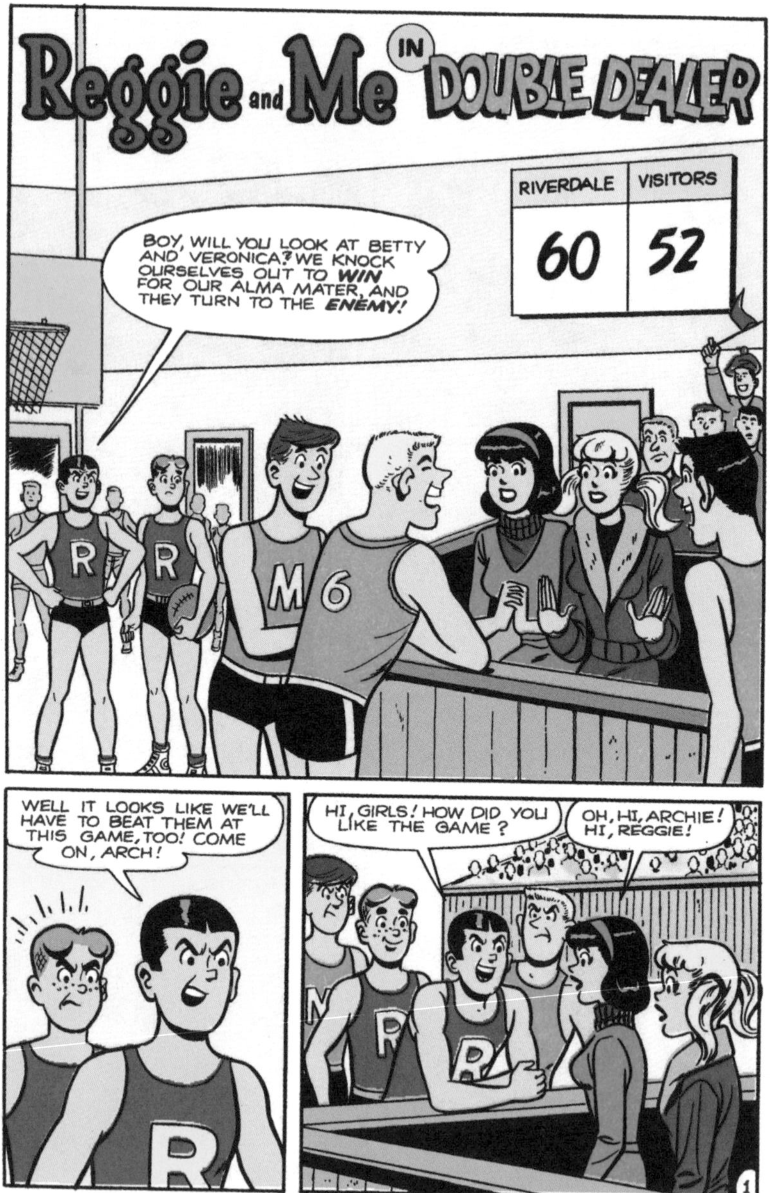
Reggie and Me IN DOUBLE DEALER
RIVERDALE VISITORS
60 52
BOY, WILL YOU LOOK AT BETTY AND VERONICA? WE KNOCK OURSELVES OUT TO WIN FOR OUR ALMA MATER, AND THEY TURN TO THE ENEMY!
R
R
M
6
WELL IT LOOKS LIKE WE'LL HAVE TO BEAT THEM AT THIS GAME, TOO! COME ON, ARCH!
R
HI, GIRLS! HOW DID YOU LIKE THE GAME?
OH, HI, ARCHIE! HI, REGGIE!
R
R
1

Story: George Gladir Pencils: Bill Vigoda
Inks & Letters: Mario Acquaviva

Originally printed in REGGIE AND ME #22, FEBRUARY 1967

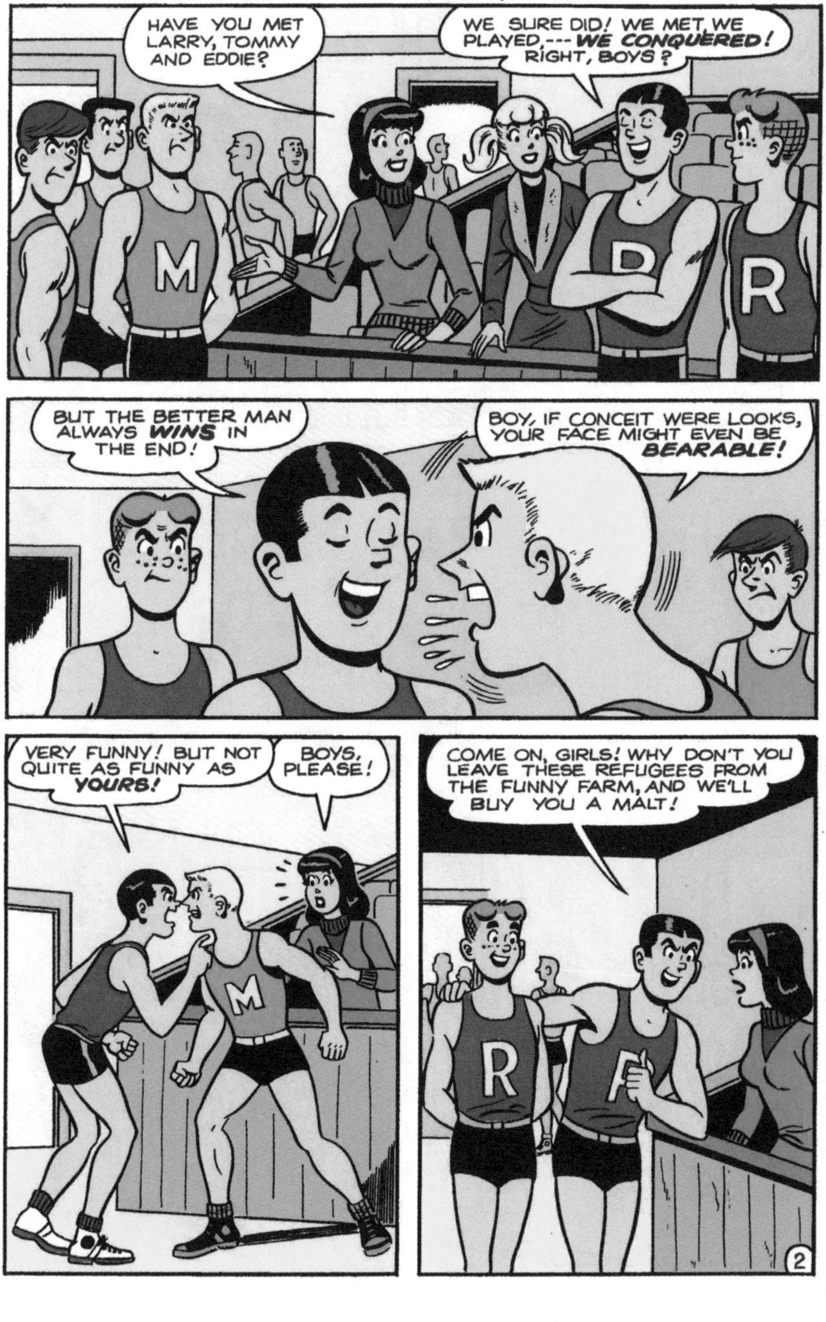
HAVE YOU MET LARRY, TOMMY AND EDDIE?
WE SURE DID! WE MET, WE PLAYED,--- WE CONQUERED! RIGHT, BOYS?
BUT THE BETTER MAN ALWAYS WINS IN THE END!
BOY, IF CONCEIT WERE LOOKS, YOUR FACE MIGHT EVEN BE BEARABLE!
VERY FUNNY! BUT NOT QUITE AS FUNNY AS YOURS!
BOYS, PLEASE!
COME ON, GIRLS! WHY DON'T YOU LEAVE THESE REFUGEES FROM THE FUNNY FARM, AND WE'LL BUY YOU A MALT!
2

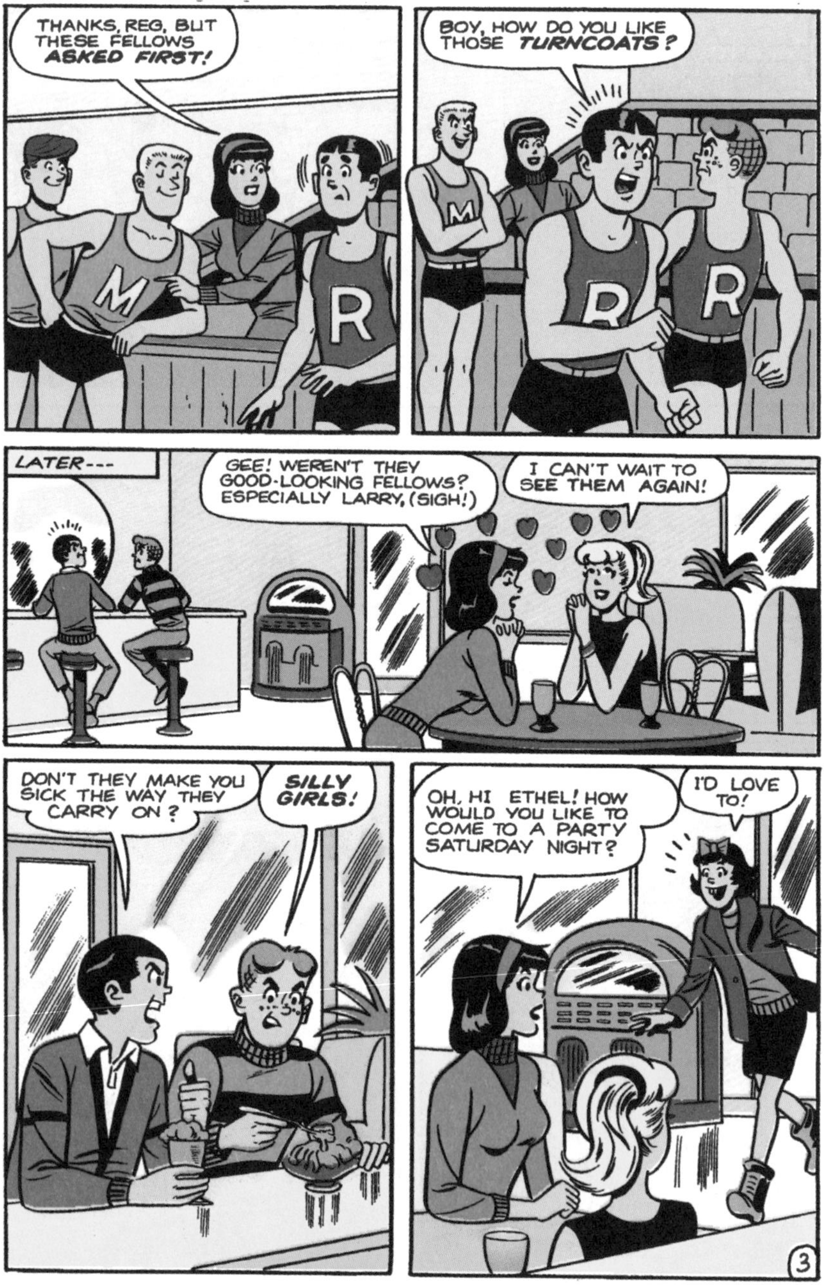
THANKS, REG, BUT THESE FELLOWS ASKED FIRST!
BOY, HOW DO YOU LIKE THOSE TURNCOATS?
LATER---
GEE! WEREN'T THEY GOOD-LOOKING FELLOWS? ESPECIALLY LARRY, (SIGH!)
I CAN'T WAIT TO SEE THEM AGAIN!
DON'T THEY MAKE YOU SICK THE WAY THEY CARRY ON?
SILLY GIRLS!
OH, HI ETHEL! HOW WOULD YOU LIKE TO COME TO A PARTY SATURDAY NIGHT?
I'D LOVE TO!
3

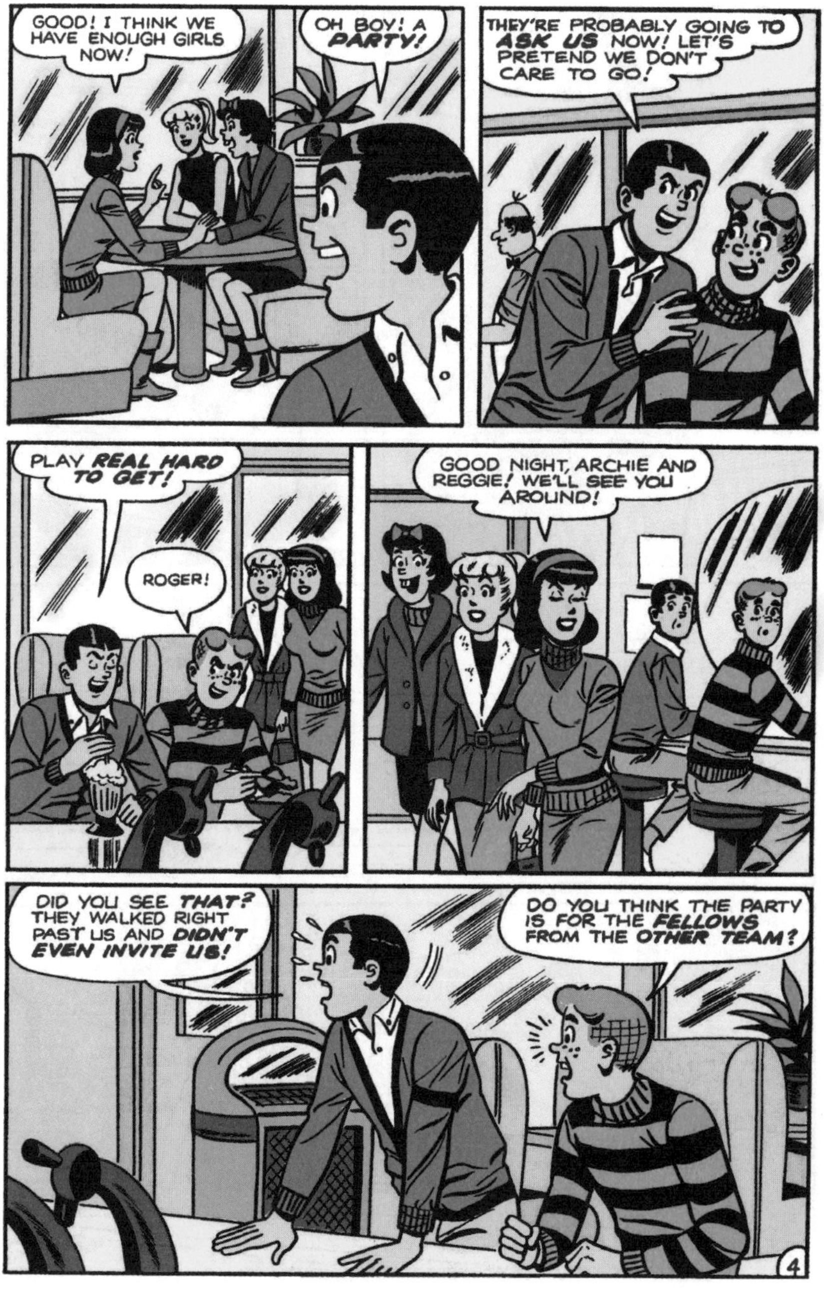
GOOD! I THINK WE HAVE ENOUGH GIRLS NOW!
OH BOY! A PARTY!
THEY'RE PROBABLY GOING TO ASK US NOW! LET'S PRETEND WE DON'T CARE TO GO!
PLAY REAL HARD TO GET!
ROGER!
GOOD NIGHT, ARCHIE AND REGGIE! WE'LL SEE YOU AROUND!
DID YOU SEE THAT? THEY WALKED RIGHT PAST US AND DIDN'T EVEN INVITE US!
DO YOU THINK THE PARTY IS FOR THE FELLOWS FROM THE OTHER TEAM?
4

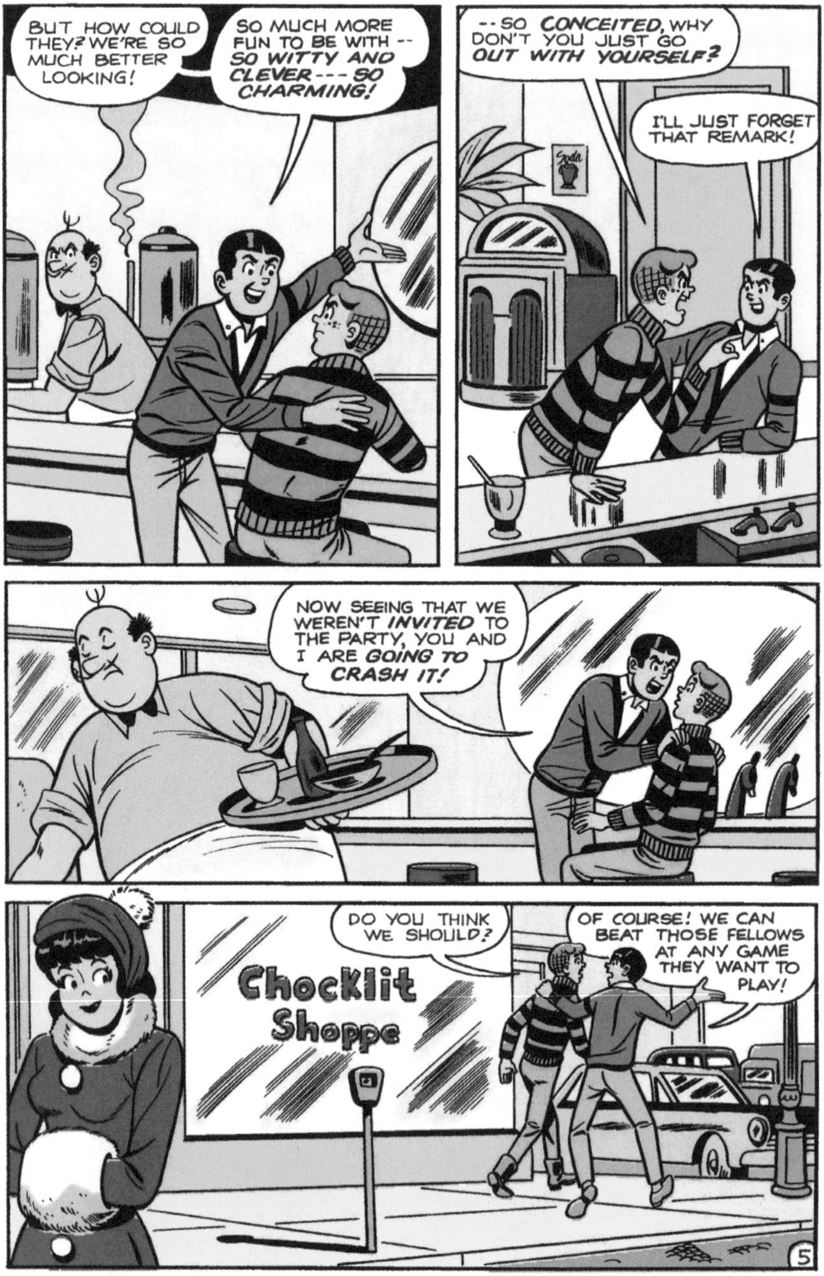
BUT HOW COULD THEY? WE'RE SO MUCH BETTER LOOKING!
SO MUCH MORE FUN TO BE WITH -- SO WITTY AND CLEVER --- SO CHARMING!
-- SO CONCEITED, WHY DON'T YOU JUST GO OUT WITH YOURSELF?
I'LL JUST FORGET THAT REMARK!
Soda
NOW SEEING THAT WE WEREN'T INVITED TO THE PARTY, YOU AND I ARE GOING TO CRASH IT!
DO YOU THINK WE SHOULD?
OF COURSE! WE CAN BEAT THOSE FELLOWS AT ANY GAME THEY WANT TO PLAY!
Chocklit Shoppe
5

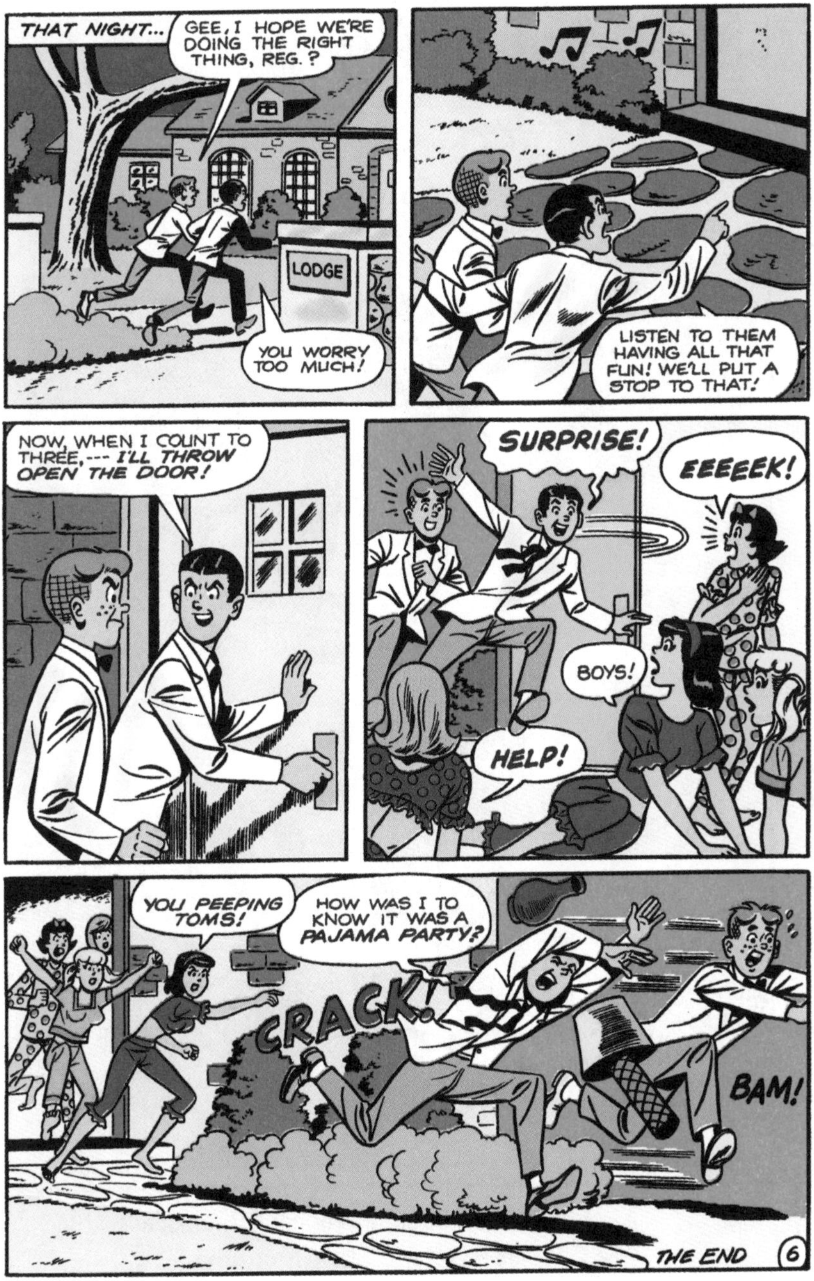
THAT NIGHT...
GEE, I HOPE WE'RE DOING THE RIGHT THING, REG.?
LODGE
YOU WORRY TOO MUCH!
LISTEN TO THEM HAVING ALL THAT FUN! WE'LL PUT A STOP TO THAT!
NOW, WHEN I COUNT TO THREE,--- I'LL THROW OPEN THE DOOR!
SURPRISE!
EEEEEK!
BOYS!
HELP!
YOU PEEPING TOMS!
HOW WAS I TO KNOW IT WAS A PAJAMA PARTY?
CRACK!
BAM!
THE END
6

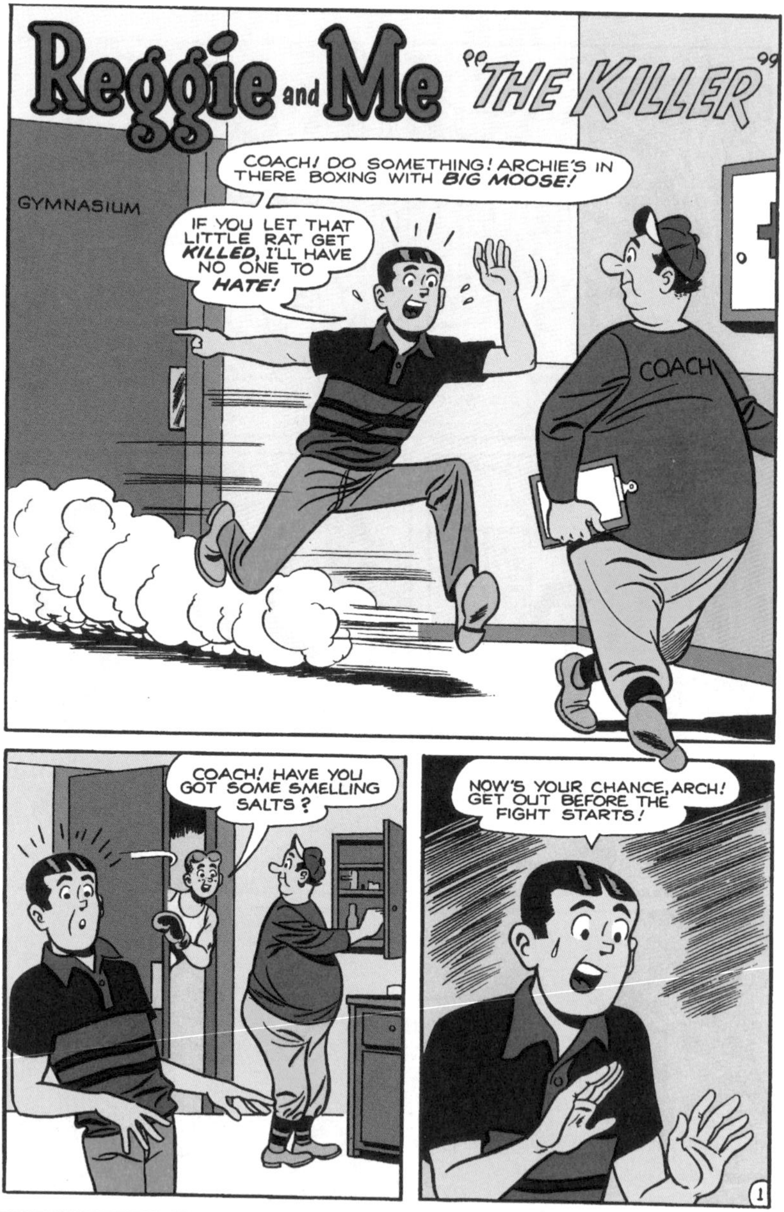
Reggie and Me
"THE KILLER"
COACH! DO SOMETHING! ARCHIE'S IN THERE BOXING WITH BIG MOOSE!
IF YOU LET THAT LITTLE RAT GET KILLED, I'LL HAVE NO ONE TO HATE!
GYMNASIUM
COACH
COACH! HAVE YOU GOT SOME SMELLING SALTS?
NOW'S YOUR CHANCE, ARCH! GET OUT BEFORE THE FIGHT STARTS!
1

Story: Frank Doyle Pencils: Bill Vigoda
Inks & Letters: Mario Acquaviva

Originally printed in REGGIE AND ME #22, FEBRUARY 1967

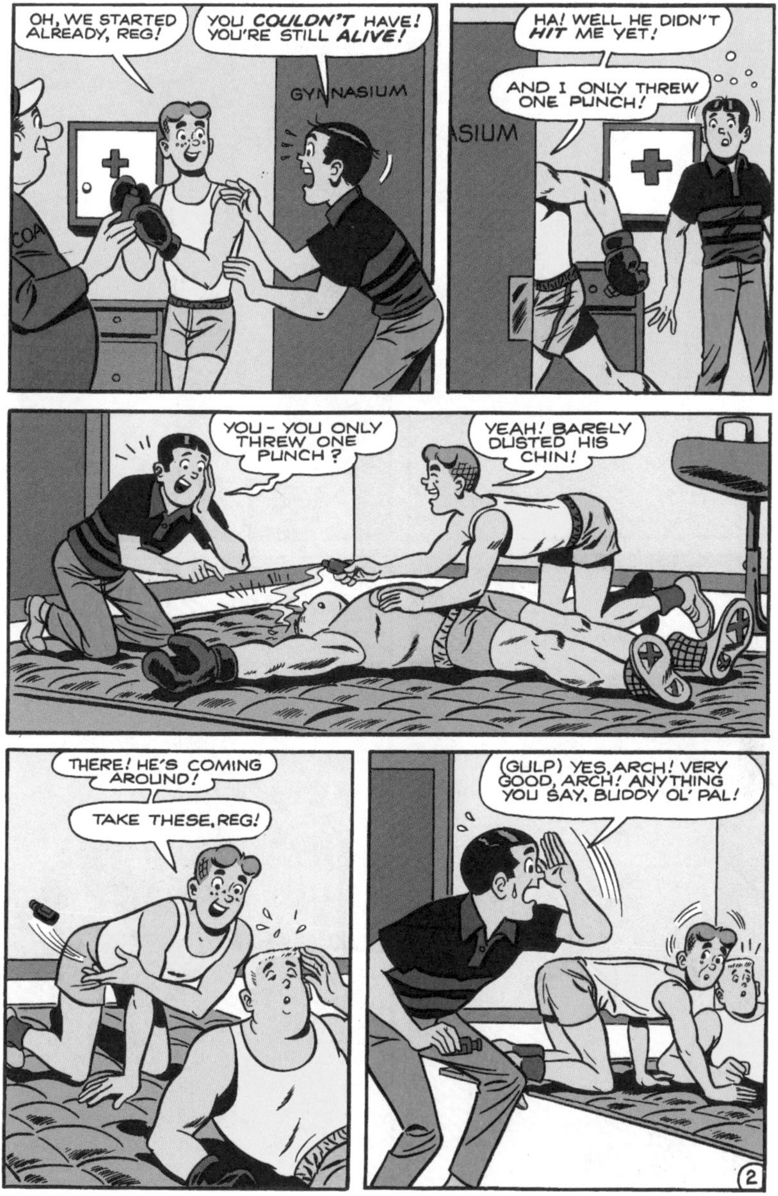
OH, WE STARTED ALREADY, REG!
YOU COULDN'T HAVE! YOU'RE STILL ALIVE!
GYMNASIUM
HA! WELL HE DIDN'T HIT ME YET!
AND I ONLY THREW ONE PUNCH!
YOU - YOU ONLY THREW ONE PUNCH?
YEAH! BARELY DUSTED HIS CHIN!
THERE! HE'S COMING AROUND!
TAKE THESE, REG!
(GULP) YES, ARCH! VERY GOOD, ARCH! ANYTHING YOU SAY, BUDDY OL' PAL!
2

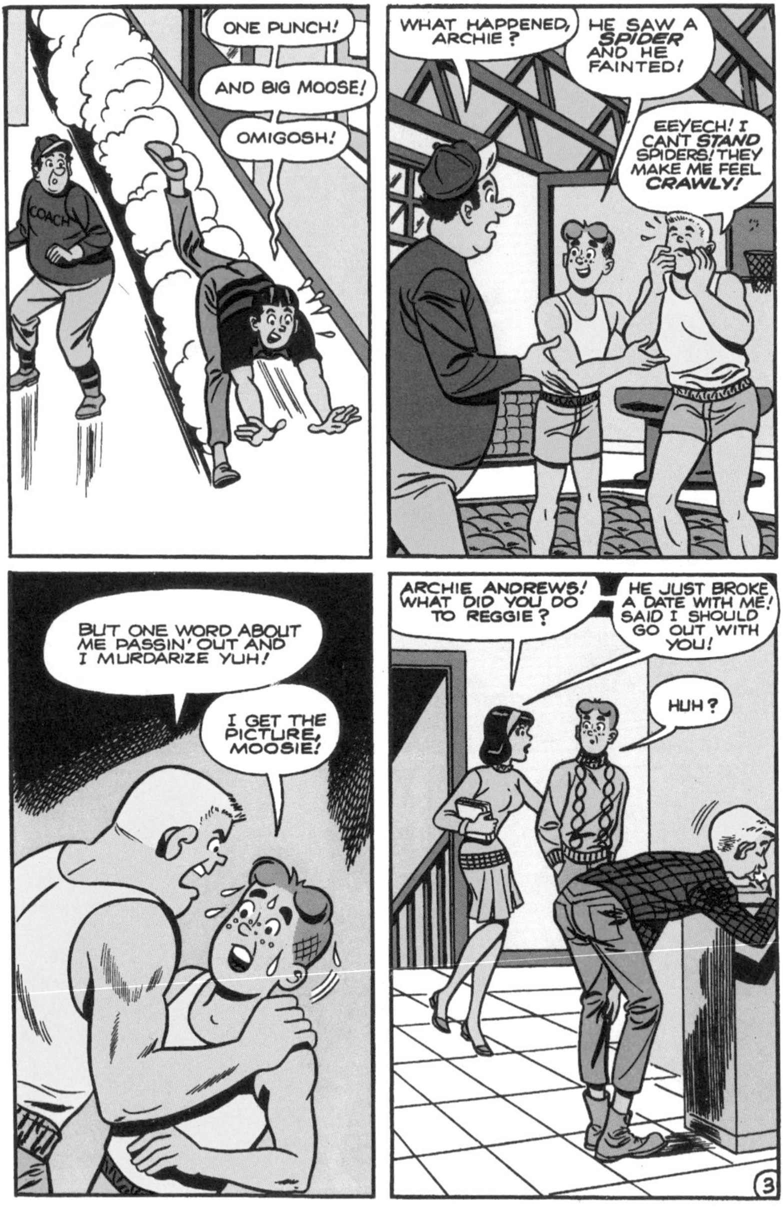
ONE PUNCH!
AND BIG MOOSE!
OMIGOSH!
COACH
WHAT HAPPENED, ARCHIE?
HE SAW A SPIDER AND HE FAINTED!
EEYECH! I CAN'T STAND SPIDERS! THEY MAKE ME FEEL CRAWLY!
BUT ONE WORD ABOUT ME PASSIN' OUT AND I MURDARIZE YUH!
I GET THE PICTURE, MOOSIE!
ARCHIE ANDREWS! WHAT DID YOU DO TO REGGIE?
HE JUST BROKE A DATE WITH ME! SAID I SHOULD GO OUT WITH YOU!
HUH?
3

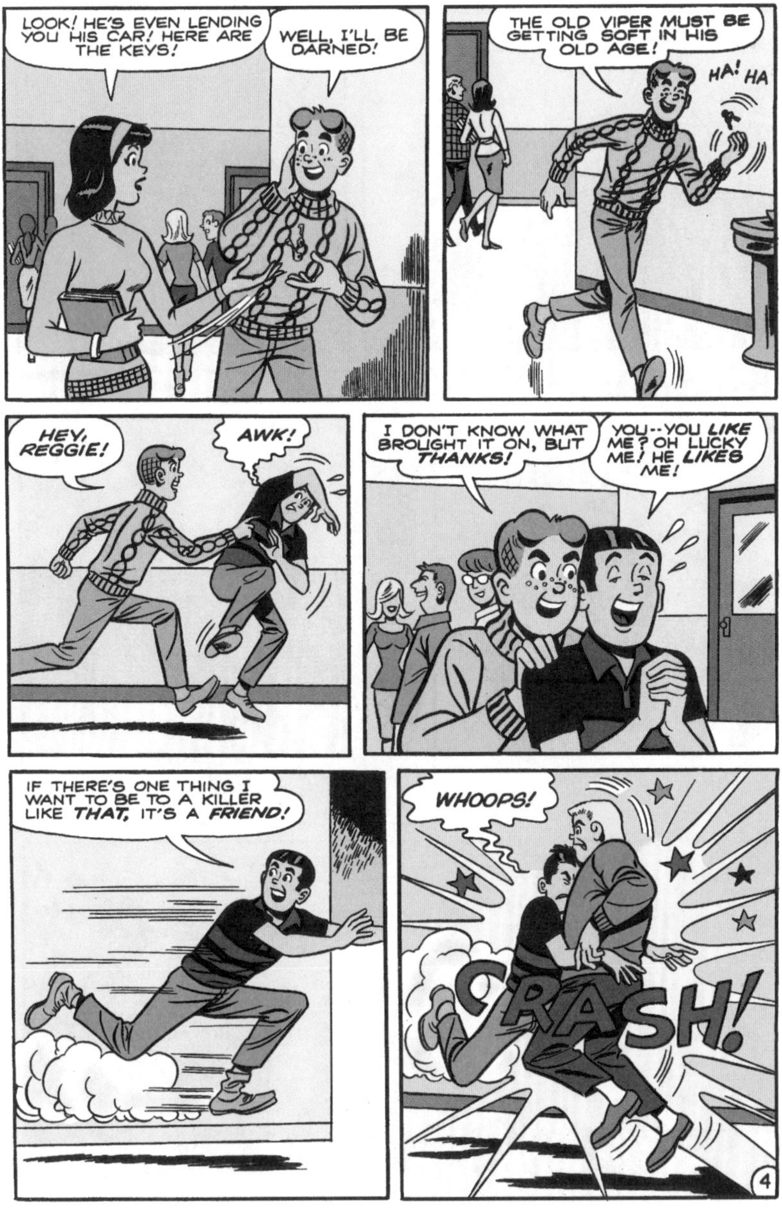
LOOK! HE'S EVEN LENDING YOU HIS CAR! HERE ARE THE KEYS!
WELL, I'LL BE DARNED!
THE OLD VIPER MUST BE GETTING SOFT IN HIS OLD AGE!
HA! HA
HEY, REGGIE!
AWK!
I DON'T KNOW WHAT BROUGHT IT ON, BUT THANKS!
YOU--YOU LIKE ME? OH LUCKY ME! HE LIKES ME!
IF THERE'S ONE THING I WANT TO BE TO A KILLER LIKE THAT, IT'S A FRIEND!
WHOOPS!
CRASH!
4

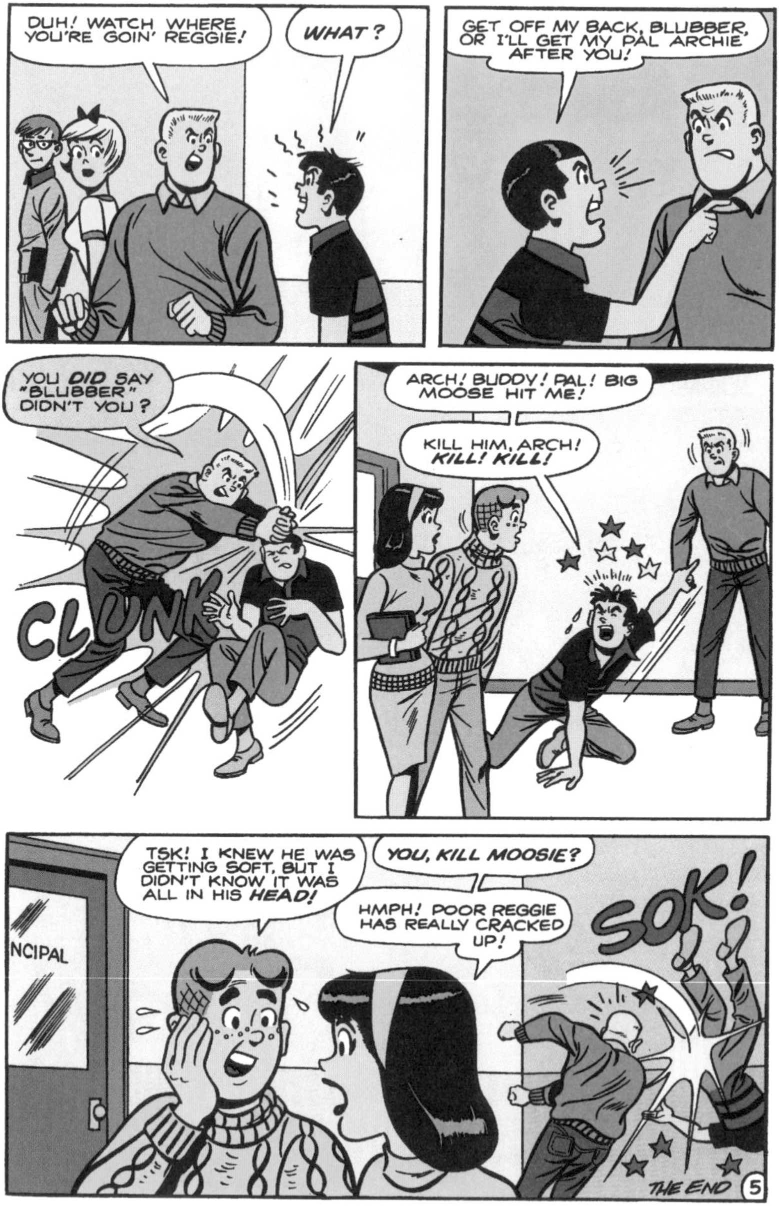
DUH! WATCH WHERE YOU'RE GOIN' REGGIE!
WHAT?
GET OFF MY BACK, BLUBBER, OR I'LL GET MY PAL ARCHIE AFTER YOU!
YOU DID SAY "BLUBBER" DIDN'T YOU?
CLUNK
ARCH! BUDDY! PAL! BIG MOOSE HIT ME!
KILL HIM, ARCH! KILL! KILL!
TSK! I KNEW HE WAS GETTING SOFT, BUT I DIDN'T KNOW IT WAS ALL IN HIS HEAD!
YOU, KILL MOOSIE?
HMPH! POOR REGGIE HAS REALLY CRACKED UP!
NCIPAL
SOK!
THE END
5

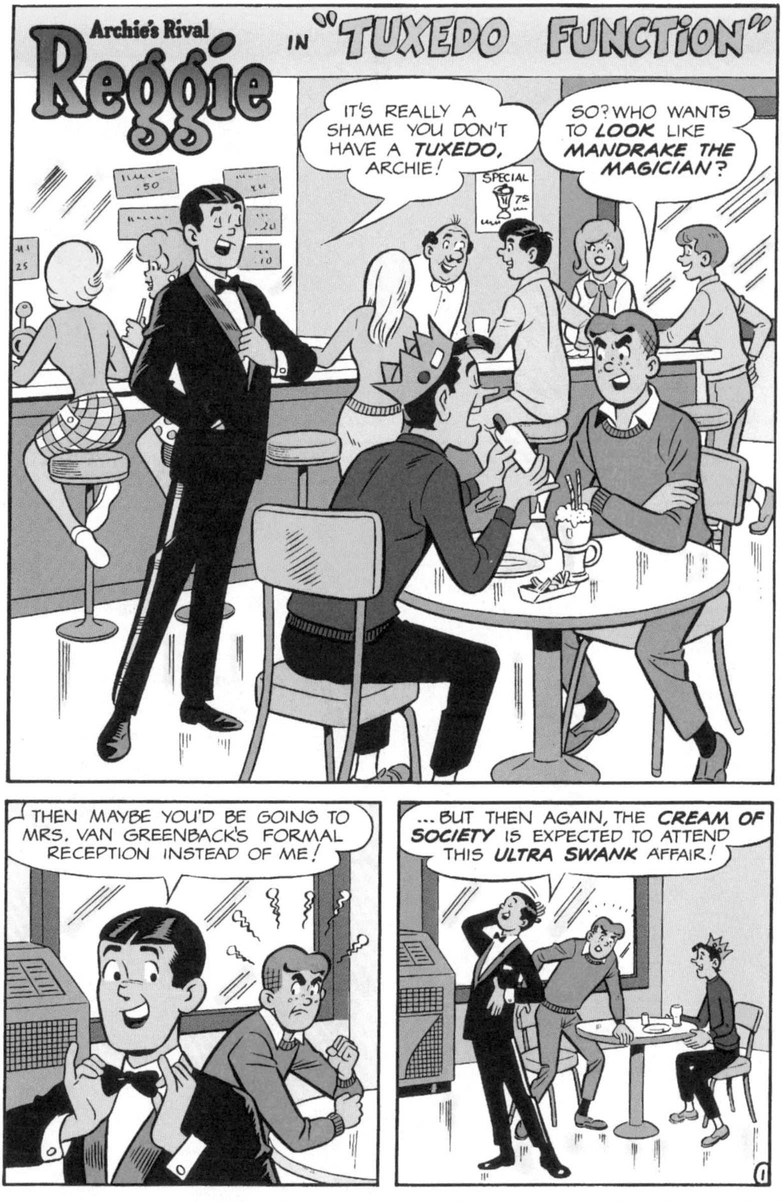
Archie's Rival Reggie IN "TUXEDO FUNCTION"
IT'S REALLY A SHAME YOU DON'T HAVE A TUXEDO, ARCHIE!
SO? WHO WANTS TO LOOK LIKE MANDRAKE THE MAGICIAN?
SPECIAL
THEN MAYBE YOU'D BE GOING TO MRS. VAN GREENBACK'S FORMAL RECEPTION INSTEAD OF ME!
...BUT THEN AGAIN, THE CREAM OF SOCIETY IS EXPECTED TO ATTEND THIS ULTRA SWANK AFFAIR!
1

Story & Pencils: Al Hartley Inks & Letters: Jon D'Agostino

Originally printed in REGGIE AND ME #24, JUNE 1967

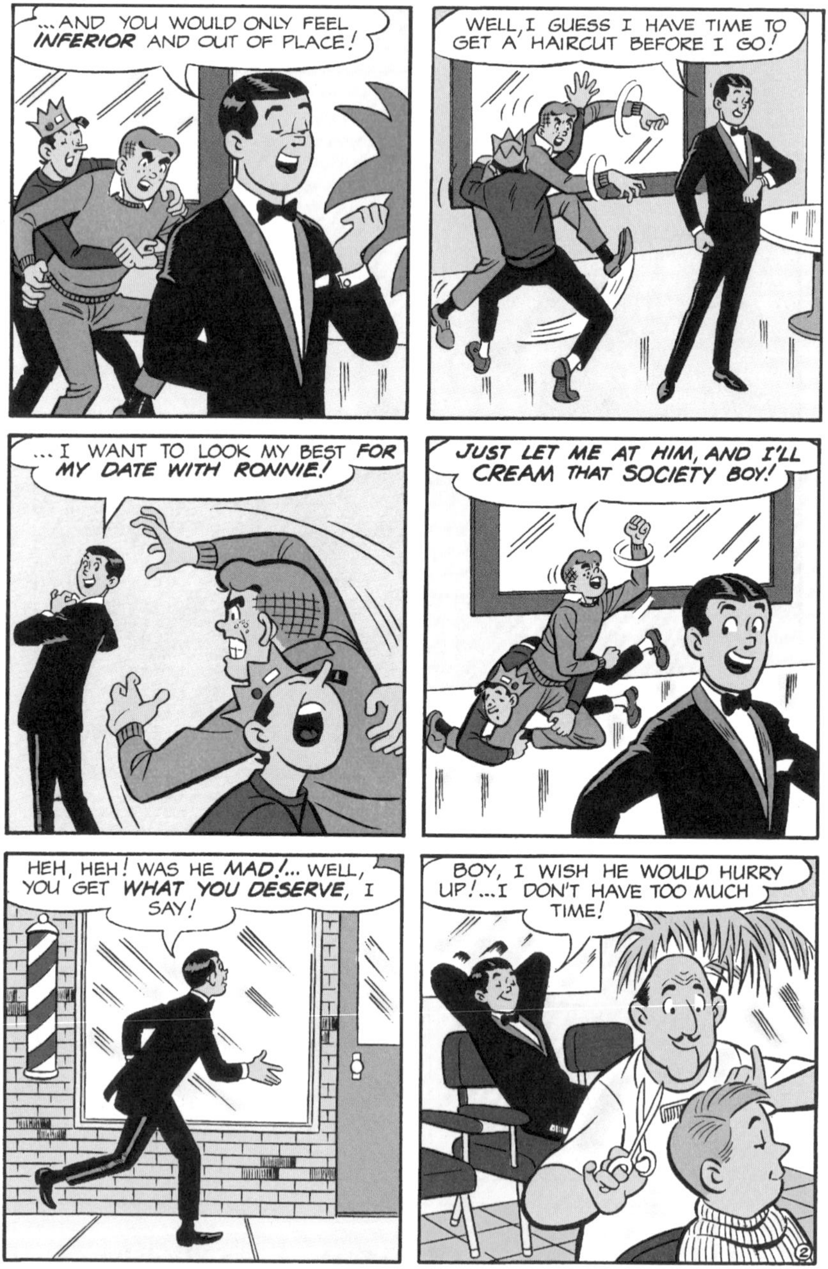
...AND YOU WOULD ONLY FEEL INFERIOR AND OUT OF PLACE!
WELL, I GUESS I HAVE TIME TO GET A HAIRCUT BEFORE I GO!
...I WANT TO LOOK MY BEST FOR MY DATE WITH RONNIE!
JUST LET ME AT HIM, AND I'LL CREAM THAT SOCIETY BOY!
HEH, HEH! WAS HE MAD!... WELL, YOU GET WHAT YOU DESERVE, I SAY!
BOY, I WISH HE WOULD HURRY UP!...I DON'T HAVE TOO MUCH TIME!
2

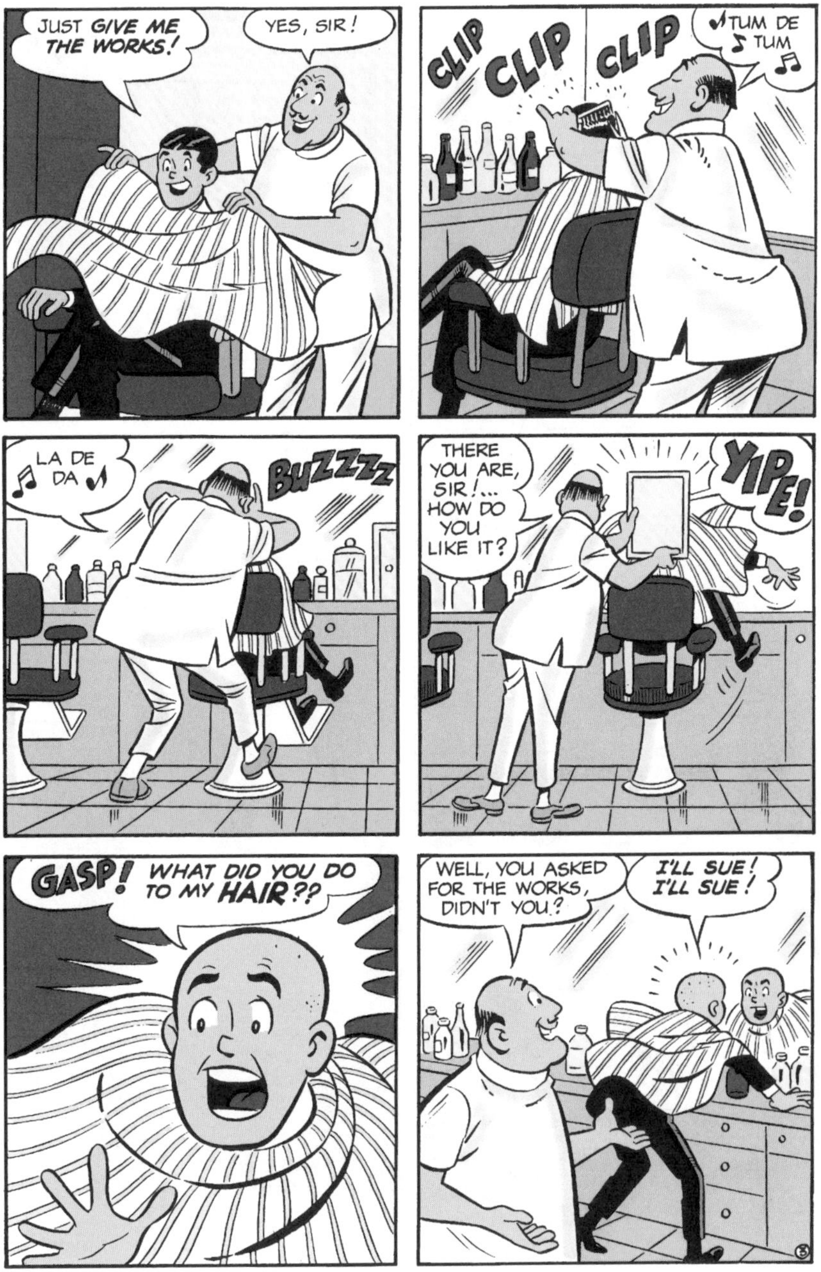
JUST GIVE ME THE WORKS!
YES, SIR!
CLIP CLIP CLIP
TUM DE TUM
LA DE DA
BUZZZZ
THERE YOU ARE, SIR!... HOW DO YOU LIKE IT?
YIPE!
GASP! WHAT DID YOU DO TO MY HAIR??
WELL, YOU ASKED FOR THE WORKS, DIDN'T YOU?
I'LL SUE! I'LL SUE!
3

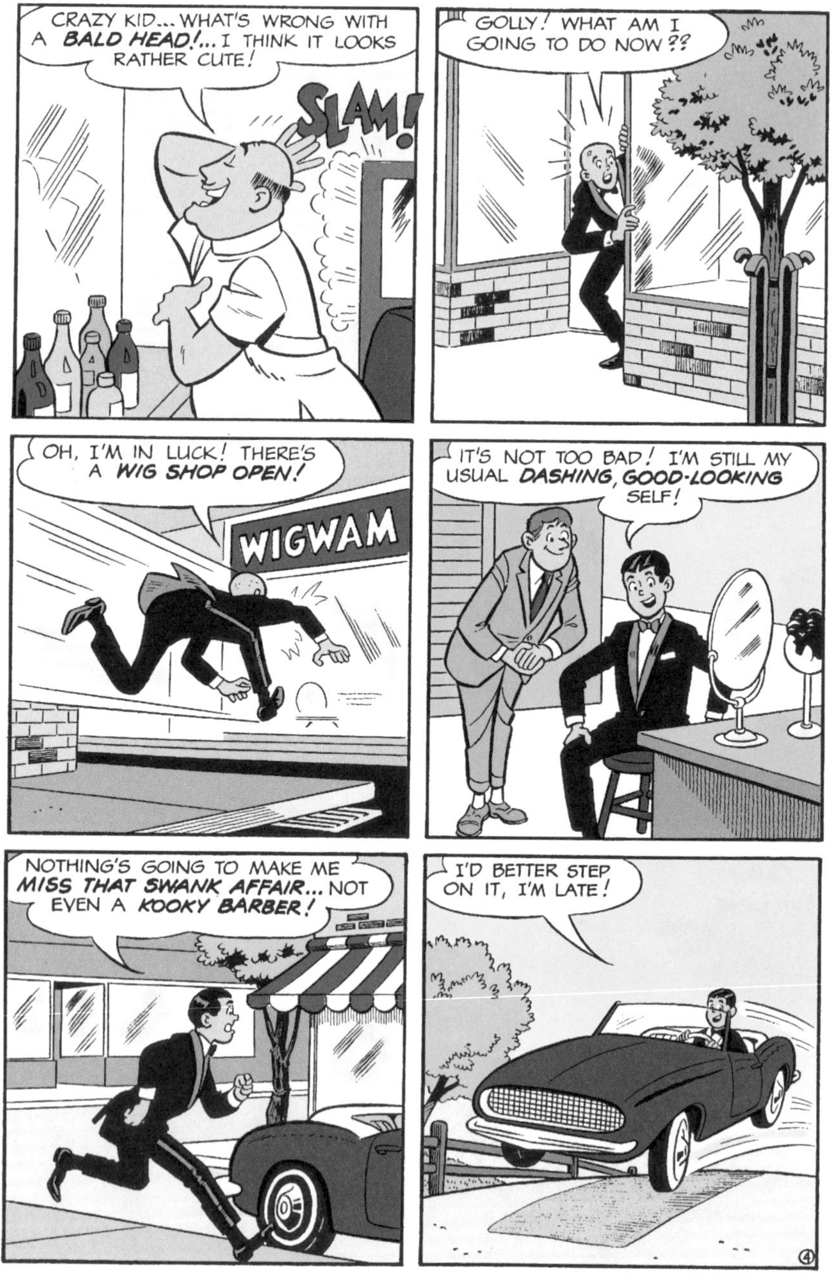
CRAZY KID... WHAT'S WRONG WITH A BALD HEAD!... I THINK IT LOOKS RATHER CUTE!
SLAM!
GOLLY! WHAT AM I GOING TO DO NOW??
OH, I'M IN LUCK! THERE'S A WIG SHOP OPEN!
WIGWAM
IT'S NOT TOO BAD! I'M STILL MY USUAL DASHING, GOOD-LOOKING SELF!
NOTHING'S GOING TO MAKE ME MISS THAT SWANK AFFAIR... NOT EVEN A KOOKY BARBER!
I'D BETTER STEP ON IT, I'M LATE!
4

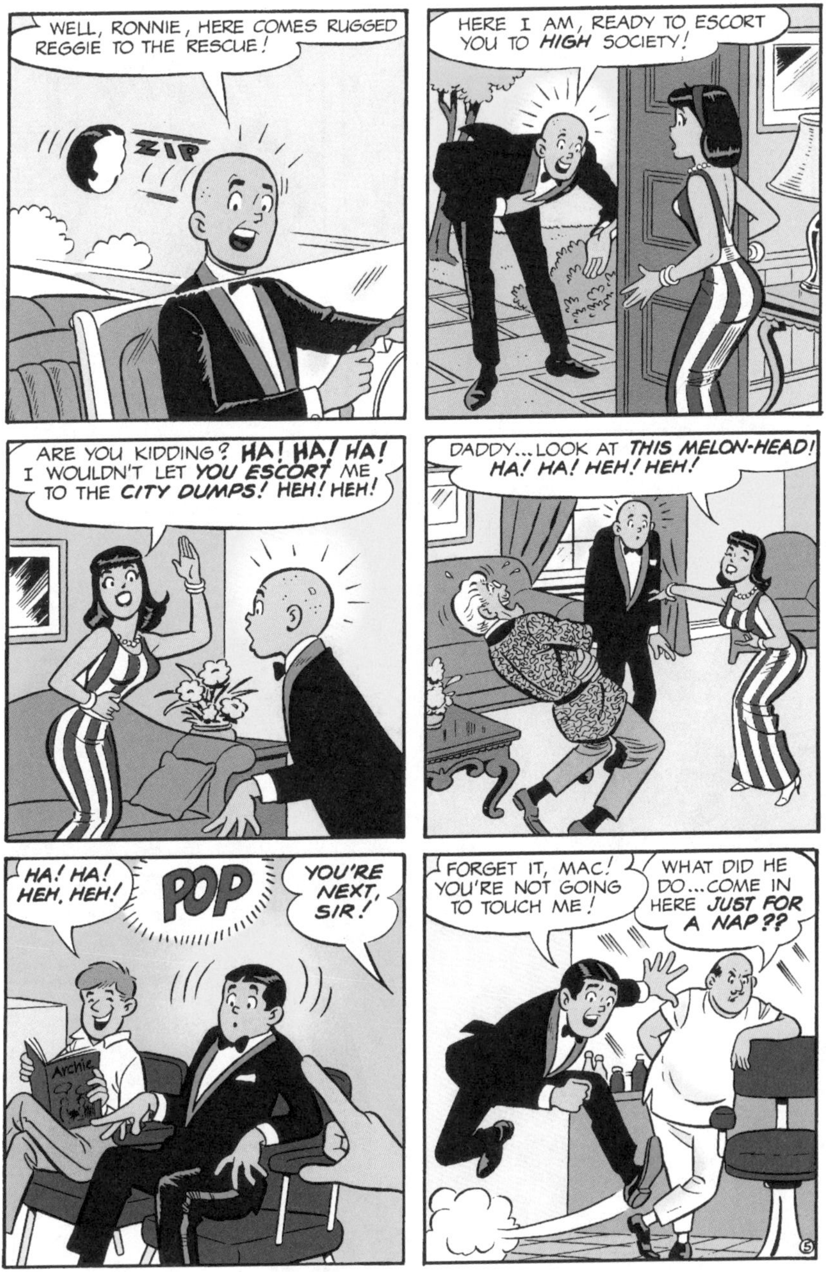
WELL, RONNIE, HERE COMES RUGGED REGGIE TO THE RESCUE!
ZIP
HERE I AM, READY TO ESCORT YOU TO HIGH SOCIETY!
ARE YOU KIDDING? HA! HA! HA! I WOULDN'T LET YOU ESCORT ME TO THE CITY DUMPS! HEH! HEH!
DADDY... LOOK AT THIS MELON-HEAD! HA! HA! HEH! HEH!
HA! HA! HEH, HEH!
POP
YOU'RE NEXT, SIR!
Archie
FORGET IT, MAC! YOU'RE NOT GOING TO TOUCH ME!
WHAT DID HE DO... COME IN HERE JUST FOR A NAP??
5

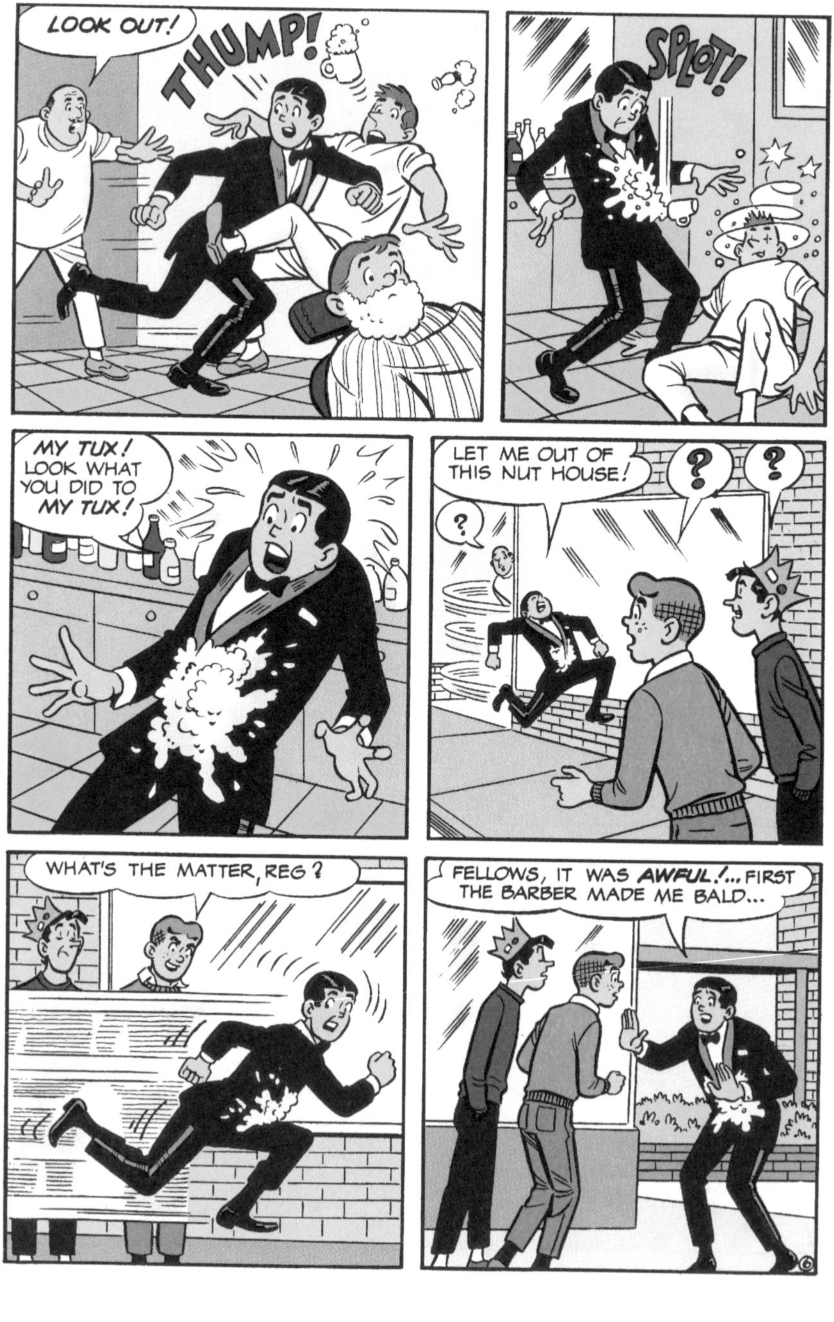
LOOK OUT!
THUMP!
SPLOT!
MY TUX! LOOK WHAT YOU DID TO MY TUX!
LET ME OUT OF THIS NUT HOUSE!
?
?
?
WHAT'S THE MATTER, REG?
FELLOWS, IT WAS AWFUL!... FIRST THE BARBER MADE ME BALD...

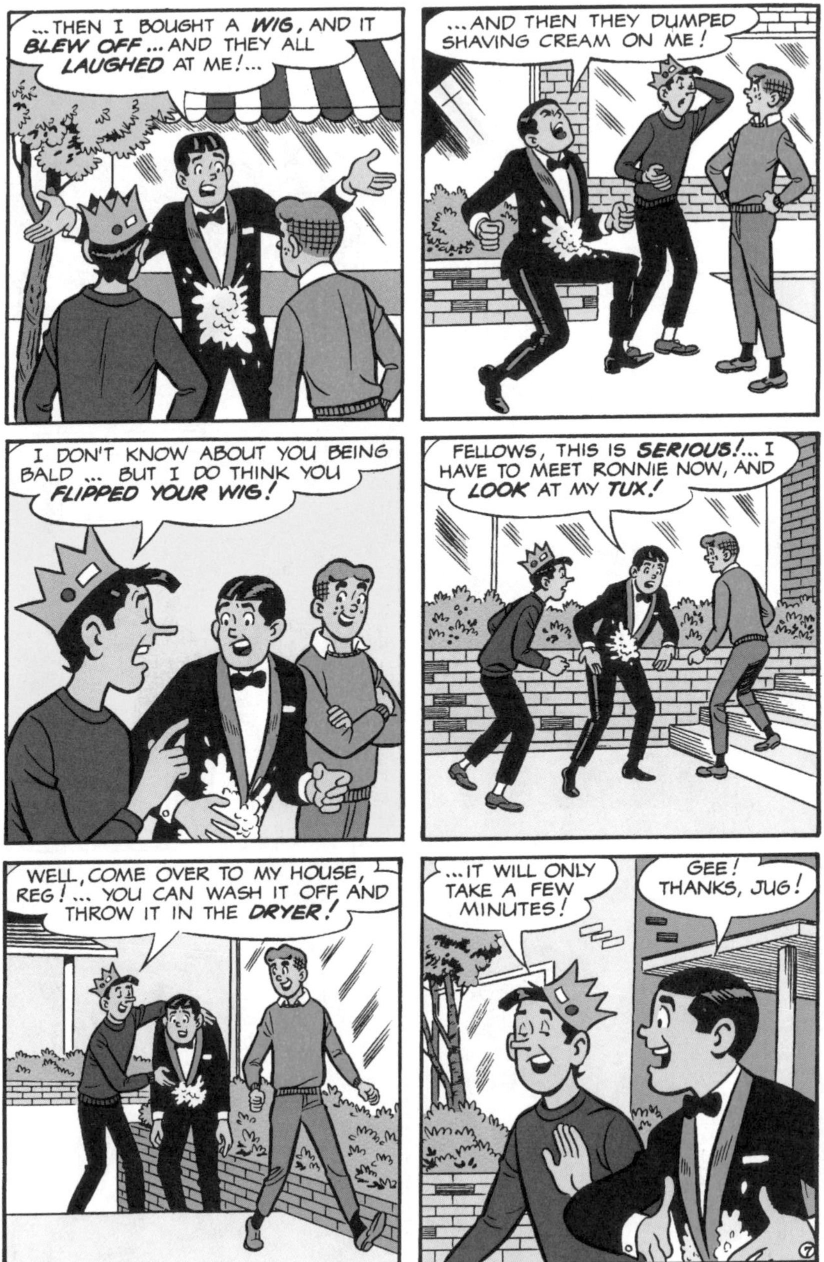
...THEN I BOUGHT A WIG, AND IT BLEW OFF ... AND THEY ALL LAUGHED AT ME!...
...AND THEN THEY DUMPED SHAVING CREAM ON ME!
I DON'T KNOW ABOUT YOU BEING BALD ... BUT I DO THINK YOU FLIPPED YOUR WIG!
FELLOWS, THIS IS SERIOUS!... I HAVE TO MEET RONNIE NOW, AND LOOK AT MY TUX!
WELL, COME OVER TO MY HOUSE, REG!... YOU CAN WASH IT OFF AND THROW IT IN THE DRYER!
...IT WILL ONLY TAKE A FEW MINUTES!
GEE! THANKS, JUG!
7

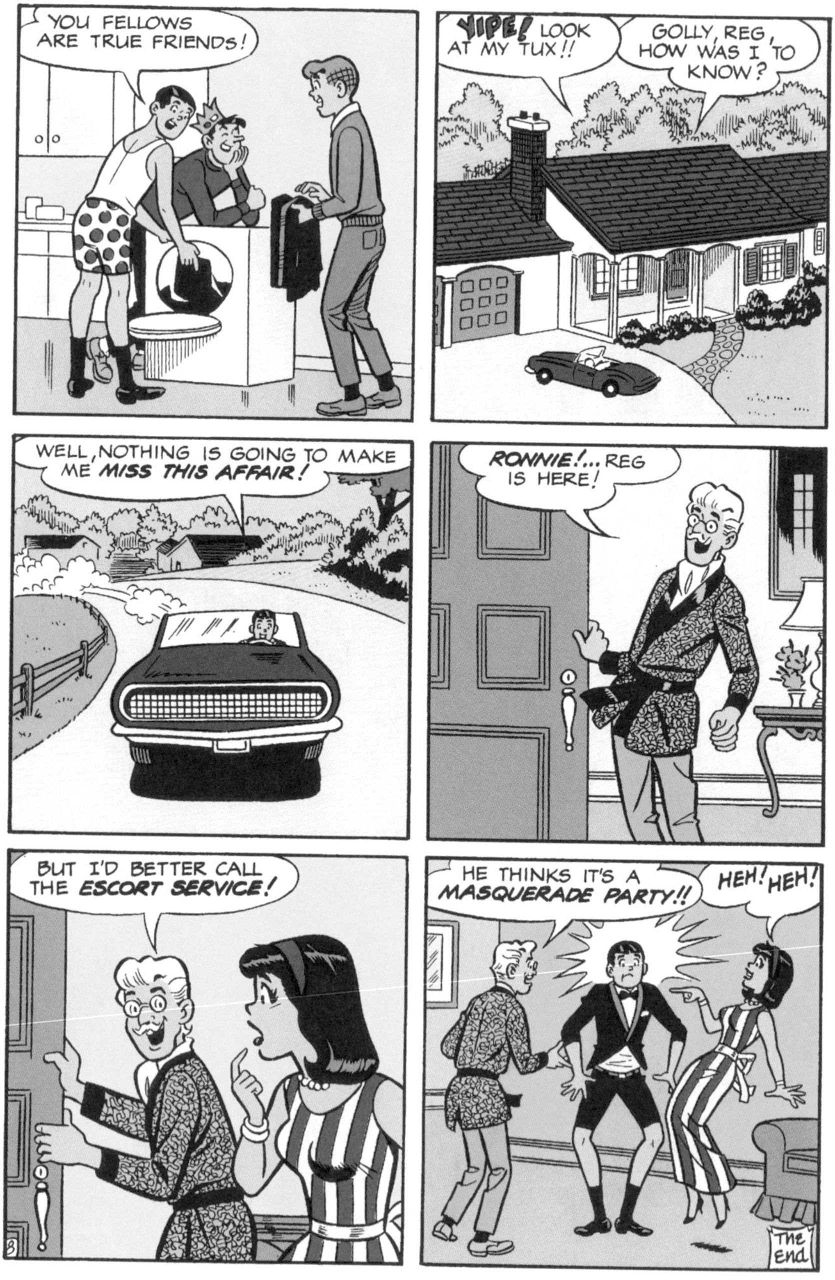
YOU FELLOWS ARE TRUE FRIENDS!
YIPE! LOOK AT MY TUX!!
GOLLY, REG, HOW WAS I TO KNOW?
WELL, NOTHING IS GOING TO MAKE ME MISS THIS AFFAIR!
RONNIE!... REG IS HERE!
BUT I'D BETTER CALL THE ESCORT SERVICE!
HE THINKS IT'S A MASQUERADE PARTY!!
HEH! HEH!
THE END

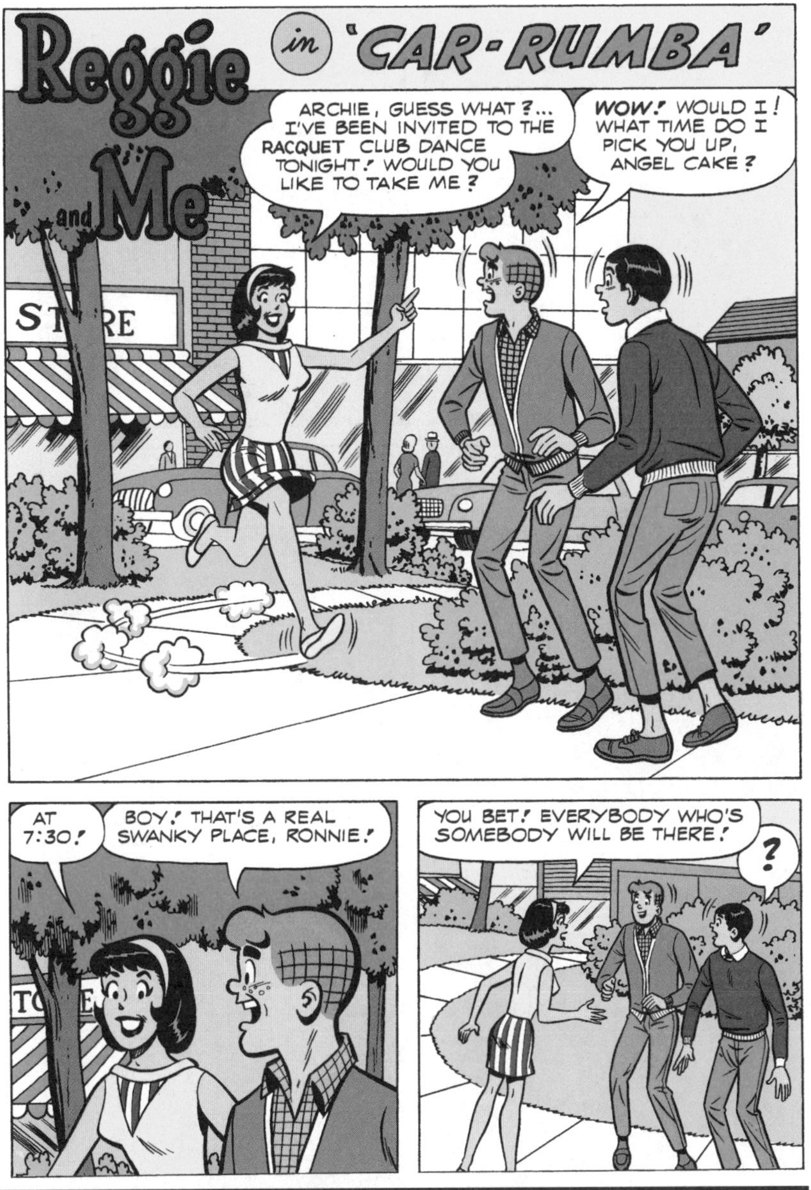
Reggie and Me
in
'CAR-RUMBA'
ARCHIE, GUESS WHAT?... I'VE BEEN INVITED TO THE RACQUET CLUB DANCE TONIGHT! WOULD YOU LIKE TO TAKE ME?
WOW! WOULD I! WHAT TIME DO I PICK YOU UP, ANGEL CAKE?
STORE
AT 7:30!
BOY! THAT'S A REAL SWANKY PLACE, RONNIE!
YOU BET! EVERYBODY WHO'S SOMEBODY WILL BE THERE!
?

Story & Pencils: Al Hartley
Inks & Letters: Jon D'Agostino

Originally printed in REGGIE AND ME #27, JANUARY 1968

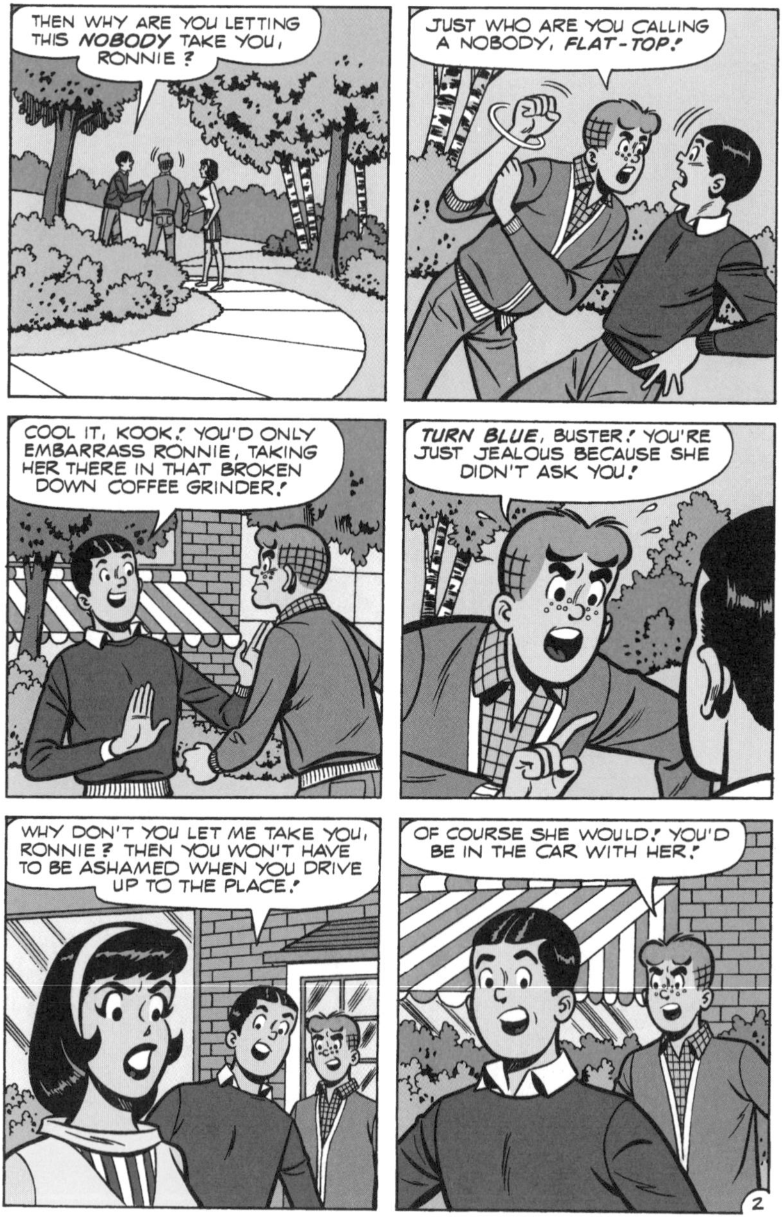
THEN WHY ARE YOU LETTING THIS NOBODY TAKE YOU, RONNIE?
JUST WHO ARE YOU CALLING A NOBODY, FLAT-TOP!
COOL IT, KOOK! YOU'D ONLY EMBARRASS RONNIE, TAKING HER THERE IN THAT BROKEN DOWN COFFEE GRINDER!
TURN BLUE, BUSTER! YOU'RE JUST JEALOUS BECAUSE SHE DIDN'T ASK YOU!
WHY DON'T YOU LET ME TAKE YOU, RONNIE? THEN YOU WON'T HAVE TO BE ASHAMED WHEN YOU DRIVE UP TO THE PLACE!
OF COURSE SHE WOULD! YOU'D BE IN THE CAR WITH HER!
2

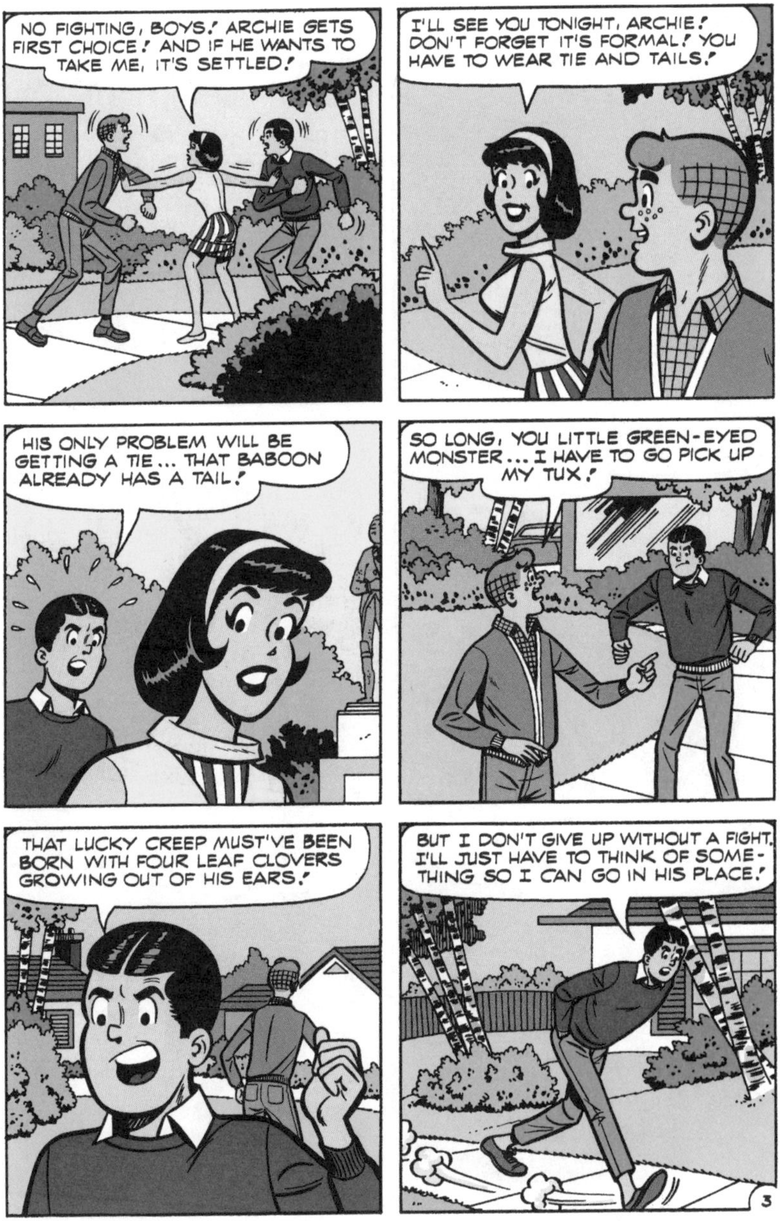
NO FIGHTING, BOYS! ARCHIE GETS FIRST CHOICE! AND IF HE WANTS TO TAKE ME, IT'S SETTLED!
I'LL SEE YOU TONIGHT, ARCHIE! DON'T FORGET IT'S FORMAL! YOU HAVE TO WEAR TIE AND TAILS!
HIS ONLY PROBLEM WILL BE GETTING A TIE... THAT BABOON ALREADY HAS A TAIL!
SO LONG, YOU LITTLE GREEN-EYED MONSTER... I HAVE TO GO PICK UP MY TUX!
THAT LUCKY CREEP MUST'VE BEEN BORN WITH FOUR LEAF CLOVERS GROWING OUT OF HIS EARS!
BUT I DON'T GIVE UP WITHOUT A FIGHT. I'LL JUST HAVE TO THINK OF SOME-THING SO I CAN GO IN HIS PLACE!
3

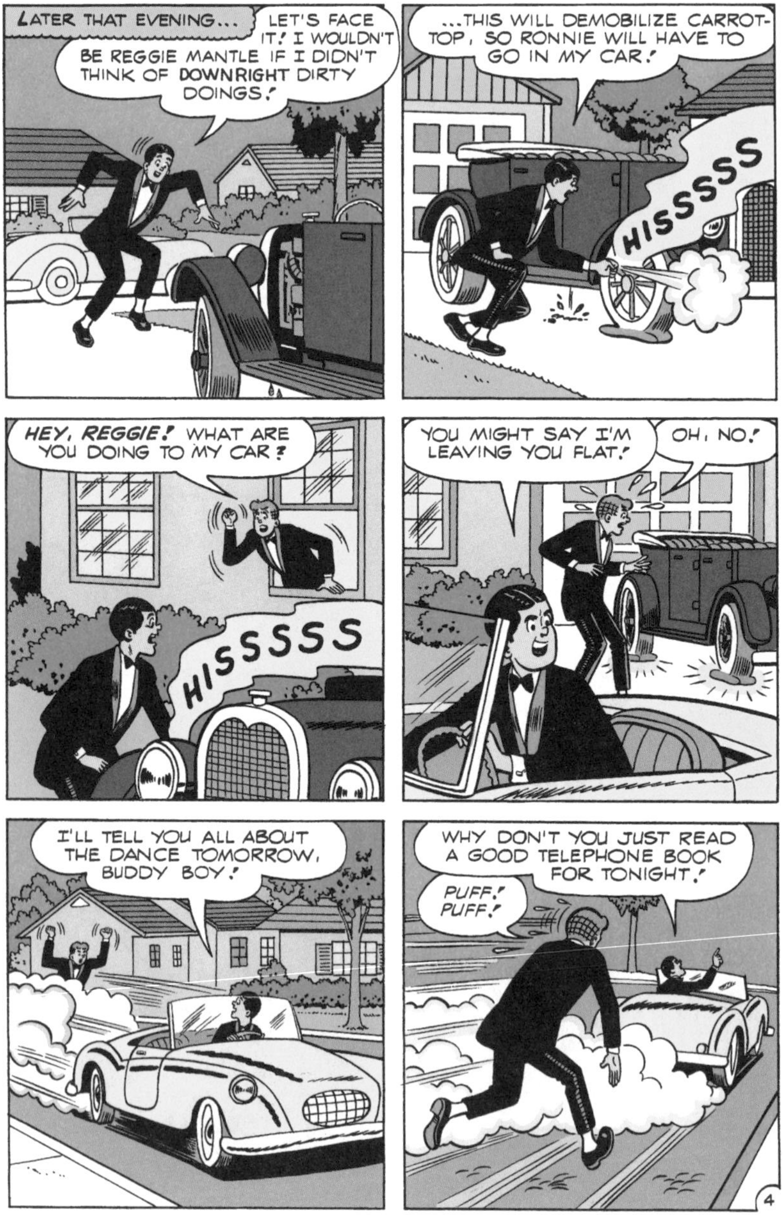
LATER THAT EVENING...
LET'S FACE IT! I WOULDN'T BE REGGIE MANTLE IF I DIDN'T THINK OF **DOWNRIGHT** DIRTY DOINGS!
...THIS WILL DEMOBILIZE CARROT-TOP, SO RONNIE WILL HAVE TO GO IN MY CAR!
HISSSSS
HEY, REGGIE! WHAT ARE YOU DOING TO MY CAR?
HISSSSSS
YOU MIGHT SAY I'M LEAVING YOU FLAT!
OH, NO!
I'LL TELL YOU ALL ABOUT THE DANCE TOMORROW, BUDDY BOY!
WHY DON'T YOU JUST READ A GOOD TELEPHONE BOOK FOR TONIGHT!
PUFF! PUFF!
4

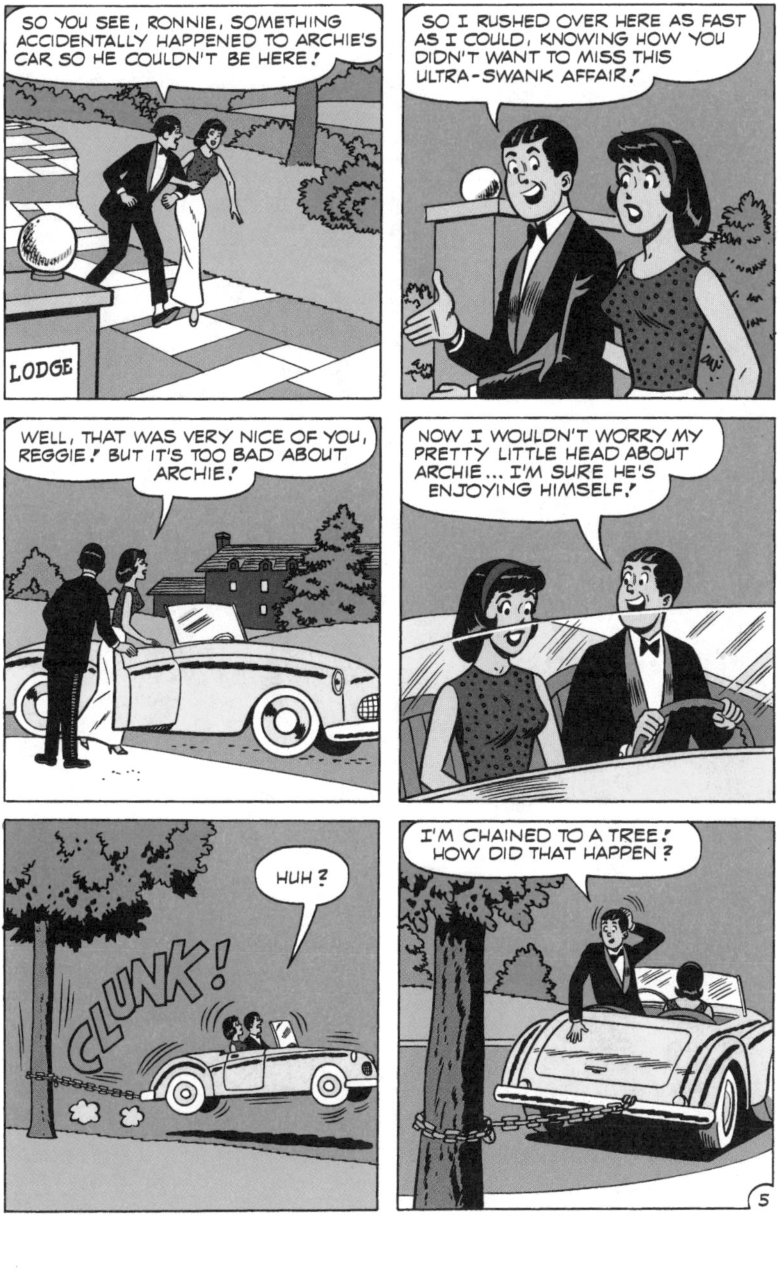
SO YOU SEE, RONNIE, SOMETHING ACCIDENTALLY HAPPENED TO ARCHIE'S CAR SO HE COULDN'T BE HERE!
LODGE
SO I RUSHED OVER HERE AS FAST AS I COULD, KNOWING HOW YOU DIDN'T WANT TO MISS THIS ULTRA-SWANK AFFAIR!
WELL, THAT WAS VERY NICE OF YOU, REGGIE! BUT IT'S TOO BAD ABOUT ARCHIE!
NOW I WOULDN'T WORRY MY PRETTY LITTLE HEAD ABOUT ARCHIE... I'M SURE HE'S ENJOYING HIMSELF!
HUH?
CLUNK!
I'M CHAINED TO A TREE! HOW DID THAT HAPPEN?
5

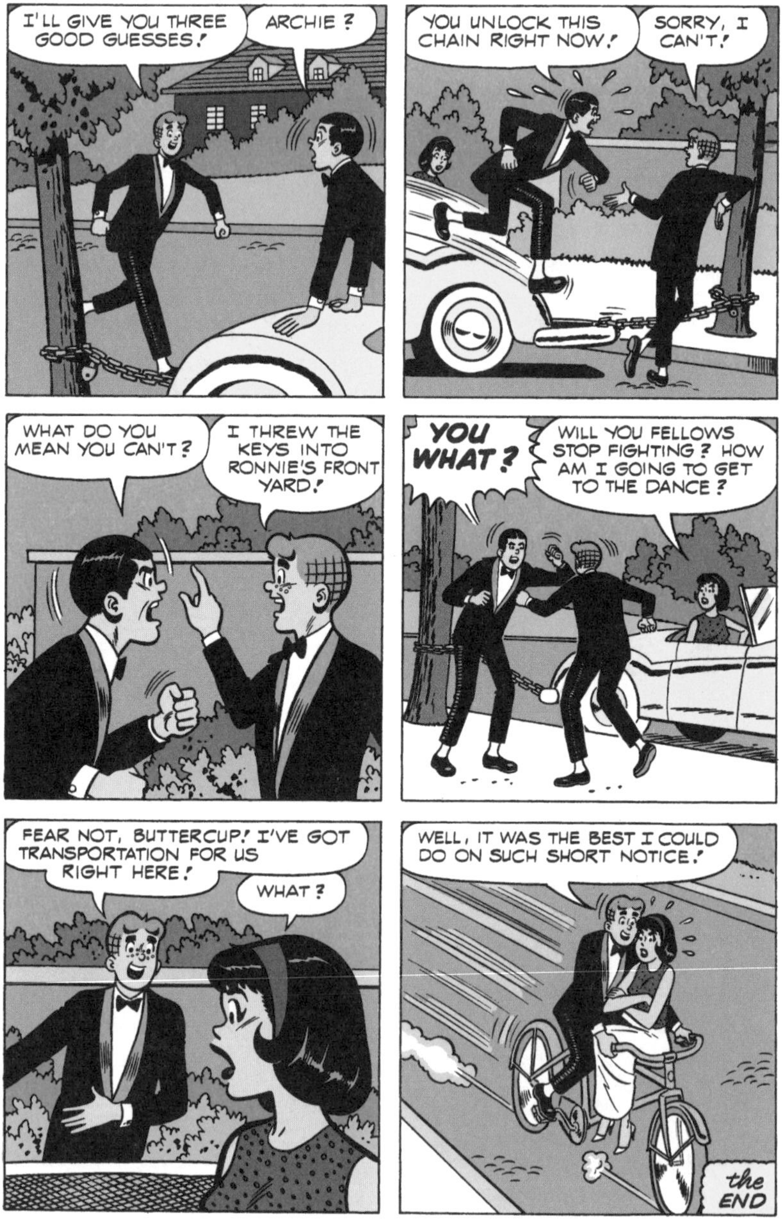
I'LL GIVE YOU THREE GOOD GUESSES!
ARCHIE?
YOU UNLOCK THIS CHAIN RIGHT NOW!
SORRY, I CAN'T!
WHAT DO YOU MEAN YOU CAN'T?
I THREW THE KEYS INTO RONNIE'S FRONT YARD!
YOU WHAT?
WILL YOU FELLOWS STOP FIGHTING? HOW AM I GOING TO GET TO THE DANCE?
FEAR NOT, BUTTERCUP! I'VE GOT TRANSPORTATION FOR US RIGHT HERE!
WHAT?
WELL, IT WAS THE BEST I COULD DO ON SUCH SHORT NOTICE!
the END

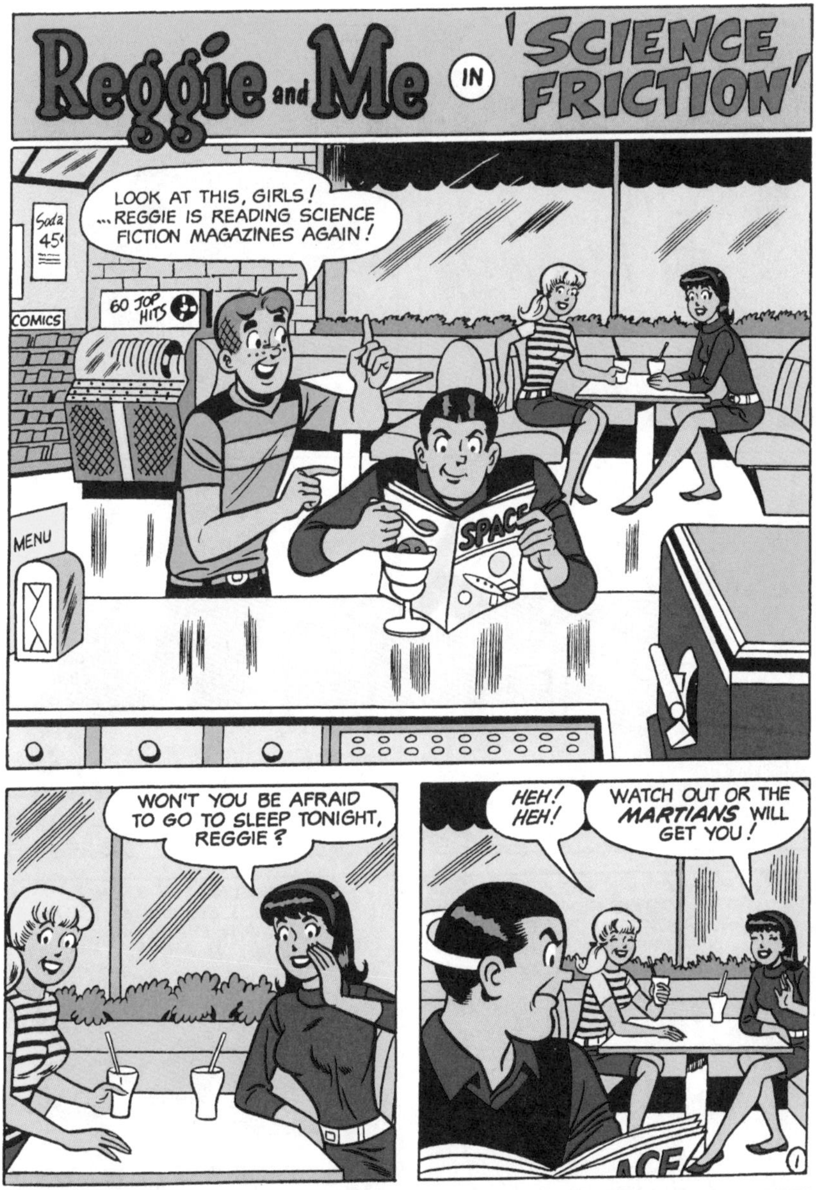
Reggie and Me IN 'SCIENCE FRICTION'
Soda 45¢
COMICS
60 TOP HITS
MENU
LOOK AT THIS, GIRLS! ...REGGIE IS READING SCIENCE FICTION MAGAZINES AGAIN!
SPACE
WON'T YOU BE AFRAID TO GO TO SLEEP TONIGHT, REGGIE?
HEH! HEH!
WATCH OUT OR THE MARTIANS WILL GET YOU!
1

Story: Frank Doyle Pencils & Inks: Bob White
Letters: Bill Yoshida

Originally printed in REGGIE AND ME #27, JANUARY 1968

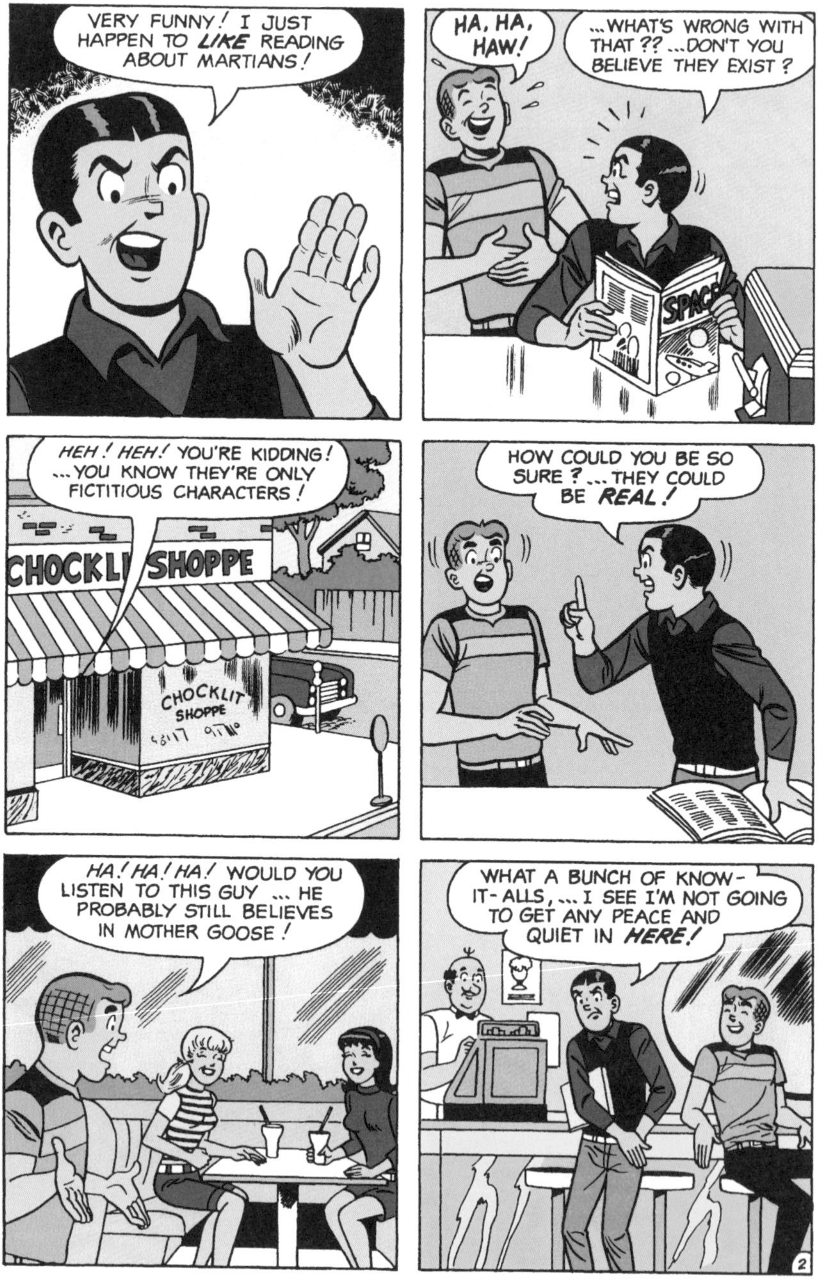
VERY FUNNY! I JUST HAPPEN TO LIKE READING ABOUT MARTIANS!
HA, HA, HAW!
...WHAT'S WRONG WITH THAT?? ...DON'T YOU BELIEVE THEY EXIST?
SPACE
HEH! HEH! YOU'RE KIDDING! ...YOU KNOW THEY'RE ONLY FICTITIOUS CHARACTERS!
CHOCKLI SHOPPE
CHOCKLIT SHOPPE
HOW COULD YOU BE SO SURE? ...THEY COULD BE REAL!
HA! HA! HA! WOULD YOU LISTEN TO THIS GUY ... HE PROBABLY STILL BELIEVES IN MOTHER GOOSE!
WHAT A BUNCH OF KNOW-IT-ALLS, ... I SEE I'M NOT GOING TO GET ANY PEACE AND QUIET IN HERE!
2

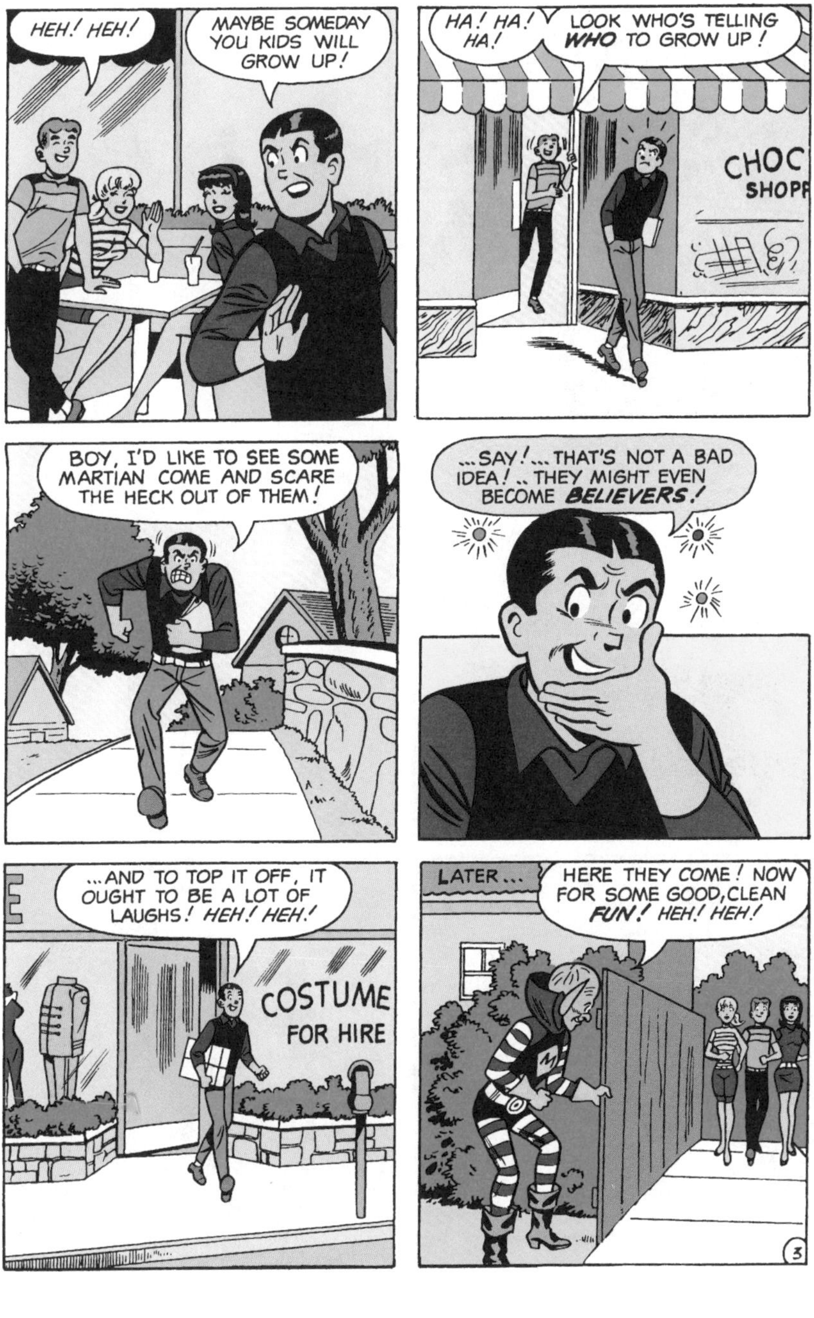
HEH! HEH!
MAYBE SOMEDAY YOU KIDS WILL GROW UP!
HA! HA! HA!
LOOK WHO'S TELLING WHO TO GROW UP!
CHOC SHOPP
BOY, I'D LIKE TO SEE SOME MARTIAN COME AND SCARE THE HECK OUT OF THEM!
...SAY!... THAT'S NOT A BAD IDEA! .. THEY MIGHT EVEN BECOME BELIEVERS!
...AND TO TOP IT OFF, IT OUGHT TO BE A LOT OF LAUGHS! HEH! HEH!
COSTUME FOR HIRE
LATER...
HERE THEY COME! NOW FOR SOME GOOD, CLEAN FUN! HEH! HEH!
3

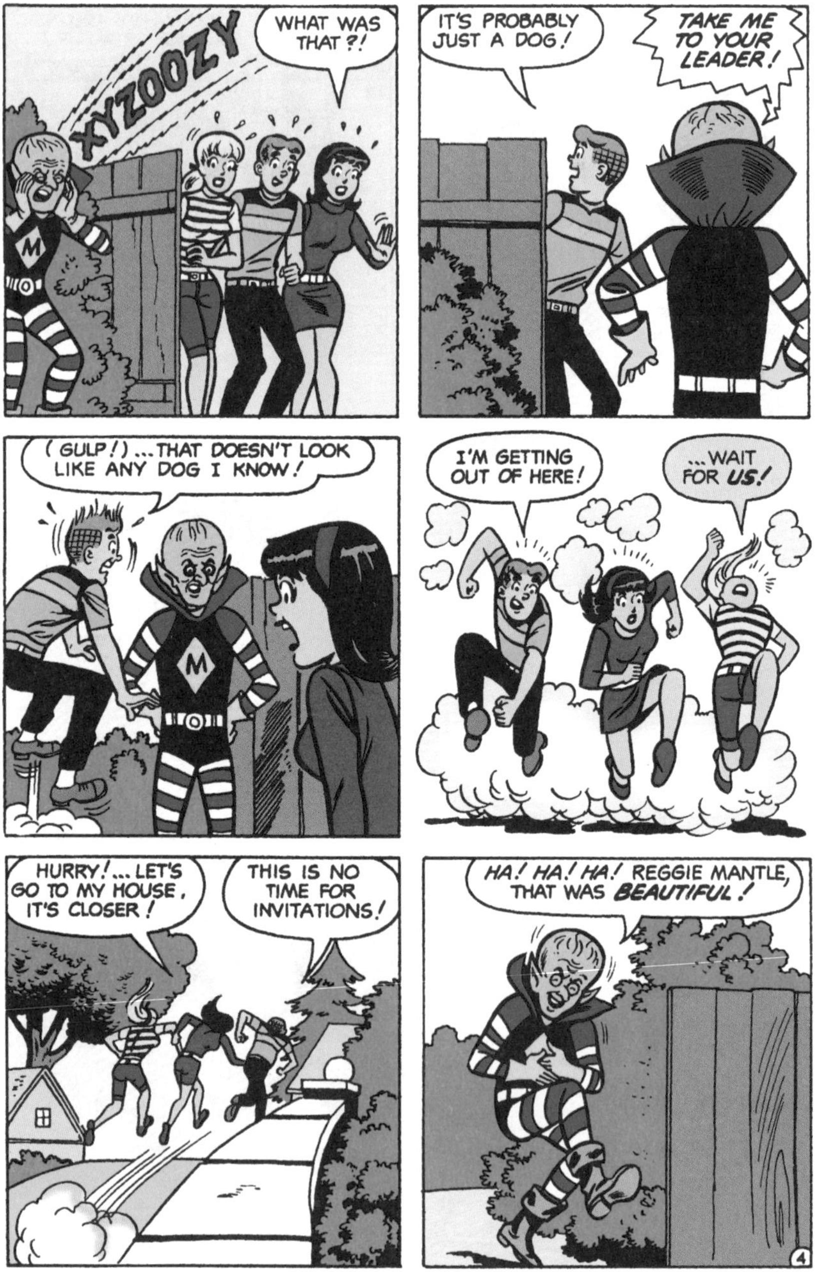
XYZOOZY
WHAT WAS THAT ?!
IT'S PROBABLY JUST A DOG !
TAKE ME TO YOUR LEADER !
(GULP !) ... THAT DOESN'T LOOK LIKE ANY DOG I KNOW !
I'M GETTING OUT OF HERE !
... WAIT FOR US !
HURRY ! ... LET'S GO TO MY HOUSE, IT'S CLOSER !
THIS IS NO TIME FOR INVITATIONS !
HA ! HA ! HA ! REGGIE MANTLE, THAT WAS BEAUTIFUL !
4

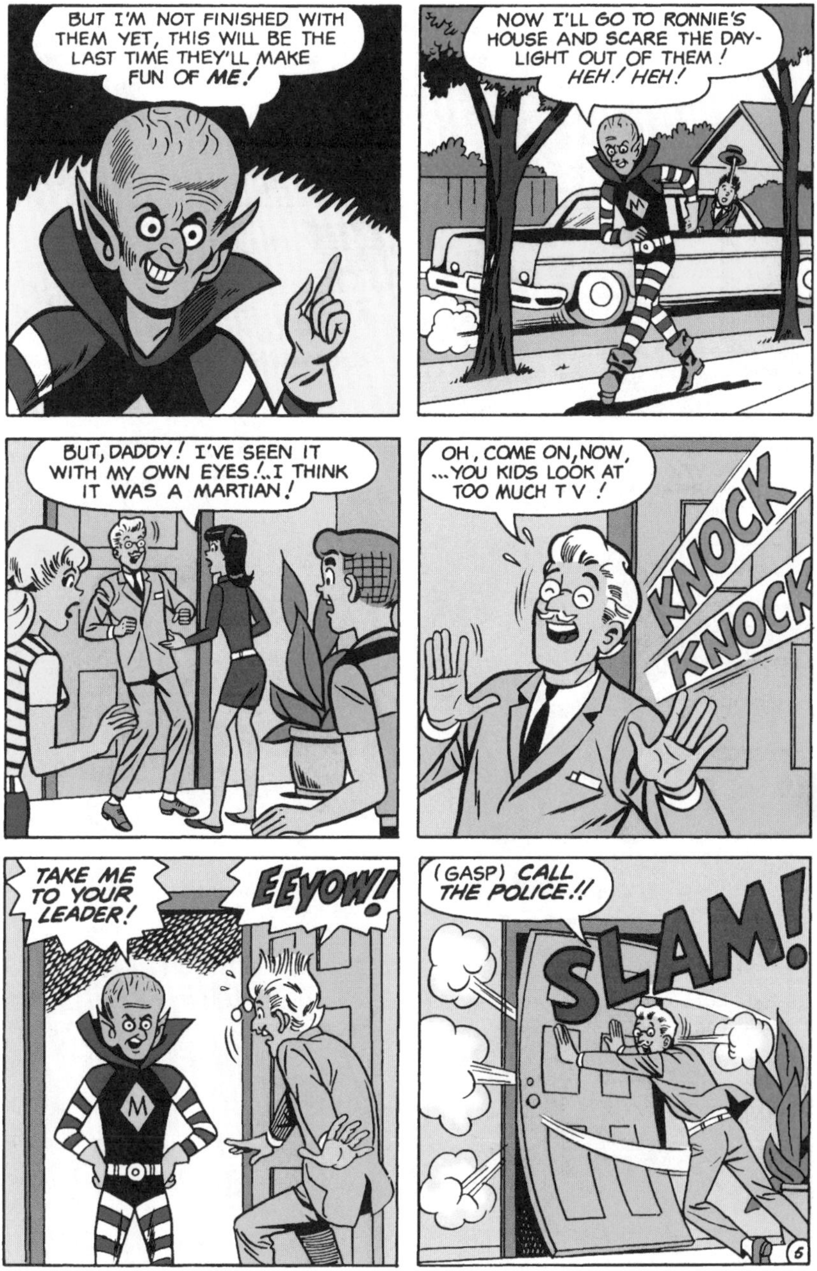
BUT I'M NOT FINISHED WITH THEM YET, THIS WILL BE THE LAST TIME THEY'LL MAKE FUN OF *ME*!
NOW I'LL GO TO RONNIE'S HOUSE AND SCARE THE DAY-LIGHT OUT OF THEM! *HEH! HEH!*
BUT, DADDY! I'VE SEEN IT WITH MY OWN EYES!..I THINK IT WAS A MARTIAN!
OH, COME ON, NOW, ...YOU KIDS LOOK AT TOO MUCH TV!
KNOCK
KNOCK
TAKE ME TO YOUR LEADER!
EEYOW!
(GASP) *CALL THE POLICE!!*
SLAM!
6

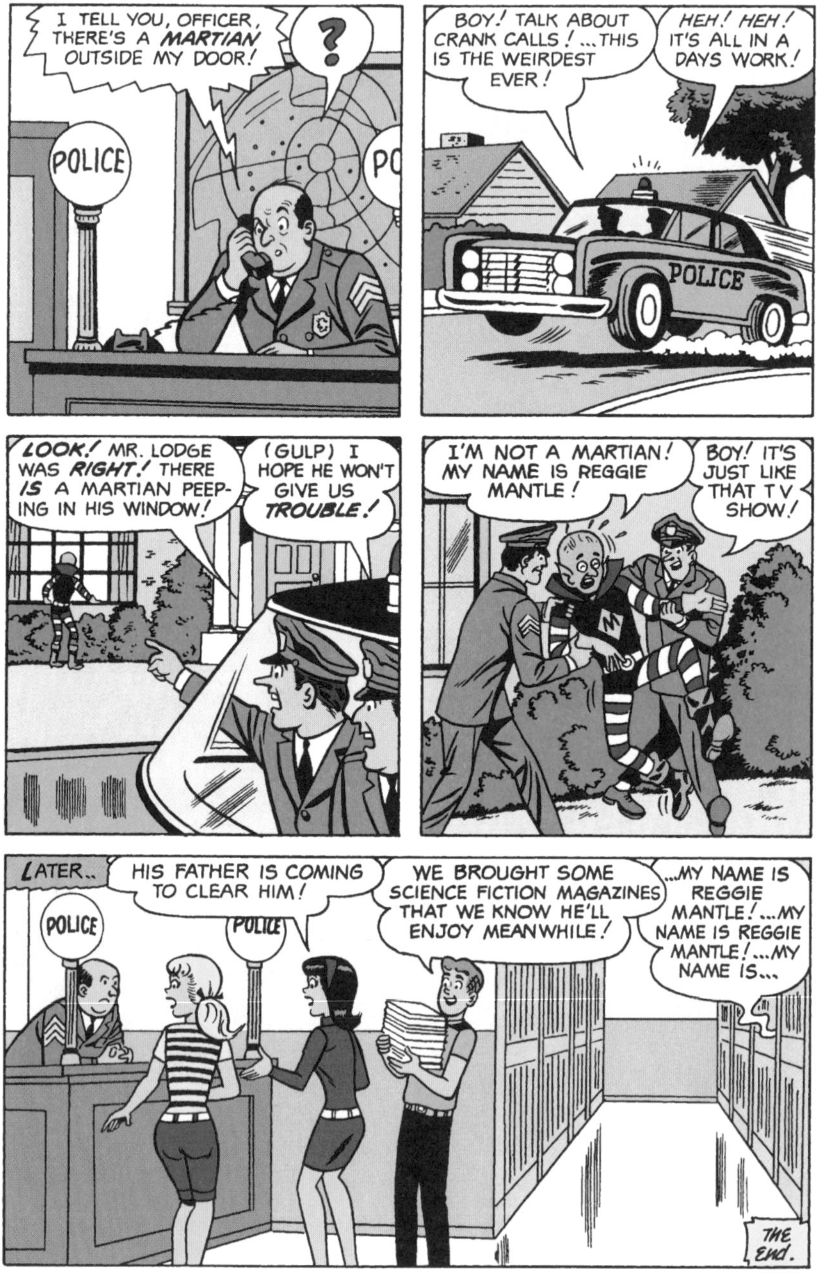
I TELL YOU, OFFICER, THERE'S A MARTIAN OUTSIDE MY DOOR!
?
POLICE
BOY! TALK ABOUT CRANK CALLS! ...THIS IS THE WEIRDEST EVER!
HEH! HEH! IT'S ALL IN A DAYS WORK!
POLICE
LOOK! MR. LODGE WAS RIGHT! THERE IS A MARTIAN PEEPING IN HIS WINDOW!
(GULP) I HOPE HE WON'T GIVE US TROUBLE!
I'M NOT A MARTIAN! MY NAME IS REGGIE MANTLE!
BOY! IT'S JUST LIKE THAT TV SHOW!
LATER..
HIS FATHER IS COMING TO CLEAR HIM!
POLICE
POLICE
WE BROUGHT SOME SCIENCE FICTION MAGAZINES THAT WE KNOW HE'LL ENJOY MEANWHILE!
...MY NAME IS REGGIE MANTLE! ...MY NAME IS REGGIE MANTLE! ...MY NAME IS...
THE End.

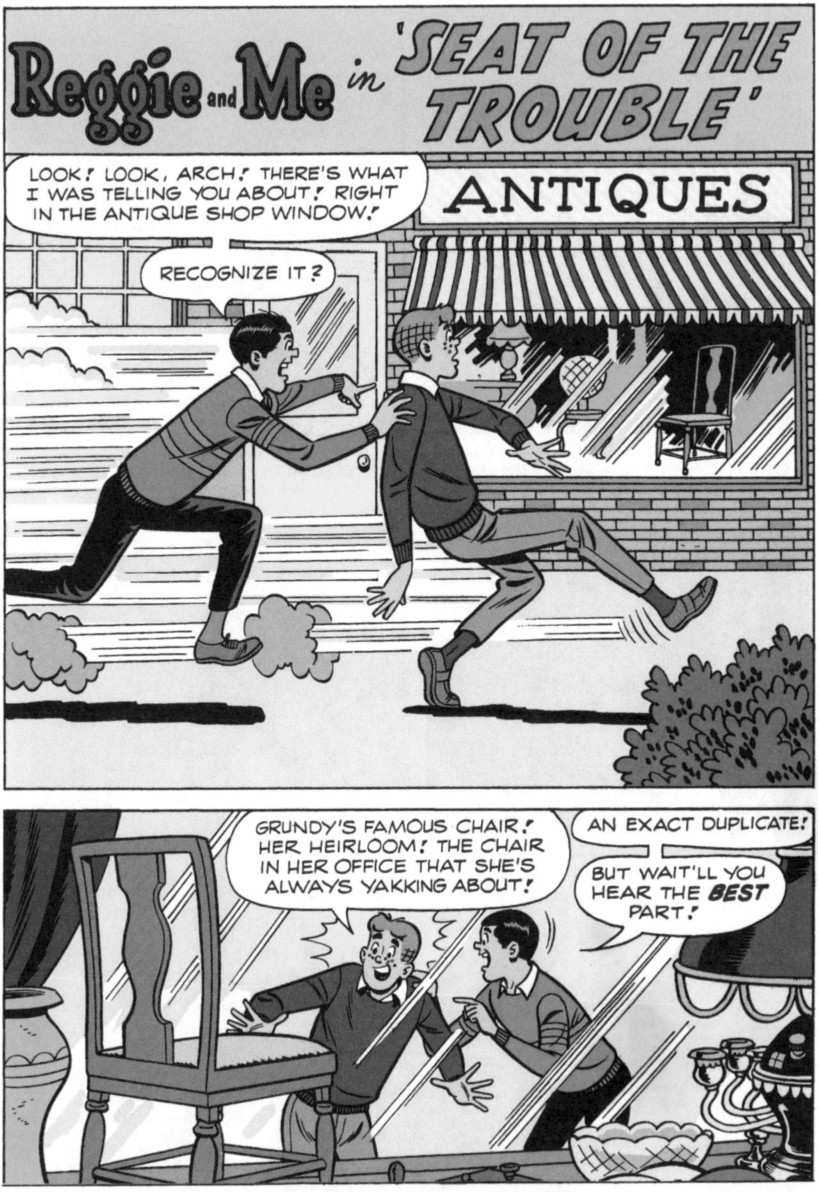
Reggie and Me in 'SEAT OF THE TROUBLE'
LOOK! LOOK, ARCH! THERE'S WHAT I WAS TELLING YOU ABOUT! RIGHT IN THE ANTIQUE SHOP WINDOW!
RECOGNIZE IT?
ANTIQUES
GRUNDY'S FAMOUS CHAIR! HER HEIRLOOM! THE CHAIR IN HER OFFICE THAT SHE'S ALWAYS YAKKING ABOUT!
AN EXACT DUPLICATE!
BUT WAIT'LL YOU HEAR THE *BEST* PART!

Story & Pencils: Al Hartley
Inks & Letters: Jon D'Agostino

Originally printed in REGGIE AND ME #29, MAY 1968

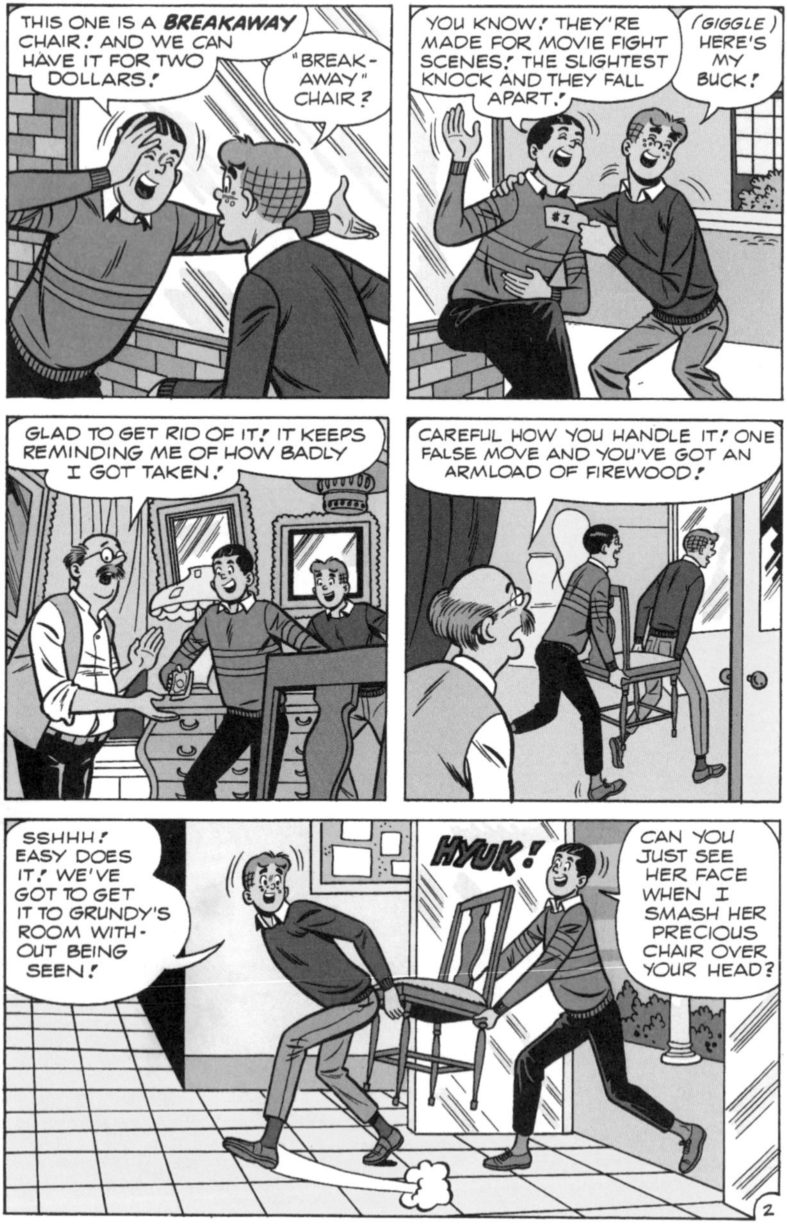
THIS ONE IS A BREAKAWAY CHAIR! AND WE CAN HAVE IT FOR TWO DOLLARS!
"BREAK-AWAY" CHAIR?
YOU KNOW! THEY'RE MADE FOR MOVIE FIGHT SCENES! THE SLIGHTEST KNOCK AND THEY FALL APART!
(GIGGLE) HERE'S MY BUCK!
#1
GLAD TO GET RID OF IT! IT KEEPS REMINDING ME OF HOW BADLY I GOT TAKEN!
CAREFUL HOW YOU HANDLE IT! ONE FALSE MOVE AND YOU'VE GOT AN ARMLOAD OF FIREWOOD!
SSHHH! EASY DOES IT! WE'VE GOT TO GET IT TO GRUNDY'S ROOM WITH-OUT BEING SEEN!
HYUK!
CAN YOU JUST SEE HER FACE WHEN I SMASH HER PRECIOUS CHAIR OVER YOUR HEAD?
2

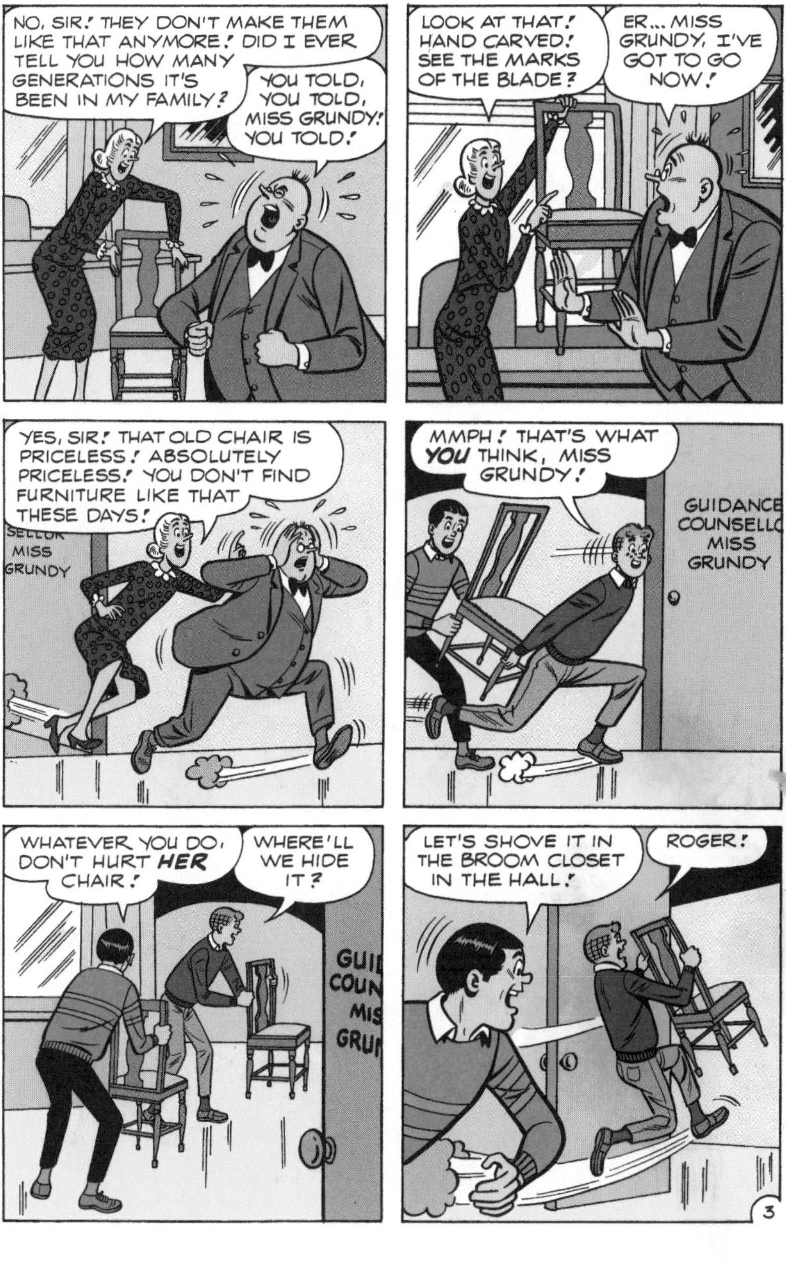
NO, SIR! THEY DON'T MAKE THEM LIKE THAT ANYMORE! DID I EVER TELL YOU HOW MANY GENERATIONS IT'S BEEN IN MY FAMILY?
YOU TOLD, YOU TOLD, MISS GRUNDY! YOU TOLD!
LOOK AT THAT! HAND CARVED! SEE THE MARKS OF THE BLADE?
ER... MISS GRUNDY, I'VE GOT TO GO NOW!
YES, SIR! THAT OLD CHAIR IS PRICELESS! ABSOLUTELY PRICELESS! YOU DON'T FIND FURNITURE LIKE THAT THESE DAYS!
MISS GRUNDY
MMPH! THAT'S WHAT YOU THINK, MISS GRUNDY!
GUIDANCE COUNSELL MISS GRUNDY
WHATEVER YOU DO, DON'T HURT HER CHAIR!
WHERE'LL WE HIDE IT?
LET'S SHOVE IT IN THE BROOM CLOSET IN THE HALL!
ROGER!
3

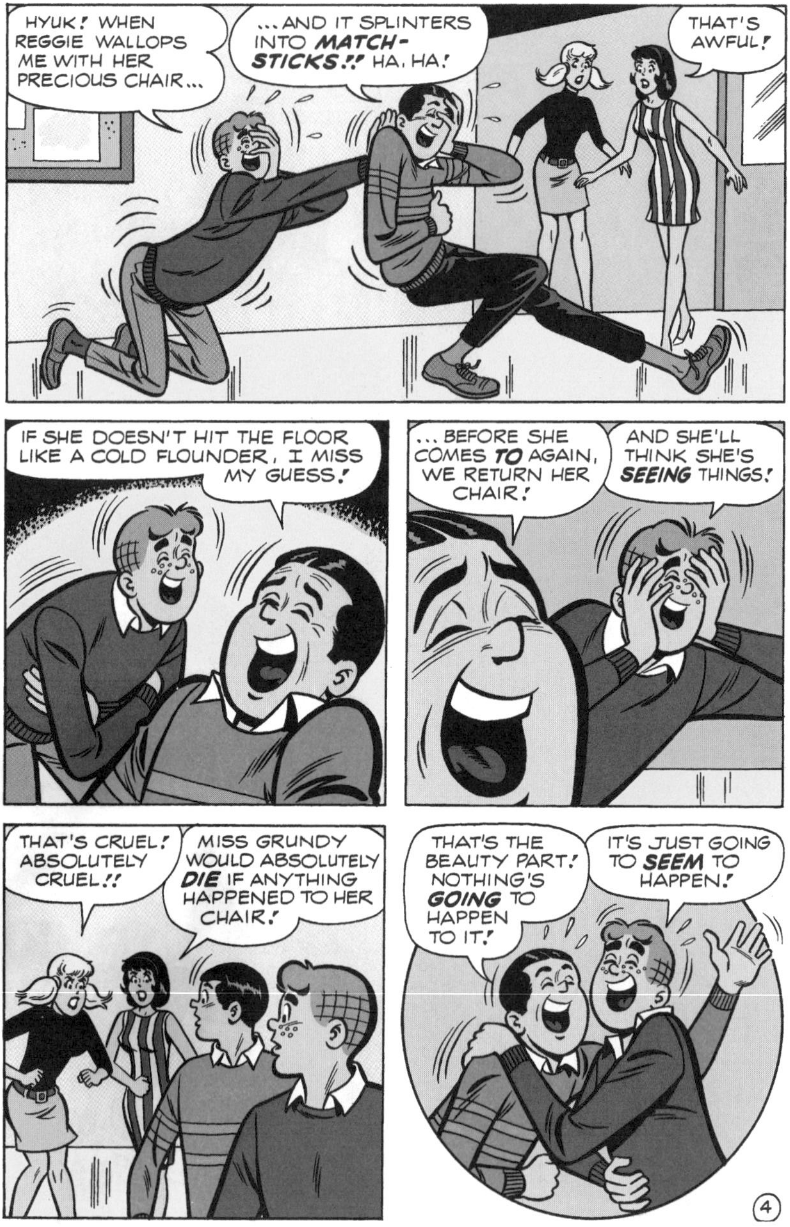
HYUK! WHEN REGGIE WALLOPS ME WITH HER PRECIOUS CHAIR...
...AND IT SPLINTERS INTO MATCH-STICKS!!! HA, HA!
THAT'S AWFUL!
IF SHE DOESN'T HIT THE FLOOR LIKE A COLD FLOUNDER, I MISS MY GUESS!
...BEFORE SHE COMES TO AGAIN, WE RETURN HER CHAIR!
AND SHE'LL THINK SHE'S SEEING THINGS!
THAT'S CRUEL! ABSOLUTELY CRUEL!!
MISS GRUNDY WOULD ABSOLUTELY DIE IF ANYTHING HAPPENED TO HER CHAIR!
THAT'S THE BEAUTY PART! NOTHING'S GOING TO HAPPEN TO IT!
IT'S JUST GOING TO SEEM TO HAPPEN!
4

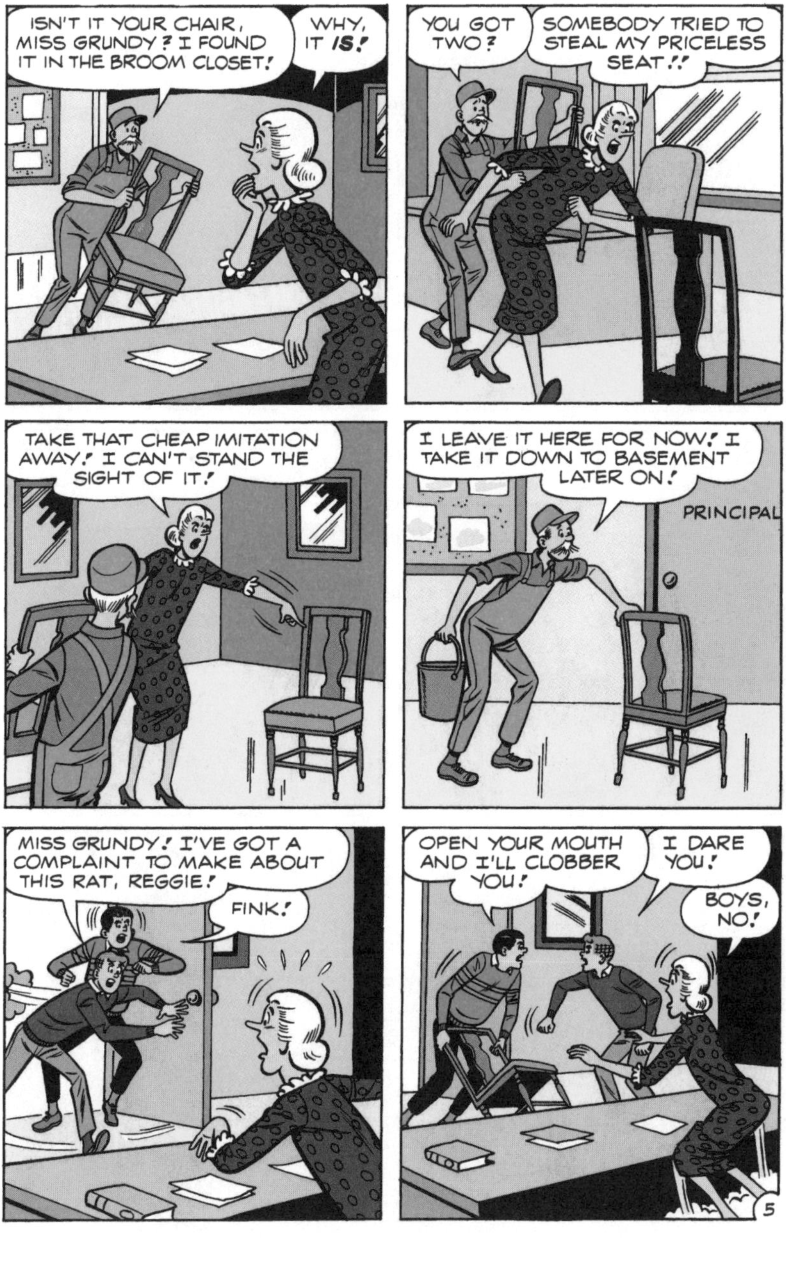
ISN'T IT YOUR CHAIR, MISS GRUNDY? I FOUND IT IN THE BROOM CLOSET!
WHY, IT IS!
YOU GOT TWO?
SOMEBODY TRIED TO STEAL MY PRICELESS SEAT!!
TAKE THAT CHEAP IMITATION AWAY! I CAN'T STAND THE SIGHT OF IT!
I LEAVE IT HERE FOR NOW! I TAKE IT DOWN TO BASEMENT LATER ON!
PRINCIPAL
MISS GRUNDY! I'VE GOT A COMPLAINT TO MAKE ABOUT THIS RAT, REGGIE!
FINK!
OPEN YOUR MOUTH AND I'LL CLOBBER YOU!
I DARE YOU!
BOYS, NO!
5

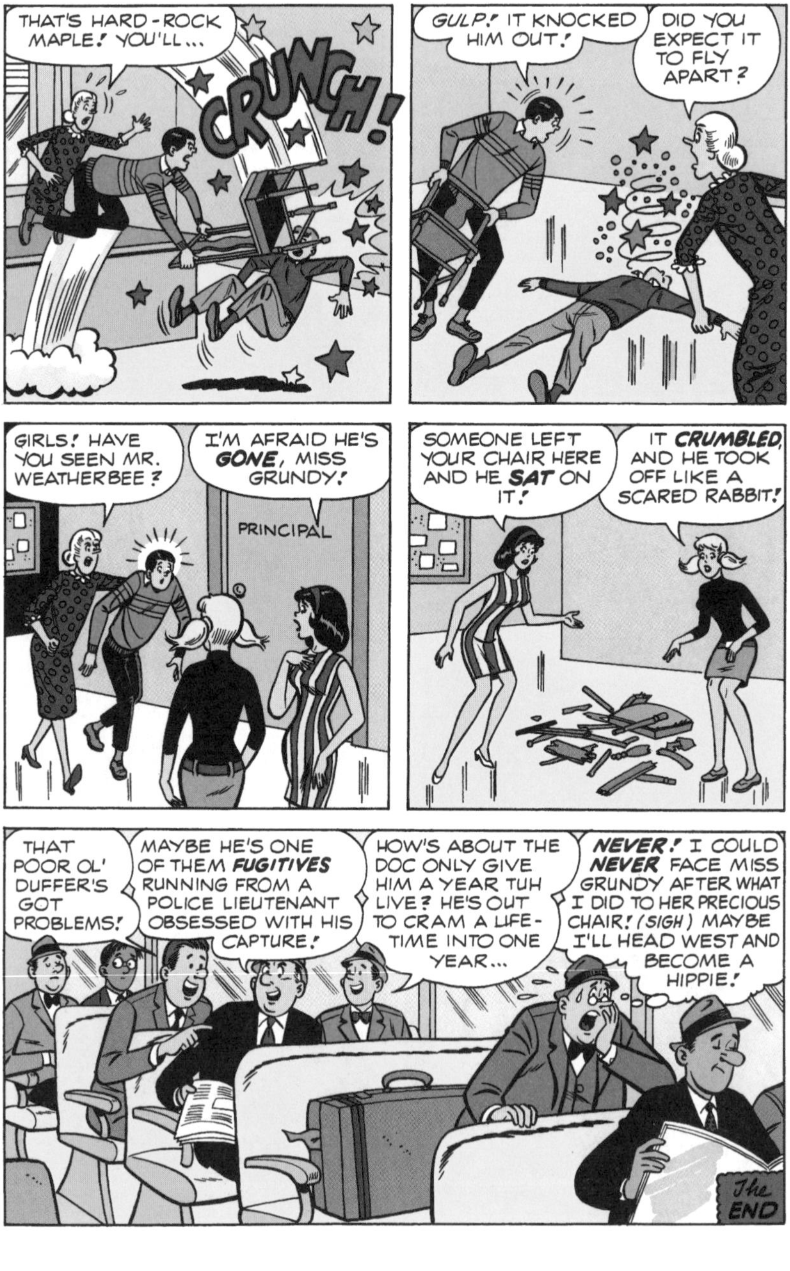
THAT'S HARD-ROCK MAPLE! YOU'LL...
CRUNCH!
GULP! IT KNOCKED HIM OUT!
DID YOU EXPECT IT TO FLY APART?
GIRLS! HAVE YOU SEEN MR. WEATHERBEE?
I'M AFRAID HE'S GONE, MISS GRUNDY!
PRINCIPAL
SOMEONE LEFT YOUR CHAIR HERE AND HE SAT ON IT!
IT CRUMBLED, AND HE TOOK OFF LIKE A SCARED RABBIT!
THAT POOR OL' DUFFER'S GOT PROBLEMS!
MAYBE HE'S ONE OF THEM FUGITIVES RUNNING FROM A POLICE LIEUTENANT OBSESSED WITH HIS CAPTURE!
HOW'S ABOUT THE DOC ONLY GIVE HIM A YEAR TUH LIVE? HE'S OUT TO CRAM A LIFE-TIME INTO ONE YEAR...
NEVER! I COULD NEVER FACE MISS GRUNDY AFTER WHAT I DID TO HER PRECIOUS CHAIR! (SIGH) MAYBE I'LL HEAD WEST AND BECOME A HIPPIE!
The END

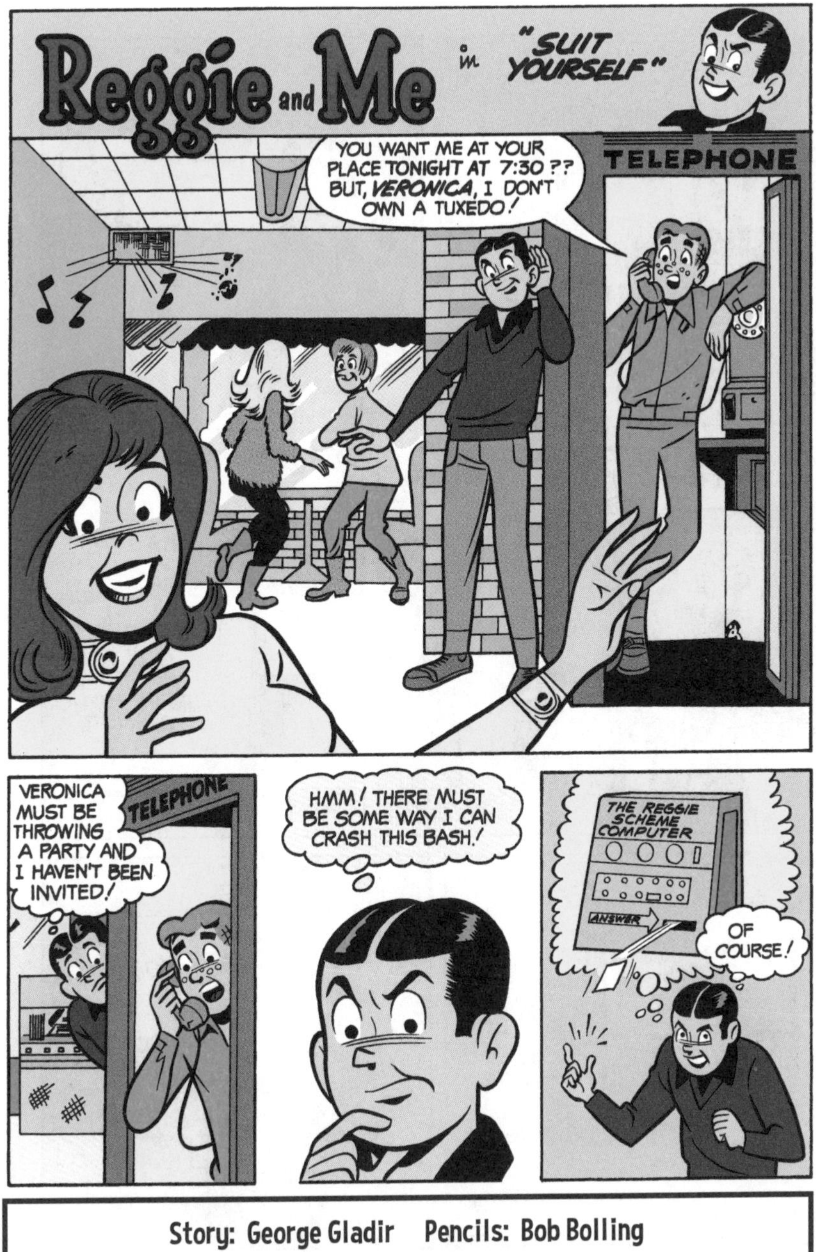
Reggie and Me
in "SUIT YOURSELF"
TELEPHONE
YOU WANT ME AT YOUR PLACE TONIGHT AT 7:30 ?? BUT, VERONICA, I DON'T OWN A TUXEDO!
TELEPHONE
VERONICA MUST BE THROWING A PARTY AND I HAVEN'T BEEN INVITED!
HMM! THERE MUST BE SOME WAY I CAN CRASH THIS BASH!
THE REGGIE SCHEME COMPUTER
ANSWER
OF COURSE!

Story: George Gladir   Pencils: Bob Bolling
Inks: Marty Epp   Letters: Bill Yoshida

Originally printed in REGGIE AND ME #29, MAY 1968

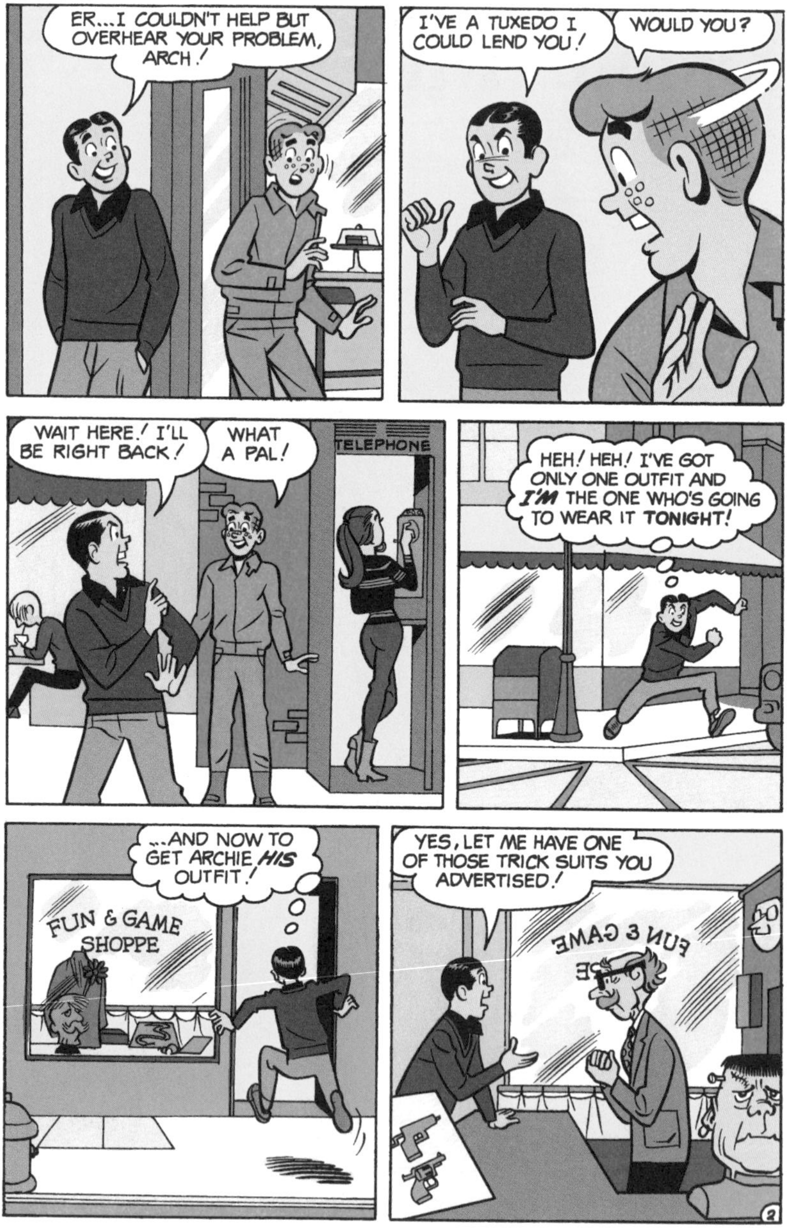
ER...I COULDN'T HELP BUT OVERHEAR YOUR PROBLEM, ARCH!
I'VE A TUXEDO I COULD LEND YOU!
WOULD YOU?
WAIT HERE! I'LL BE RIGHT BACK!
WHAT A PAL!
TELEPHONE
HEH! HEH! I'VE GOT ONLY ONE OUTFIT AND I'M THE ONE WHO'S GOING TO WEAR IT TONIGHT!
...AND NOW TO GET ARCHIE HIS OUTFIT!
FUN & GAME SHOPPE
YES, LET ME HAVE ONE OF THOSE TRICK SUITS YOU ADVERTISED!
2

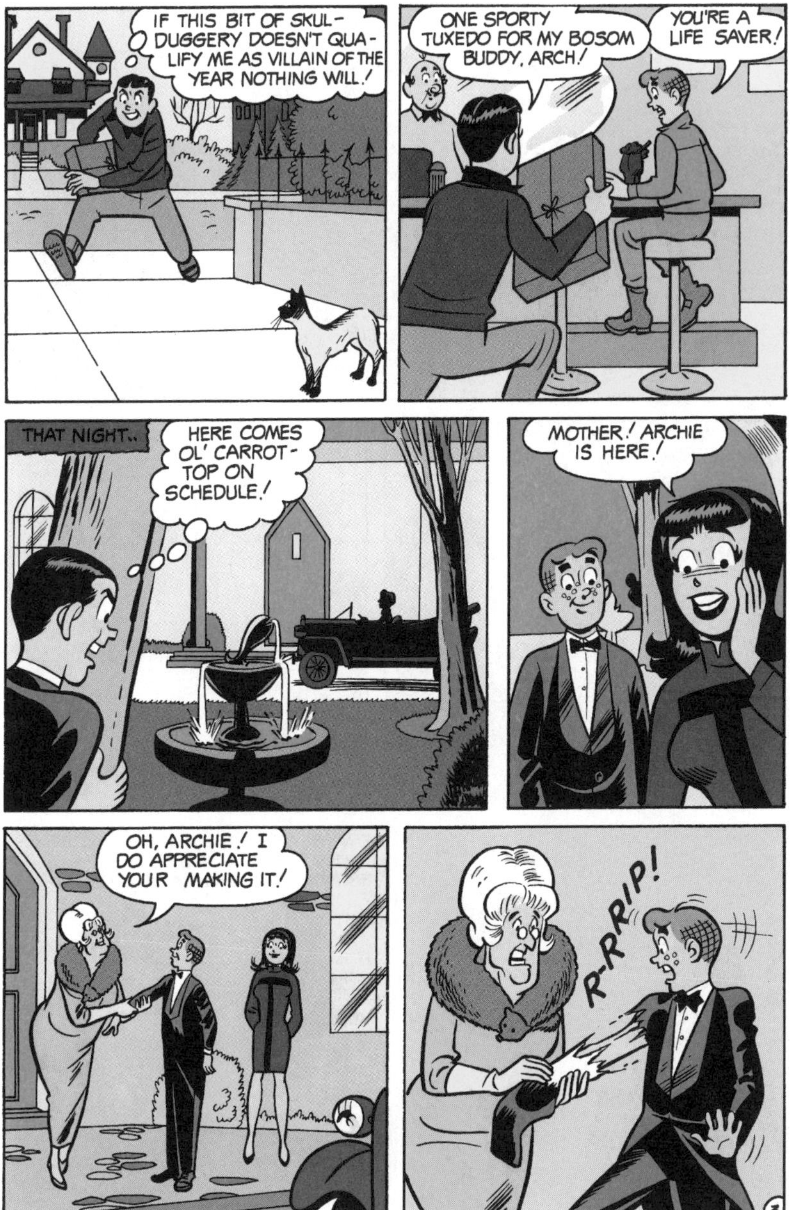
IF THIS BIT OF SKUL-DUGGERY DOESN'T QUA-LIFY ME AS VILLAIN OF THE YEAR NOTHING WILL!
ONE SPORTY TUXEDO FOR MY BOSOM BUDDY, ARCH!
YOU'RE A LIFE SAVER!
THAT NIGHT..
HERE COMES OL' CARROT-TOP ON SCHEDULE!
MOTHER! ARCHIE IS HERE!
OH, ARCHIE! I DO APPRECIATE YOUR MAKING IT!
R-R-RIP!
3

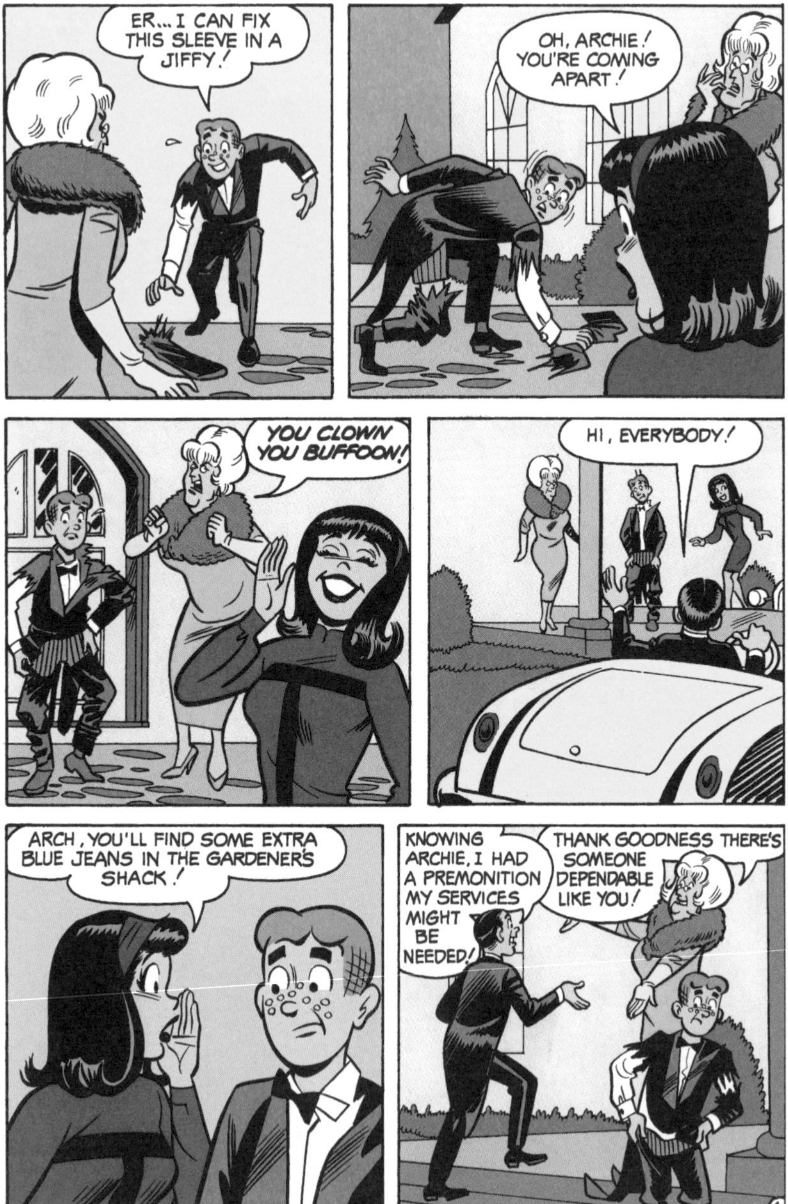
ER... I CAN FIX THIS SLEEVE IN A JIFFY!
OH, ARCHIE! YOU'RE COMING APART!
YOU CLOWN YOU BUFFOON!
HI, EVERYBODY!
ARCH, YOU'LL FIND SOME EXTRA BLUE JEANS IN THE GARDENER'S SHACK!
KNOWING ARCHIE, I HAD A PREMONITION MY SERVICES MIGHT BE NEEDED!
THANK GOODNESS THERE'S SOMEONE DEPENDABLE LIKE YOU!
4

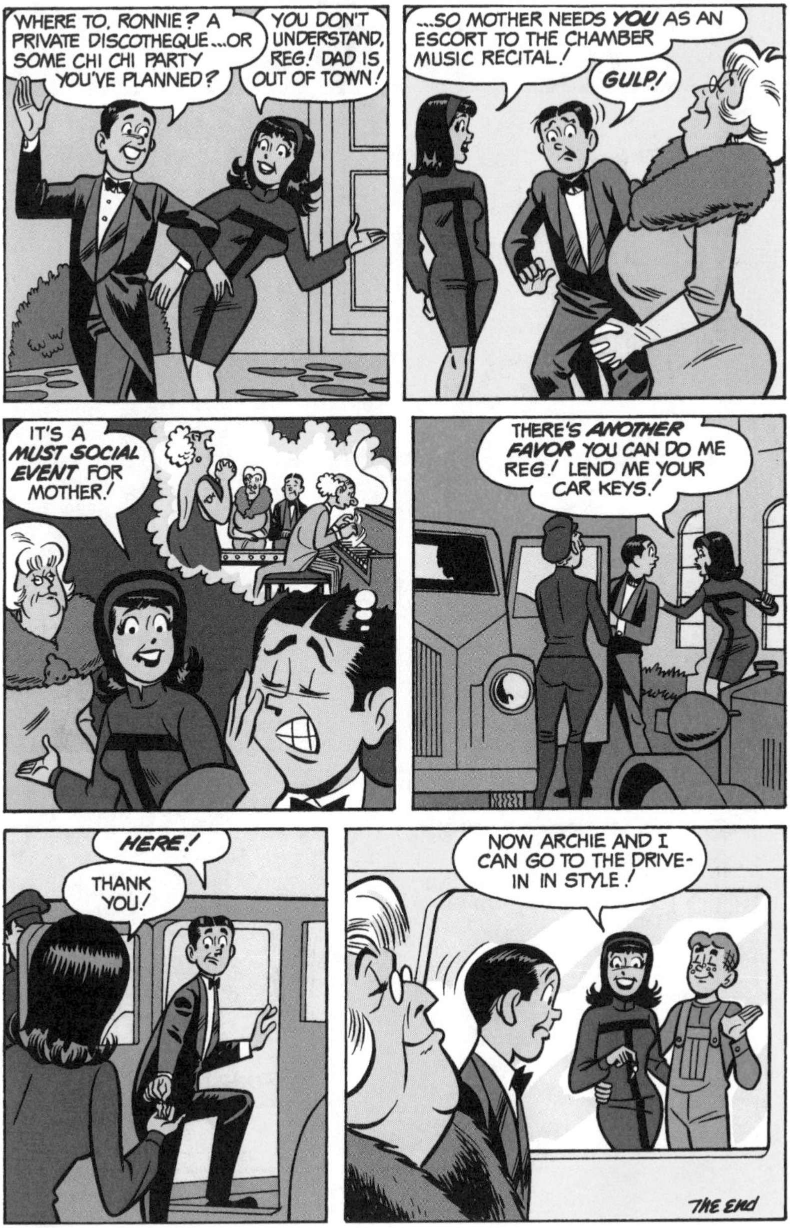
WHERE TO, RONNIE? A PRIVATE DISCOTHEQUE...OR SOME CHI CHI PARTY YOU'VE PLANNED?
YOU DON'T UNDERSTAND, REG! DAD IS OUT OF TOWN!
...SO MOTHER NEEDS YOU AS AN ESCORT TO THE CHAMBER MUSIC RECITAL!
GULP!
IT'S A MUST SOCIAL EVENT FOR MOTHER!
THERE'S ANOTHER FAVOR YOU CAN DO ME REG! LEND ME YOUR CAR KEYS!
HERE!
THANK YOU!
NOW ARCHIE AND I CAN GO TO THE DRIVE-IN IN STYLE!
THE END

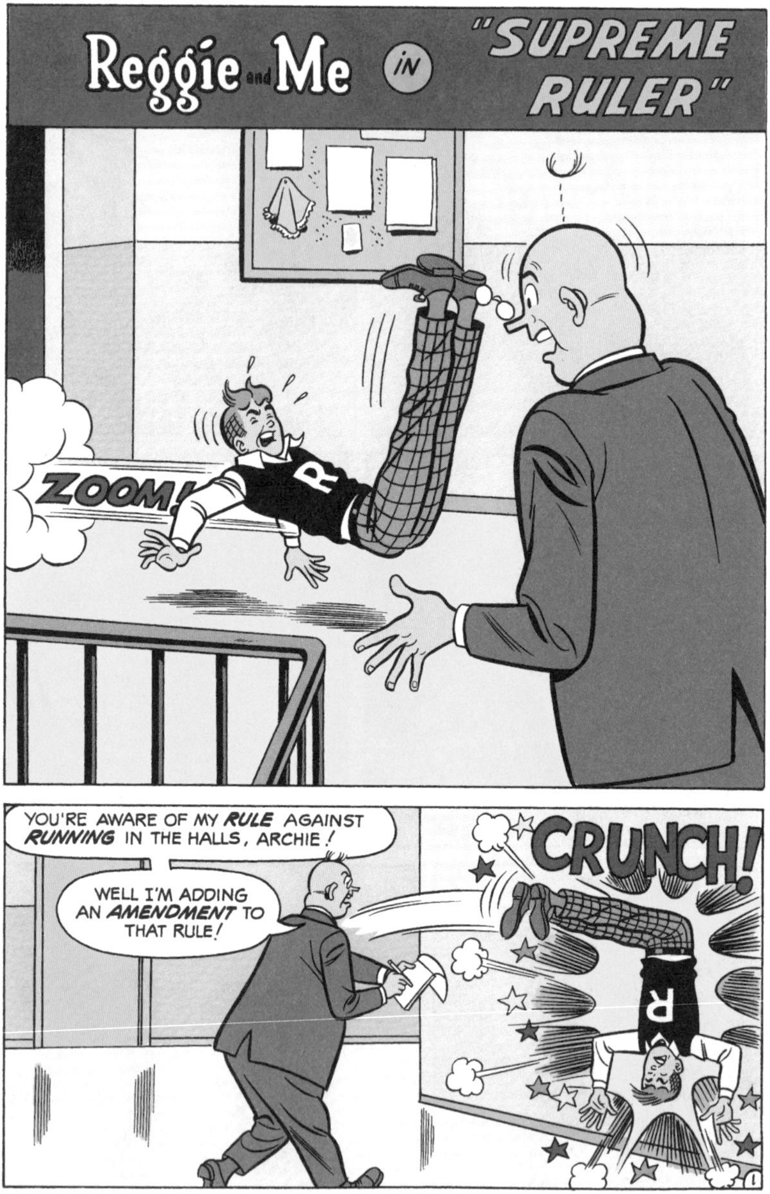
Reggie and Me
in
"SUPREME RULER"
ZOOM!
YOU'RE AWARE OF MY RULE AGAINST RUNNING IN THE HALLS, ARCHIE!
WELL I'M ADDING AN AMENDMENT TO THAT RULE!
CRUNCH!

Story: Frank Doyle Pencils & Inks: Bob White
Letters: Bill Yoshida

Originally printed in REGGIE AND ME #30, JULY 1968

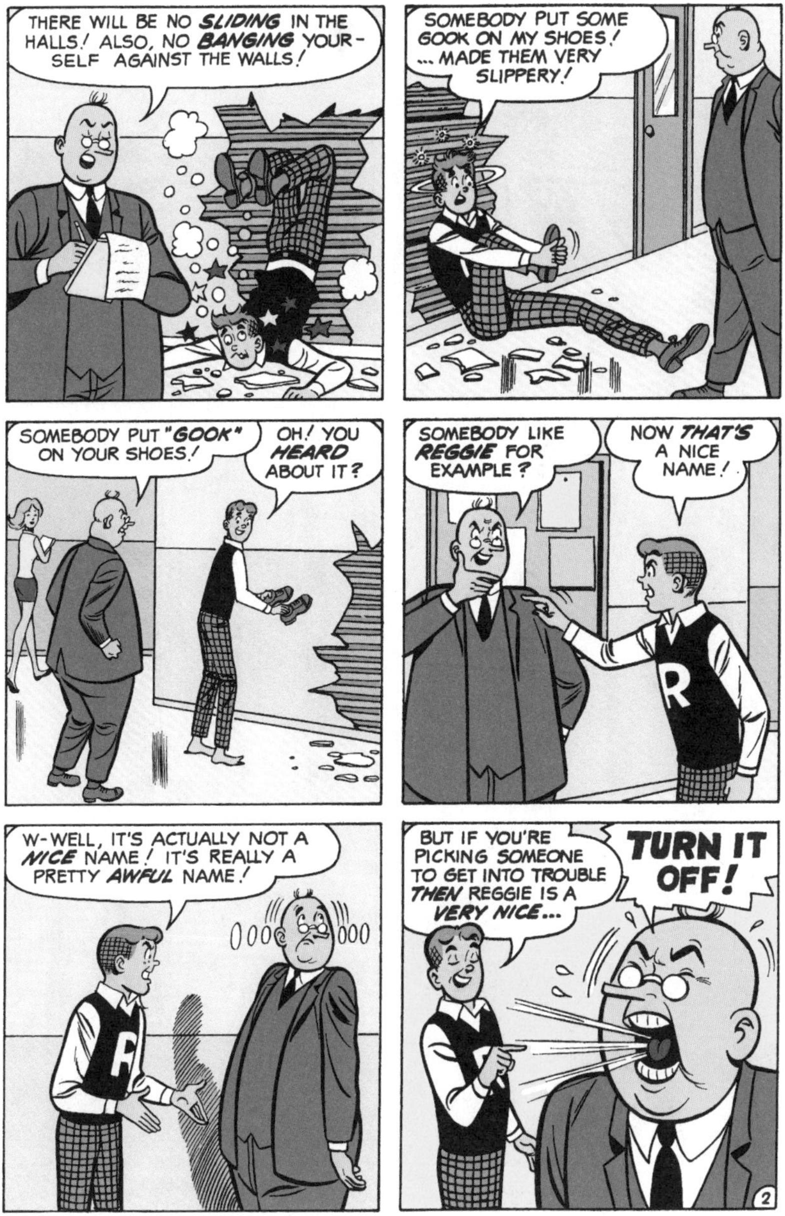
THERE WILL BE NO SLIDING IN THE HALLS! ALSO, NO BANGING YOURSELF AGAINST THE WALLS!
SOMEBODY PUT SOME GOOK ON MY SHOES! ... MADE THEM VERY SLIPPERY!
SOMEBODY PUT "GOOK" ON YOUR SHOES!
OH! YOU HEARD ABOUT IT?
SOMEBODY LIKE REGGIE FOR EXAMPLE?
NOW THAT'S A NICE NAME!
W-WELL, IT'S ACTUALLY NOT A NICE NAME! IT'S REALLY A PRETTY AWFUL NAME!
BUT IF YOU'RE PICKING SOMEONE TO GET INTO TROUBLE THEN REGGIE IS A VERY NICE...
TURN IT OFF!
2

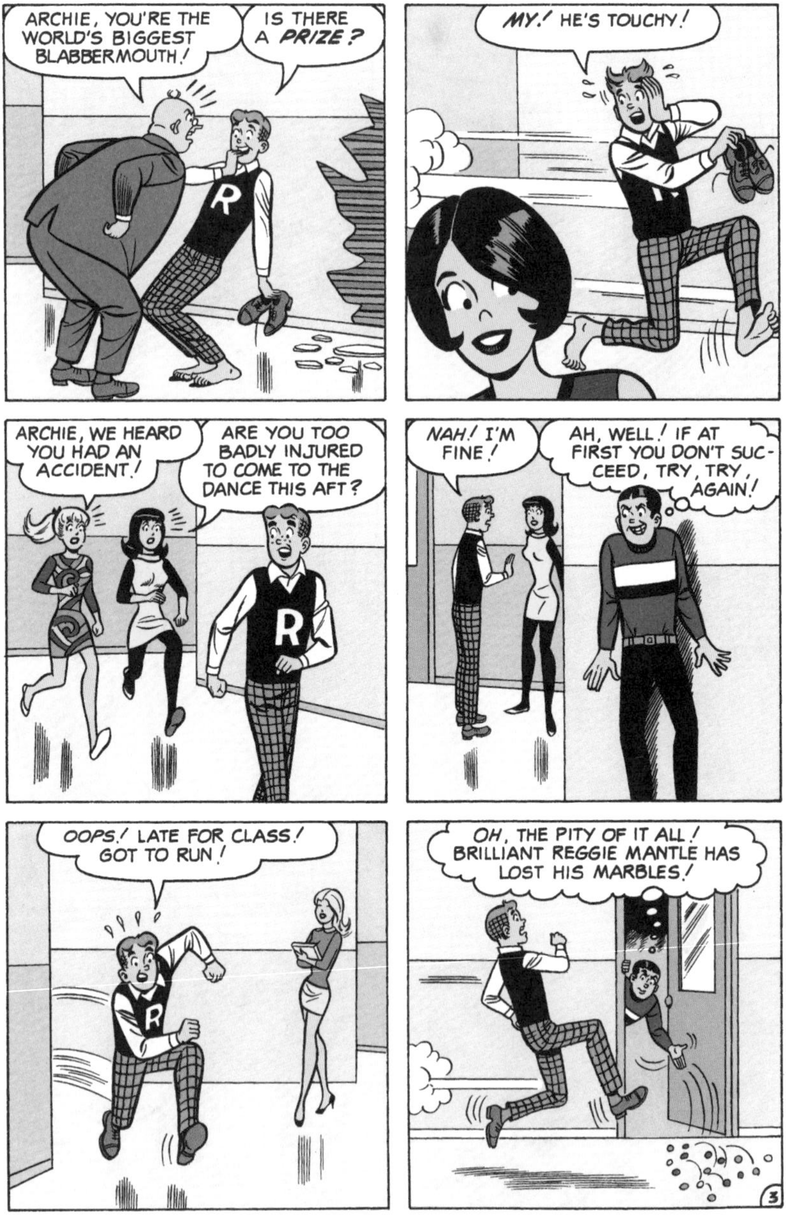
ARCHIE, YOU'RE THE WORLD'S BIGGEST BLABBERMOUTH!
IS THERE A PRIZE?
MY! HE'S TOUCHY!
ARCHIE, WE HEARD YOU HAD AN ACCIDENT!
ARE YOU TOO BADLY INJURED TO COME TO THE DANCE THIS AFT?
NAH! I'M FINE!
AH, WELL! IF AT FIRST YOU DON'T SUCCEED, TRY, TRY, AGAIN!
OOPS! LATE FOR CLASS! GOT TO RUN!
OH, THE PITY OF IT ALL! BRILLIANT REGGIE MANTLE HAS LOST HIS MARBLES!
3

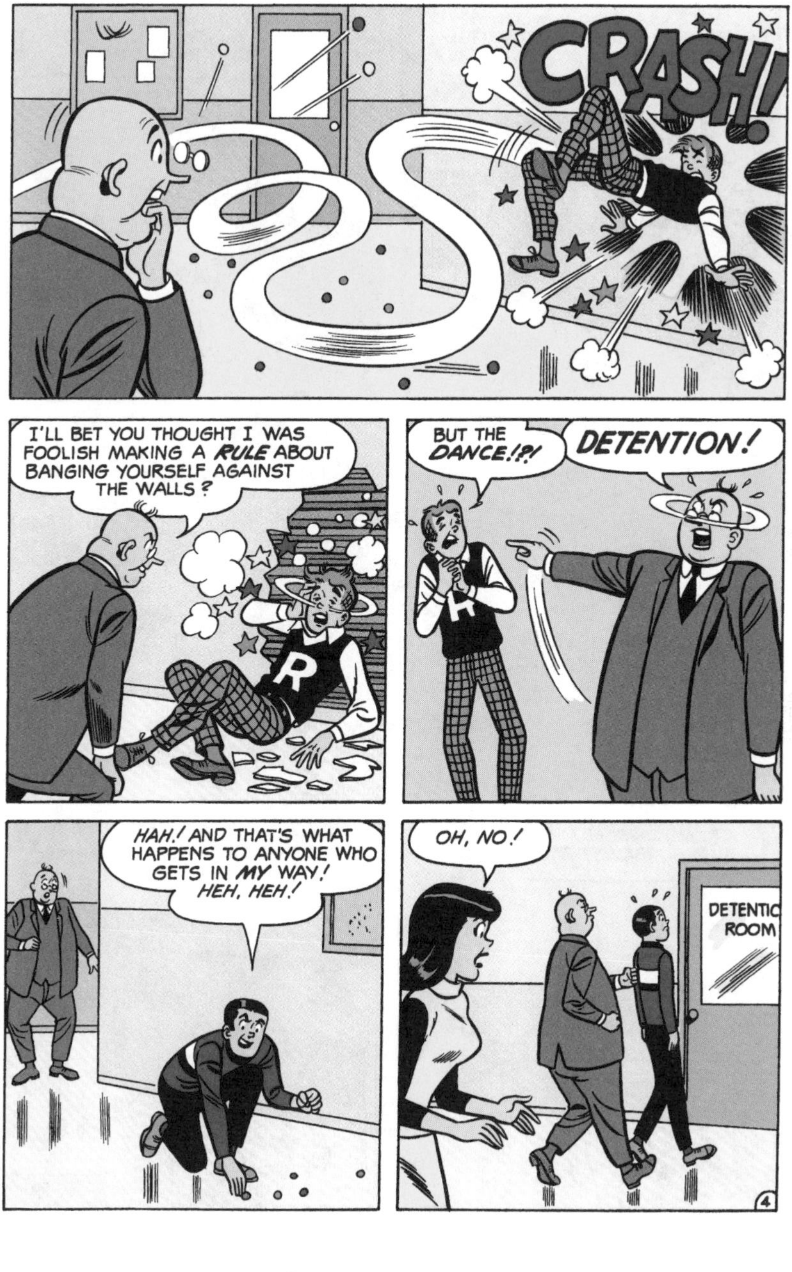
CRASH!
I'LL BET YOU THOUGHT I WAS FOOLISH MAKING A RULE ABOUT BANGING YOURSELF AGAINST THE WALLS?
BUT THE DANCE!?!
DETENTION!
HAH! AND THAT'S WHAT HAPPENS TO ANYONE WHO GETS IN MY WAY! HEH, HEH!
OH, NO!
DETENTIC ROOM
4

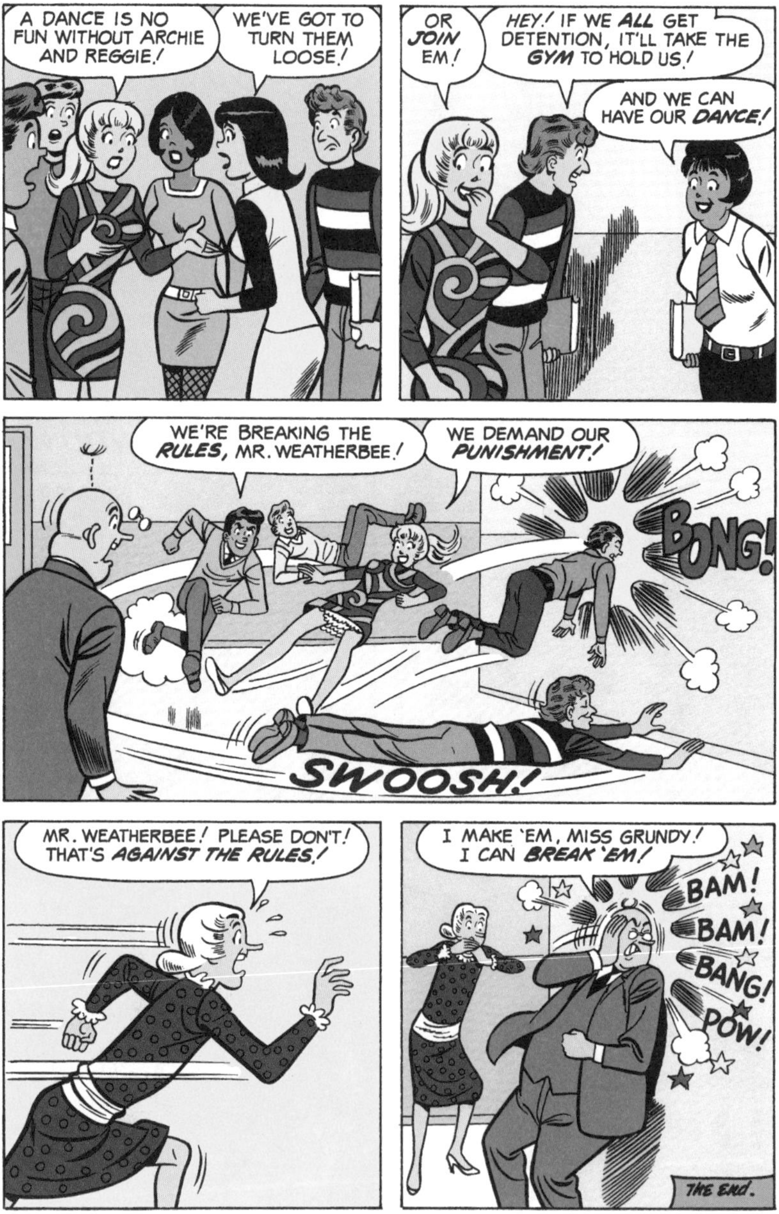

A DANCE IS NO FUN WITHOUT ARCHIE AND REGGIE!
WE'VE GOT TO TURN THEM LOOSE!
OR JOIN EM!
HEY! IF WE ALL GET DETENTION, IT'LL TAKE THE GYM TO HOLD US!
AND WE CAN HAVE OUR DANCE!
WE'RE BREAKING THE RULES, MR. WEATHERBEE!
WE DEMAND OUR PUNISHMENT!
BONG!
SWOOSH!
MR. WEATHERBEE! PLEASE DON'T! THAT'S AGAINST THE RULES!
I MAKE 'EM, MISS GRUNDY! I CAN BREAK 'EM!
BAM!
BAM!
BANG!
POW!
THE END.

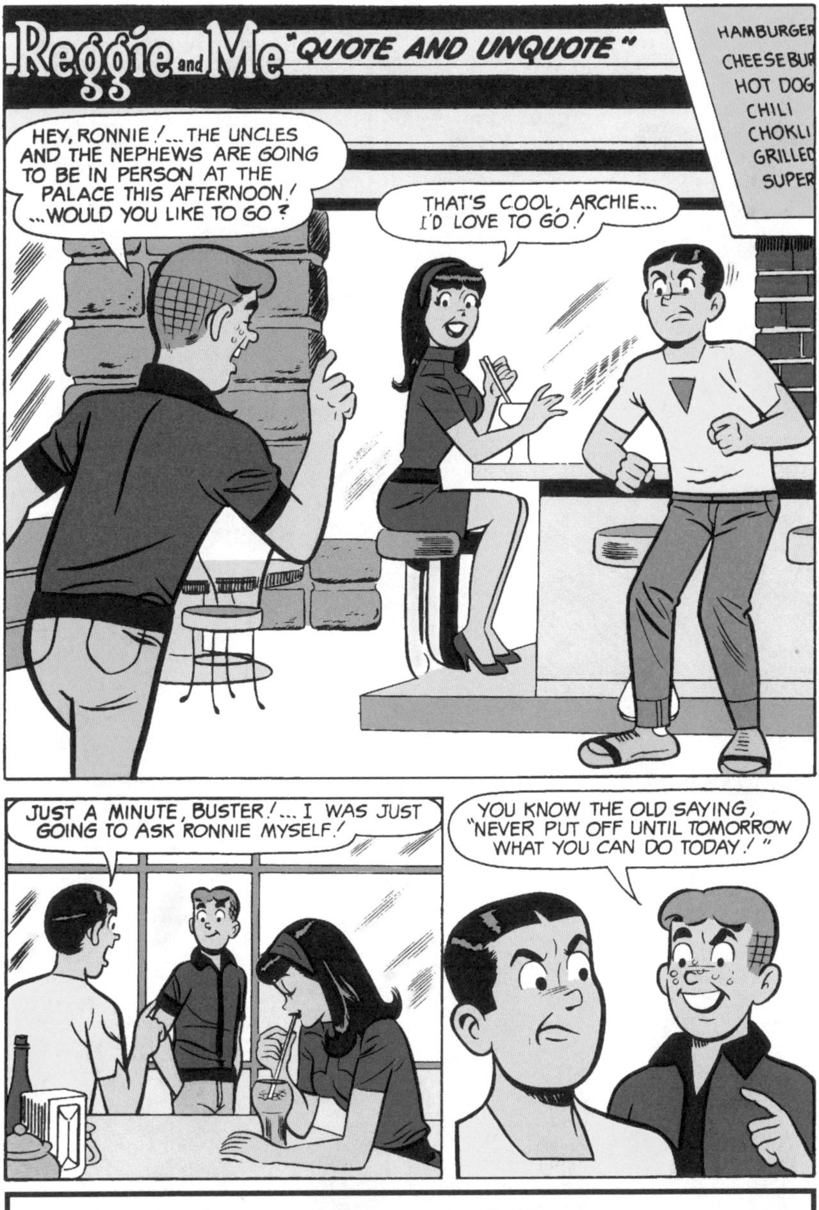
Reggie and Me "QUOTE AND UNQUOTE"
HAMBURGER
CHEESEBUR
HOT DOG
CHILI
CHOKLI
GRILLED
SUPER
HEY, RONNIE!... THE UNCLES AND THE NEPHEWS ARE GOING TO BE IN PERSON AT THE PALACE THIS AFTERNOON! ...WOULD YOU LIKE TO GO?
THAT'S COOL, ARCHIE... I'D LOVE TO GO!
JUST A MINUTE, BUSTER!... I WAS JUST GOING TO ASK RONNIE MYSELF!
YOU KNOW THE OLD SAYING, "NEVER PUT OFF UNTIL TOMORROW WHAT YOU CAN DO TODAY!"

Story & Pencils: Bob Bolling
Letters: Bill Yoshida Colors: Barry Grossman

Originally printed in REGGIE AND ME #31, SEPTEMBER 1968

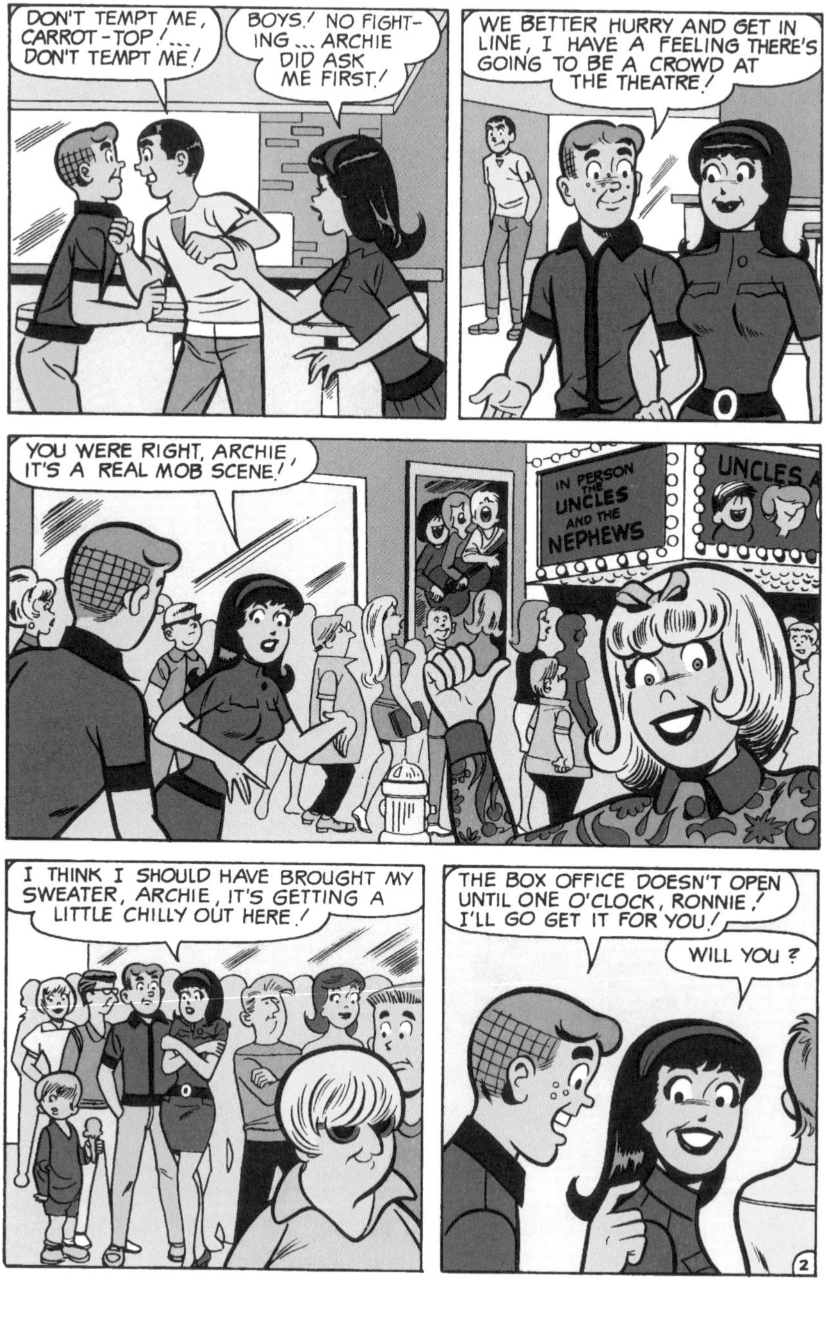
DON'T TEMPT ME, CARROT-TOP!... DON'T TEMPT ME!
BOYS! NO FIGHT-ING... ARCHIE DID ASK ME FIRST!
WE BETTER HURRY AND GET IN LINE, I HAVE A FEELING THERE'S GOING TO BE A CROWD AT THE THEATRE!
YOU WERE RIGHT, ARCHIE, IT'S A REAL MOB SCENE!
IN PERSON THE UNCLES AND THE NEPHEWS
UNCLES A
I THINK I SHOULD HAVE BROUGHT MY SWEATER, ARCHIE, IT'S GETTING A LITTLE CHILLY OUT HERE!
THE BOX OFFICE DOESN'T OPEN UNTIL ONE O'CLOCK, RONNIE! I'LL GO GET IT FOR YOU!
WILL YOU?
2

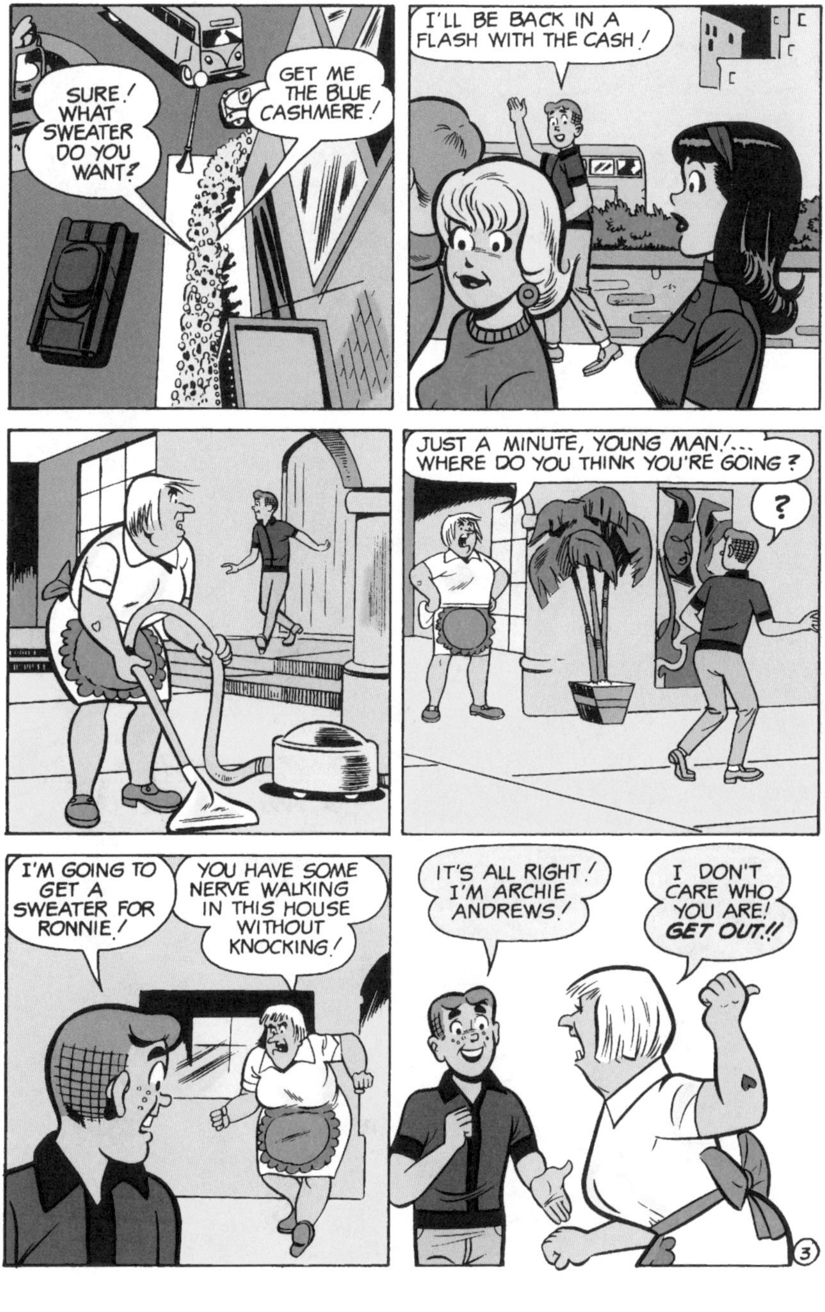
SURE! WHAT SWEATER DO YOU WANT?
GET ME THE BLUE CASHMERE!
I'LL BE BACK IN A FLASH WITH THE CASH!
JUST A MINUTE, YOUNG MAN!... WHERE DO YOU THINK YOU'RE GOING?
?
I'M GOING TO GET A SWEATER FOR RONNIE!
YOU HAVE SOME NERVE WALKING IN THIS HOUSE WITHOUT KNOCKING!
IT'S ALL RIGHT! I'M ARCHIE ANDREWS!
I DON'T CARE WHO YOU ARE! **GET OUT!!**
3

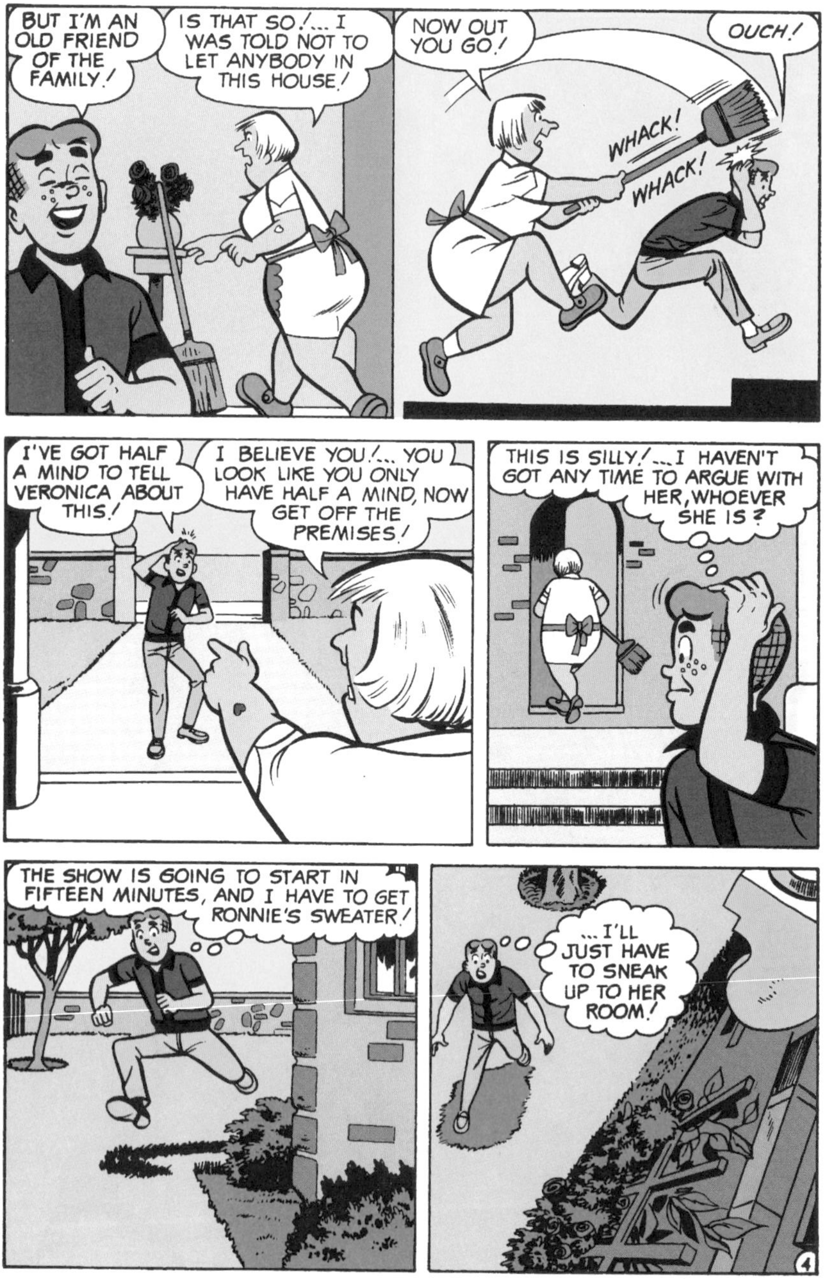
BUT I'M AN OLD FRIEND OF THE FAMILY!
IS THAT SO!... I WAS TOLD NOT TO LET ANYBODY IN THIS HOUSE!
NOW OUT YOU GO!
OUCH!
WHACK!
WHACK!
I'VE GOT HALF A MIND TO TELL VERONICA ABOUT THIS!
I BELIEVE YOU!... YOU LOOK LIKE YOU ONLY HAVE HALF A MIND, NOW GET OFF THE PREMISES!
THIS IS SILLY!... I HAVEN'T GOT ANY TIME TO ARGUE WITH HER, WHOEVER SHE IS?
THE SHOW IS GOING TO START IN FIFTEEN MINUTES, AND I HAVE TO GET RONNIE'S SWEATER!
... I'LL JUST HAVE TO SNEAK UP TO HER ROOM!
4

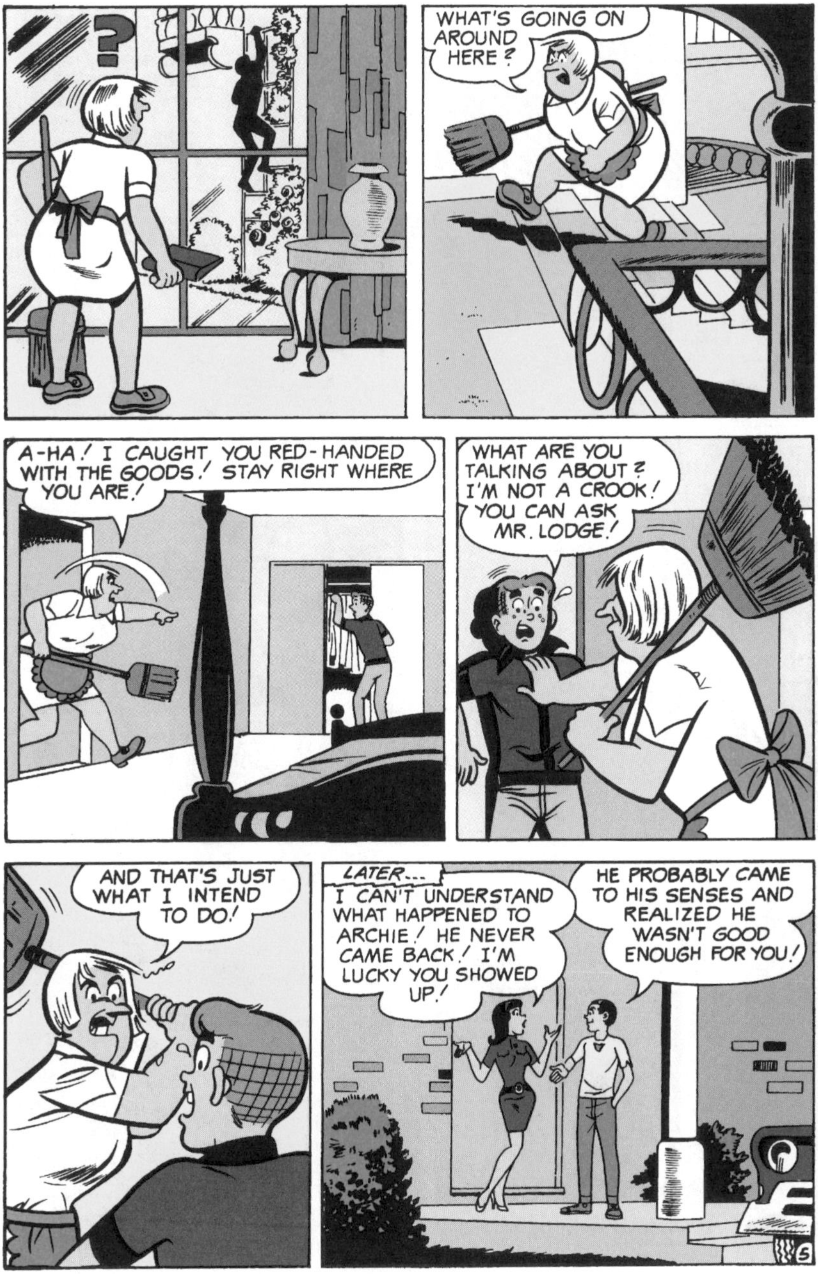
?
WHAT'S GOING ON AROUND HERE?
A-HA! I CAUGHT YOU RED-HANDED WITH THE GOODS! STAY RIGHT WHERE YOU ARE!
WHAT ARE YOU TALKING ABOUT? I'M NOT A CROOK! YOU CAN ASK MR. LODGE!
AND THAT'S JUST WHAT I INTEND TO DO!
LATER...
I CAN'T UNDERSTAND WHAT HAPPENED TO ARCHIE! HE NEVER CAME BACK! I'M LUCKY YOU SHOWED UP!
HE PROBABLY CAME TO HIS SENSES AND REALIZED HE WASN'T GOOD ENOUGH FOR YOU!
5

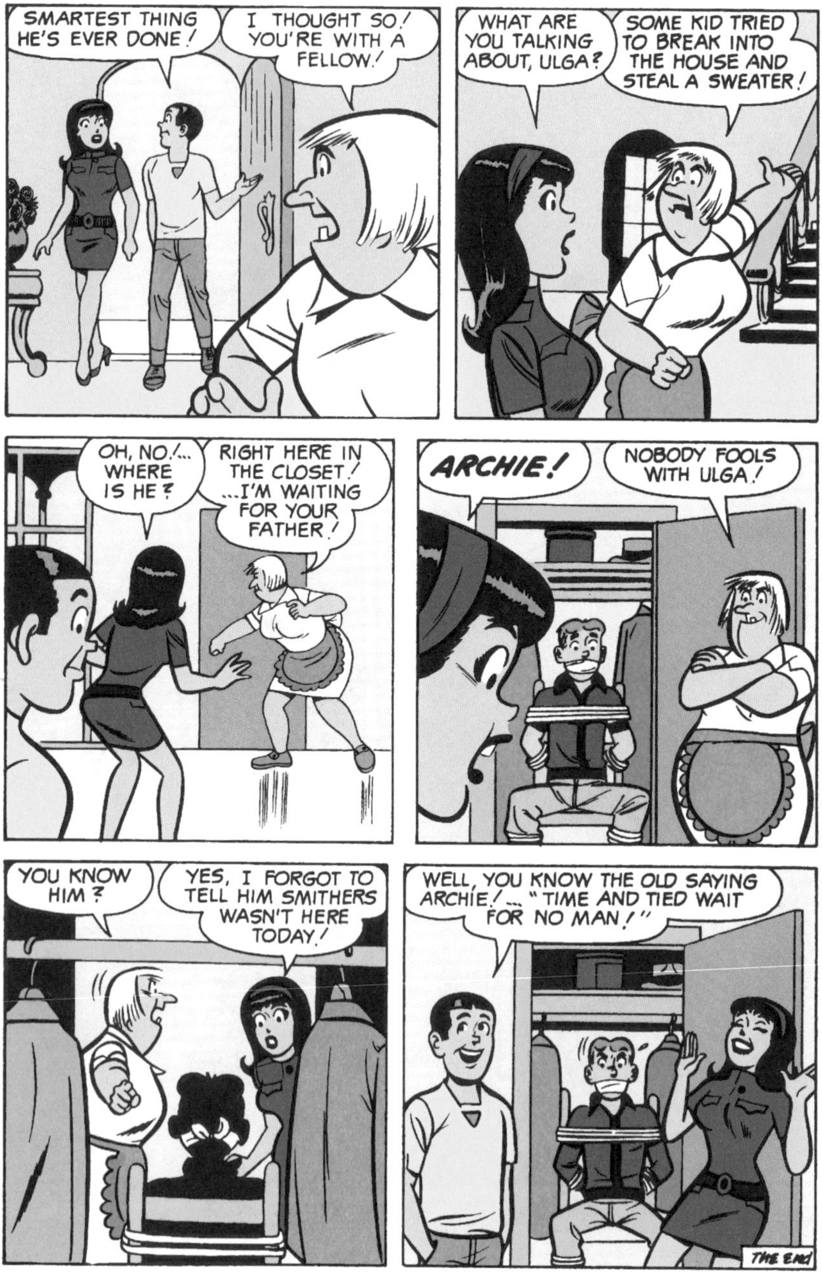
SMARTEST THING HE'S EVER DONE!
I THOUGHT SO! YOU'RE WITH A FELLOW!
WHAT ARE YOU TALKING ABOUT, ULGA?
SOME KID TRIED TO BREAK INTO THE HOUSE AND STEAL A SWEATER!
OH, NO!... WHERE IS HE?
RIGHT HERE IN THE CLOSET! ...I'M WAITING FOR YOUR FATHER!
ARCHIE!
NOBODY FOOLS WITH ULGA!
YOU KNOW HIM?
YES, I FORGOT TO TELL HIM SMITHERS WASN'T HERE TODAY!
WELL, YOU KNOW THE OLD SAYING ARCHIE!... "TIME AND TIED WAIT FOR NO MAN!"
THE END

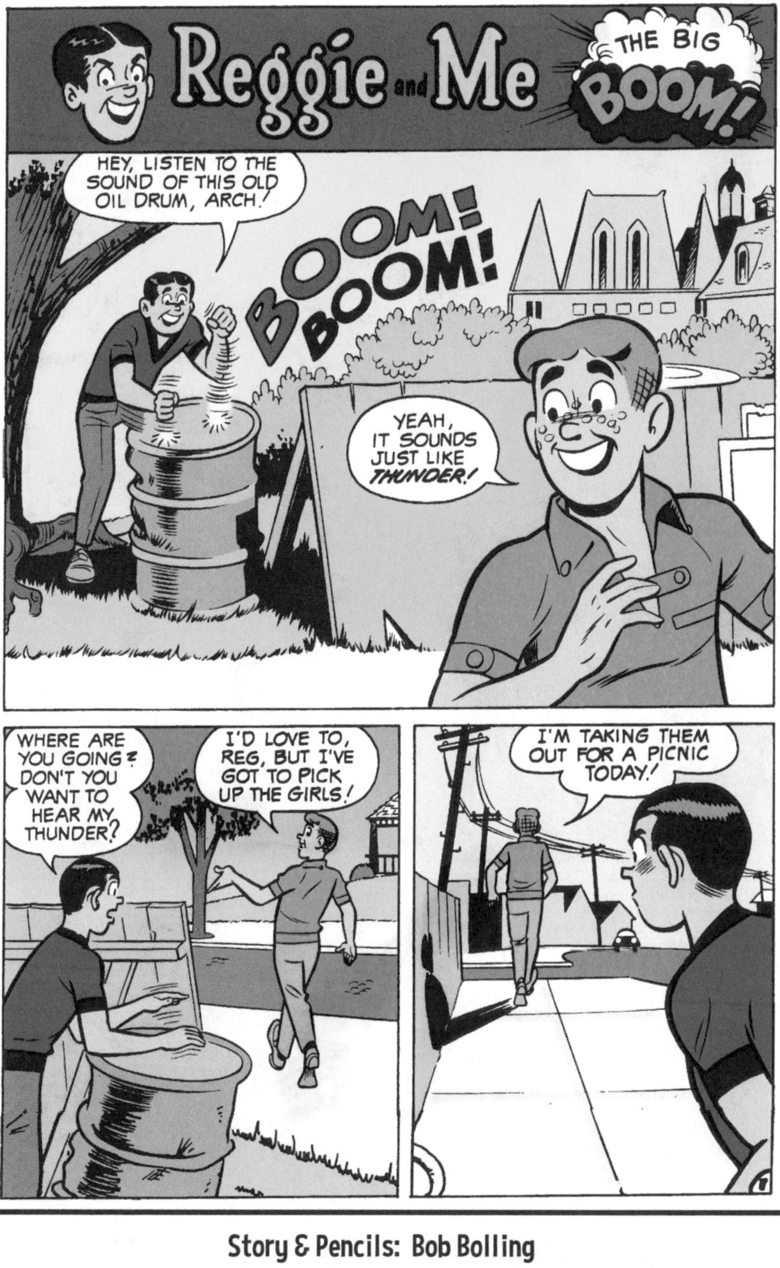
Reggie and Me
THE BIG BOOM!
HEY, LISTEN TO THE SOUND OF THIS OLD OIL DRUM, ARCH.!
BOOM! BOOM!
YEAH, IT SOUNDS JUST LIKE THUNDER!
WHERE ARE YOU GOING? DON'T YOU WANT TO HEAR MY THUNDER?
I'D LOVE TO, REG, BUT I'VE GOT TO PICK UP THE GIRLS!
I'M TAKING THEM OUT FOR A PICNIC TODAY!

Story & Pencils: Bob Bolling
Letters: Bill Yoshida Colors: Barry Grossman

Originally printed in REGGIE AND ME #32, NOVEMBER 1968

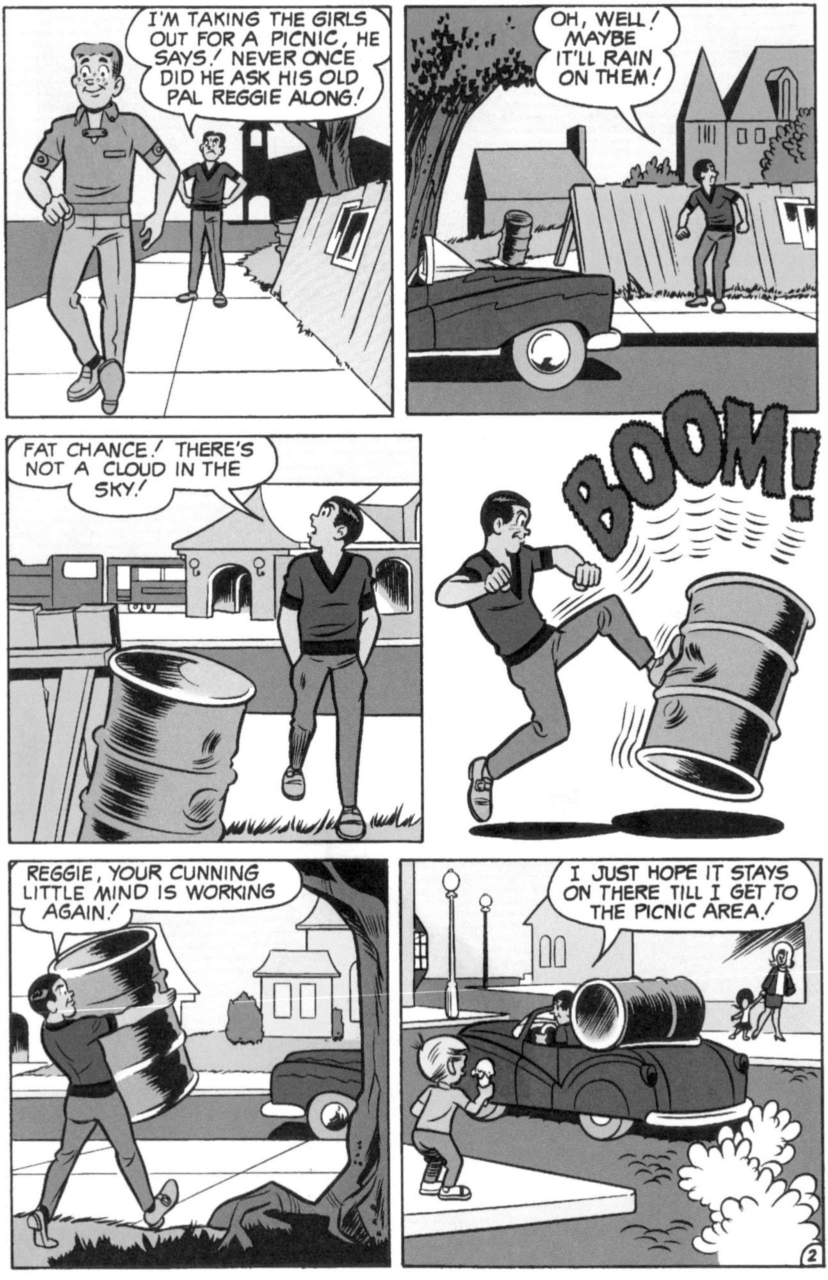
I'M TAKING THE GIRLS OUT FOR A PICNIC, HE SAYS! NEVER ONCE DID HE ASK HIS OLD PAL REGGIE ALONG!
OH, WELL! MAYBE IT'LL RAIN ON THEM!
FAT CHANCE! THERE'S NOT A CLOUD IN THE SKY!
BOOM!
REGGIE, YOUR CUNNING LITTLE MIND IS WORKING AGAIN!
I JUST HOPE IT STAYS ON THERE TILL I GET TO THE PICNIC AREA!
2

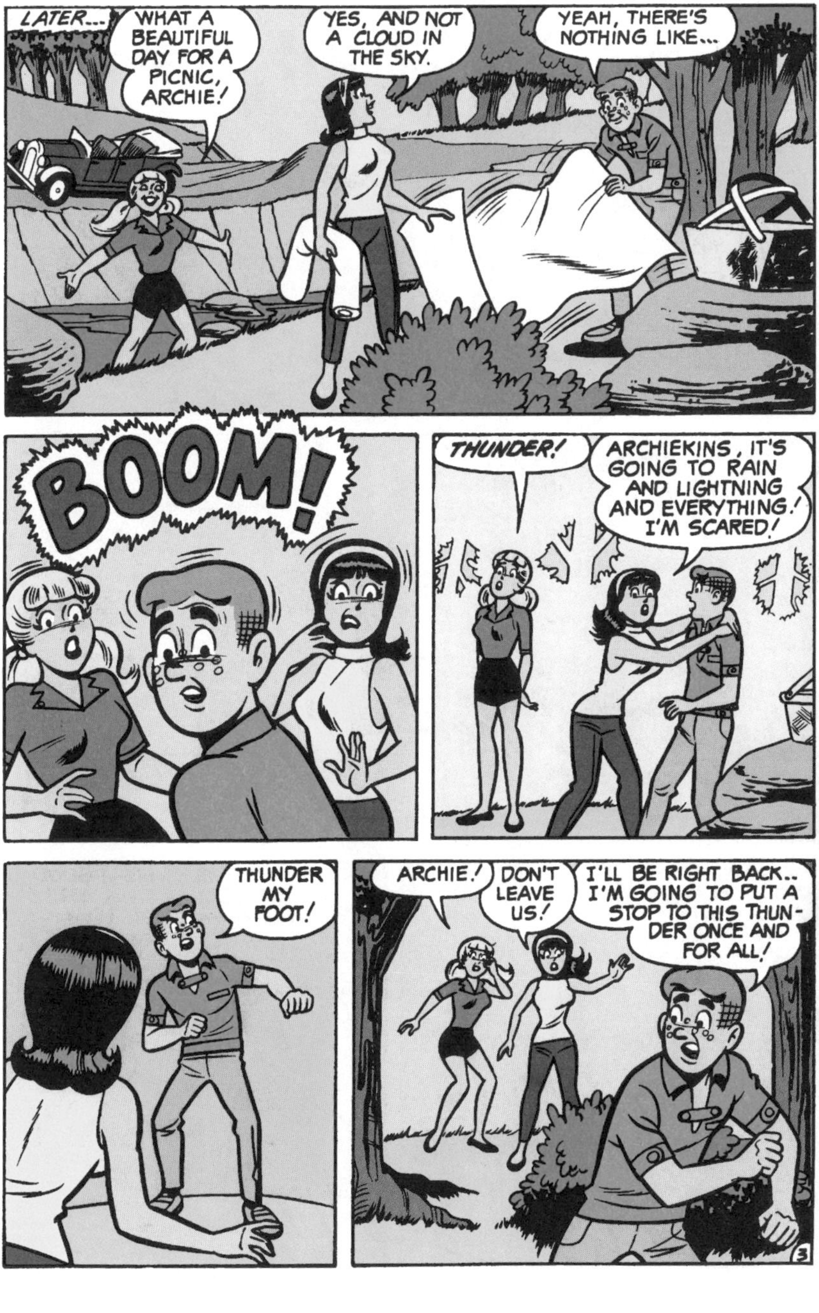
LATER...
WHAT A BEAUTIFUL DAY FOR A PICNIC, ARCHIE!
YES, AND NOT A CLOUD IN THE SKY.
YEAH, THERE'S NOTHING LIKE...
BOOM!
THUNDER!
ARCHIEKINS, IT'S GOING TO RAIN AND LIGHTNING AND EVERYTHING! I'M SCARED!
THUNDER MY FOOT!
ARCHIE!
DON'T LEAVE US!
I'LL BE RIGHT BACK.. I'M GOING TO PUT A STOP TO THIS THUNDER ONCE AND FOR ALL!
3

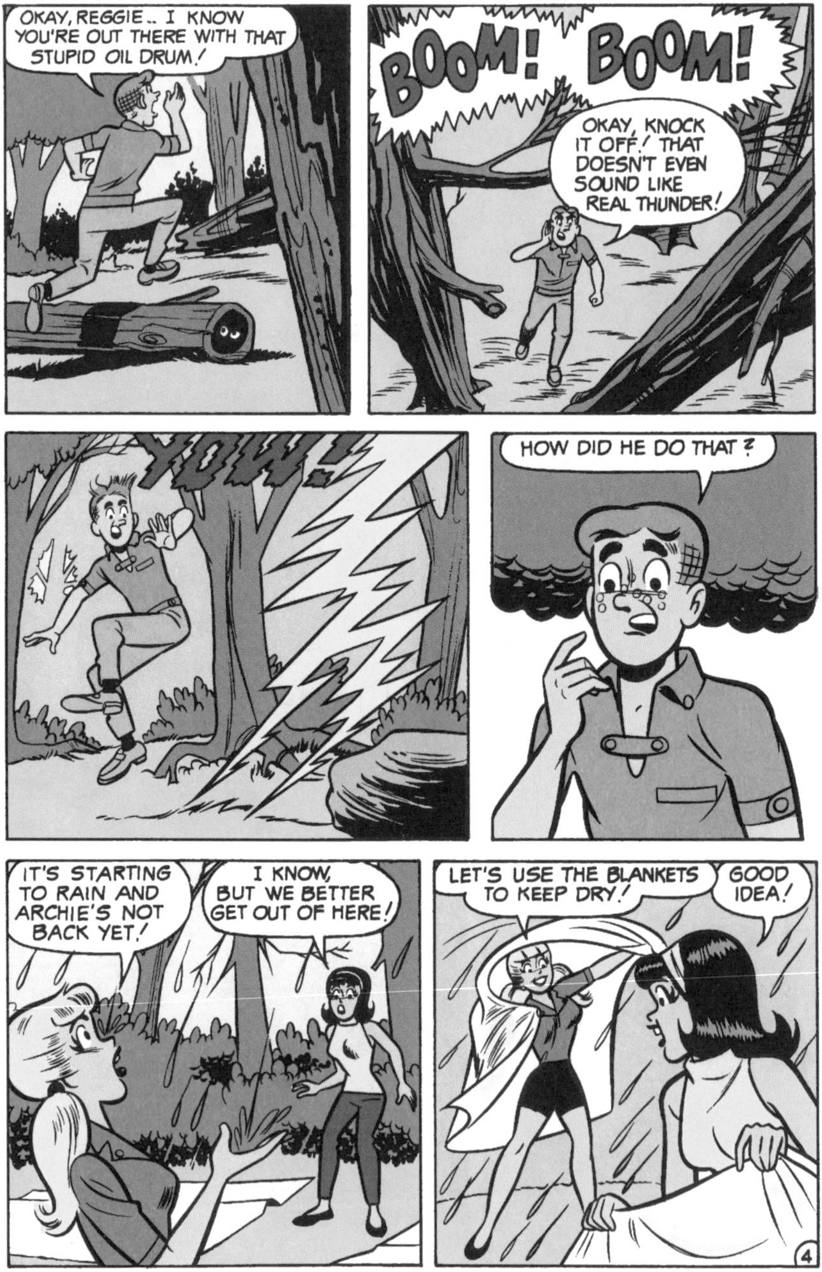
OKAY, REGGIE.. I KNOW YOU'RE OUT THERE WITH THAT STUPID OIL DRUM!
BOOM! BOOM!
OKAY, KNOCK IT OFF! THAT DOESN'T EVEN SOUND LIKE REAL THUNDER!
YOW!
HOW DID HE DO THAT?
IT'S STARTING TO RAIN AND ARCHIE'S NOT BACK YET!
I KNOW, BUT WE BETTER GET OUT OF HERE!
LET'S USE THE BLANKETS TO KEEP DRY!
GOOD IDEA!
4

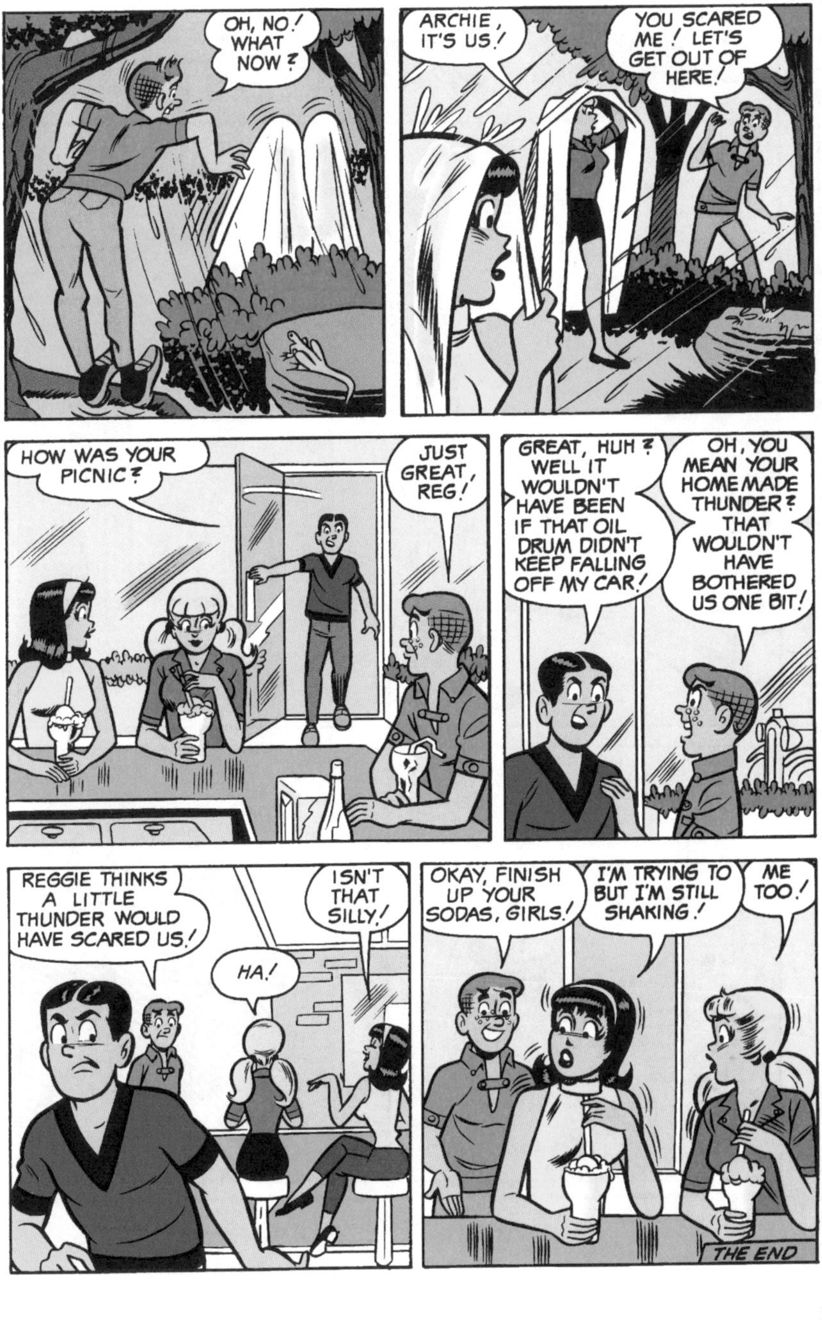
OH, NO! WHAT NOW?
ARCHIE, IT'S US!
YOU SCARED ME! LET'S GET OUT OF HERE!
HOW WAS YOUR PICNIC?
JUST GREAT, REG!
GREAT, HUH? WELL IT WOULDN'T HAVE BEEN IF THAT OIL DRUM DIDN'T KEEP FALLING OFF MY CAR!
OH, YOU MEAN YOUR HOME MADE THUNDER? THAT WOULDN'T HAVE BOTHERED US ONE BIT!
REGGIE THINKS A LITTLE THUNDER WOULD HAVE SCARED US!
HA!
ISN'T THAT SILLY!
OKAY, FINISH UP YOUR SODAS, GIRLS!
I'M TRYING TO BUT I'M STILL SHAKING!
ME TOO!
THE END

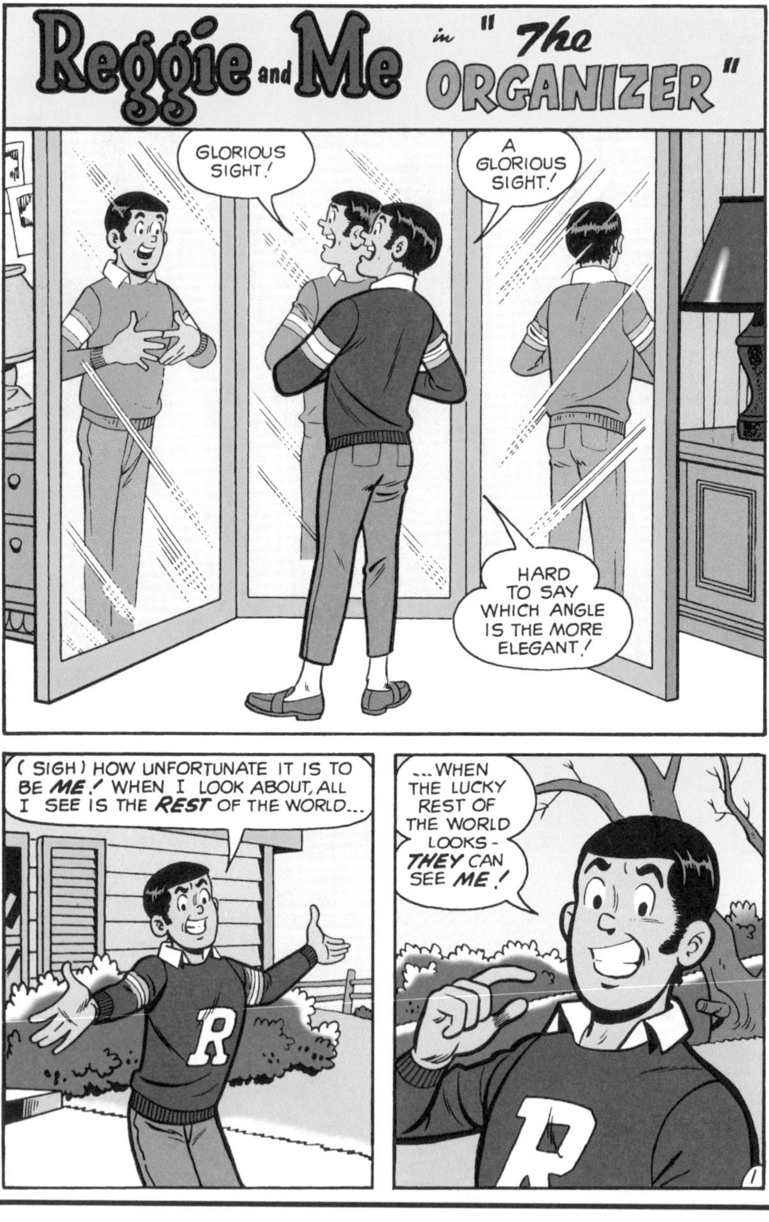
Reggie and Me
in "The ORGANIZER"
GLORIOUS SIGHT!
A GLORIOUS SIGHT!
HARD TO SAY WHICH ANGLE IS THE MORE ELEGANT!
(SIGH) HOW UNFORTUNATE IT IS TO BE *ME*! WHEN I LOOK ABOUT, ALL I SEE IS THE *REST* OF THE WORLD...
...WHEN THE LUCKY REST OF THE WORLD LOOKS - *THEY* CAN SEE *ME*!

Story & Pencils: Al Hartley
Inks: Jon D'Agostino Letters: Bill Yoshida

Originally printed in REGGIE AND ME #34, MARCH 1969

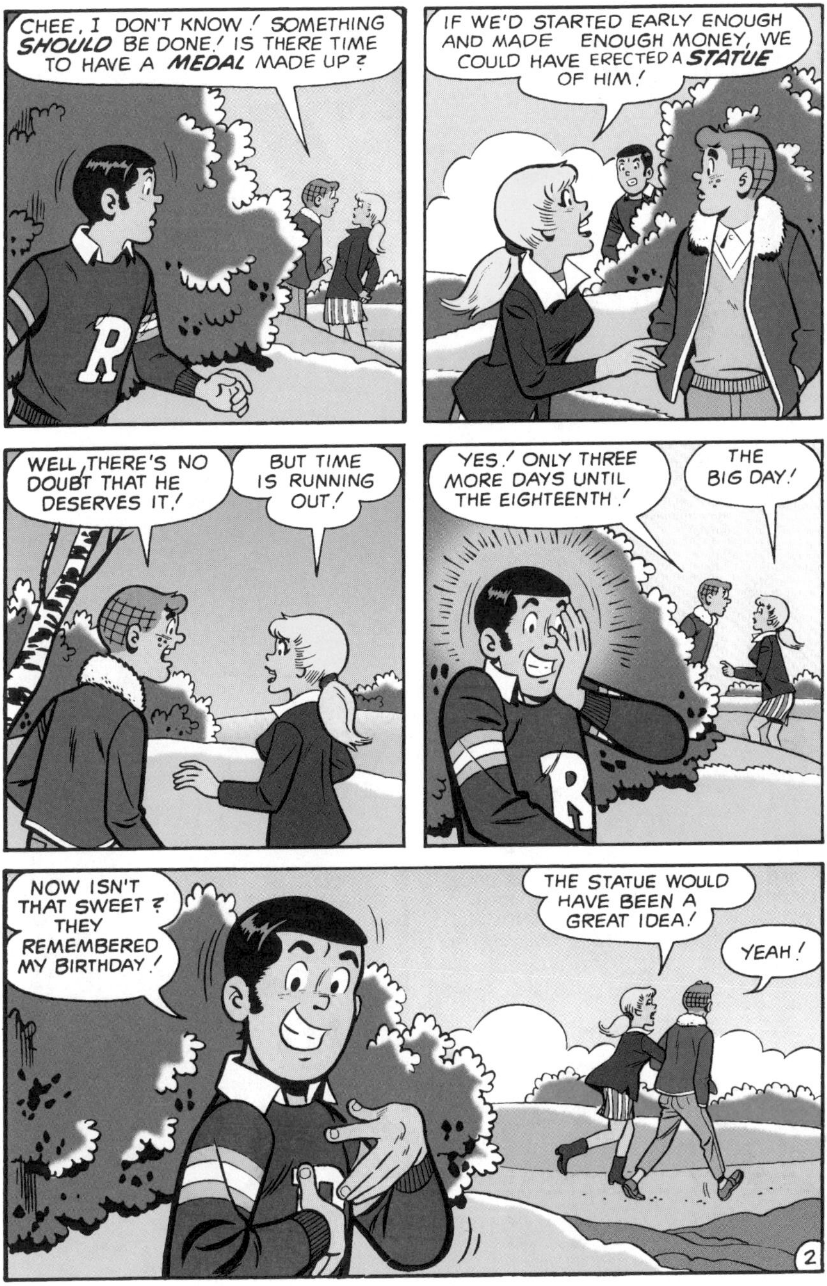
CHEE, I DON'T KNOW! SOMETHING SHOULD BE DONE! IS THERE TIME TO HAVE A MEDAL MADE UP?
IF WE'D STARTED EARLY ENOUGH AND MADE ENOUGH MONEY, WE COULD HAVE ERECTED A STATUE OF HIM!
WELL, THERE'S NO DOUBT THAT HE DESERVES IT!
BUT TIME IS RUNNING OUT!
YES! ONLY THREE MORE DAYS UNTIL THE EIGHTEENTH!
THE BIG DAY!
NOW ISN'T THAT SWEET? THEY REMEMBERED MY BIRTHDAY!
THE STATUE WOULD HAVE BEEN A GREAT IDEA!
YEAH!
2

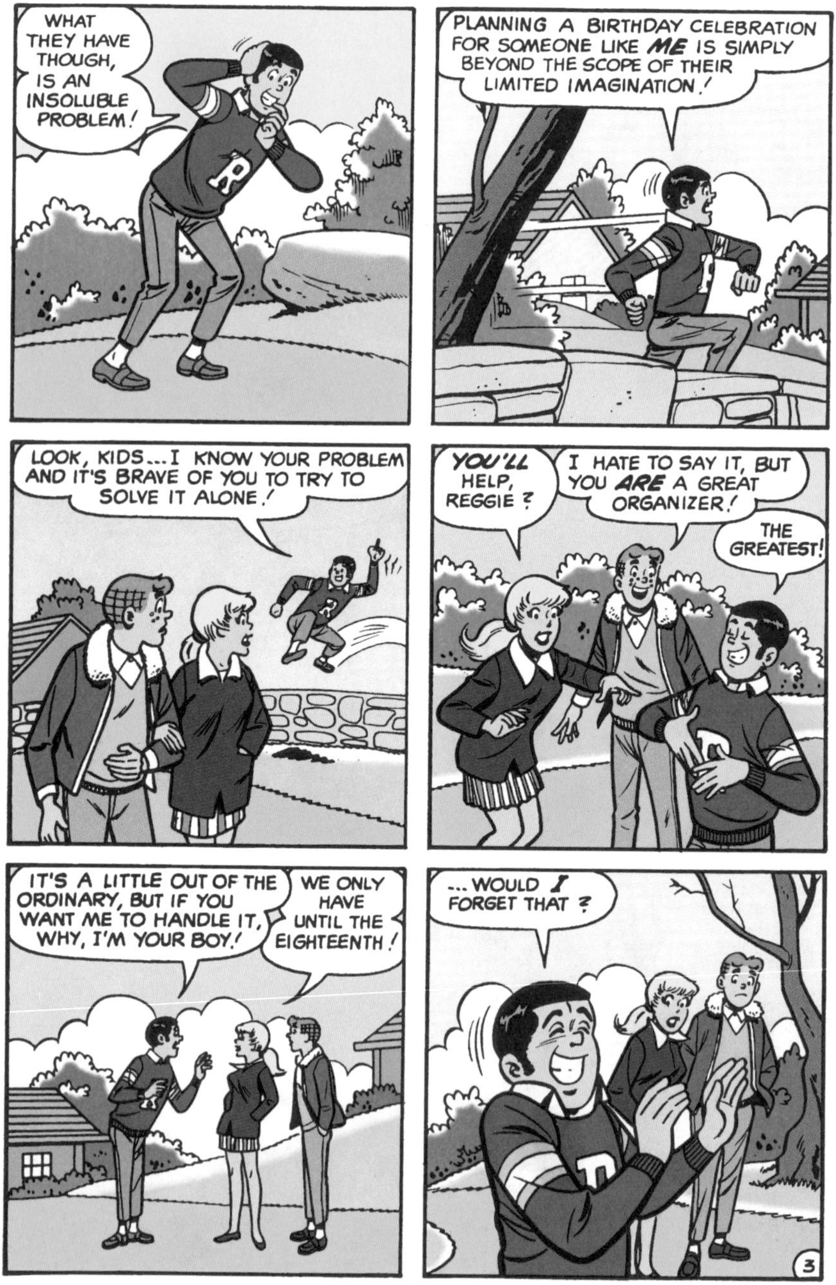
WHAT THEY HAVE THOUGH, IS AN INSOLUBLE PROBLEM!
PLANNING A BIRTHDAY CELEBRATION FOR SOMEONE LIKE ME IS SIMPLY BEYOND THE SCOPE OF THEIR LIMITED IMAGINATION!
LOOK, KIDS...I KNOW YOUR PROBLEM AND IT'S BRAVE OF YOU TO TRY TO SOLVE IT ALONE!
YOU'LL HELP, REGGIE?
I HATE TO SAY IT, BUT YOU ARE A GREAT ORGANIZER!
THE GREATEST!
IT'S A LITTLE OUT OF THE ORDINARY, BUT IF YOU WANT ME TO HANDLE IT, WHY, I'M YOUR BOY!
WE ONLY HAVE UNTIL THE EIGHTEENTH!
...WOULD I FORGET THAT?
3

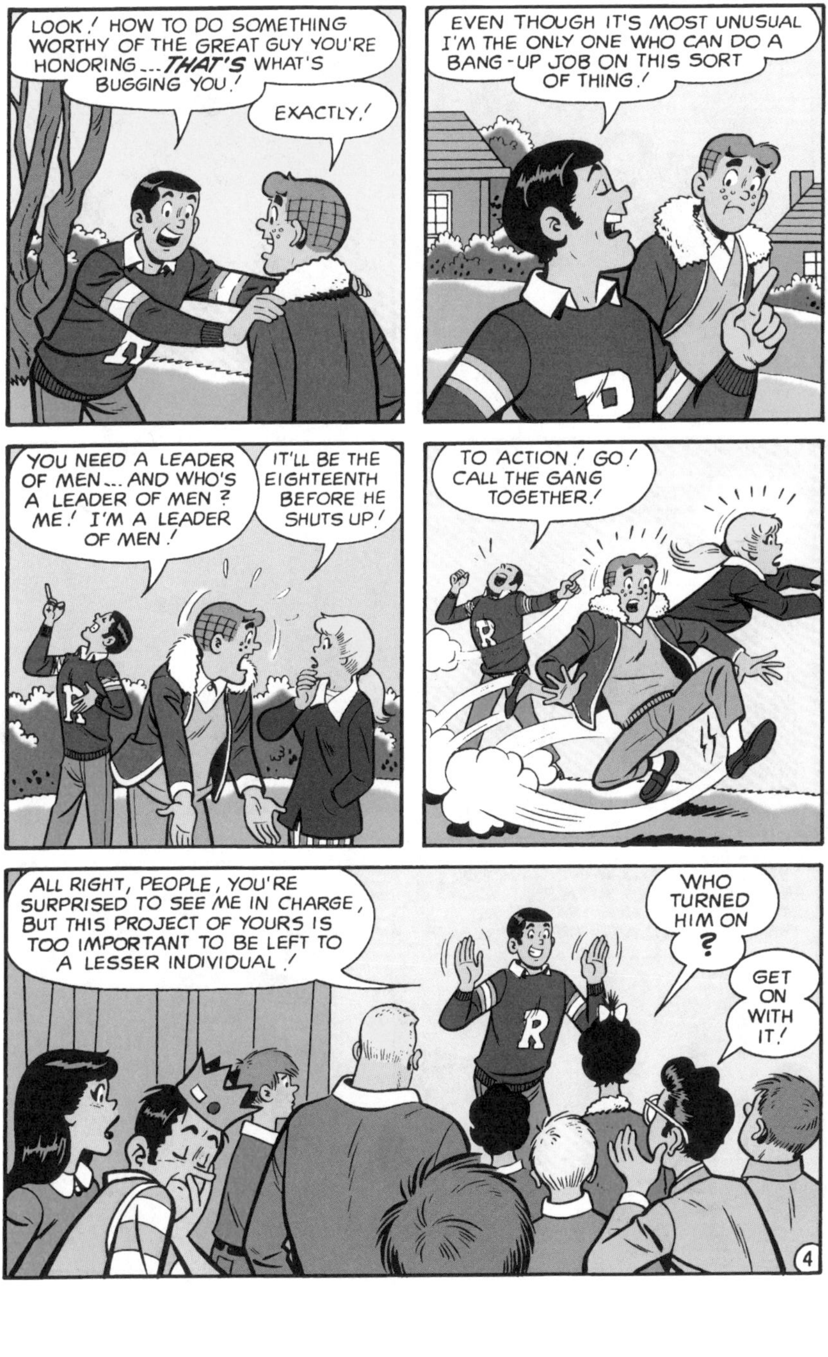
LOOK! HOW TO DO SOMETHING WORTHY OF THE GREAT GUY YOU'RE HONORING ... *THAT'S* WHAT'S BUGGING YOU!
EXACTLY!
EVEN THOUGH IT'S MOST UNUSUAL I'M THE ONLY ONE WHO CAN DO A BANG-UP JOB ON THIS SORT OF THING!
YOU NEED A LEADER OF MEN ... AND WHO'S A LEADER OF MEN? ME! I'M A LEADER OF MEN!
IT'LL BE THE EIGHTEENTH BEFORE HE SHUTS UP!
TO ACTION! GO! CALL THE GANG TOGETHER!
ALL RIGHT, PEOPLE, YOU'RE SURPRISED TO SEE ME IN CHARGE, BUT THIS PROJECT OF YOURS IS TOO IMPORTANT TO BE LEFT TO A LESSER INDIVIDUAL!
WHO TURNED HIM ON?
GET ON WITH IT!
4

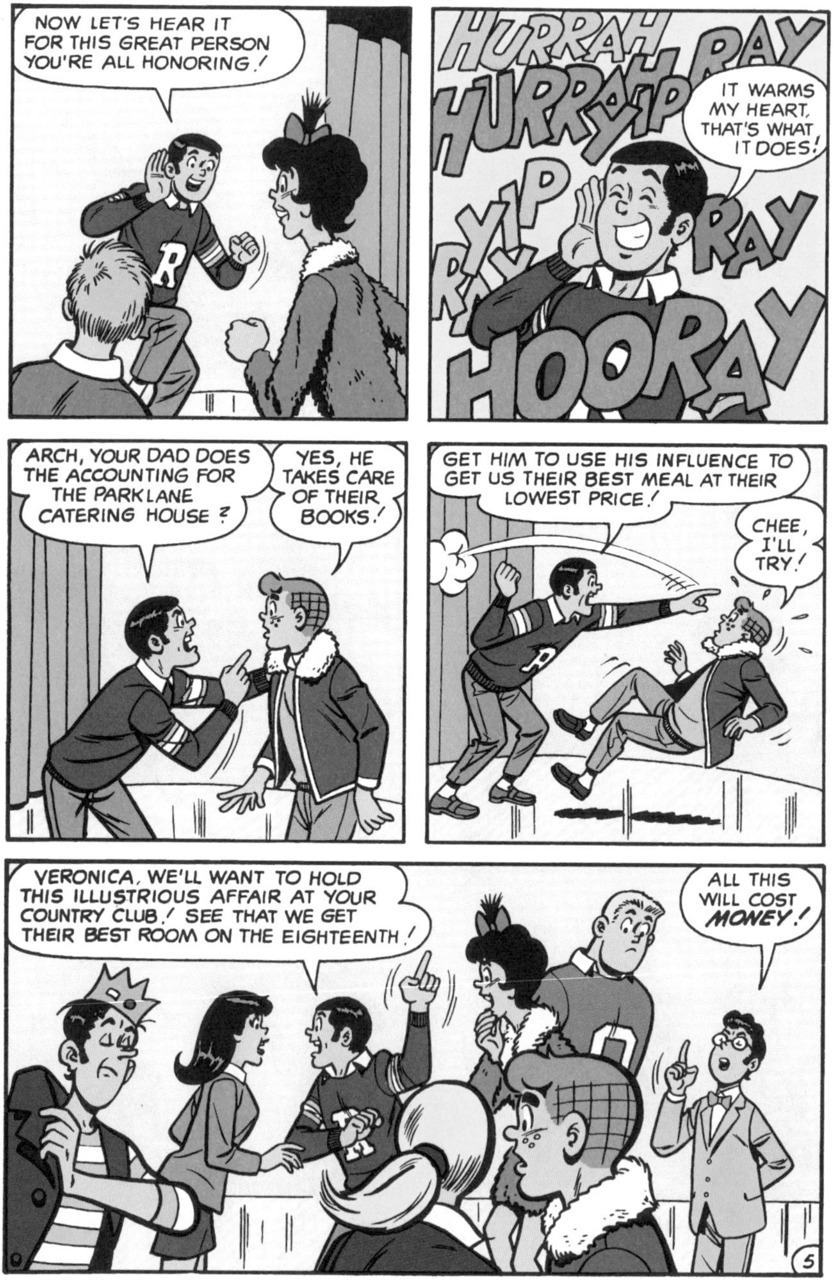
NOW LET'S HEAR IT FOR THIS GREAT PERSON YOU'RE ALL HONORING!
HURRAH
HURRAH
YIP
RAY
IT WARMS MY HEART, THAT'S WHAT IT DOES!
YIP
YIP
RAY
RAY
HOORAY
ARCH, YOUR DAD DOES THE ACCOUNTING FOR THE PARKLANE CATERING HOUSE?
YES, HE TAKES CARE OF THEIR BOOKS!
GET HIM TO USE HIS INFLUENCE TO GET US THEIR BEST MEAL AT THEIR LOWEST PRICE!
CHEE, I'LL TRY!
VERONICA, WE'LL WANT TO HOLD THIS ILLUSTRIOUS AFFAIR AT YOUR COUNTRY CLUB! SEE THAT WE GET THEIR BEST ROOM ON THE EIGHTEENTH!
ALL THIS WILL COST MONEY!
5

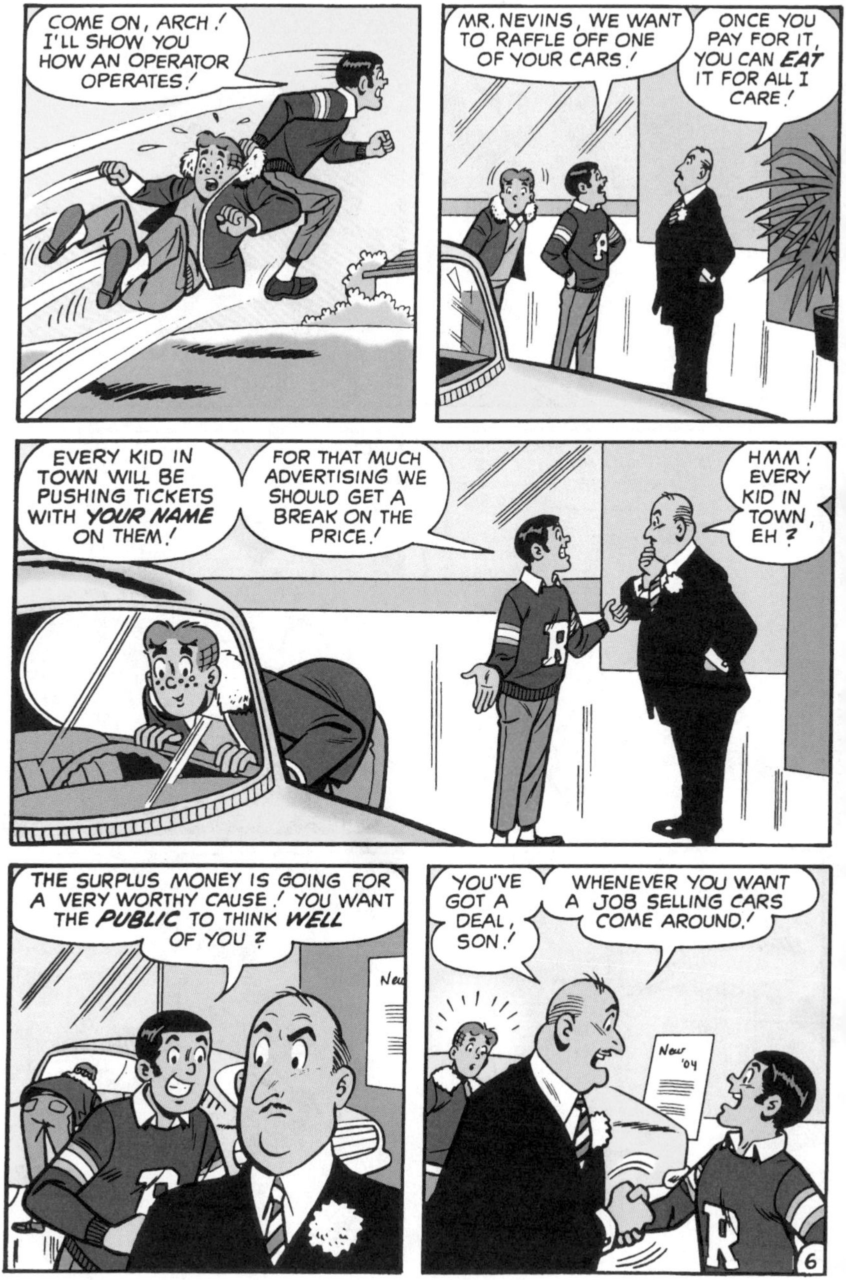
COME ON, ARCH! I'LL SHOW YOU HOW AN OPERATOR OPERATES!
MR. NEVINS, WE WANT TO RAFFLE OFF ONE OF YOUR CARS!
ONCE YOU PAY FOR IT, YOU CAN EAT IT FOR ALL I CARE!
EVERY KID IN TOWN WILL BE PUSHING TICKETS WITH YOUR NAME ON THEM!
FOR THAT MUCH ADVERTISING WE SHOULD GET A BREAK ON THE PRICE!
HMM! EVERY KID IN TOWN, EH?
THE SURPLUS MONEY IS GOING FOR A VERY WORTHY CAUSE! YOU WANT THE PUBLIC TO THINK WELL OF YOU?
YOU'VE GOT A DEAL, SON!
WHENEVER YOU WANT A JOB SELLING CARS COME AROUND!
New '04
6

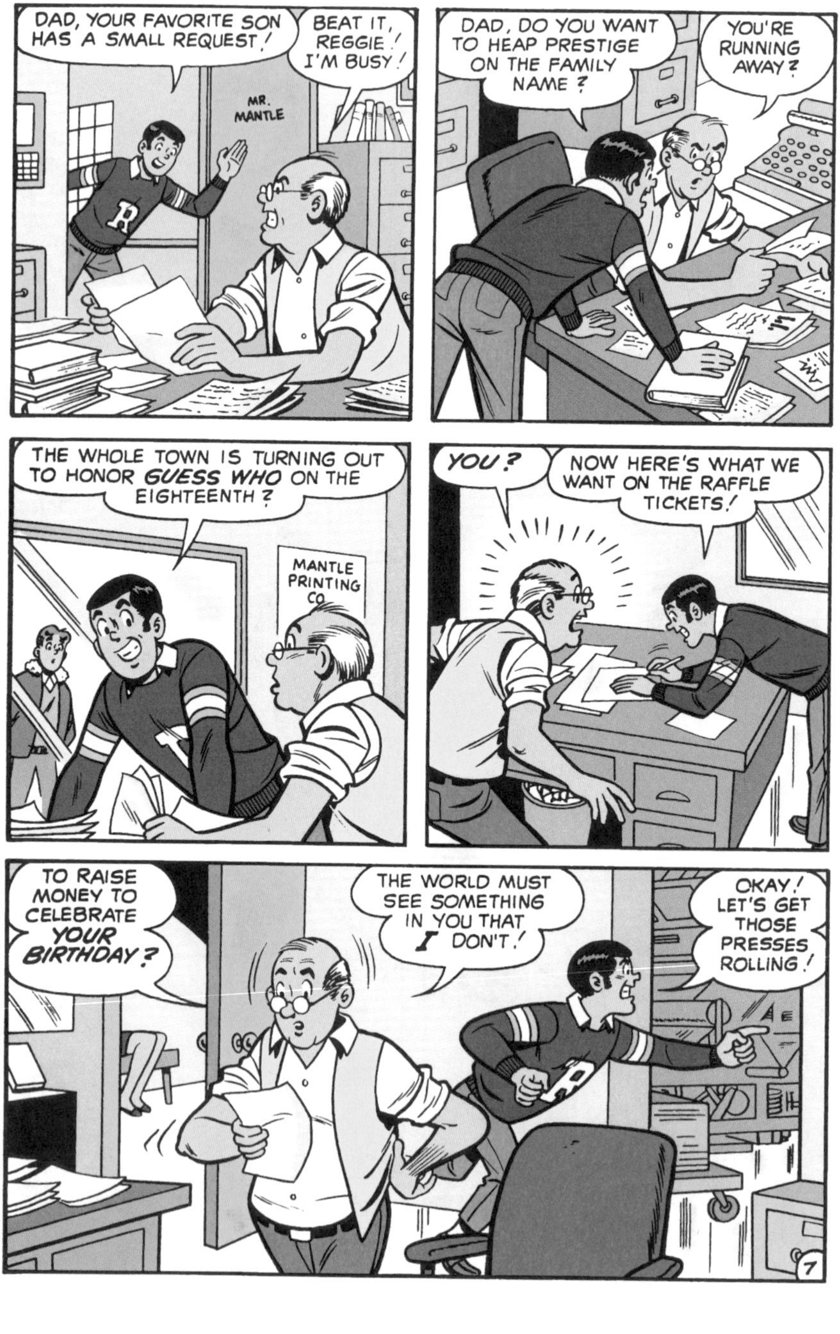
DAD, YOUR FAVORITE SON HAS A SMALL REQUEST!
BEAT IT, REGGIE! I'M BUSY!
MR. MANTLE
DAD, DO YOU WANT TO HEAP PRESTIGE ON THE FAMILY NAME?
YOU'RE RUNNING AWAY?
THE WHOLE TOWN IS TURNING OUT TO HONOR GUESS WHO ON THE EIGHTEENTH?
MANTLE PRINTING CO
YOU?
NOW HERE'S WHAT WE WANT ON THE RAFFLE TICKETS!
TO RAISE MONEY TO CELEBRATE YOUR BIRTHDAY?
THE WORLD MUST SEE SOMETHING IN YOU THAT I DON'T!
OKAY! LET'S GET THOSE PRESSES ROLLING!
7

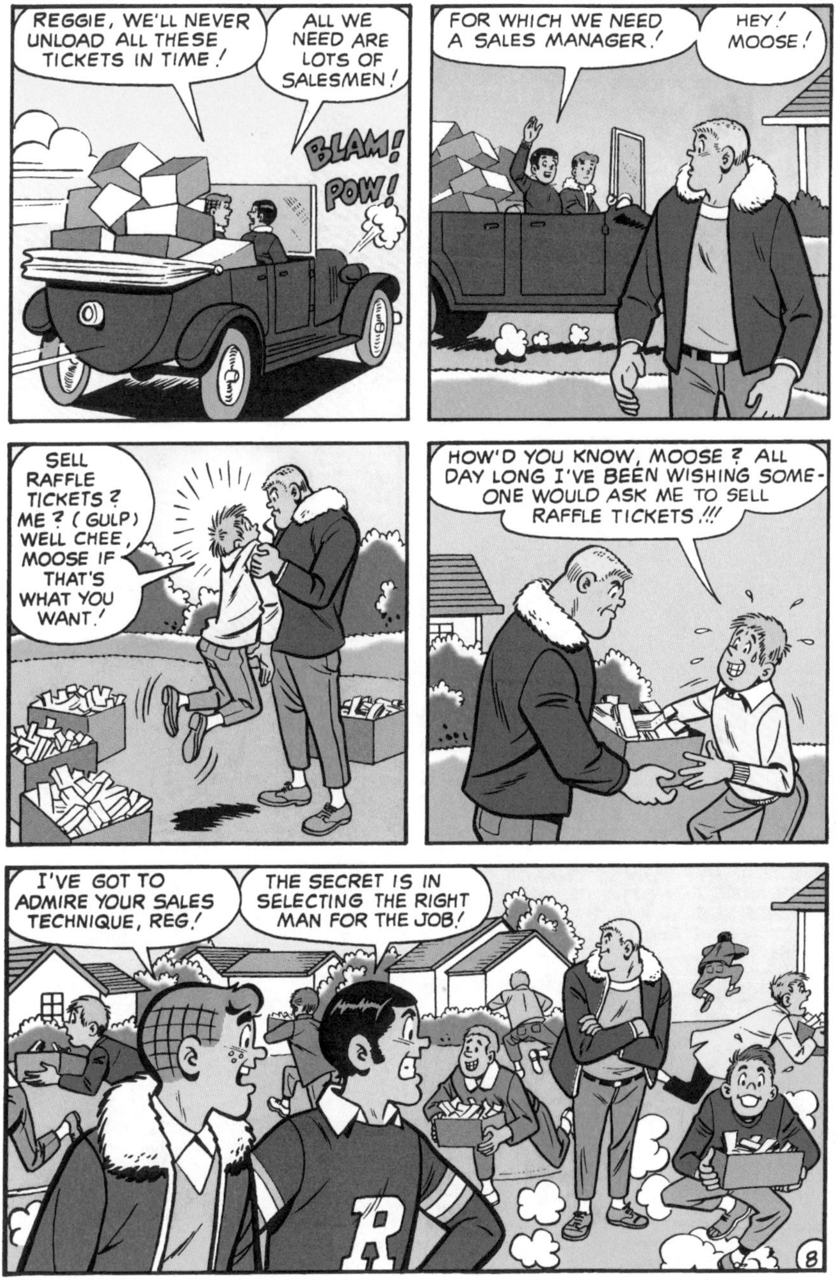
REGGIE, WE'LL NEVER UNLOAD ALL THESE TICKETS IN TIME!
ALL WE NEED ARE LOTS OF SALESMEN!
BLAM!
POW!
FOR WHICH WE NEED A SALES MANAGER!
HEY! MOOSE!
SELL RAFFLE TICKETS? ME? (GULP) WELL CHEE, MOOSE IF THAT'S WHAT YOU WANT!
HOW'D YOU KNOW, MOOSE? ALL DAY LONG I'VE BEEN WISHING SOME-ONE WOULD ASK ME TO SELL RAFFLE TICKETS!!!
I'VE GOT TO ADMIRE YOUR SALES TECHNIQUE, REG!
THE SECRET IS IN SELECTING THE RIGHT MAN FOR THE JOB!
8

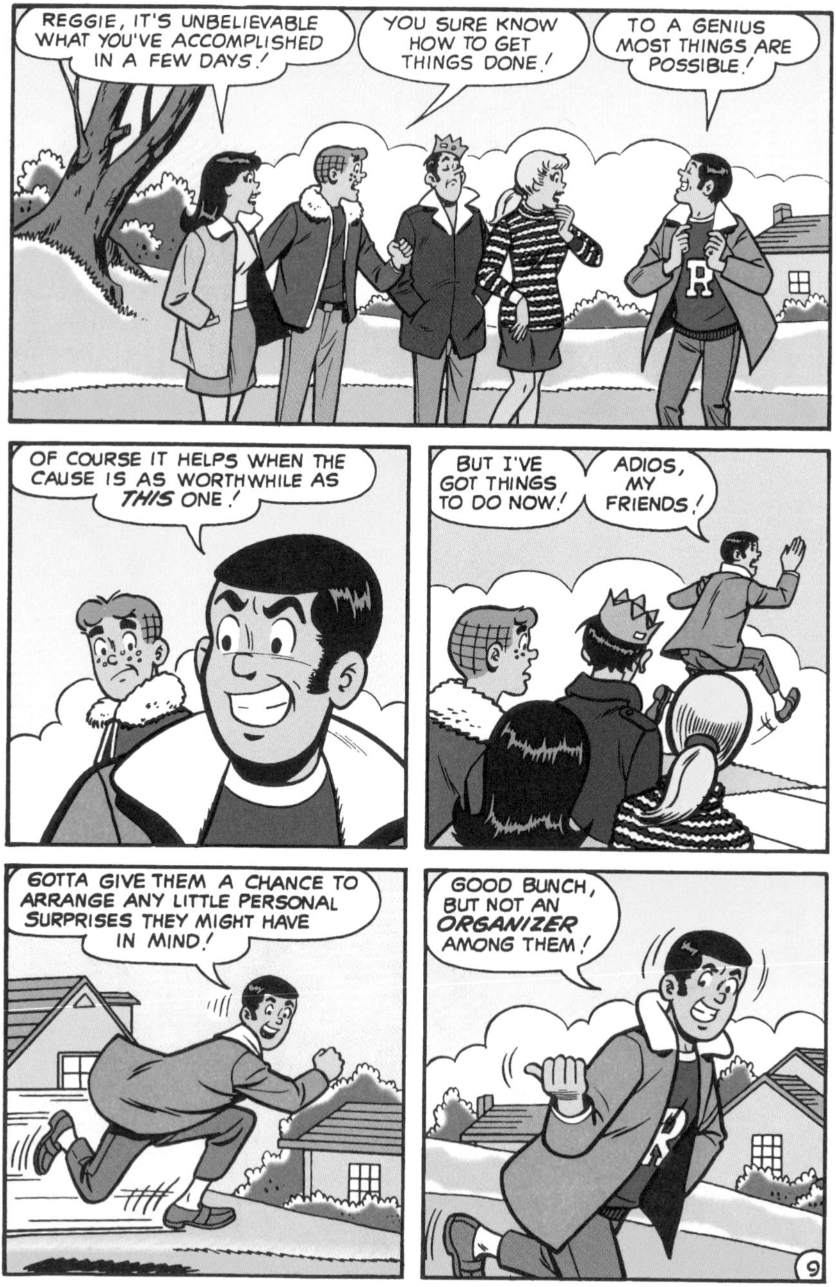

REGGIE, IT'S UNBELIEVABLE WHAT YOU'VE ACCOMPLISHED IN A FEW DAYS!
YOU SURE KNOW HOW TO GET THINGS DONE!
TO A GENIUS MOST THINGS ARE POSSIBLE!
OF COURSE IT HELPS WHEN THE CAUSE IS AS WORTHWHILE AS THIS ONE!
BUT I'VE GOT THINGS TO DO NOW!
ADIOS, MY FRIENDS!
GOTTA GIVE THEM A CHANCE TO ARRANGE ANY LITTLE PERSONAL SURPRISES THEY MIGHT HAVE IN MIND!
GOOD BUNCH, BUT NOT AN ORGANIZER AMONG THEM!
9

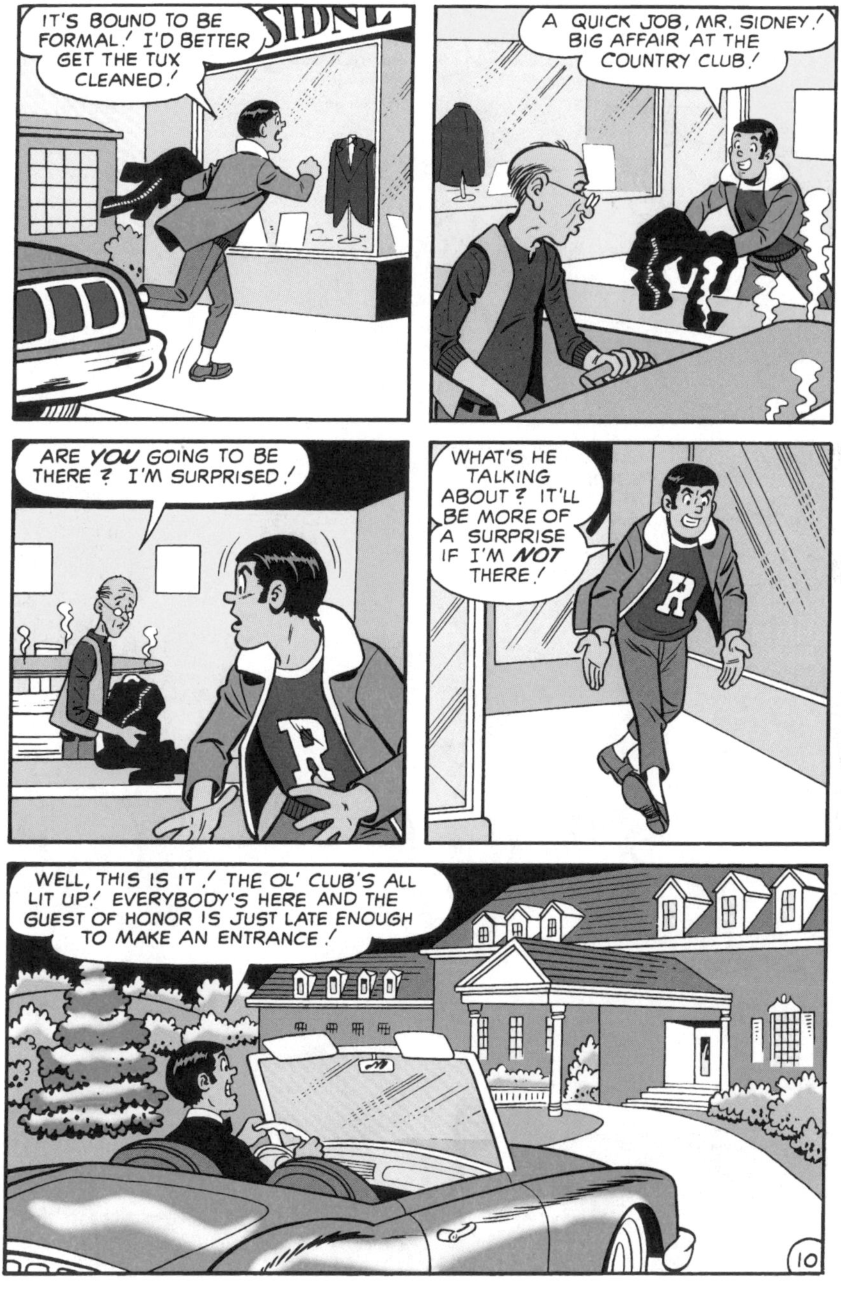

SIDNE
IT'S BOUND TO BE FORMAL! I'D BETTER GET THE TUX CLEANED!
A QUICK JOB, MR. SIDNEY! BIG AFFAIR AT THE COUNTRY CLUB!
ARE YOU GOING TO BE THERE? I'M SURPRISED!
WHAT'S HE TALKING ABOUT? IT'LL BE MORE OF A SURPRISE IF I'M NOT THERE!
WELL, THIS IS IT! THE OL' CLUB'S ALL LIT UP! EVERYBODY'S HERE AND THE GUEST OF HONOR IS JUST LATE ENOUGH TO MAKE AN ENTRANCE!
10

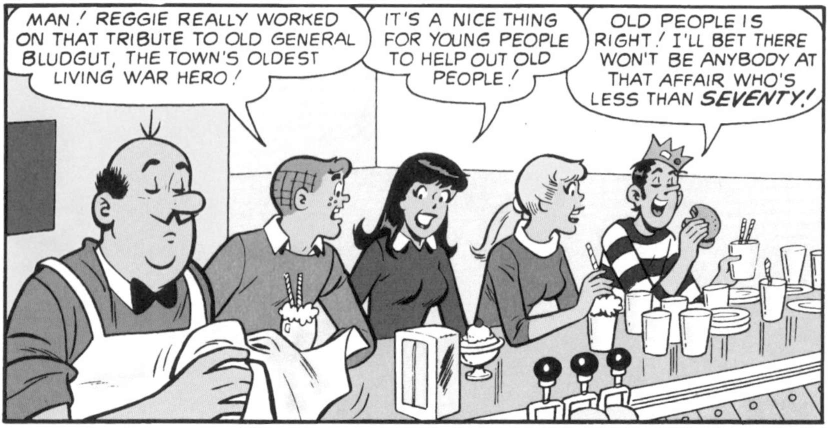
MAN! REGGIE REALLY WORKED ON THAT TRIBUTE TO OLD GENERAL BLUDGUT, THE TOWN'S OLDEST LIVING WAR HERO!
IT'S A NICE THING FOR YOUNG PEOPLE TO HELP OUT OLD PEOPLE!
OLD PEOPLE IS RIGHT! I'LL BET THERE WON'T BE ANYBODY AT THAT AFFAIR WHO'S LESS THAN SEVENTY!

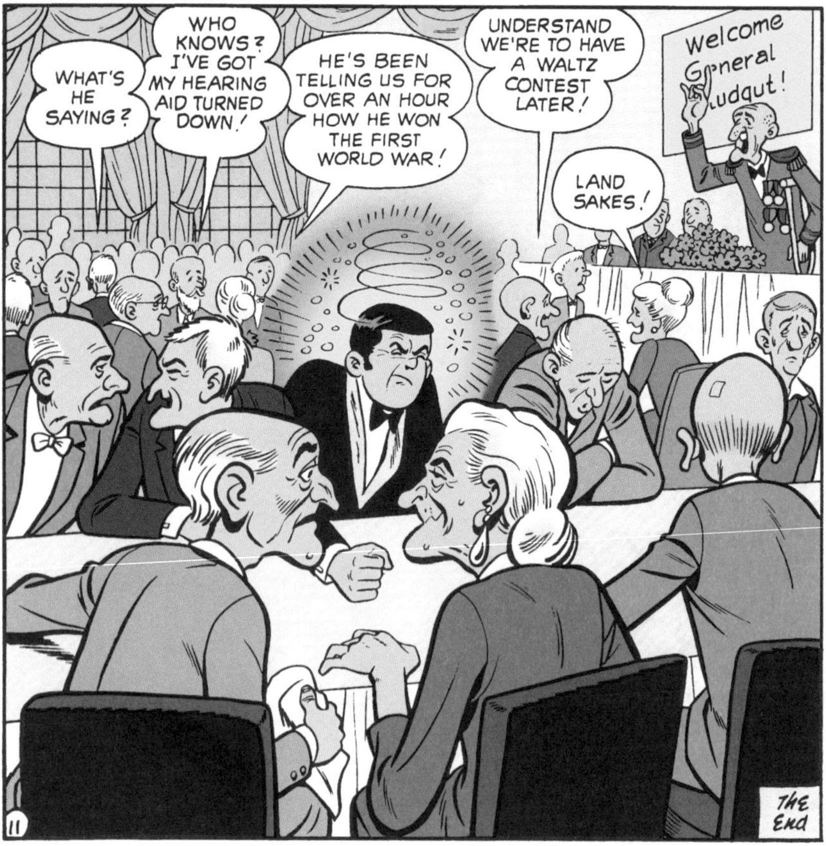
WHAT'S HE SAYING?
WHO KNOWS? I'VE GOT MY HEARING AID TURNED DOWN!
HE'S BEEN TELLING US FOR OVER AN HOUR HOW HE WON THE FIRST WORLD WAR!
UNDERSTAND WE'RE TO HAVE A WALTZ CONTEST LATER!
LAND SAKES!
11
THE End

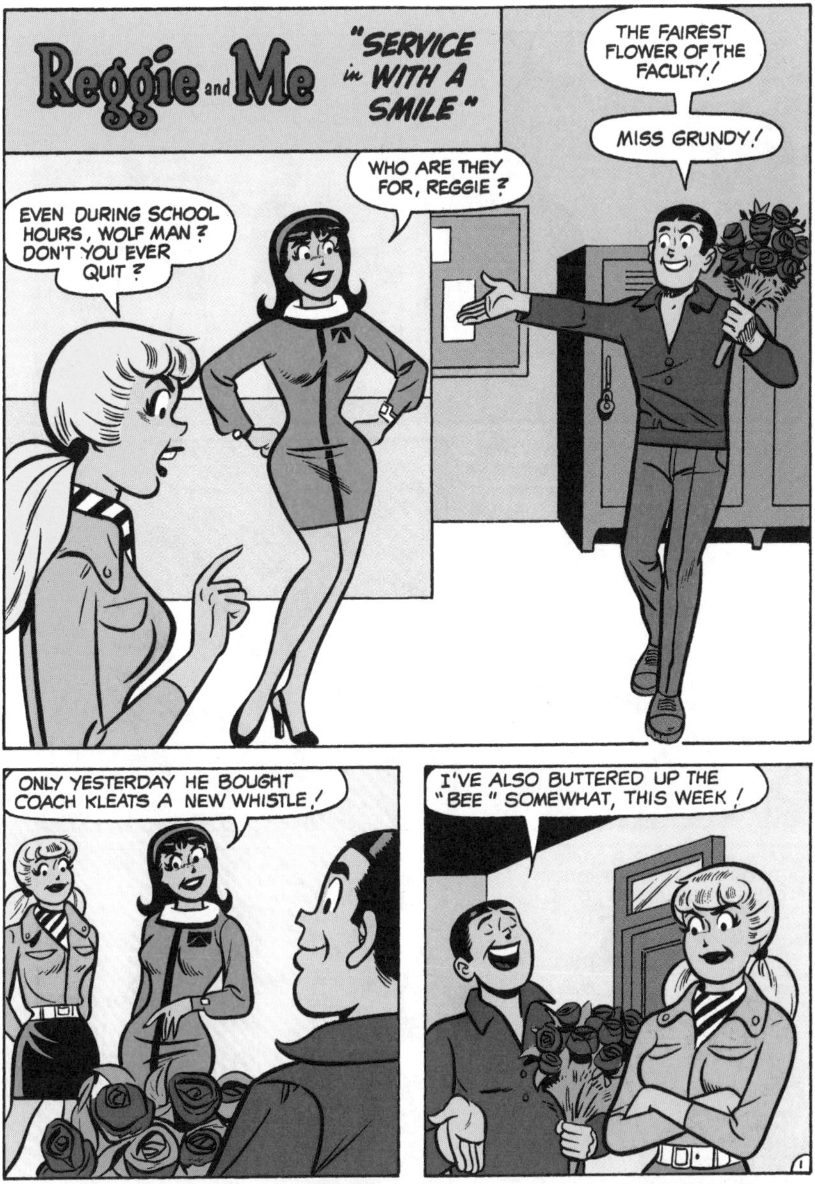
Reggie and Me
"SERVICE WITH A SMILE"
THE FAIREST FLOWER OF THE FACULTY!
MISS GRUNDY!
WHO ARE THEY FOR, REGGIE?
EVEN DURING SCHOOL HOURS, WOLF MAN? DON'T YOU EVER QUIT?
ONLY YESTERDAY HE BOUGHT COACH KLEATS A NEW WHISTLE!
I'VE ALSO BUTTERED UP THE "BEE" SOMEWHAT, THIS WEEK!
1

Story: Frank Doyle Pencils: Bob Bolling
Inks: Rudy Lapick Letters: Bill Yoshida

Originally printed in REGGIE AND ME #34, MARCH 1969

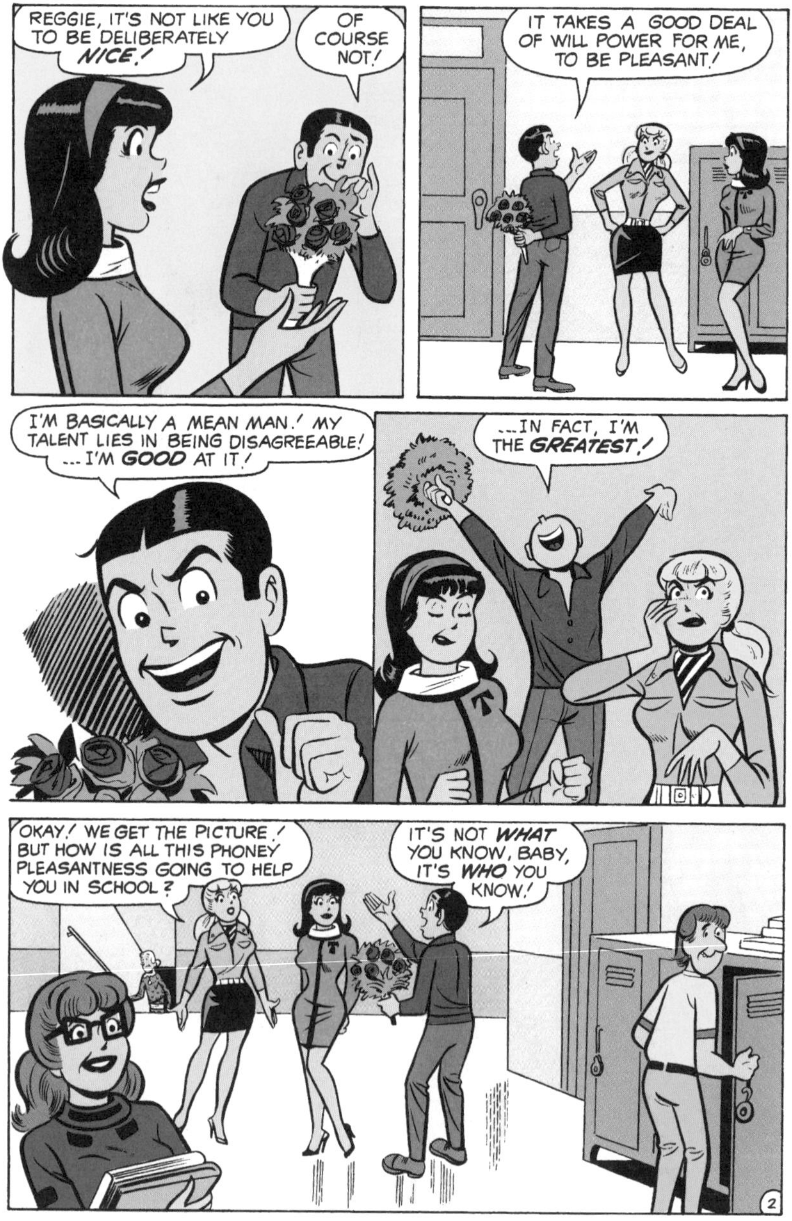
REGGIE, IT'S NOT LIKE YOU TO BE DELIBERATELY *NICE*!
OF COURSE NOT!
IT TAKES A GOOD DEAL OF WILL POWER FOR ME, TO BE PLEASANT!
I'M BASICALLY A MEAN MAN! MY TALENT LIES IN BEING DISAGREEABLE! ...I'M *GOOD* AT IT!
...IN FACT, I'M THE *GREATEST*!
OKAY! WE GET THE PICTURE! BUT HOW IS ALL THIS PHONEY PLEASANTNESS GOING TO HELP YOU IN SCHOOL?
IT'S NOT *WHAT* YOU KNOW, BABY, IT'S *WHO* YOU KNOW!
2

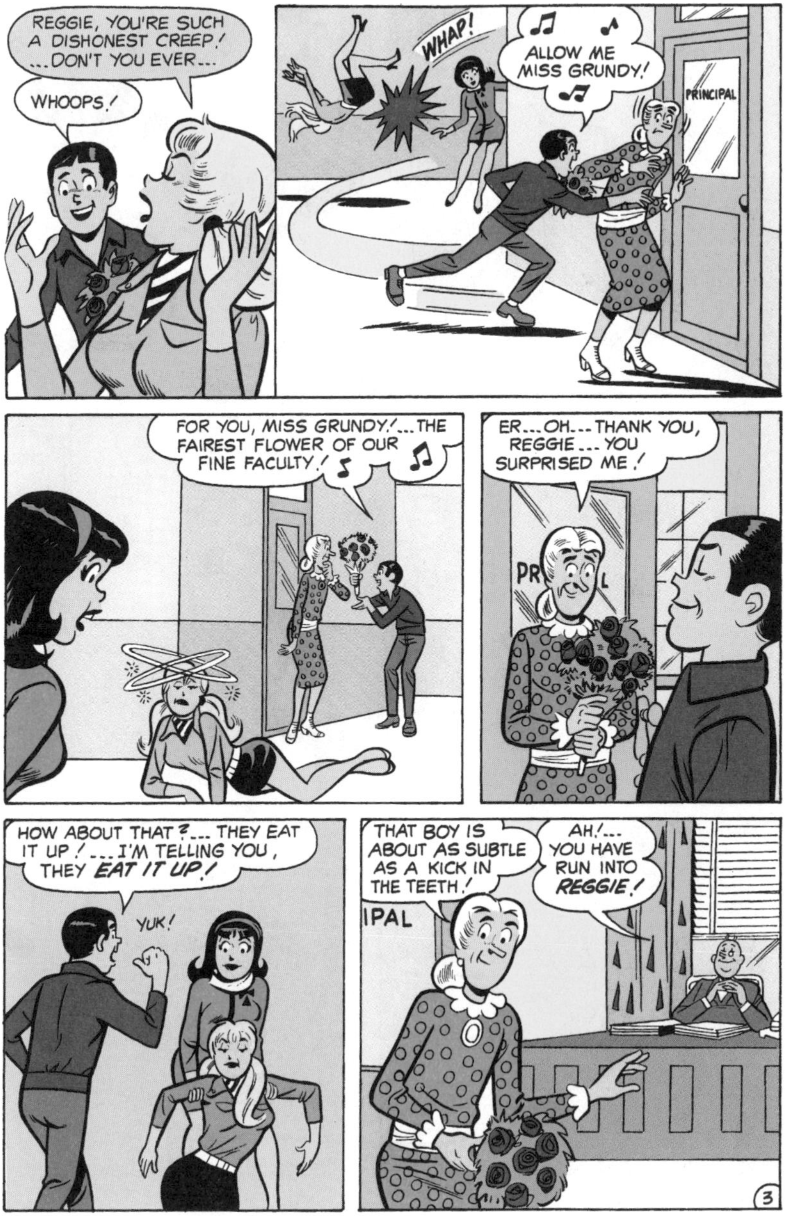
REGGIE, YOU'RE SUCH A DISHONEST CREEP! ...DON'T YOU EVER...
WHOOPS!
WHAP!
ALLOW ME MISS GRUNDY!
PRINCIPAL
FOR YOU, MISS GRUNDY!... THE FAIREST FLOWER OF OUR FINE FACULTY!
ER...OH...THANK YOU, REGGIE... YOU SURPRISED ME!
PR
L
HOW ABOUT THAT?... THEY EAT IT UP!... I'M TELLING YOU, THEY EAT IT UP!
YUK!
THAT BOY IS ABOUT AS SUBTLE AS A KICK IN THE TEETH!
AH!... YOU HAVE RUN INTO REGGIE!
IPAL
3

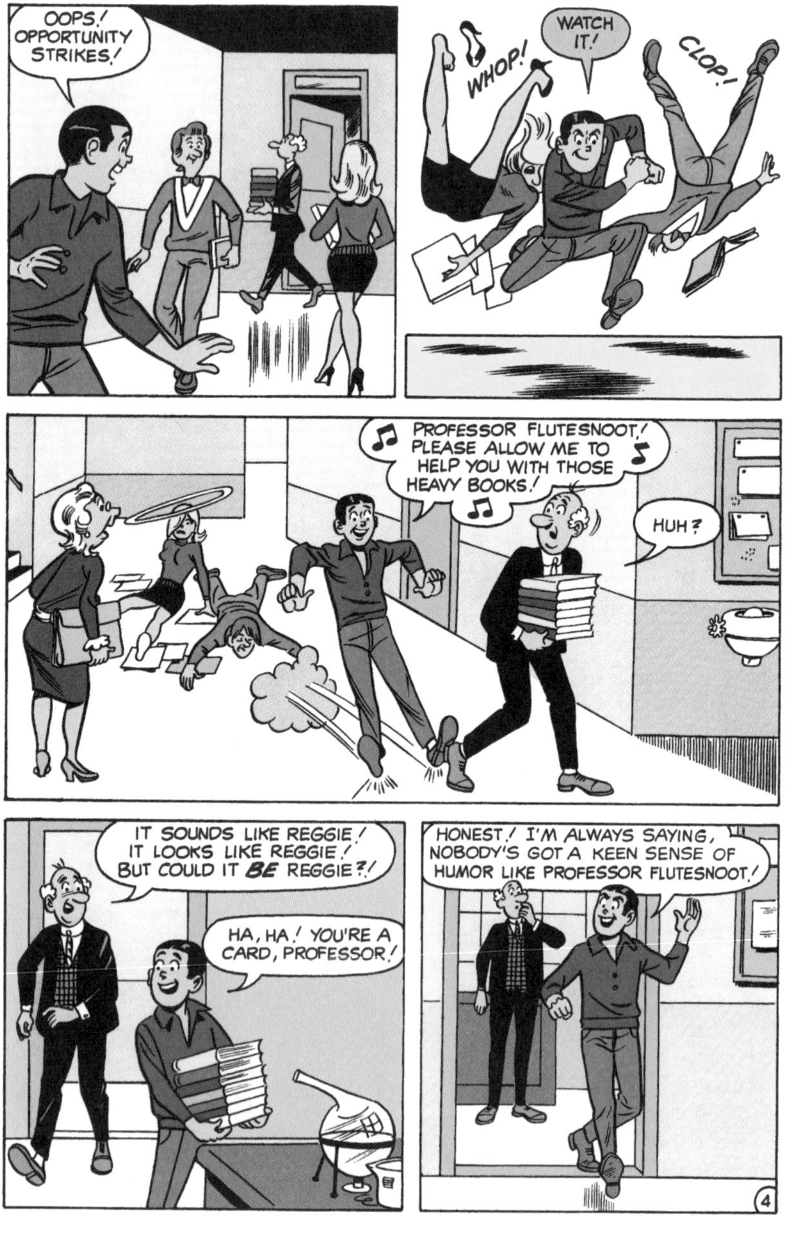
OOPS! OPPORTUNITY STRIKES!
WHOP!
WATCH IT!
CLOP!
PROFESSOR FLUTESNOOT! PLEASE ALLOW ME TO HELP YOU WITH THOSE HEAVY BOOKS!
HUH?
IT SOUNDS LIKE REGGIE! IT LOOKS LIKE REGGIE! BUT COULD IT BE REGGIE?!
HA, HA! YOU'RE A CARD, PROFESSOR!
HONEST! I'M ALWAYS SAYING, NOBODY'S GOT A KEEN SENSE OF HUMOR LIKE PROFESSOR FLUTESNOOT!
4

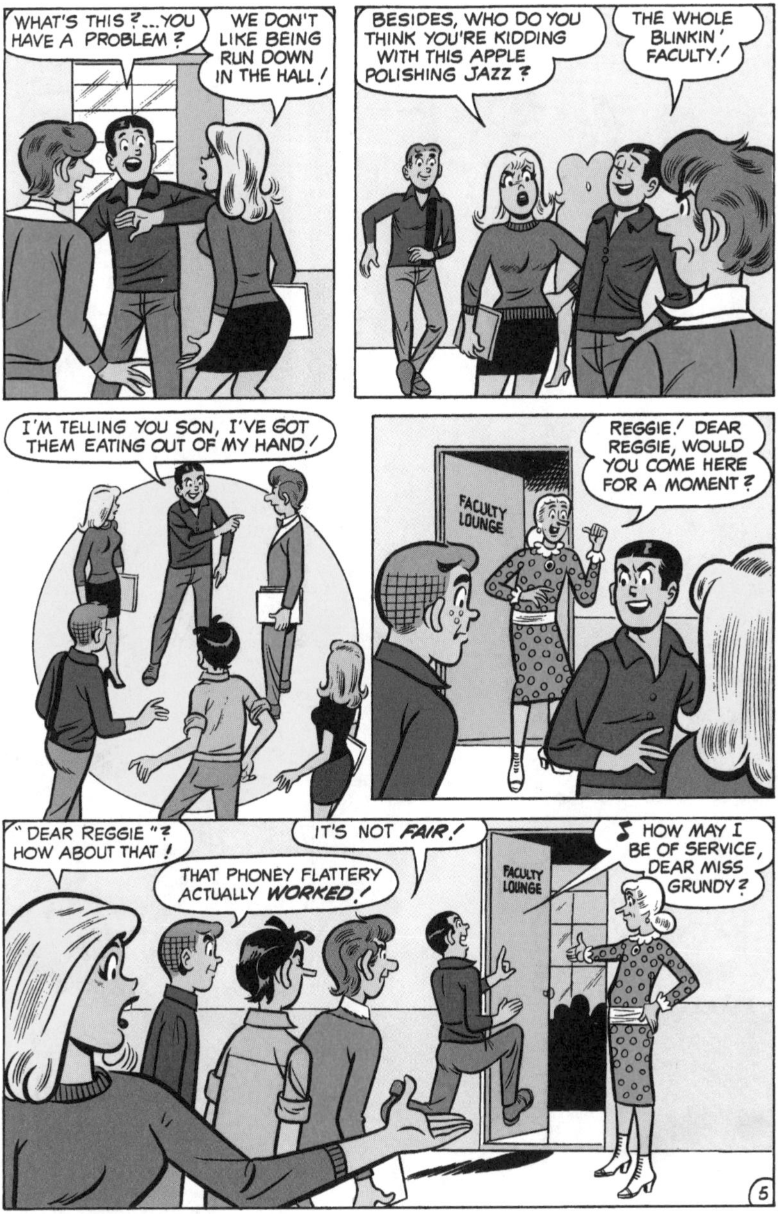
WHAT'S THIS ?...YOU HAVE A PROBLEM ?
WE DON'T LIKE BEING RUN DOWN IN THE HALL !
BESIDES, WHO DO YOU THINK YOU'RE KIDDING WITH THIS APPLE POLISHING JAZZ ?
THE WHOLE BLINKIN' FACULTY !
I'M TELLING YOU SON, I'VE GOT THEM EATING OUT OF MY HAND !
FACULTY LOUNGE
REGGIE ! DEAR REGGIE, WOULD YOU COME HERE FOR A MOMENT ?
"DEAR REGGIE"? HOW ABOUT THAT !
THAT PHONEY FLATTERY ACTUALLY WORKED !
IT'S NOT FAIR !
FACULTY LOUNGE
HOW MAY I BE OF SERVICE, DEAR MISS GRUNDY ?
5

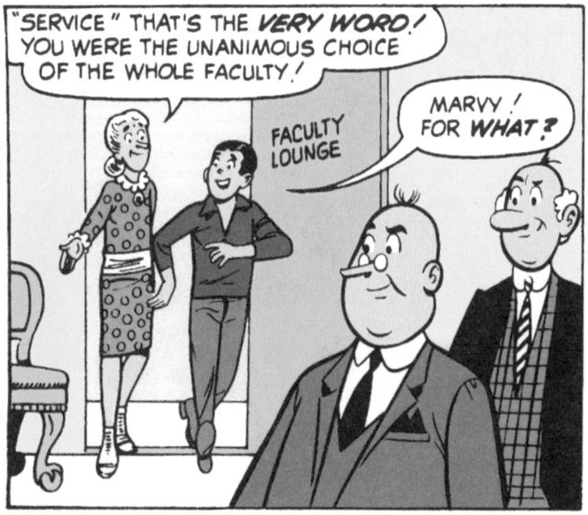
"SERVICE" THAT'S THE VERY WORD! YOU WERE THE UNANIMOUS CHOICE OF THE WHOLE FACULTY!
FACULTY LOUNGE
MARVY! FOR WHAT?

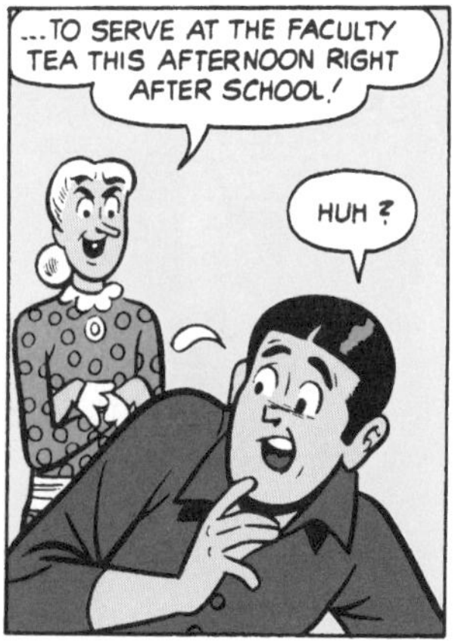
...TO SERVE AT THE FACULTY TEA THIS AFTERNOON RIGHT AFTER SCHOOL!
HUH?

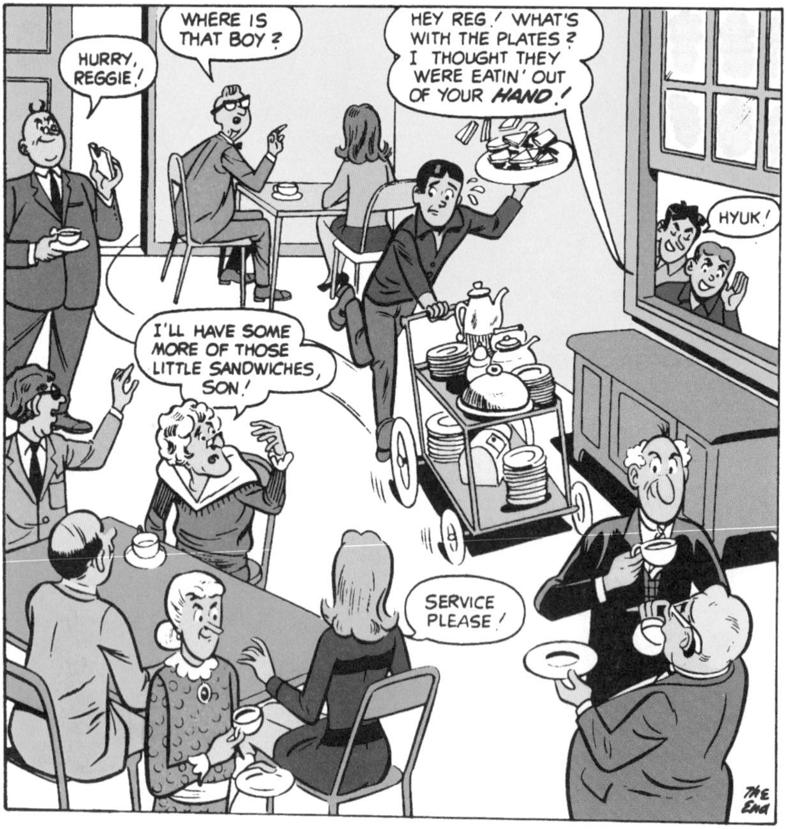
HURRY, REGGIE!
WHERE IS THAT BOY?
HEY REG! WHAT'S WITH THE PLATES? I THOUGHT THEY WERE EATIN' OUT OF YOUR HAND!
HYUK!
I'LL HAVE SOME MORE OF THOSE LITTLE SANDWICHES, SON!
SERVICE PLEASE!
THE End

Reggie and Me in the "INCREDIBILITY GAP"

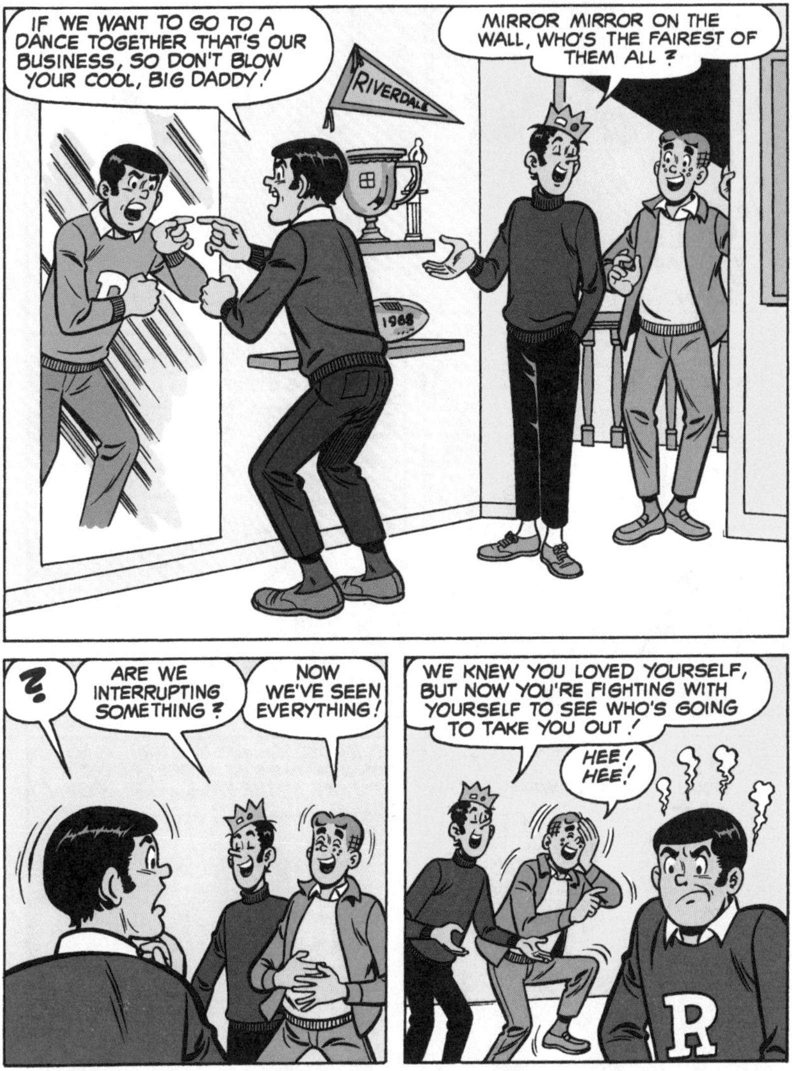
IF WE WANT TO GO TO A DANCE TOGETHER THAT'S OUR BUSINESS, SO DON'T BLOW YOUR COOL, BIG DADDY!
RIVERDALE
1968
MIRROR MIRROR ON THE WALL, WHO'S THE FAIREST OF THEM ALL?
?
ARE WE INTERRUPTING SOMETHING?
NOW WE'VE SEEN EVERYTHING!
WE KNEW YOU LOVED YOURSELF, BUT NOW YOU'RE FIGHTING WITH YOURSELF TO SEE WHO'S GOING TO TAKE YOU OUT!
HEE! HEE!
R

Story & Pencils: Al Hartley
Inks: Jon D'Agostino Letters: Bill Yoshida

Originally printed in REGGIE AND ME #35, MAY 1969

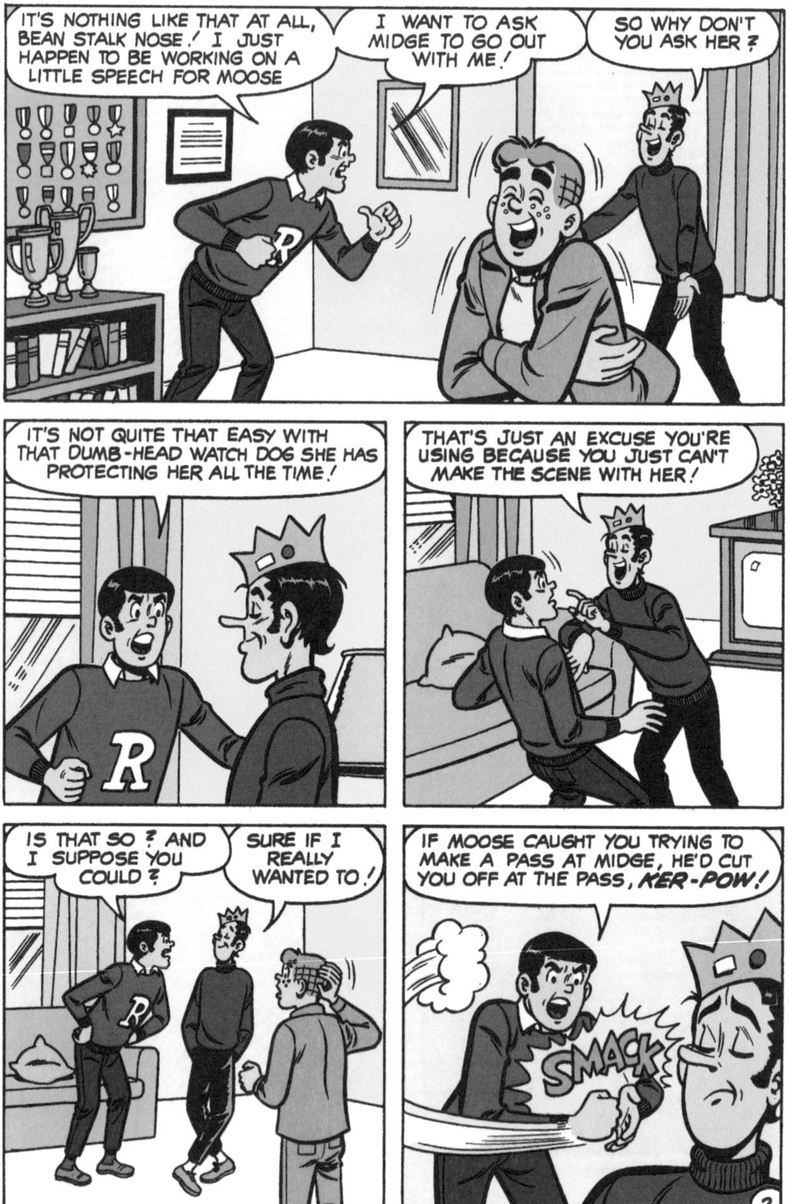
IT'S NOTHING LIKE THAT AT ALL, BEAN STALK NOSE! I JUST HAPPEN TO BE WORKING ON A LITTLE SPEECH FOR MOOSE
I WANT TO ASK MIDGE TO GO OUT WITH ME!
SO WHY DON'T YOU ASK HER ?
IT'S NOT QUITE THAT EASY WITH THAT DUMB-HEAD WATCH DOG SHE HAS PROTECTING HER ALL THE TIME!
THAT'S JUST AN EXCUSE YOU'RE USING BECAUSE YOU JUST CAN'T MAKE THE SCENE WITH HER!
IS THAT SO ? AND I SUPPOSE YOU COULD ?
SURE IF I REALLY WANTED TO!
IF MOOSE CAUGHT YOU TRYING TO MAKE A PASS AT MIDGE, HE'D CUT YOU OFF AT THE PASS, KER-POW!
SMACK
2

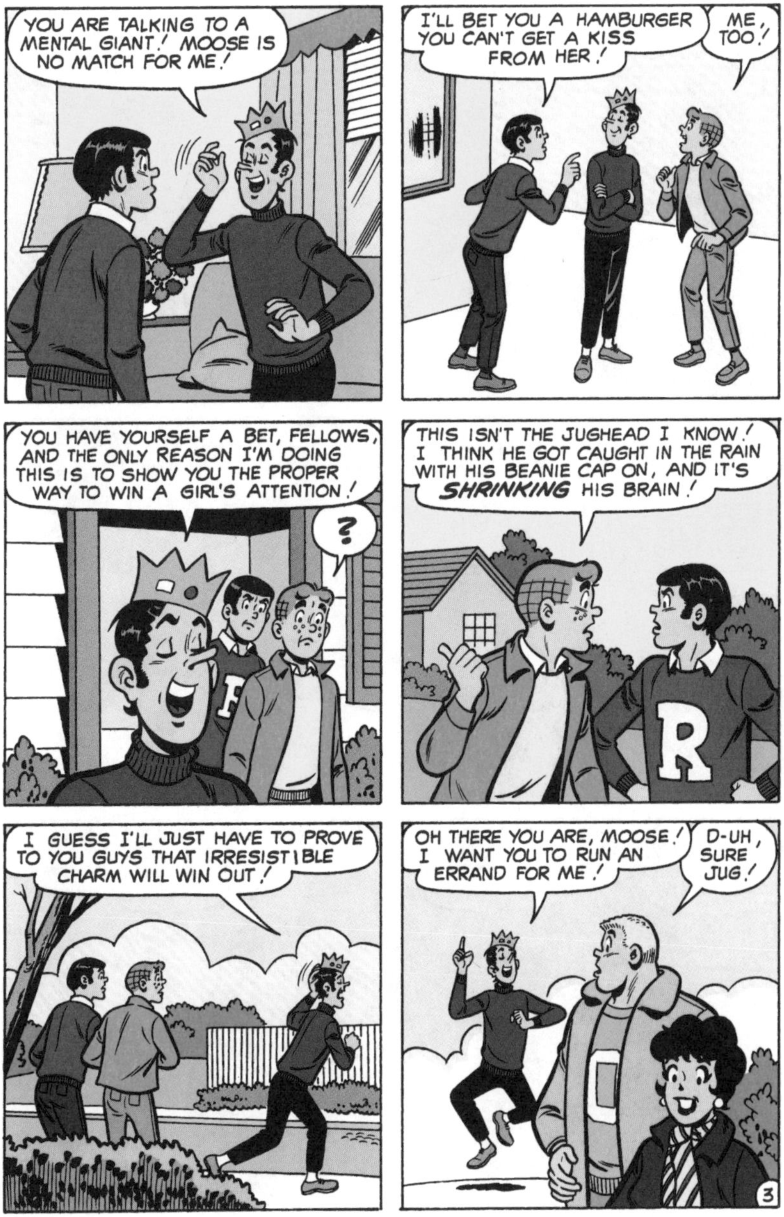
YOU ARE TALKING TO A MENTAL GIANT! MOOSE IS NO MATCH FOR ME!
I'LL BET YOU A HAMBURGER YOU CAN'T GET A KISS FROM HER!
ME, TOO!
YOU HAVE YOURSELF A BET, FELLOWS, AND THE ONLY REASON I'M DOING THIS IS TO SHOW YOU THE PROPER WAY TO WIN A GIRL'S ATTENTION!
?
THIS ISN'T THE JUGHEAD I KNOW! I THINK HE GOT CAUGHT IN THE RAIN WITH HIS BEANIE CAP ON, AND IT'S SHRINKING HIS BRAIN!
I GUESS I'LL JUST HAVE TO PROVE TO YOU GUYS THAT IRRESISTIBLE CHARM WILL WIN OUT!
OH THERE YOU ARE, MOOSE! I WANT YOU TO RUN AN ERRAND FOR ME!
D-UH, SURE JUG!
3

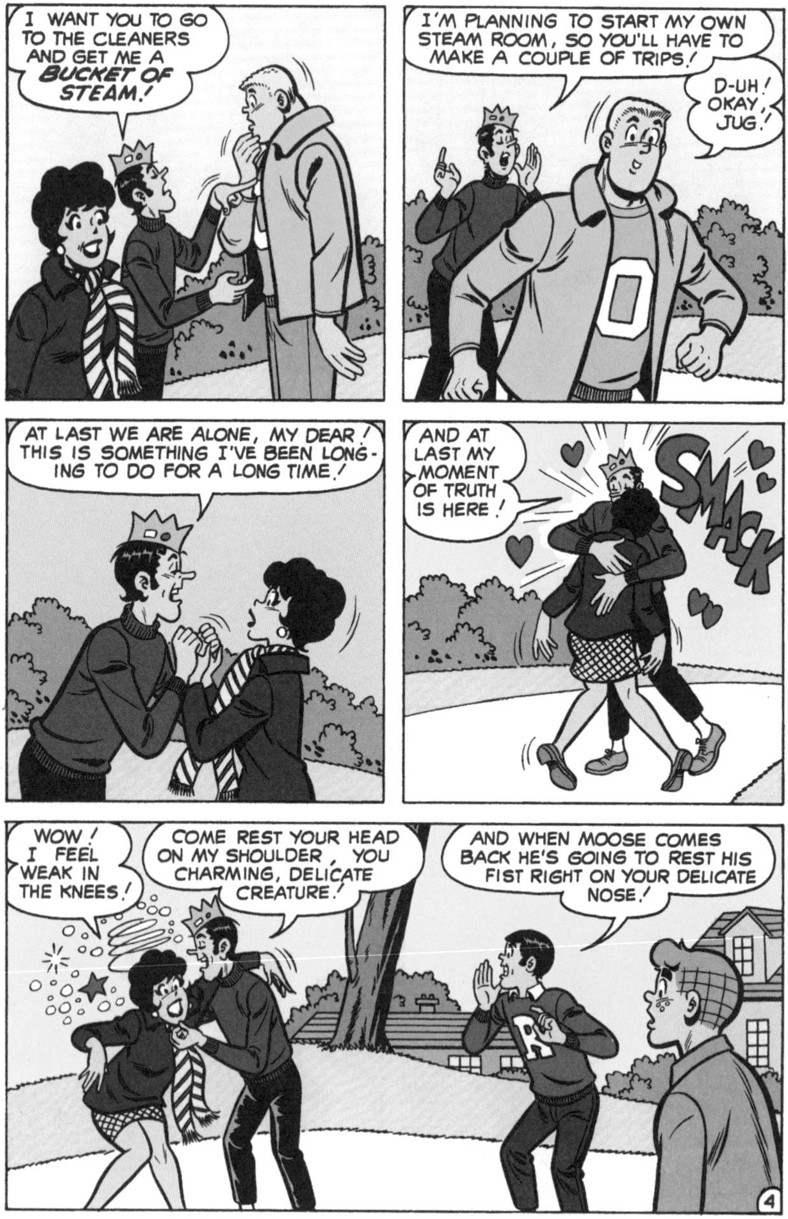
I WANT YOU TO GO TO THE CLEANERS AND GET ME A BUCKET OF STEAM!
I'M PLANNING TO START MY OWN STEAM ROOM, SO YOU'LL HAVE TO MAKE A COUPLE OF TRIPS!
D-UH! OKAY, JUG!
AT LAST WE ARE ALONE, MY DEAR! THIS IS SOMETHING I'VE BEEN LONG-ING TO DO FOR A LONG TIME!
AND AT LAST MY MOMENT OF TRUTH IS HERE!
SMACK
WOW! I FEEL WEAK IN THE KNEES!
COME REST YOUR HEAD ON MY SHOULDER, YOU CHARMING, DELICATE CREATURE!
AND WHEN MOOSE COMES BACK HE'S GOING TO REST HIS FIST RIGHT ON YOUR DELICATE NOSE!
4

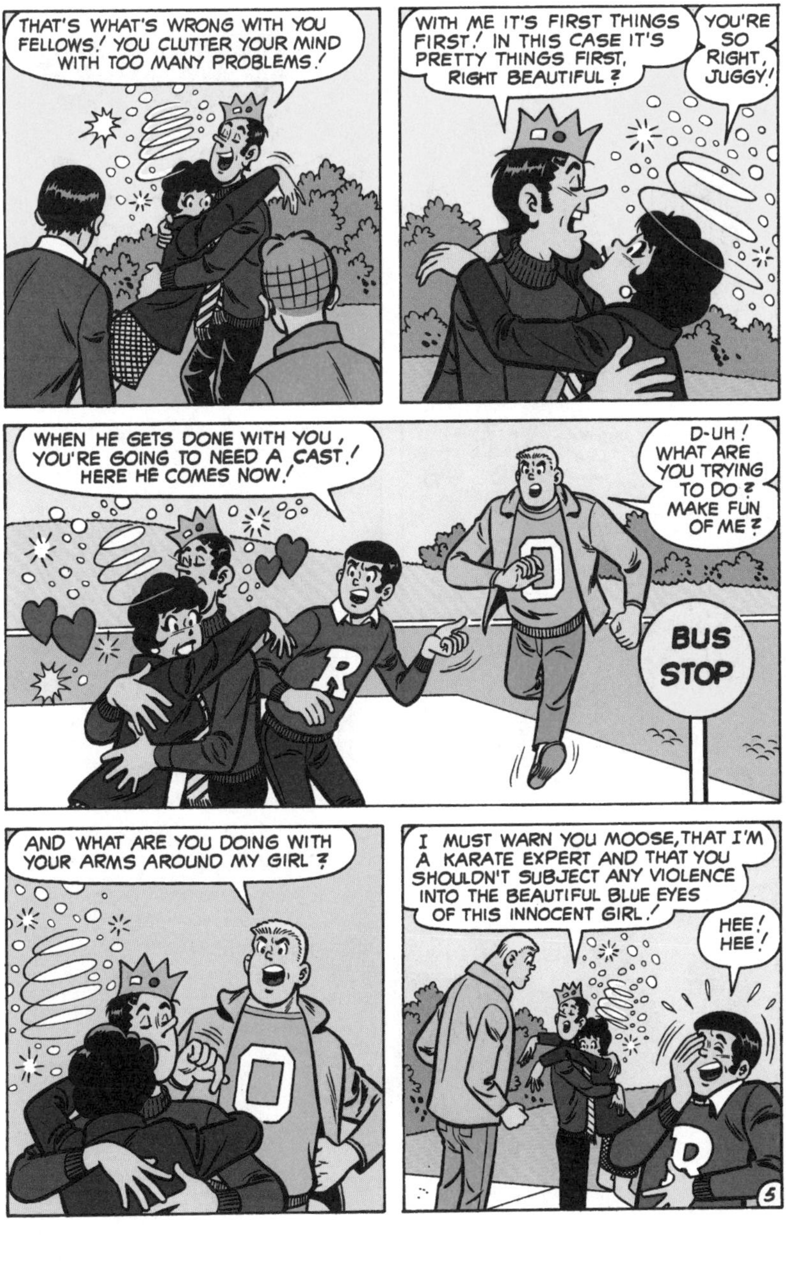
THAT'S WHAT'S WRONG WITH YOU FELLOWS! YOU CLUTTER YOUR MIND WITH TOO MANY PROBLEMS!
WITH ME IT'S FIRST THINGS FIRST! IN THIS CASE IT'S PRETTY THINGS FIRST, RIGHT BEAUTIFUL?
YOU'RE SO RIGHT, JUGGY!
WHEN HE GETS DONE WITH YOU, YOU'RE GOING TO NEED A CAST! HERE HE COMES NOW!
D-UH! WHAT ARE YOU TRYING TO DO? MAKE FUN OF ME?
BUS STOP
AND WHAT ARE YOU DOING WITH YOUR ARMS AROUND MY GIRL?
I MUST WARN YOU MOOSE, THAT I'M A KARATE EXPERT AND THAT YOU SHOULDN'T SUBJECT ANY VIOLENCE INTO THE BEAUTIFUL BLUE EYES OF THIS INNOCENT GIRL!
HEE! HEE!
5

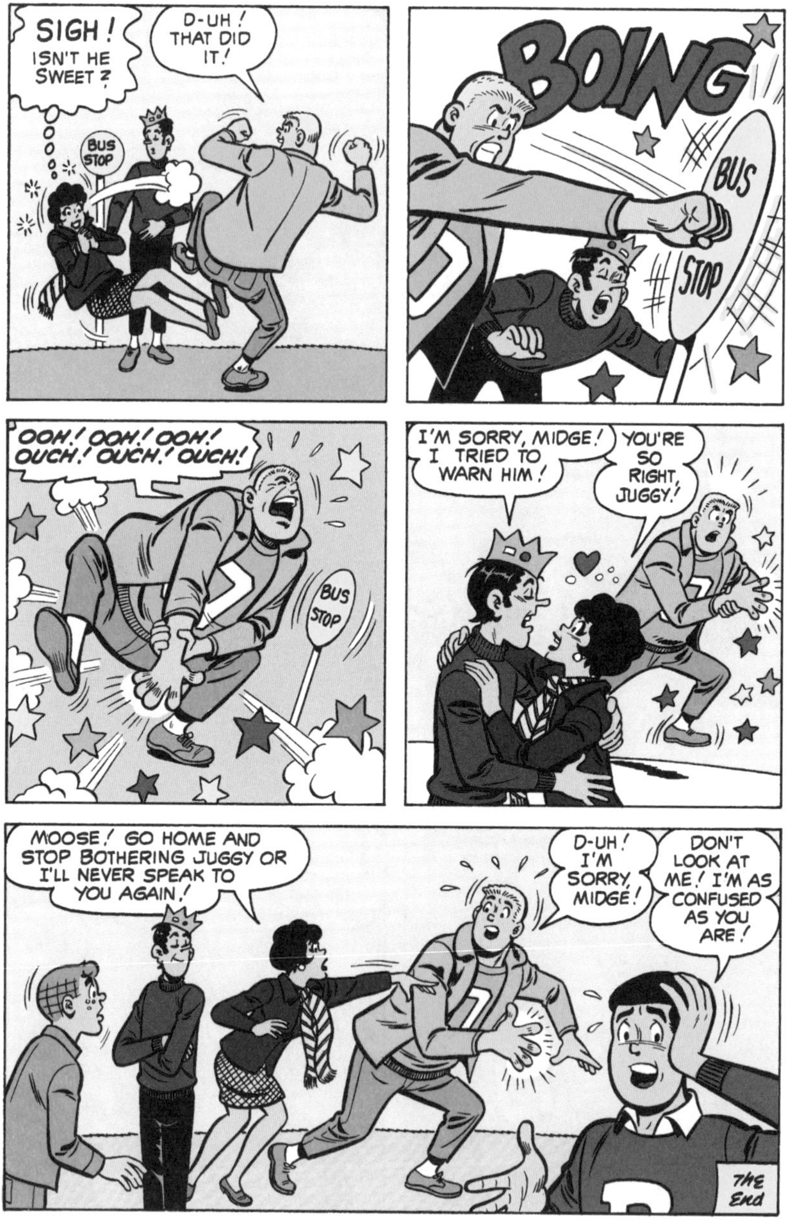
SIGH! ISN'T HE SWEET?
D-UH! THAT DID IT!
BUS STOP
BOING
BUS STOP
OOH! OOH! OOH! OUCH! OUCH! OUCH!
BUS STOP
I'M SORRY, MIDGE! I TRIED TO WARN HIM!
YOU'RE SO RIGHT, JUGGY!
MOOSE! GO HOME AND STOP BOTHERING JUGGY OR I'LL NEVER SPEAK TO YOU AGAIN!
D-UH! I'M SORRY, MIDGE!
DON'T LOOK AT ME! I'M AS CONFUSED AS YOU ARE!
THE End

Reggie and Me "THE FINAL OBSTACLE"

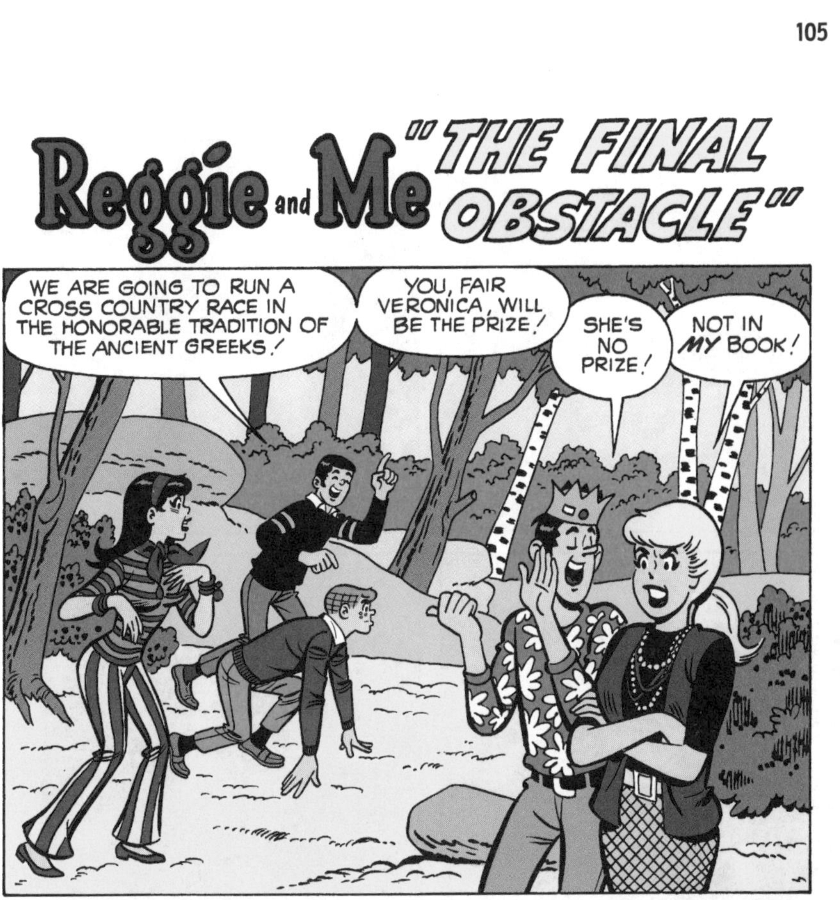
WE ARE GOING TO RUN A CROSS COUNTRY RACE IN THE HONORABLE TRADITION OF THE ANCIENT GREEKS!
YOU, FAIR VERONICA, WILL BE THE PRIZE!
SHE'S NO PRIZE!
NOT IN *MY* BOOK!

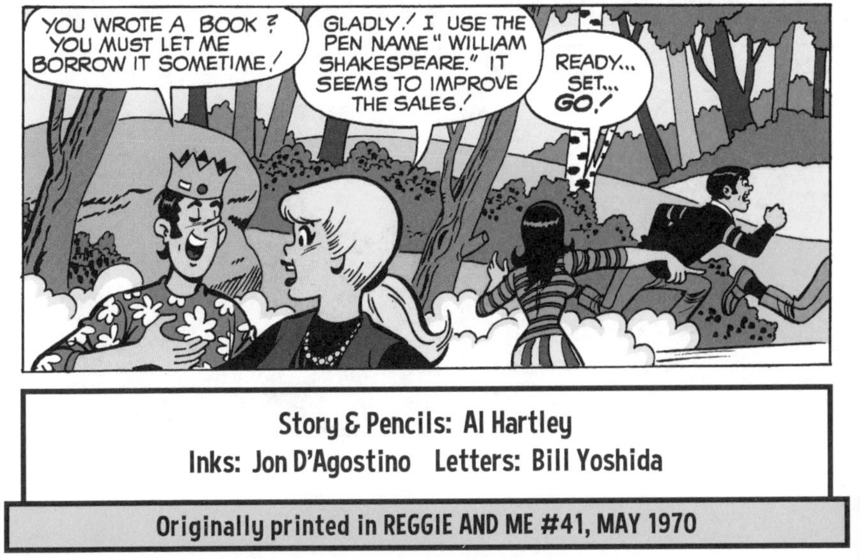
YOU WROTE A BOOK? YOU MUST LET ME BORROW IT SOMETIME!
GLADLY! I USE THE PEN NAME "WILLIAM SHAKESPEARE." IT SEEMS TO IMPROVE THE SALES!
READY... SET... *GO!*

Story & Pencils: Al Hartley

Inks: Jon D'Agostino Letters: Bill Yoshida

Originally printed in REGGIE AND ME #41, MAY 1970

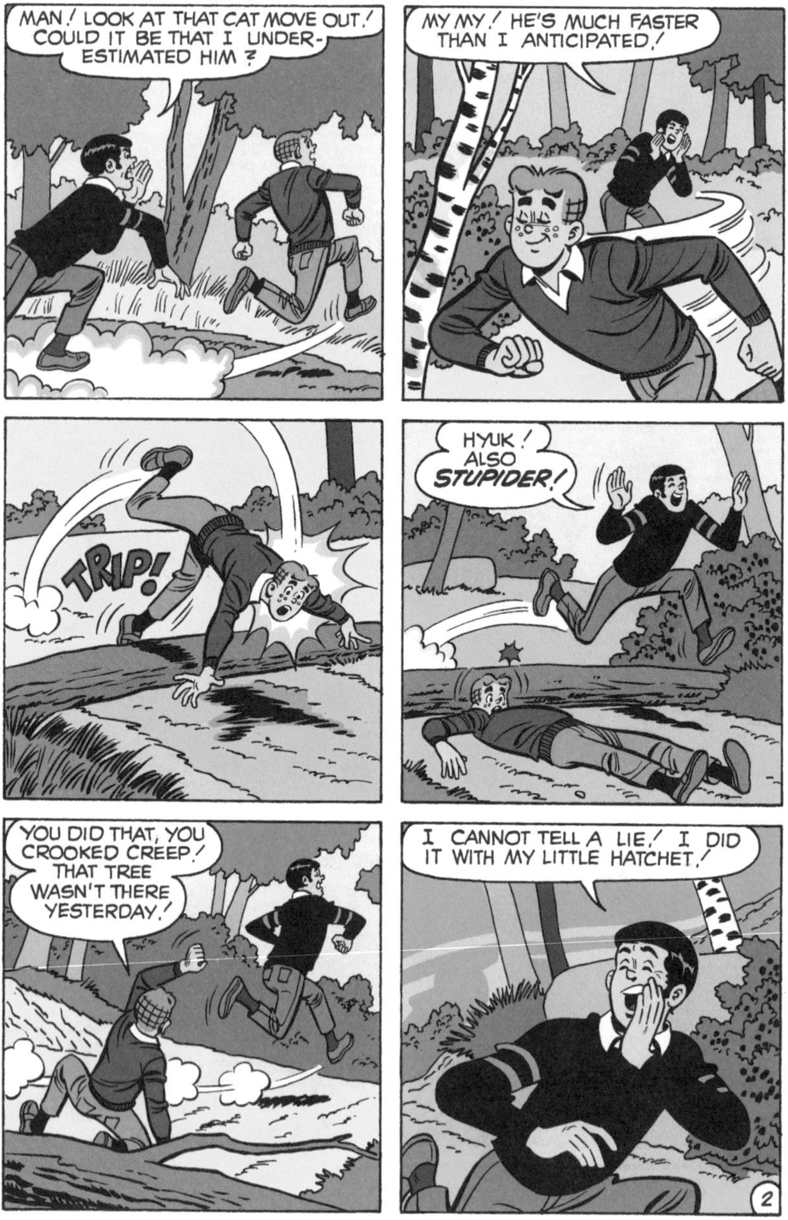
MAN! LOOK AT THAT CAT MOVE OUT! COULD IT BE THAT I UNDER-ESTIMATED HIM?
MY MY! HE'S MUCH FASTER THAN I ANTICIPATED!
TRIP!
HYUK! ALSO STUPIDER!
YOU DID THAT, YOU CROOKED CREEP! THAT TREE WASN'T THERE YESTERDAY!
I CANNOT TELL A LIE! I DID IT WITH MY LITTLE HATCHET!
2

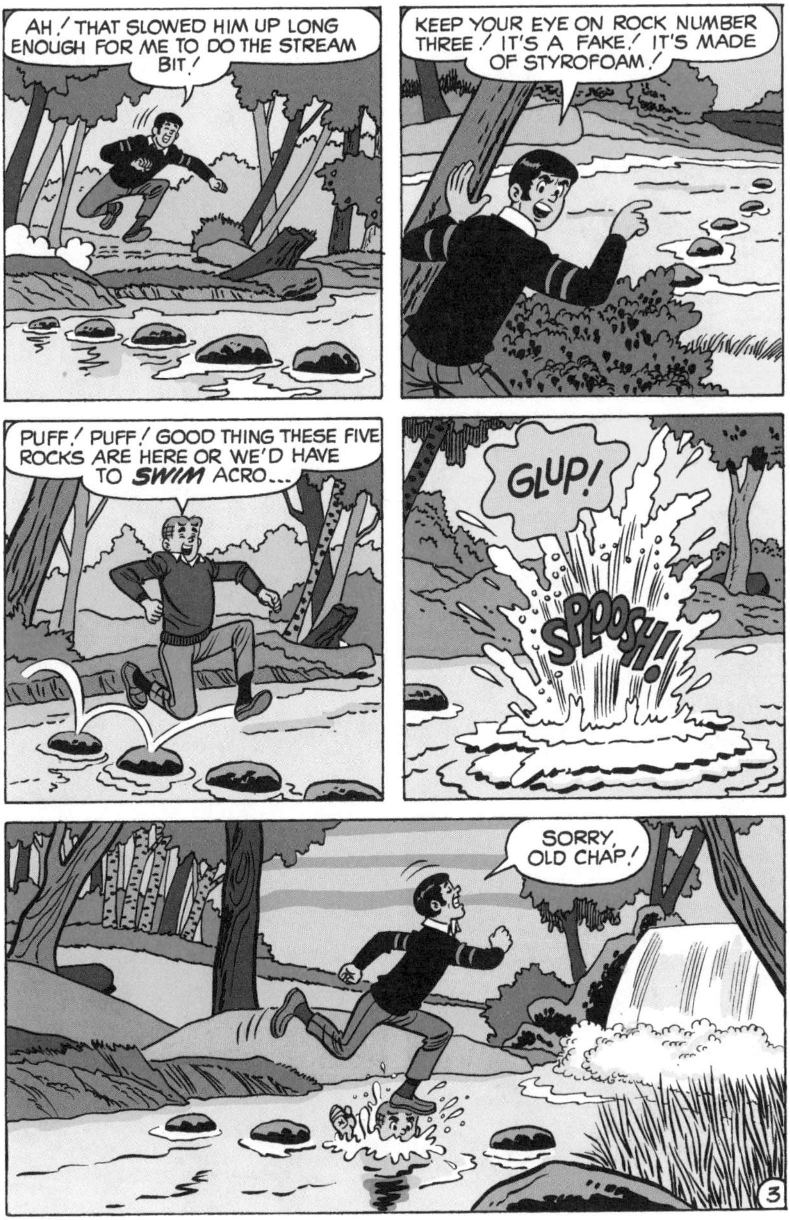
AH! THAT SLOWED HIM UP LONG ENOUGH FOR ME TO DO THE STREAM BIT!
KEEP YOUR EYE ON ROCK NUMBER THREE! IT'S A FAKE! IT'S MADE OF STYROFOAM!
PUFF! PUFF! GOOD THING THESE FIVE ROCKS ARE HERE OR WE'D HAVE TO SWIM ACRO...
GLUP!
SPLOOSH!
SORRY, OLD CHAP!
3

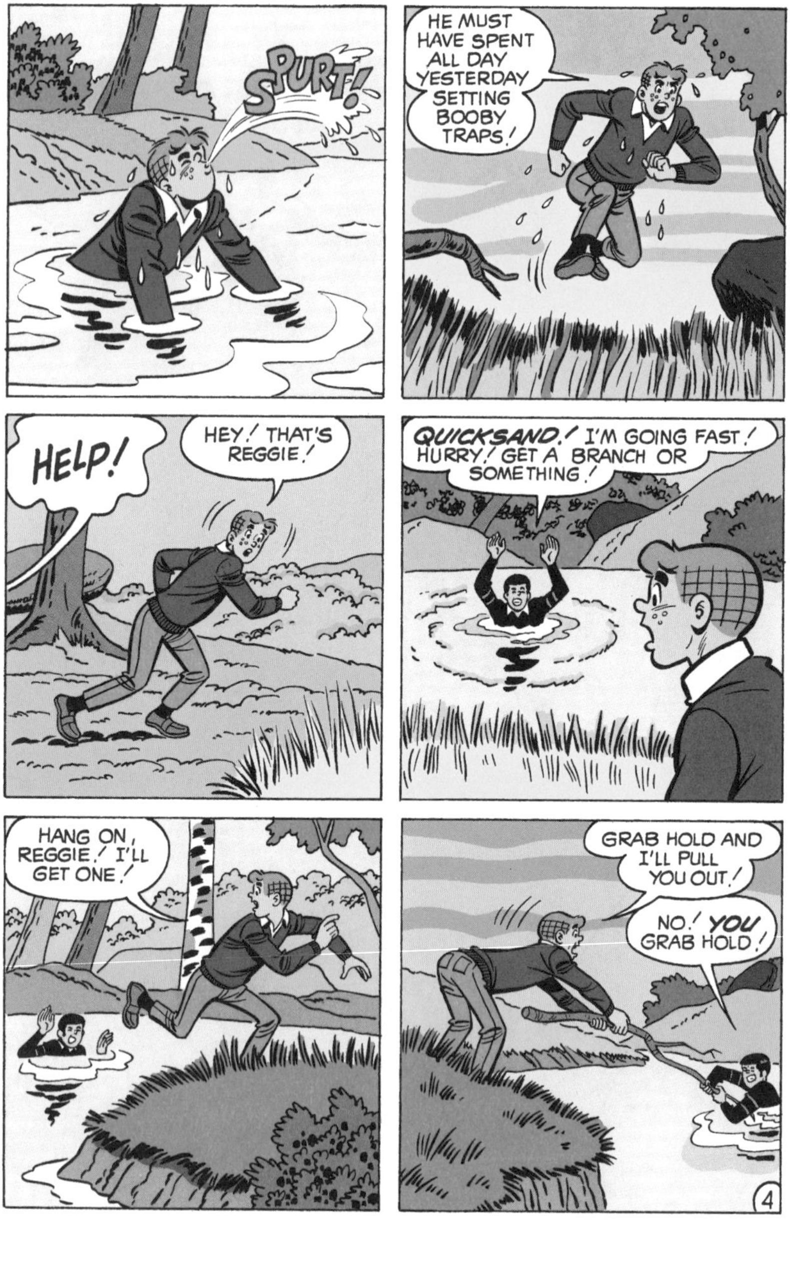
SPURT!
HE MUST HAVE SPENT ALL DAY YESTERDAY SETTING BOOBY TRAPS!
HELP!
HEY! THAT'S REGGIE!
QUICKSAND! I'M GOING FAST! HURRY! GET A BRANCH OR SOMETHING!
HANG ON, REGGIE! I'LL GET ONE!
GRAB HOLD AND I'LL PULL YOU OUT!
NO! YOU GRAB HOLD!
4

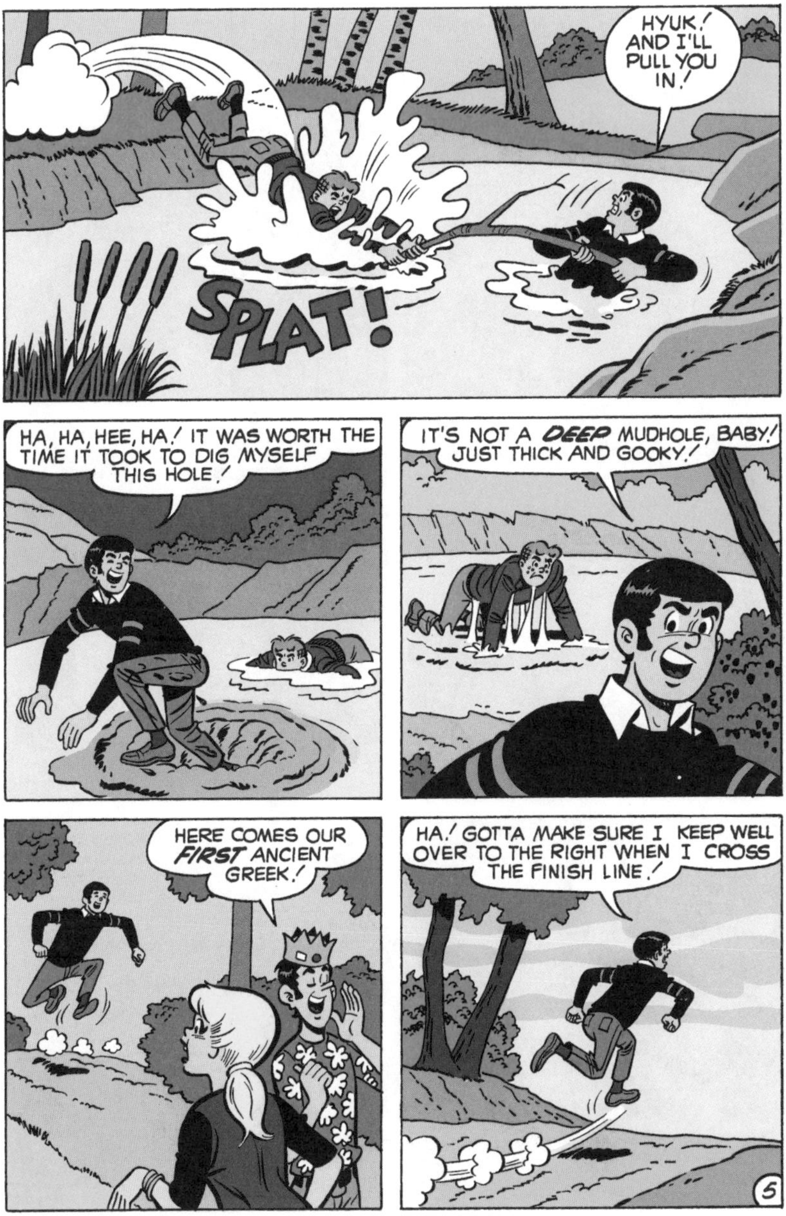
HYUK! AND I'LL PULL YOU IN!
SPLAT!
HA, HA, HEE, HA! IT WAS WORTH THE TIME IT TOOK TO DIG MYSELF THIS HOLE!
IT'S NOT A DEEP MUDHOLE, BABY! JUST THICK AND GOOKY!
HERE COMES OUR FIRST ANCIENT GREEK!
HA! GOTTA MAKE SURE I KEEP WELL OVER TO THE RIGHT WHEN I CROSS THE FINISH LINE!
5

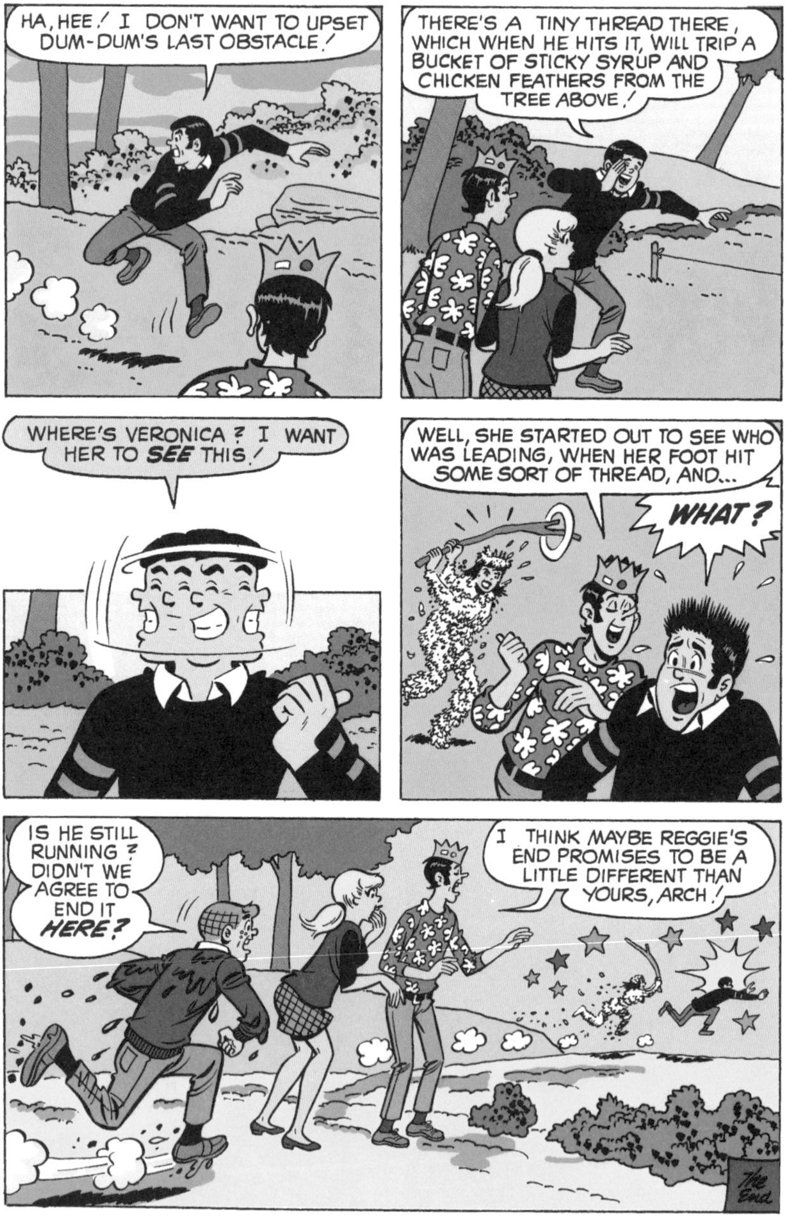
HA, HEE! I DON'T WANT TO UPSET DUM-DUM'S LAST OBSTACLE!
THERE'S A TINY THREAD THERE, WHICH WHEN HE HITS IT, WILL TRIP A BUCKET OF STICKY SYRUP AND CHICKEN FEATHERS FROM THE TREE ABOVE!
WHERE'S VERONICA? I WANT HER TO SEE THIS!
WELL, SHE STARTED OUT TO SEE WHO WAS LEADING, WHEN HER FOOT HIT SOME SORT OF THREAD, AND...
WHAT?
IS HE STILL RUNNING? DIDN'T WE AGREE TO END IT HERE?
I THINK MAYBE REGGIE'S END PROMISES TO BE A LITTLE DIFFERENT THAN YOURS, ARCH!
The End

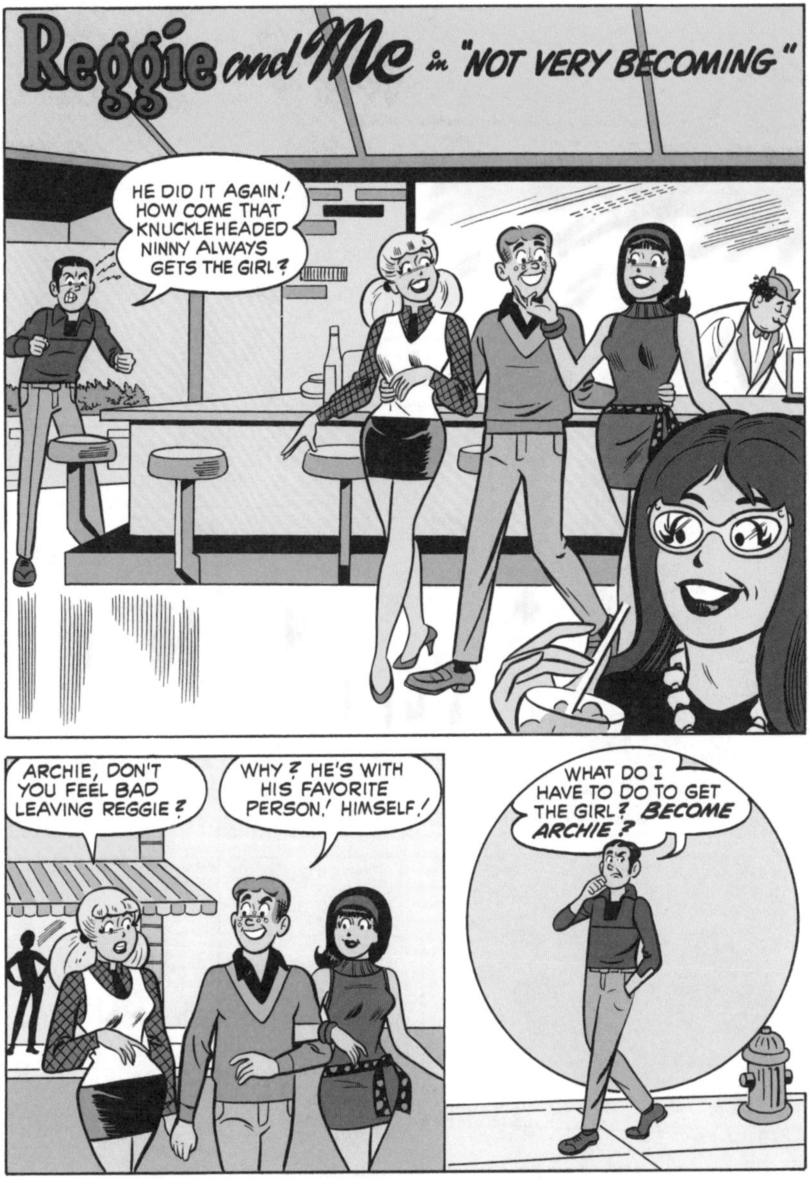
Reggie and Me in "NOT VERY BECOMING"
HE DID IT AGAIN! HOW COME THAT KNUCKLEHEADED NINNY ALWAYS GETS THE GIRL?
ARCHIE, DON'T YOU FEEL BAD LEAVING REGGIE?
WHY? HE'S WITH HIS FAVORITE PERSON! HIMSELF!
WHAT DO I HAVE TO DO TO GET THE GIRL? BECOME ARCHIE?

Story: Frank Doyle Pencils & Inks: Bob Bolling
Letters: Bill Yoshida

Originally printed in REGGIE AND ME #41, MAY 1970

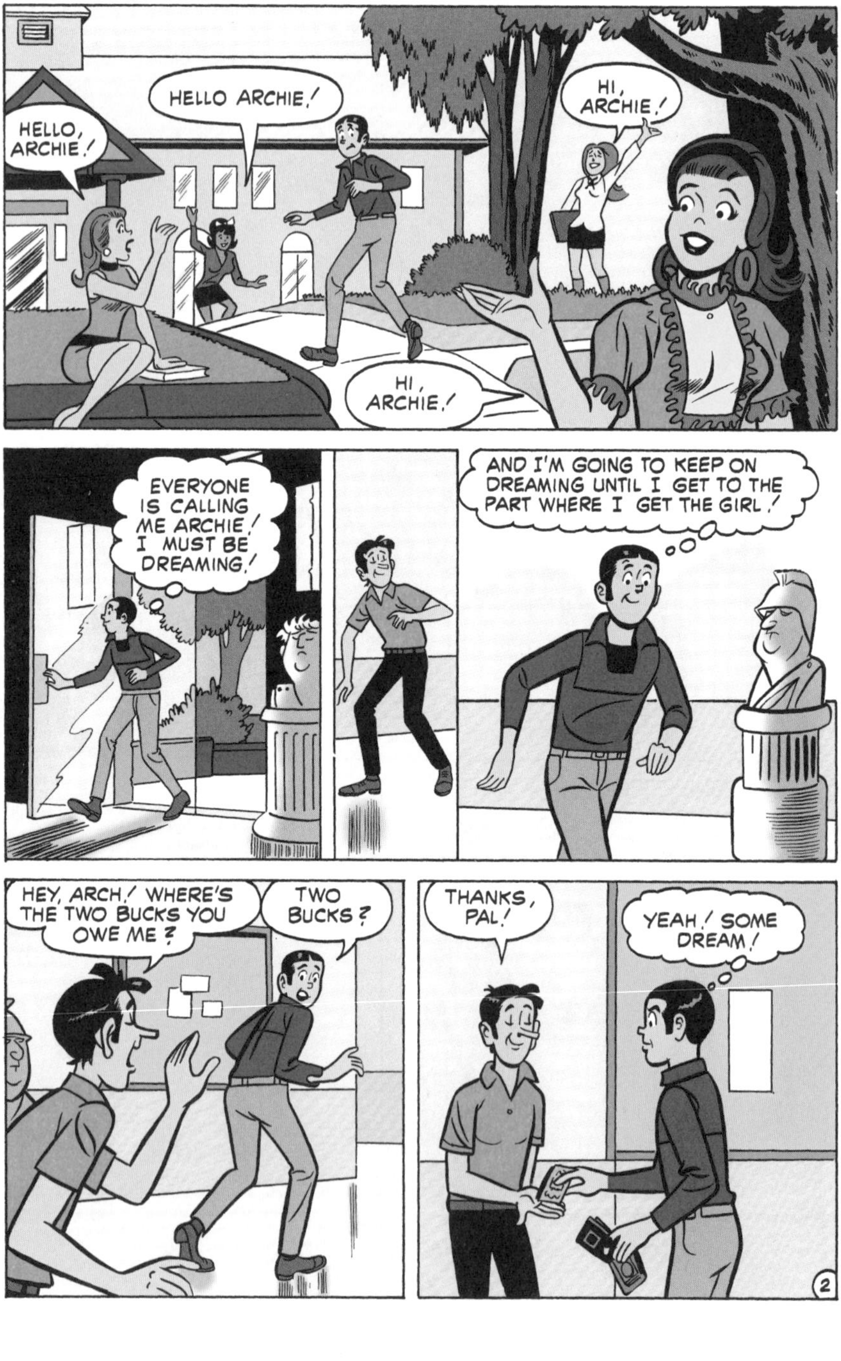
HELLO, ARCHIE!
HELLO ARCHIE!
HI, ARCHIE!
HI ARCHIE!
EVERYONE IS CALLING ME ARCHIE! I MUST BE DREAMING!
AND I'M GOING TO KEEP ON DREAMING UNTIL I GET TO THE PART WHERE I GET THE GIRL!
HEY, ARCH! WHERE'S THE TWO BUCKS YOU OWE ME?
TWO BUCKS?
THANKS, PAL!
YEAH! SOME DREAM!
2

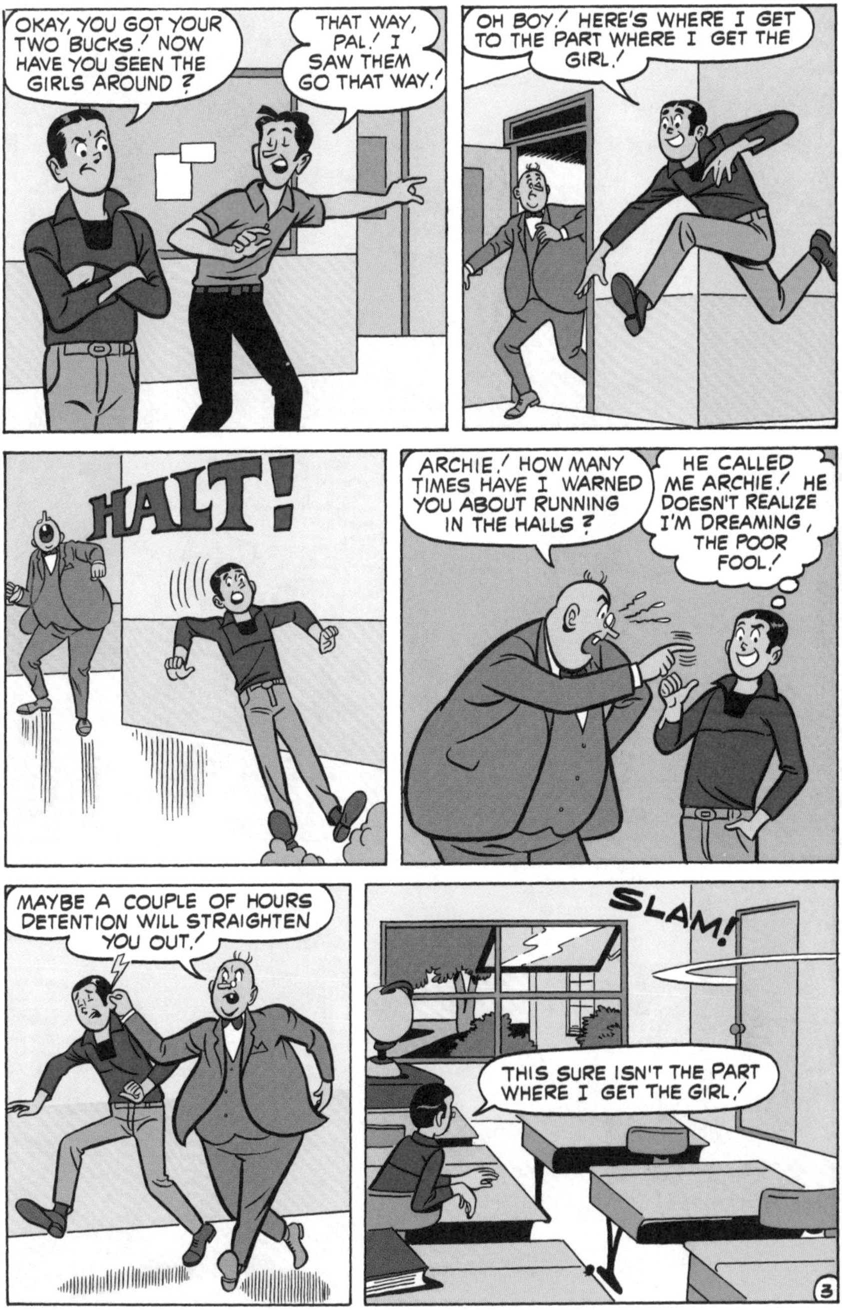
OKAY, YOU GOT YOUR TWO BUCKS! NOW HAVE YOU SEEN THE GIRLS AROUND ?
THAT WAY, PAL! I SAW THEM GO THAT WAY!
OH BOY! HERE'S WHERE I GET TO THE PART WHERE I GET THE GIRL!
HALT!
ARCHIE! HOW MANY TIMES HAVE I WARNED YOU ABOUT RUNNING IN THE HALLS ?
HE CALLED ME ARCHIE! HE DOESN'T REALIZE I'M DREAMING, THE POOR FOOL!
MAYBE A COUPLE OF HOURS DETENTION WILL STRAIGHTEN YOU OUT!
SLAM!
THIS SURE ISN'T THE PART WHERE I GET THE GIRL!
3

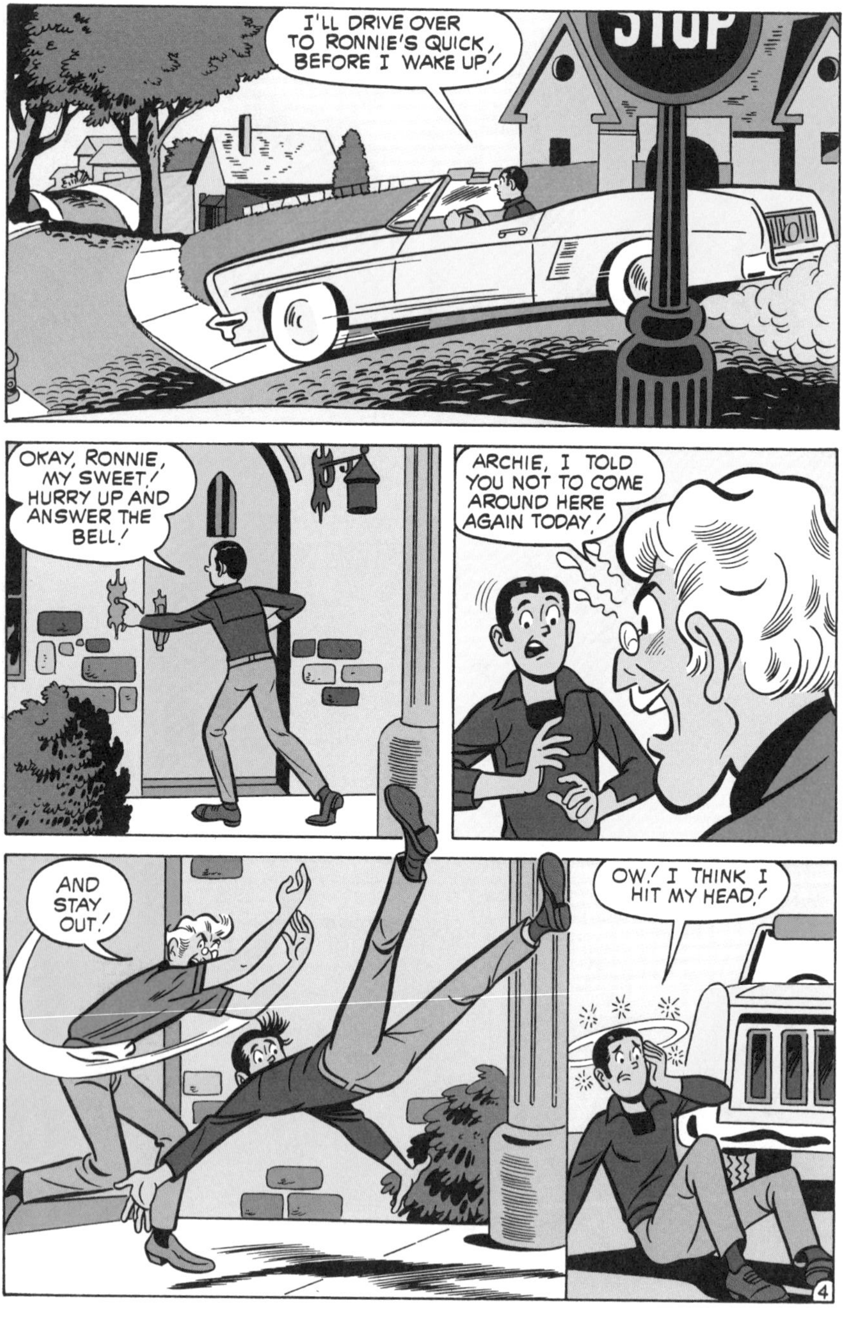
I'LL DRIVE OVER TO RONNIE'S QUICK, BEFORE I WAKE UP!
STOP
OKAY, RONNIE, MY SWEET! HURRY UP AND ANSWER THE BELL!
ARCHIE, I TOLD YOU NOT TO COME AROUND HERE AGAIN TODAY!
AND STAY OUT!
OW! I THINK I HIT MY HEAD!
4

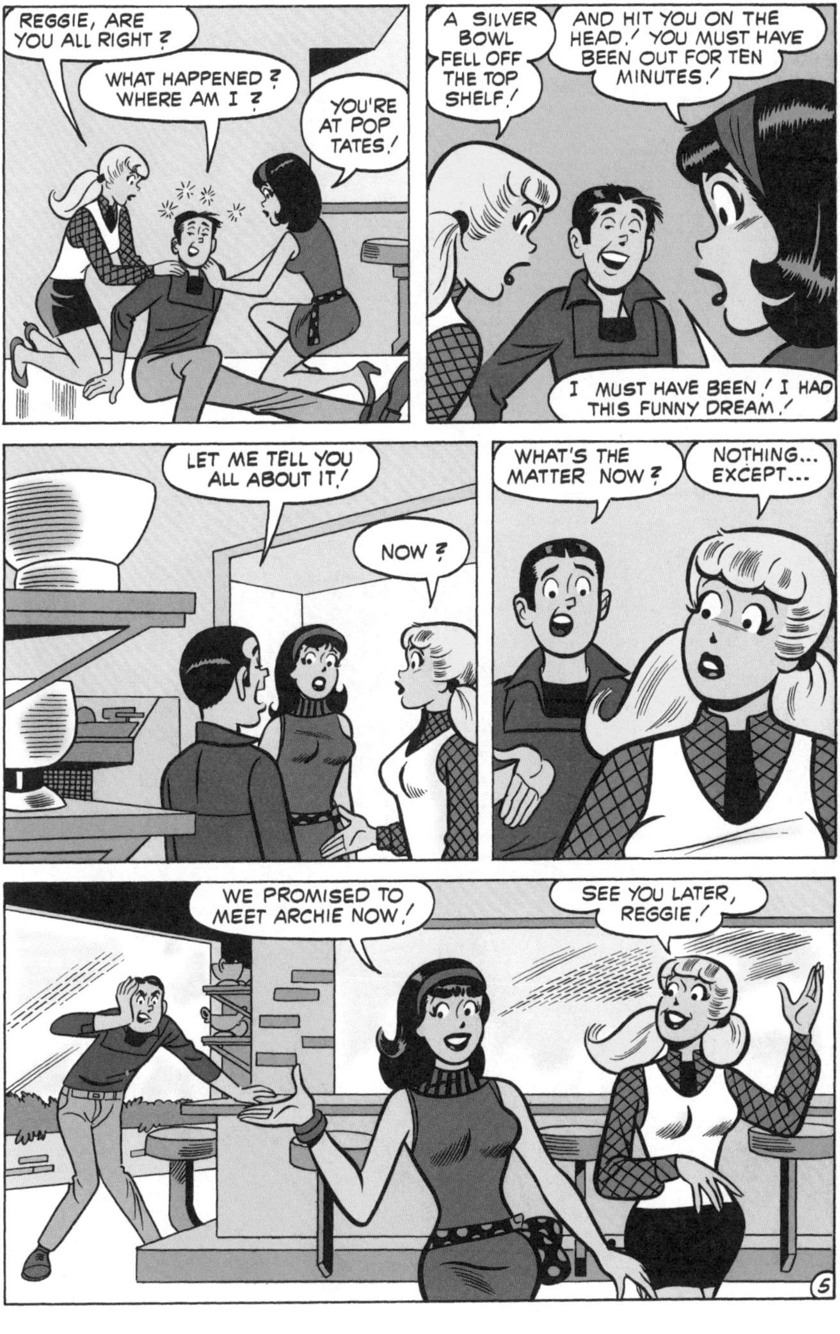
REGGIE, ARE YOU ALL RIGHT?
WHAT HAPPENED? WHERE AM I?
YOU'RE AT POP TATES!
A SILVER BOWL FELL OFF THE TOP SHELF!
AND HIT YOU ON THE HEAD! YOU MUST HAVE BEEN OUT FOR TEN MINUTES!
I MUST HAVE BEEN! I HAD THIS FUNNY DREAM!
LET ME TELL YOU ALL ABOUT IT!
NOW?
WHAT'S THE MATTER NOW?
NOTHING... EXCEPT...
WE PROMISED TO MEET ARCHIE NOW!
SEE YOU LATER, REGGIE!
5

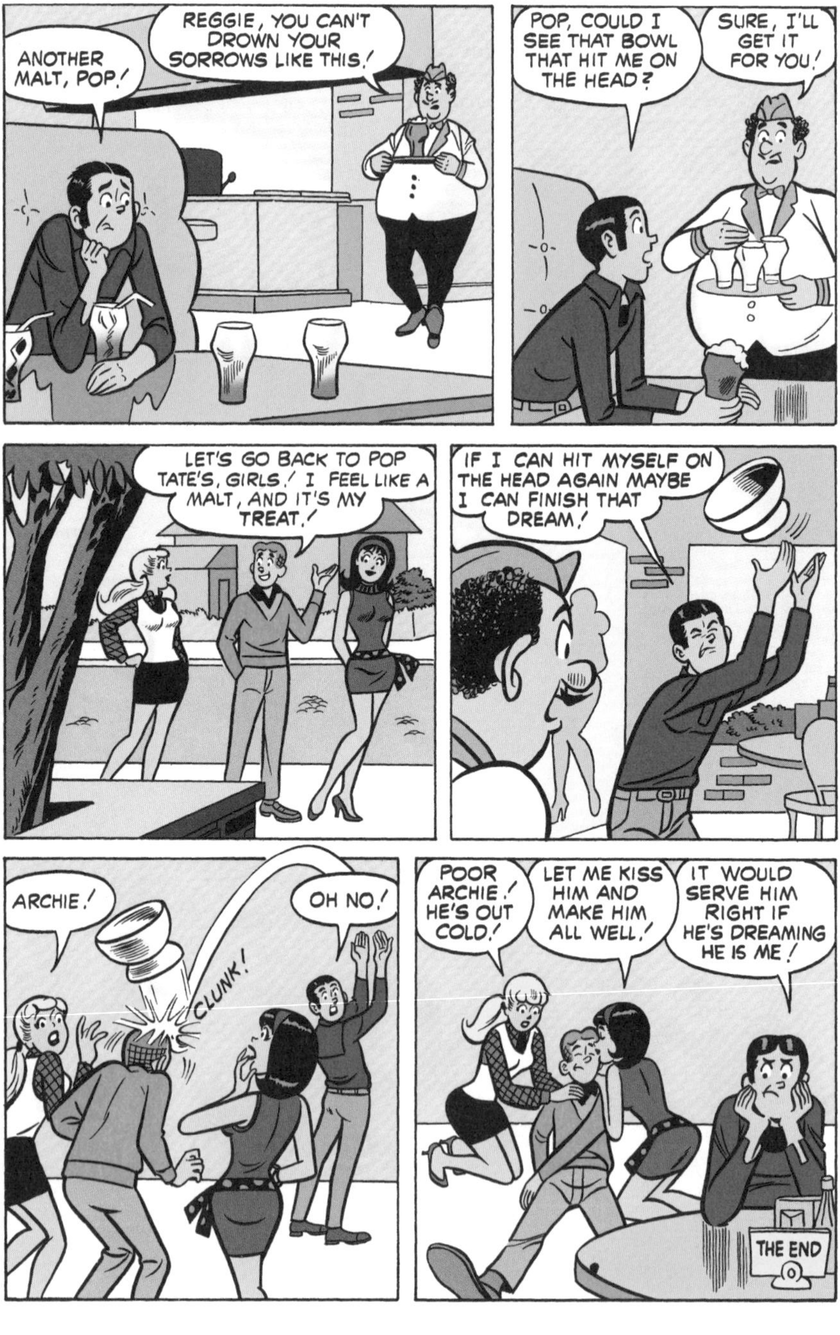
ANOTHER MALT, POP!
REGGIE, YOU CAN'T DROWN YOUR SORROWS LIKE THIS!
POP, COULD I SEE THAT BOWL THAT HIT ME ON THE HEAD?
SURE, I'LL GET IT FOR YOU!
LET'S GO BACK TO POP TATE'S, GIRLS! I FEEL LIKE A MALT, AND IT'S MY TREAT!
IF I CAN HIT MYSELF ON THE HEAD AGAIN MAYBE I CAN FINISH THAT DREAM!
ARCHIE!
OH NO!
CLUNK!
POOR ARCHIE! HE'S OUT COLD!
LET ME KISS HIM AND MAKE HIM ALL WELL!
IT WOULD SERVE HIM RIGHT IF HE'S DREAMING HE IS ME!
THE END

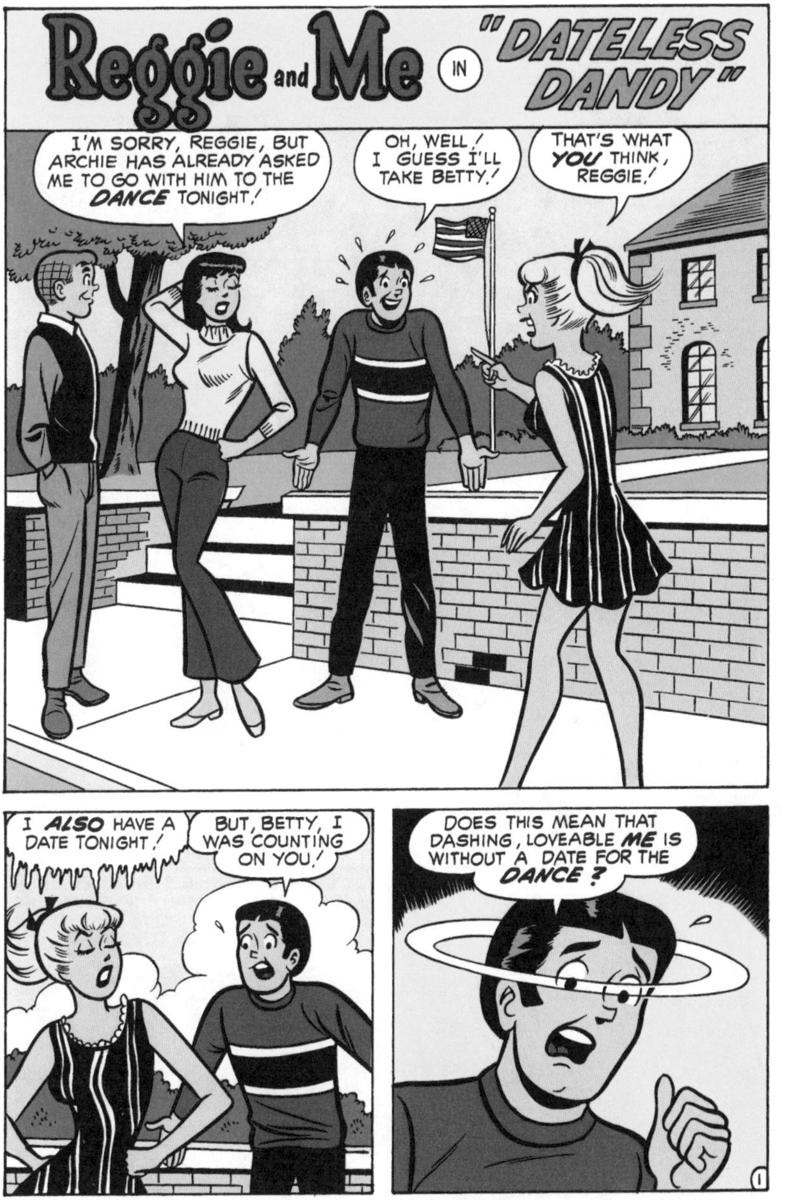
Reggie and Me
IN
"DATELESS DANDY"
I'M SORRY, REGGIE, BUT ARCHIE HAS ALREADY ASKED ME TO GO WITH HIM TO THE DANCE TONIGHT!
OH, WELL! I GUESS I'LL TAKE BETTY!
THAT'S WHAT YOU THINK, REGGIE!
I ALSO HAVE A DATE TONIGHT!
BUT, BETTY, I WAS COUNTING ON YOU!
DOES THIS MEAN THAT DASHING, LOVEABLE ME IS WITHOUT A DATE FOR THE DANCE?
1

Story: George Gladir Pencils: Bob White
Inks: Rudy Lapick Letters: Bill Yoshida

Originally printed in REGGIE AND ME #42, JULY 1970

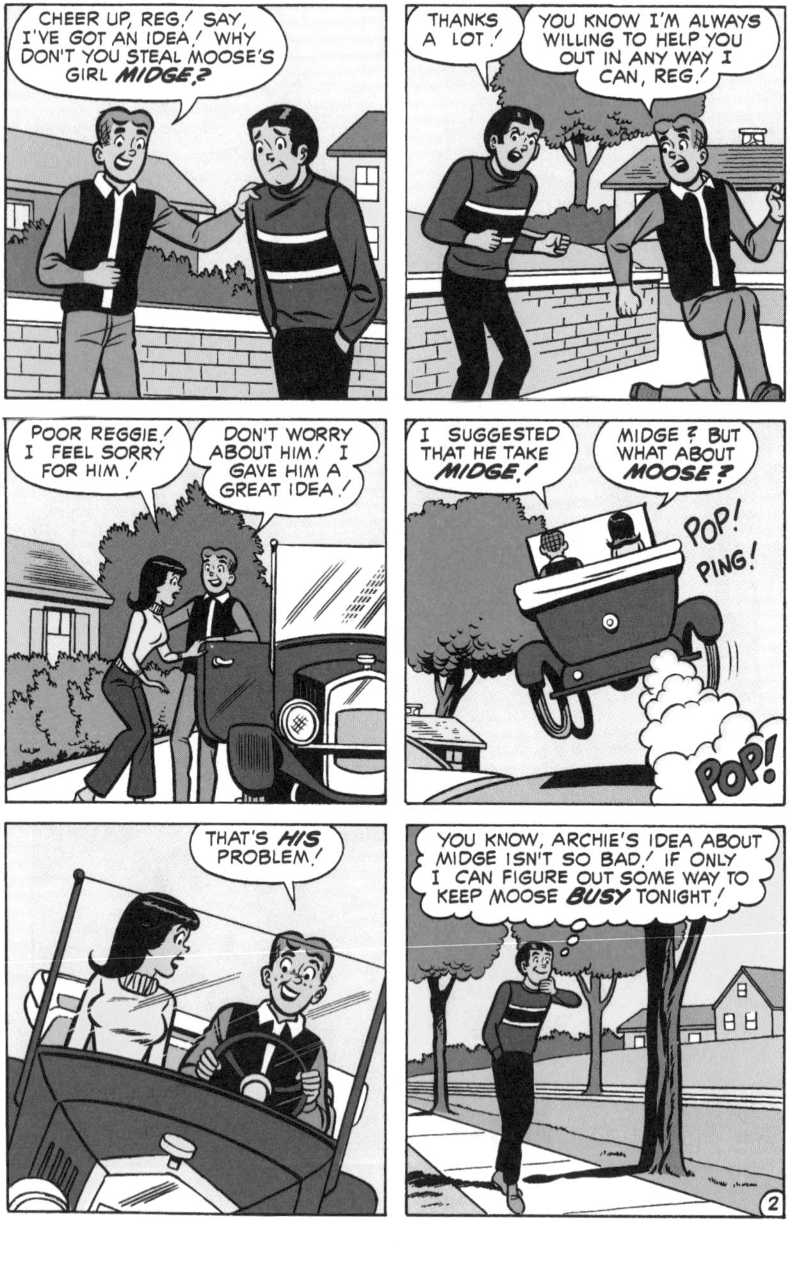
CHEER UP, REG.! SAY, I'VE GOT AN IDEA! WHY DON'T YOU STEAL MOOSE'S GIRL MIDGE?
THANKS A LOT!
YOU KNOW I'M ALWAYS WILLING TO HELP YOU OUT IN ANY WAY I CAN, REG.!
POOR REGGIE! I FEEL SORRY FOR HIM!
DON'T WORRY ABOUT HIM! I GAVE HIM A GREAT IDEA!
I SUGGESTED THAT HE TAKE MIDGE!
MIDGE? BUT WHAT ABOUT MOOSE?
POP!
PING!
POP!
THAT'S HIS PROBLEM!
YOU KNOW, ARCHIE'S IDEA ABOUT MIDGE ISN'T SO BAD! IF ONLY I CAN FIGURE OUT SOME WAY TO KEEP MOOSE BUSY TONIGHT!
2

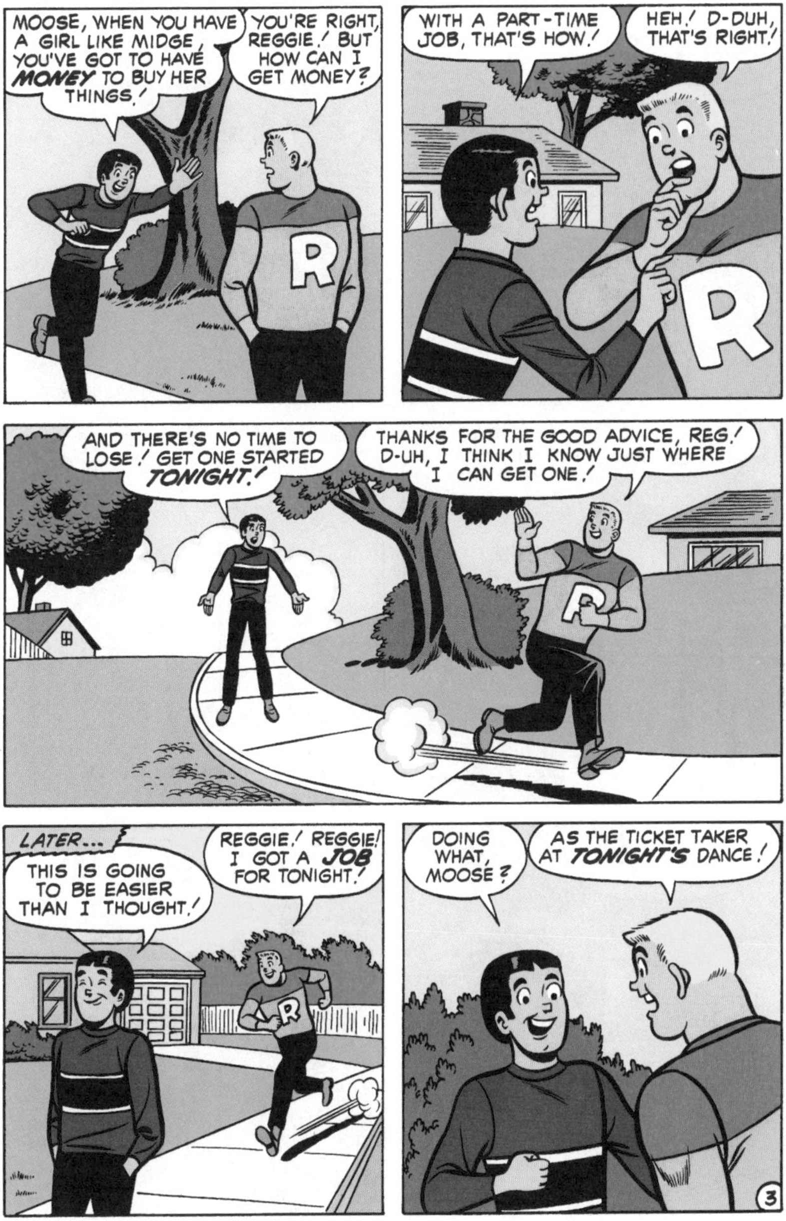
MOOSE, WHEN YOU HAVE A GIRL LIKE MIDGE, YOU'VE GOT TO HAVE MONEY TO BUY HER THINGS!
YOU'RE RIGHT, REGGIE! BUT HOW CAN I GET MONEY?
WITH A PART-TIME JOB, THAT'S HOW!
HEH! D-DUH, THAT'S RIGHT!
AND THERE'S NO TIME TO LOSE! GET ONE STARTED TONIGHT!
THANKS FOR THE GOOD ADVICE, REG! D-UH, I THINK I KNOW JUST WHERE I CAN GET ONE!
LATER...
THIS IS GOING TO BE EASIER THAN I THOUGHT!
REGGIE! REGGIE! I GOT A JOB FOR TONIGHT!
DOING WHAT, MOOSE?
AS THE TICKET TAKER AT TONIGHT'S DANCE!
3

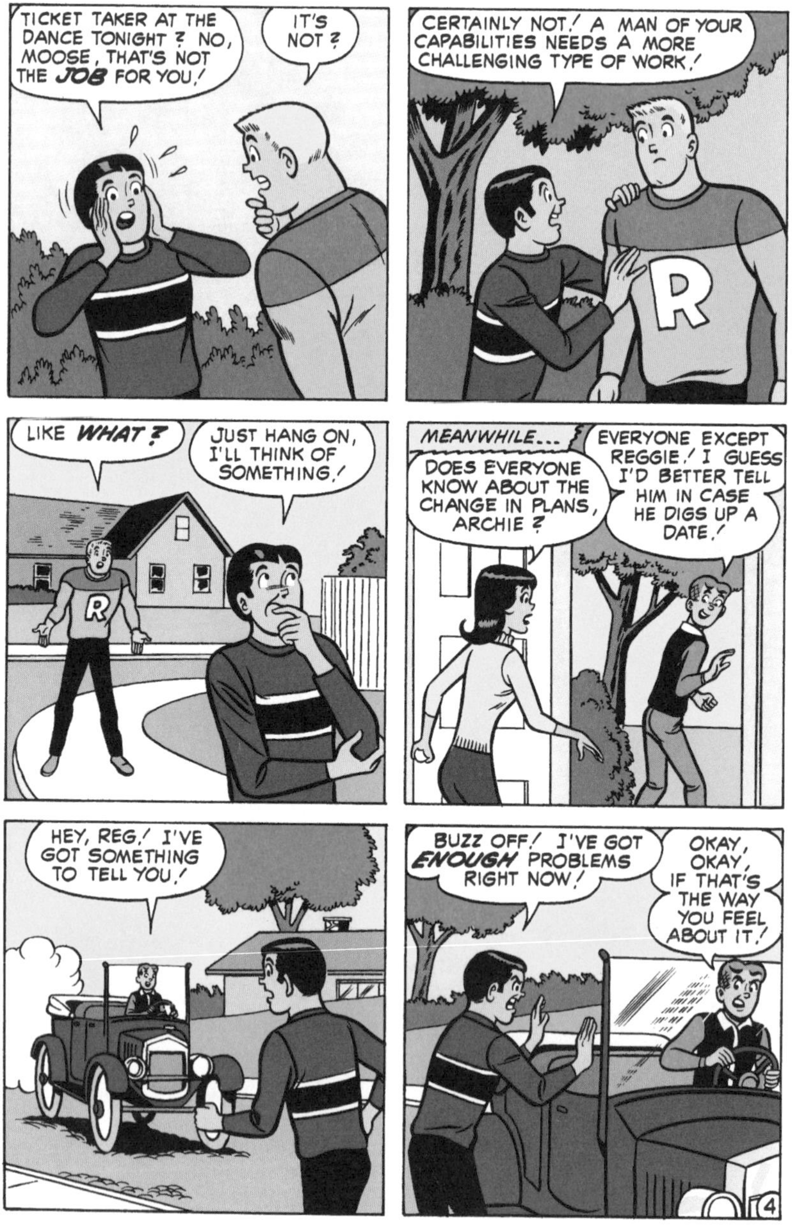
TICKET TAKER AT THE DANCE TONIGHT ? NO, MOOSE, THAT'S NOT THE JOB FOR YOU!
IT'S NOT ?
CERTAINLY NOT! A MAN OF YOUR CAPABILITIES NEEDS A MORE CHALLENGING TYPE OF WORK!
LIKE WHAT ?
JUST HANG ON, I'LL THINK OF SOMETHING!
MEANWHILE...
DOES EVERYONE KNOW ABOUT THE CHANGE IN PLANS, ARCHIE ?
EVERYONE EXCEPT REGGIE! I GUESS I'D BETTER TELL HIM IN CASE HE DIGS UP A DATE!
HEY, REG! I'VE GOT SOMETHING TO TELL YOU!
BUZZ OFF! I'VE GOT ENOUGH PROBLEMS RIGHT NOW!
OKAY, OKAY, IF THAT'S THE WAY YOU FEEL ABOUT IT!
4

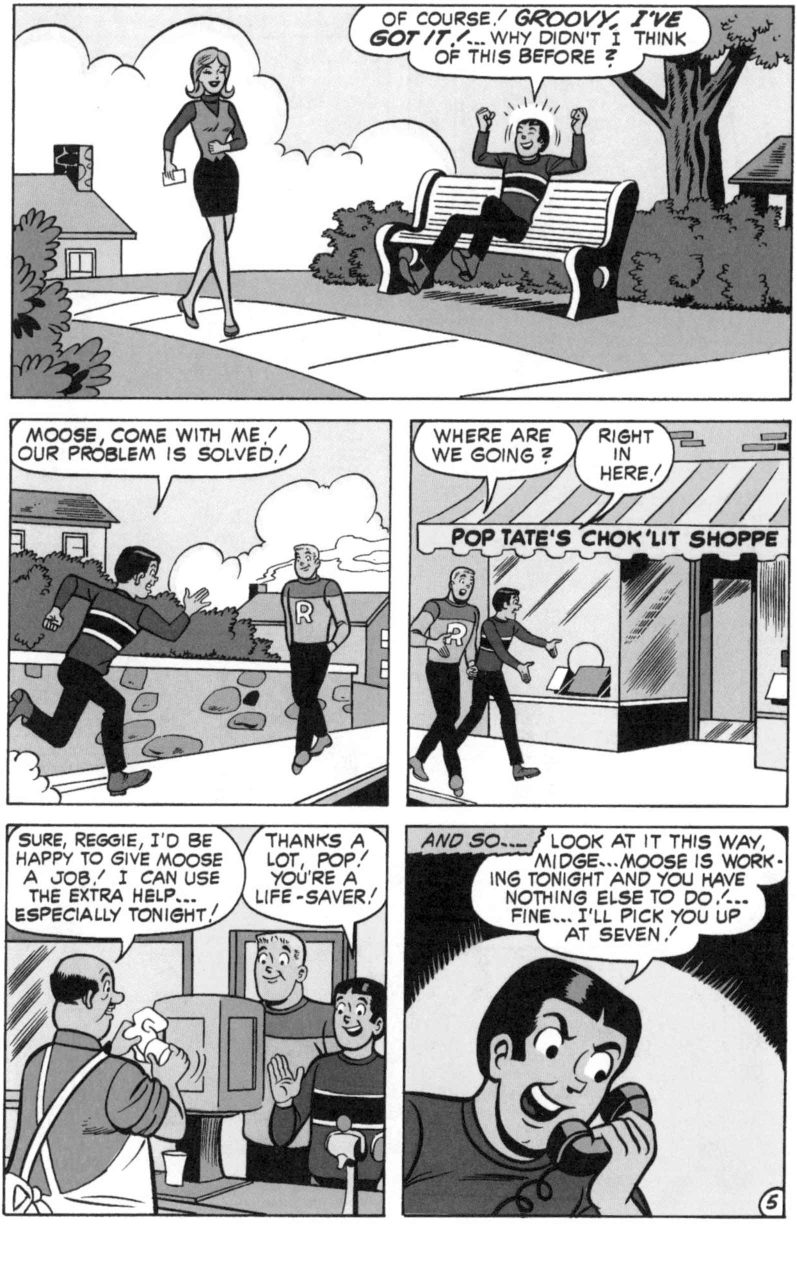
OF COURSE! GROOVY, I'VE GOT IT!... WHY DIDN'T I THINK OF THIS BEFORE?
MOOSE, COME WITH ME! OUR PROBLEM IS SOLVED!
WHERE ARE WE GOING?
RIGHT IN HERE!
POP TATE'S CHOK'LIT SHOPPE
SURE, REGGIE, I'D BE HAPPY TO GIVE MOOSE A JOB! I CAN USE THE EXTRA HELP... ESPECIALLY TONIGHT!
THANKS A LOT, POP! YOU'RE A LIFE-SAVER!
AND SO...
LOOK AT IT THIS WAY, MIDGE...MOOSE IS WORKING TONIGHT AND YOU HAVE NOTHING ELSE TO DO!... FINE... I'LL PICK YOU UP AT SEVEN!
5

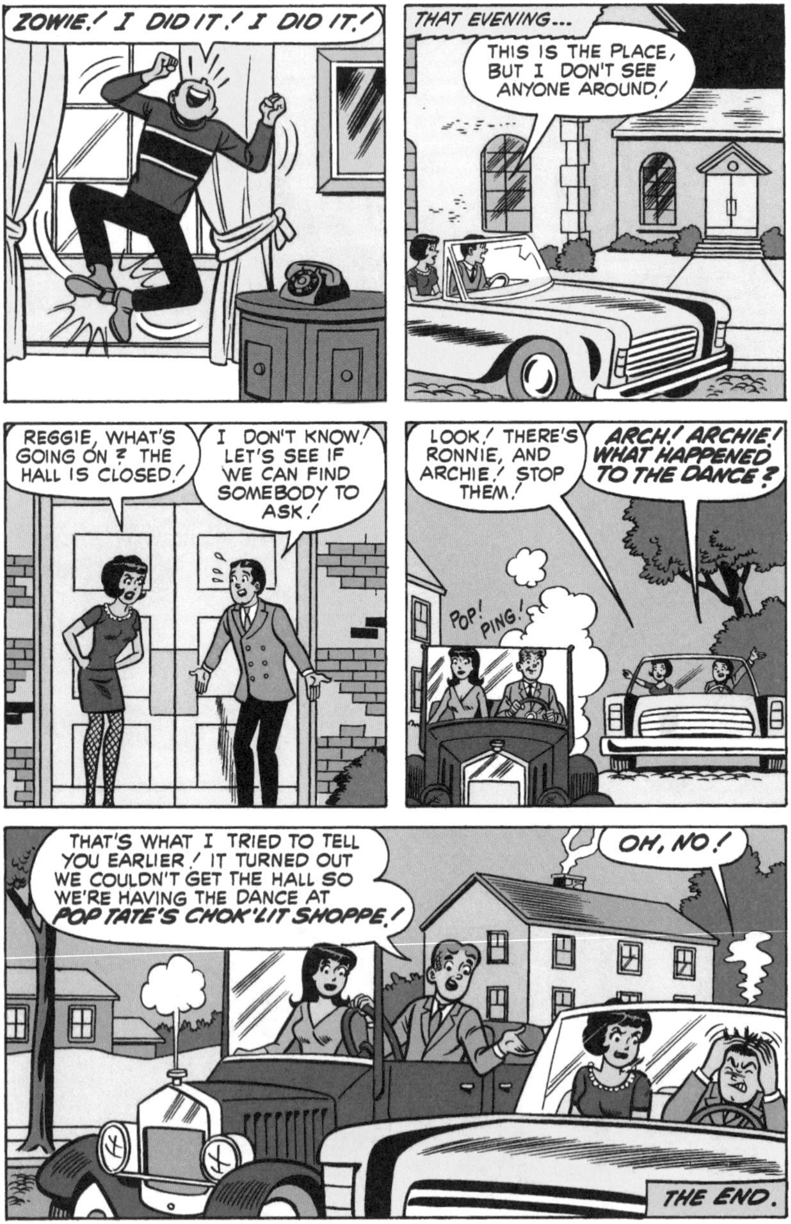
ZOWIE! I DID IT! I DID IT!
THAT EVENING...
THIS IS THE PLACE, BUT I DON'T SEE ANYONE AROUND!
REGGIE, WHAT'S GOING ON? THE HALL IS CLOSED!
I DON'T KNOW! LET'S SEE IF WE CAN FIND SOMEBODY TO ASK!
LOOK! THERE'S RONNIE, AND ARCHIE! STOP THEM!
ARCH! ARCHIE! WHAT HAPPENED TO THE DANCE?
POP! PING!
THAT'S WHAT I TRIED TO TELL YOU EARLIER! IT TURNED OUT WE COULDN'T GET THE HALL SO WE'RE HAVING THE DANCE AT POP TATE'S CHOK'LIT SHOPPE!
OH, NO!
THE END.

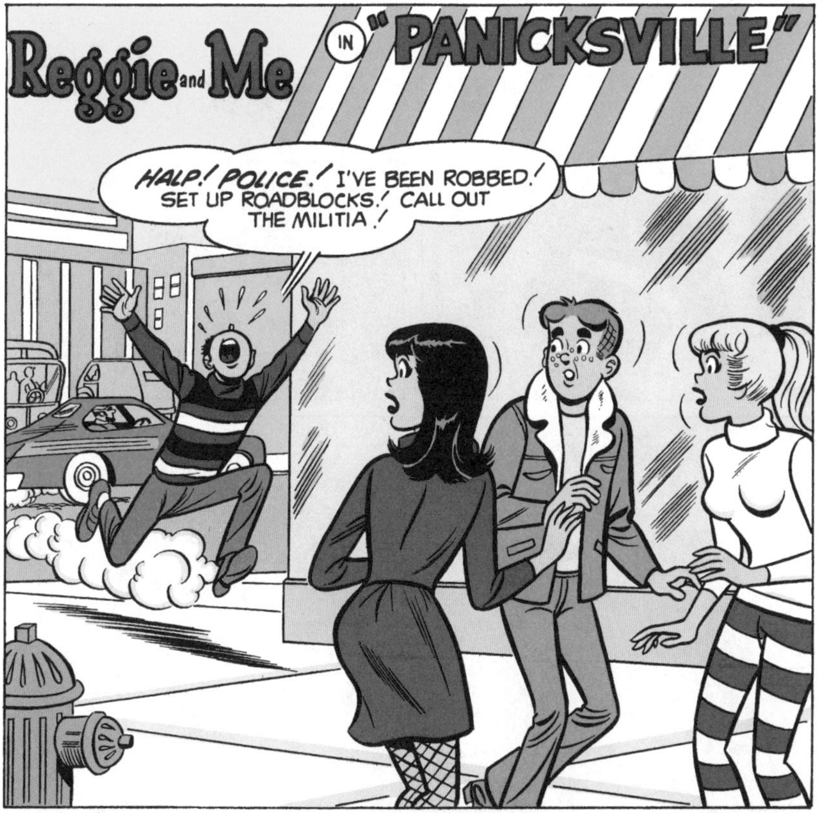
Reggie and Me
IN "PANICKSVILLE"
HALP! POLICE! I'VE BEEN ROBBED! SET UP ROADBLOCKS! CALL OUT THE MILITIA!

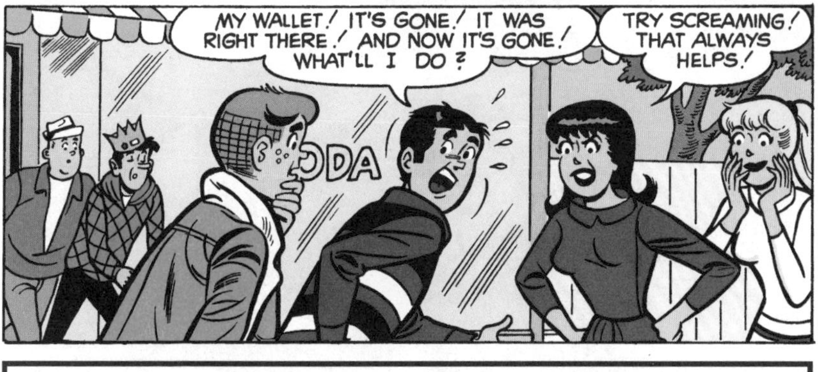
MY WALLET! IT'S GONE! IT WAS RIGHT THERE! AND NOW IT'S GONE! WHAT'LL I DO?
TRY SCREAMING! THAT ALWAYS HELPS!
ODA

Story: Frank Doyle Pencils: Bill Vigoda
Inks: Mario Acquaviva Letters: Bill Yoshida

Originally printed in REGGIE AND ME #42, JULY 1970

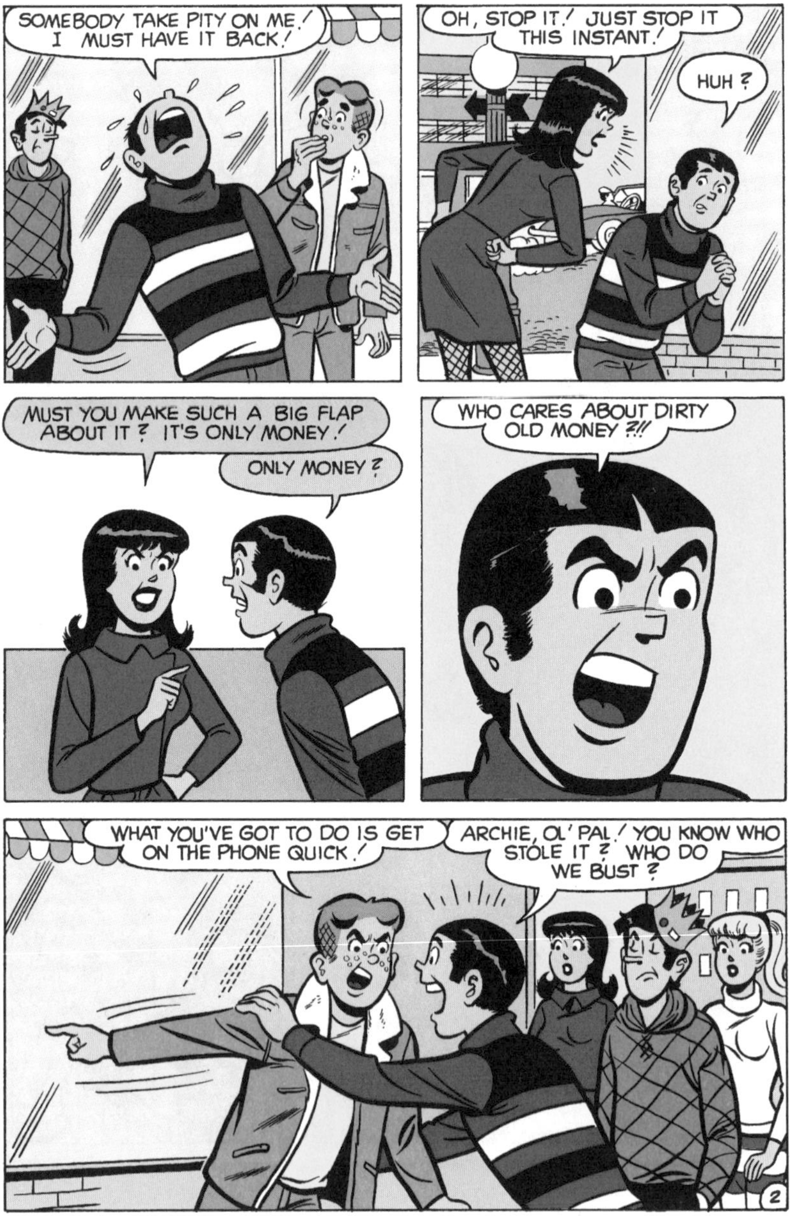
SOMEBODY TAKE PITY ON ME! I MUST HAVE IT BACK!
OH, STOP IT! JUST STOP IT THIS INSTANT!
HUH?
MUST YOU MAKE SUCH A BIG FLAP ABOUT IT? IT'S ONLY MONEY!
ONLY MONEY?
WHO CARES ABOUT DIRTY OLD MONEY?!!
WHAT YOU'VE GOT TO DO IS GET ON THE PHONE QUICK!
ARCHIE, OL' PAL! YOU KNOW WHO STOLE IT? WHO DO WE BUST?
2

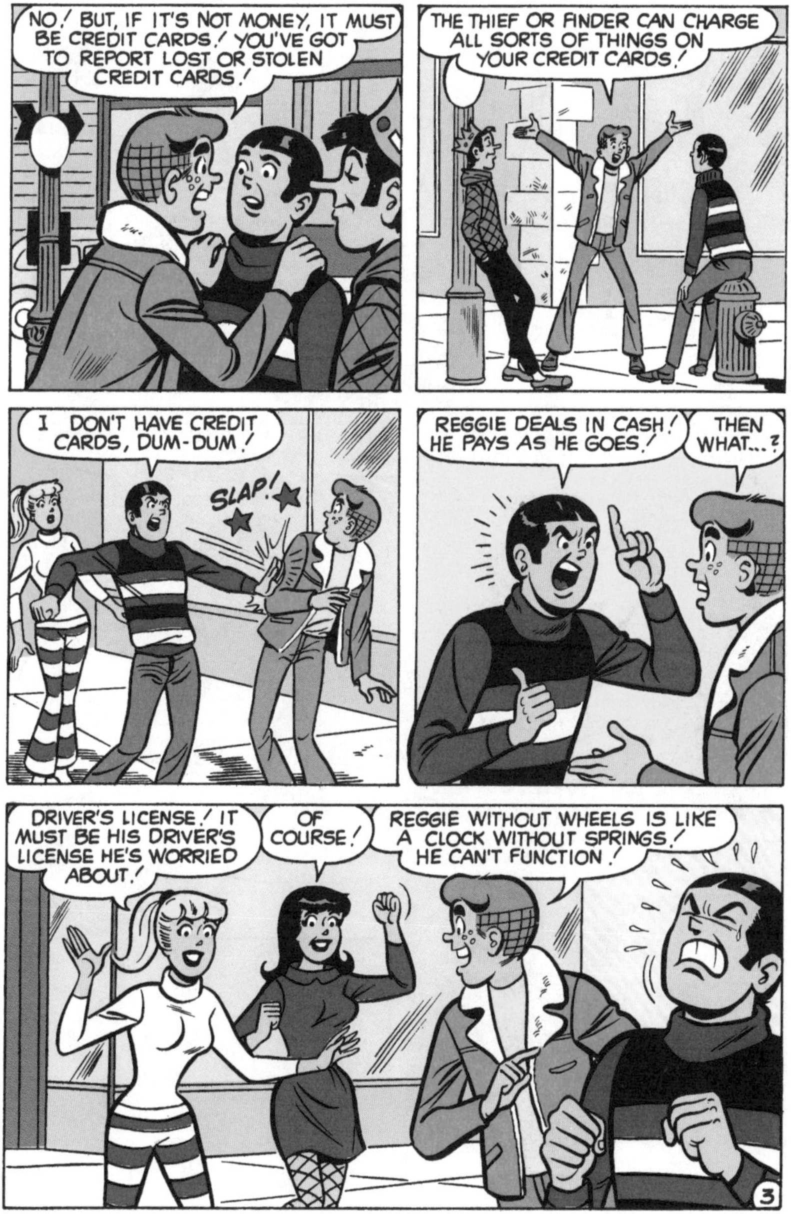
NO! BUT, IF IT'S NOT MONEY, IT MUST BE CREDIT CARDS! YOU'VE GOT TO REPORT LOST OR STOLEN CREDIT CARDS!
THE THIEF OR FINDER CAN CHARGE ALL SORTS OF THINGS ON YOUR CREDIT CARDS!
I DON'T HAVE CREDIT CARDS, DUM-DUM!
SLAP!
REGGIE DEALS IN CASH! HE PAYS AS HE GOES!
THEN WHAT...?
DRIVER'S LICENSE! IT MUST BE HIS DRIVER'S LICENSE HE'S WORRIED ABOUT!
OF COURSE!
REGGIE WITHOUT WHEELS IS LIKE A CLOCK WITHOUT SPRINGS! HE CAN'T FUNCTION!
3

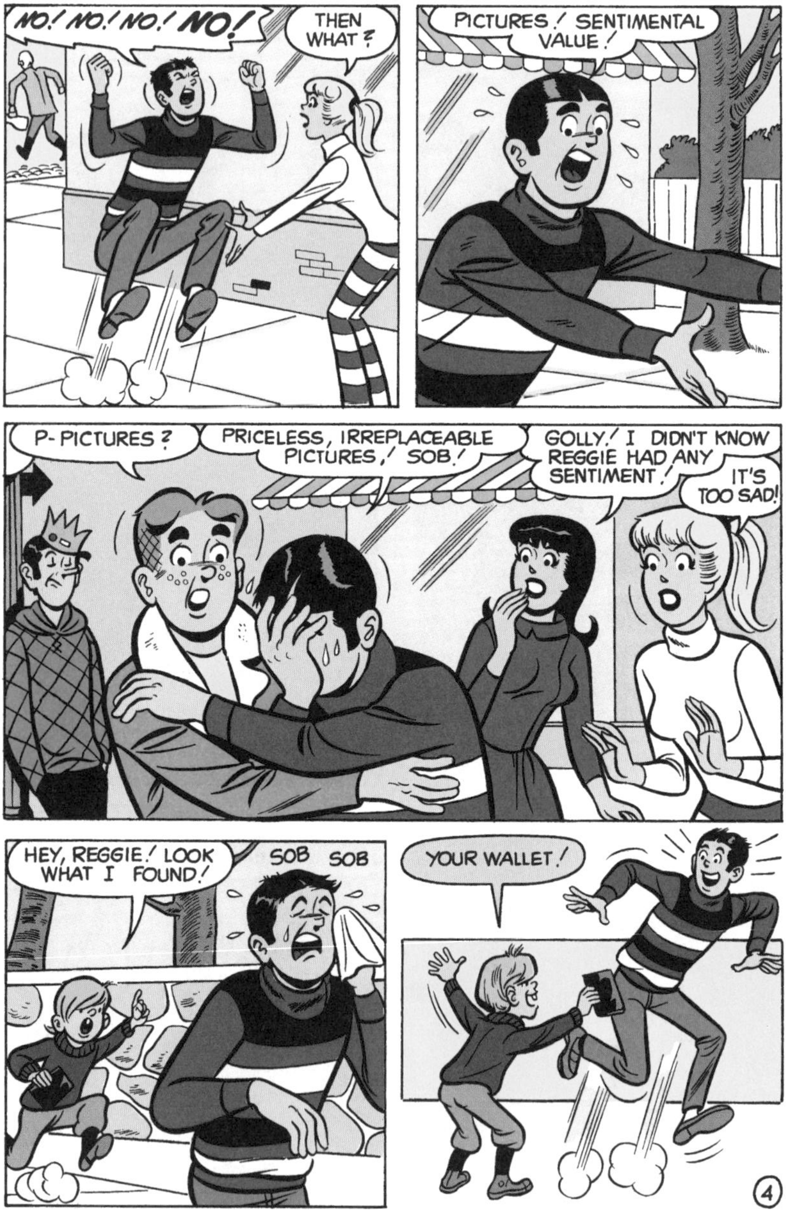
NO! NO! NO! NO!
THEN WHAT?
PICTURES! SENTIMENTAL VALUE!
P-PICTURES?
PRICELESS, IRREPLACEABLE PICTURES! SOB!
GOLLY! I DIDN'T KNOW REGGIE HAD ANY SENTIMENT!
IT'S TOO SAD!
HEY, REGGIE! LOOK WHAT I FOUND!
SOB SOB
YOUR WALLET!
4

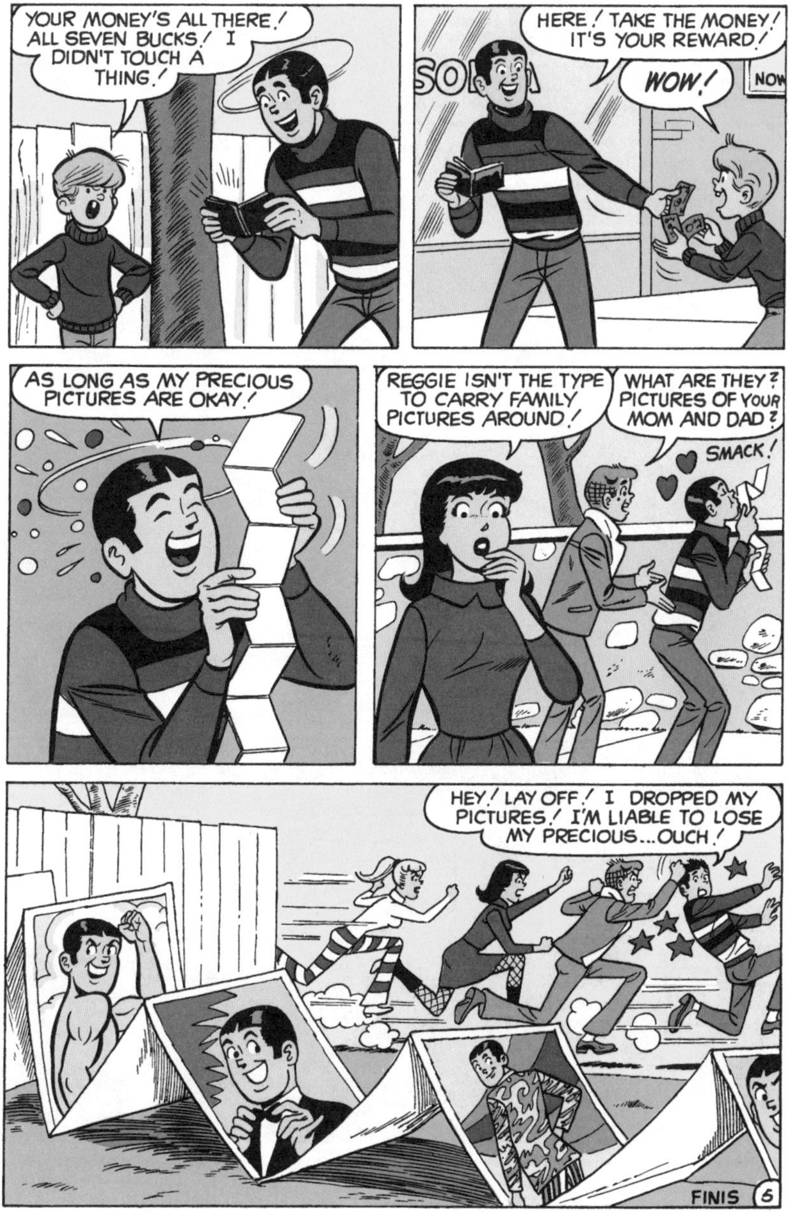
YOUR MONEY'S ALL THERE! ALL SEVEN BUCKS! I DIDN'T TOUCH A THING!
HERE! TAKE THE MONEY! IT'S YOUR REWARD!
WOW!
SO
NOW
AS LONG AS MY PRECIOUS PICTURES ARE OKAY!
REGGIE ISN'T THE TYPE TO CARRY FAMILY PICTURES AROUND!
WHAT ARE THEY? PICTURES OF YOUR MOM AND DAD?
SMACK!
HEY! LAY OFF! I DROPPED MY PICTURES! I'M LIABLE TO LOSE MY PRECIOUS...OUCH!
FINIS
5

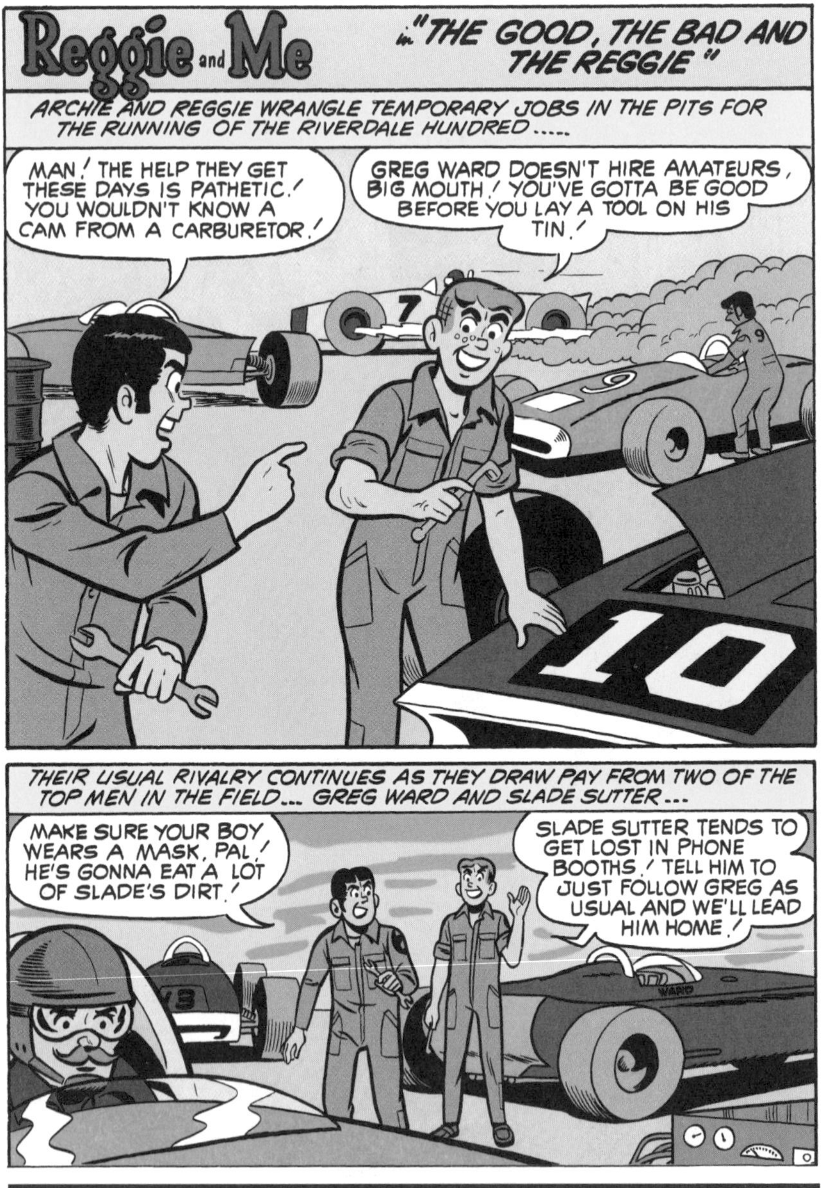
Reggie and Me
in "THE GOOD, THE BAD AND THE REGGIE"
ARCHIE AND REGGIE WRANGLE TEMPORARY JOBS IN THE PITS FOR THE RUNNING OF THE RIVERDALE HUNDRED.....
MAN! THE HELP THEY GET THESE DAYS IS PATHETIC! YOU WOULDN'T KNOW A CAM FROM A CARBURETOR!
GREG WARD DOESN'T HIRE AMATEURS, BIG MOUTH! YOU'VE GOTTA BE GOOD BEFORE YOU LAY A TOOL ON HIS TIN!
7
9
10
THEIR USUAL RIVALRY CONTINUES AS THEY DRAW PAY FROM TWO OF THE TOP MEN IN THE FIELD... GREG WARD AND SLADE SUTTER...
MAKE SURE YOUR BOY WEARS A MASK, PAL! HE'S GONNA EAT A LOT OF SLADE'S DIRT!
SLADE SUTTER TENDS TO GET LOST IN PHONE BOOTHS! TELL HIM TO JUST FOLLOW GREG AS USUAL AND WE'LL LEAD HIM HOME!
WARD

Story: George Gladir Pencils: Bob Bolling

Inks: Rudy Lapick Letters: Bill Yoshida Colors: Barry Grossman

Originally printed in REGGIE AND ME #43, SEPTEMBER 1970

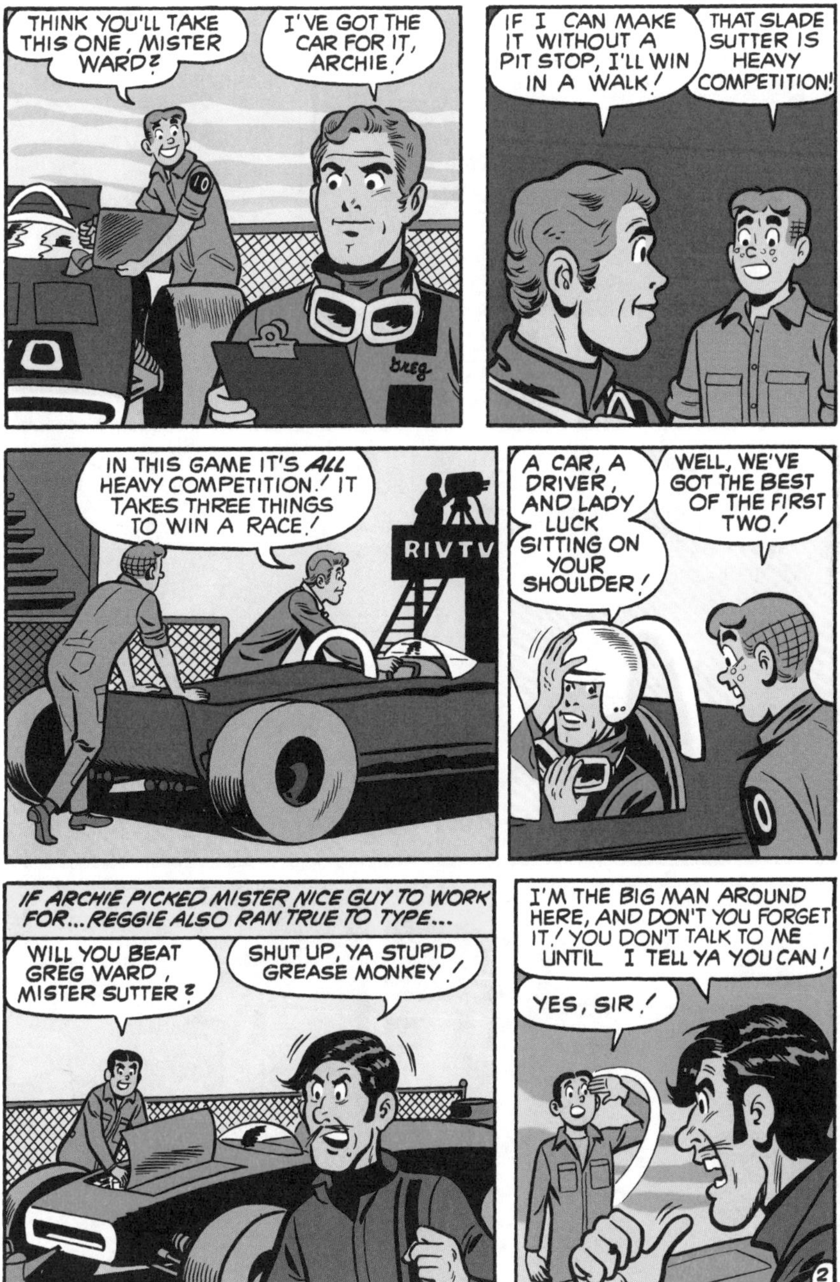
THINK YOU'LL TAKE THIS ONE, MISTER WARD?
I'VE GOT THE CAR FOR IT, ARCHIE!
IF I CAN MAKE IT WITHOUT A PIT STOP, I'LL WIN IN A WALK!
THAT SLADE SUTTER IS HEAVY COMPETITION!
IN THIS GAME IT'S ALL HEAVY COMPETITION! IT TAKES THREE THINGS TO WIN A RACE!
RIVTV
A CAR, A DRIVER, AND LADY LUCK SITTING ON YOUR SHOULDER!
WELL, WE'VE GOT THE BEST OF THE FIRST TWO!
IF ARCHIE PICKED MISTER NICE GUY TO WORK FOR...REGGIE ALSO RAN TRUE TO TYPE...
WILL YOU BEAT GREG WARD, MISTER SUTTER?
SHUT UP, YA STUPID GREASE MONKEY!
I'M THE BIG MAN AROUND HERE, AND DON'T YOU FORGET IT! YOU DON'T TALK TO ME UNTIL I TELL YA YOU CAN!
YES, SIR!
2

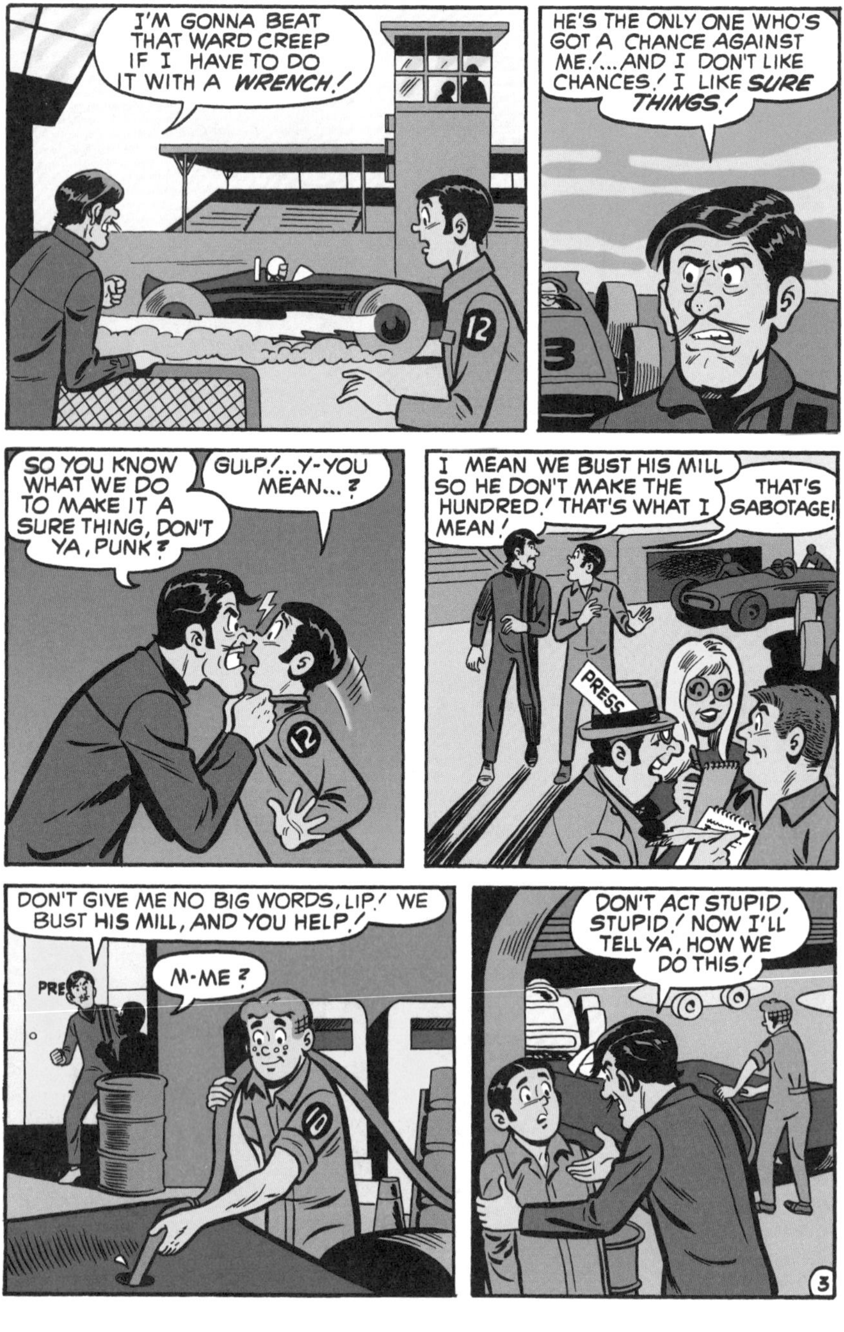
I'M GONNA BEAT THAT WARD CREEP IF I HAVE TO DO IT WITH A *WRENCH*!
HE'S THE ONLY ONE WHO'S GOT A CHANCE AGAINST ME!...AND I DON'T LIKE CHANCES! I LIKE *SURE THINGS*!
12
3
SO YOU KNOW WHAT WE DO TO MAKE IT A SURE THING, DON'T YA, PUNK?
GULP!...Y-YOU MEAN...?
12
I MEAN WE BUST HIS MILL SO HE DON'T MAKE THE HUNDRED! THAT'S WHAT I MEAN!
THAT'S SABOTAGE!
PRESS
DON'T GIVE ME NO BIG WORDS, LIP! WE BUST HIS MILL, AND YOU HELP!
M-ME?
PRE
10
DON'T ACT STUPID, STUPID! NOW I'LL TELL YA, HOW WE DO THIS!
3

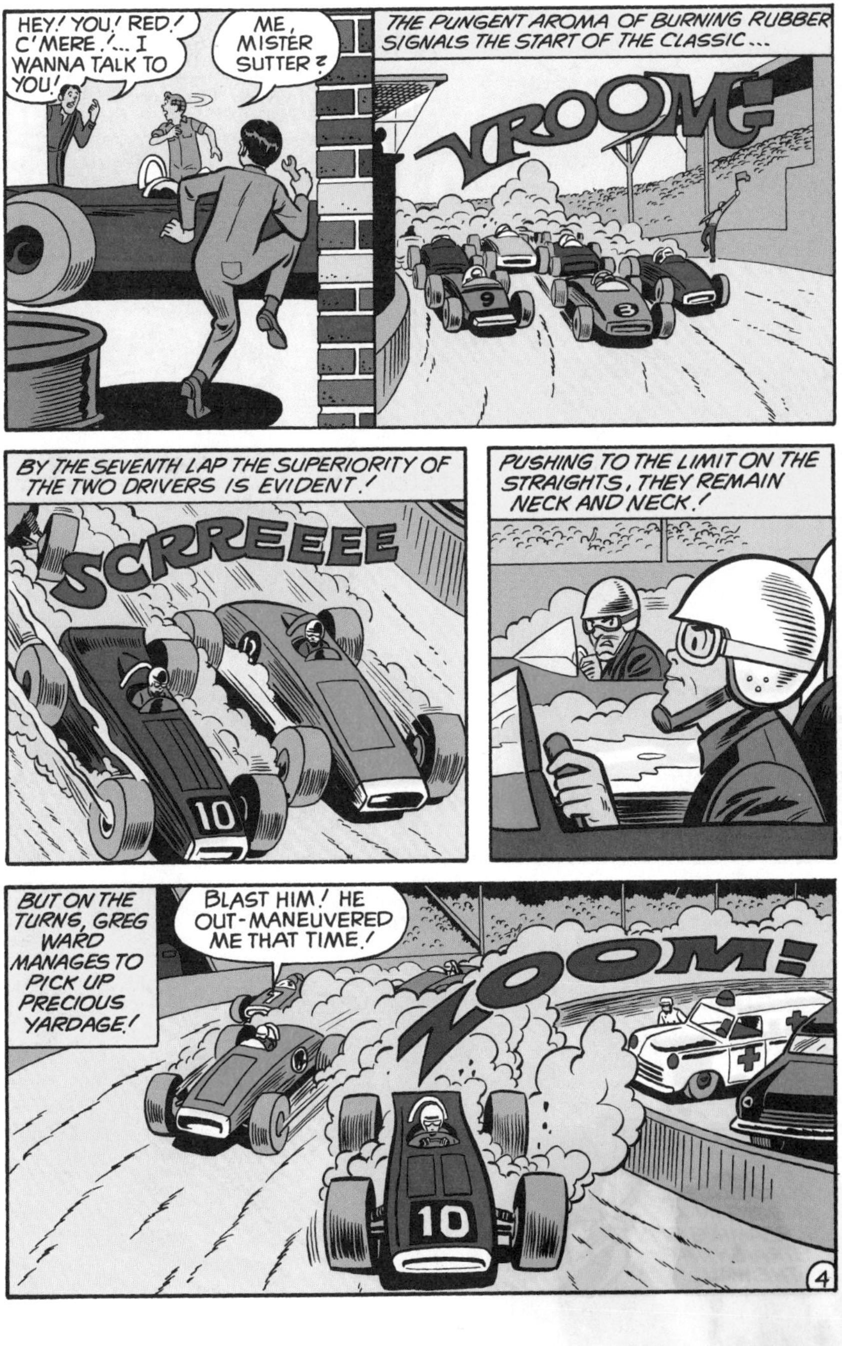
HEY! YOU! RED! C'MERE!... I WANNA TALK TO YOU!
ME, MISTER SUTTER?
THE PUNGENT AROMA OF BURNING RUBBER SIGNALS THE START OF THE CLASSIC...
VROOM!
BY THE SEVENTH LAP THE SUPERIORITY OF THE TWO DRIVERS IS EVIDENT!
SCRREEEE
PUSHING TO THE LIMIT ON THE STRAIGHTS, THEY REMAIN NECK AND NECK!
BUT ON THE TURNS, GREG WARD MANAGES TO PICK UP PRECIOUS YARDAGE!
BLAST HIM! HE OUT-MANEUVERED ME THAT TIME!
ZOOM!
4

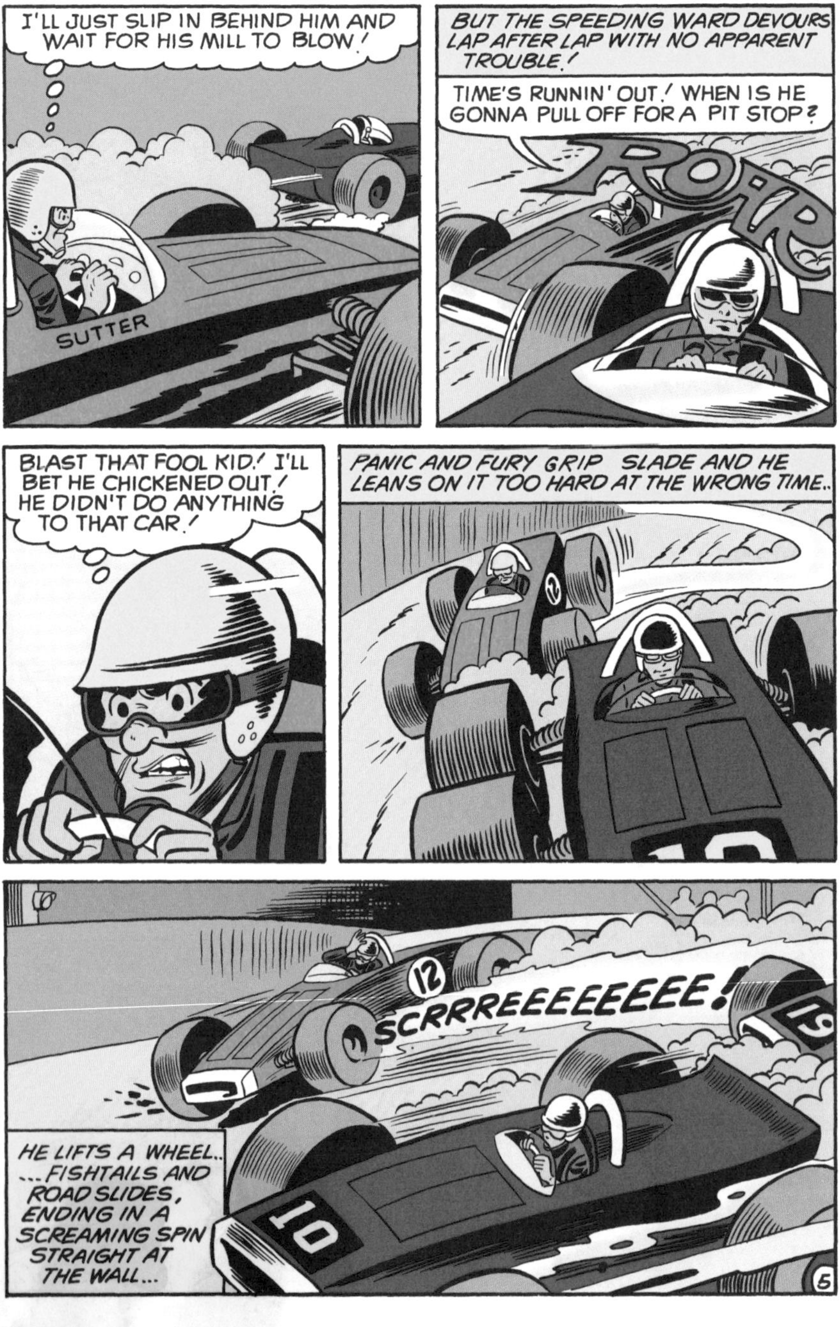
I'LL JUST SLIP IN BEHIND HIM AND WAIT FOR HIS MILL TO BLOW!
SUTTER
BUT THE SPEEDING WARD DEVOURS LAP AFTER LAP WITH NO APPARENT TROUBLE!
TIME'S RUNNIN' OUT! WHEN IS HE GONNA PULL OFF FOR A PIT STOP?
ROAR
BLAST THAT FOOL KID! I'LL BET HE CHICKENED OUT! HE DIDN'T DO ANYTHING TO THAT CAR!
PANIC AND FURY GRIP SLADE AND HE LEANS ON IT TOO HARD AT THE WRONG TIME..
12
12
SCRRREEEEEEEEE!
19
10
HE LIFTS A WHEEL.. ...FISHTAILS AND ROAD SLIDES, ENDING IN A SCREAMING SPIN STRAIGHT AT THE WALL...
5

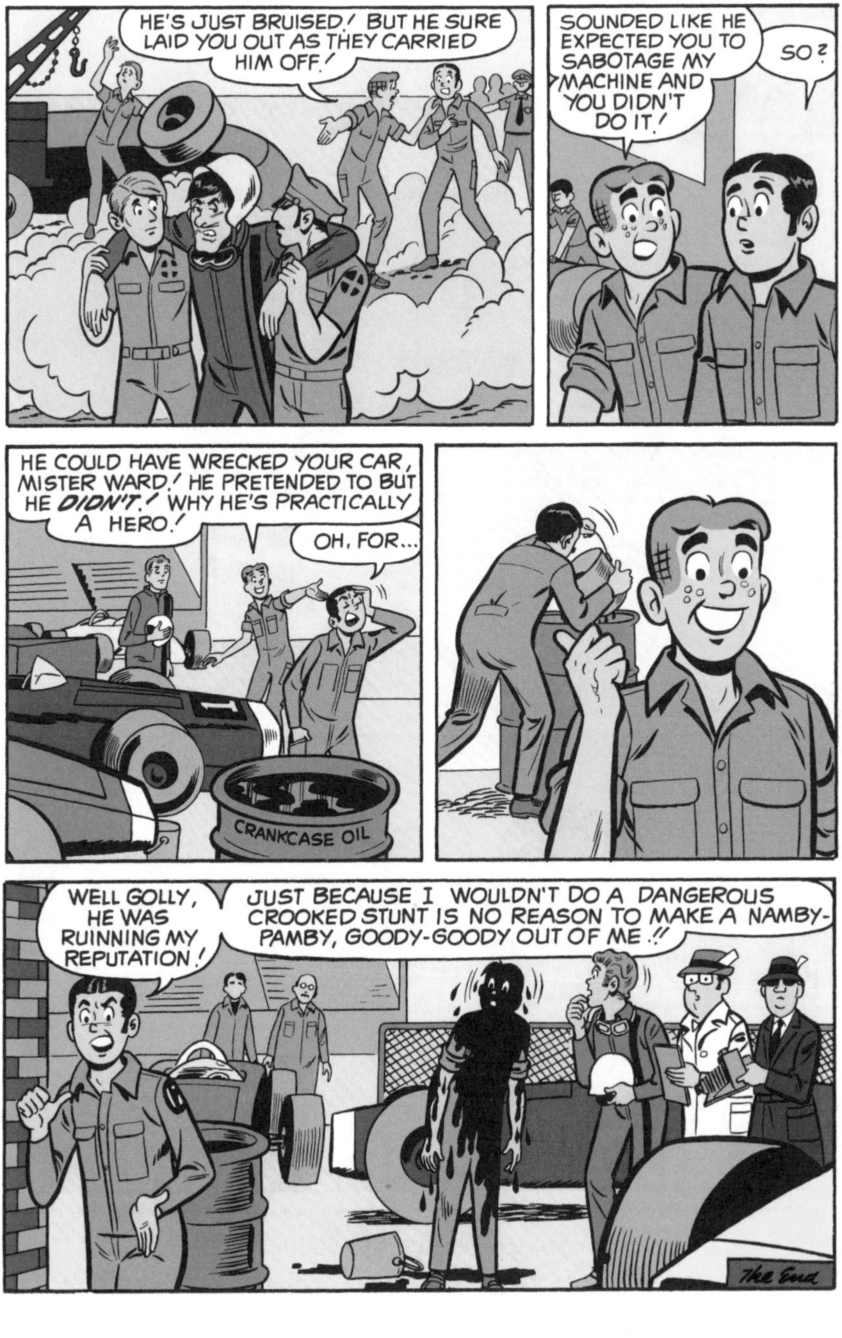

HE'S JUST BRUISED! BUT HE SURE LAID YOU OUT AS THEY CARRIED HIM OFF!
SOUNDED LIKE HE EXPECTED YOU TO SABOTAGE MY MACHINE AND YOU DIDN'T DO IT!
SO?
HE COULD HAVE WRECKED YOUR CAR, MISTER WARD! HE PRETENDED TO BUT HE DIDN'T! WHY HE'S PRACTICALLY A HERO!
OH, FOR...
CRANKCASE OIL
WELL GOLLY, HE WAS RUINNING MY REPUTATION!
JUST BECAUSE I WOULDN'T DO A DANGEROUS CROOKED STUNT IS NO REASON TO MAKE A NAMBY-PAMBY, GOODY-GOODY OUT OF ME.!!
The End

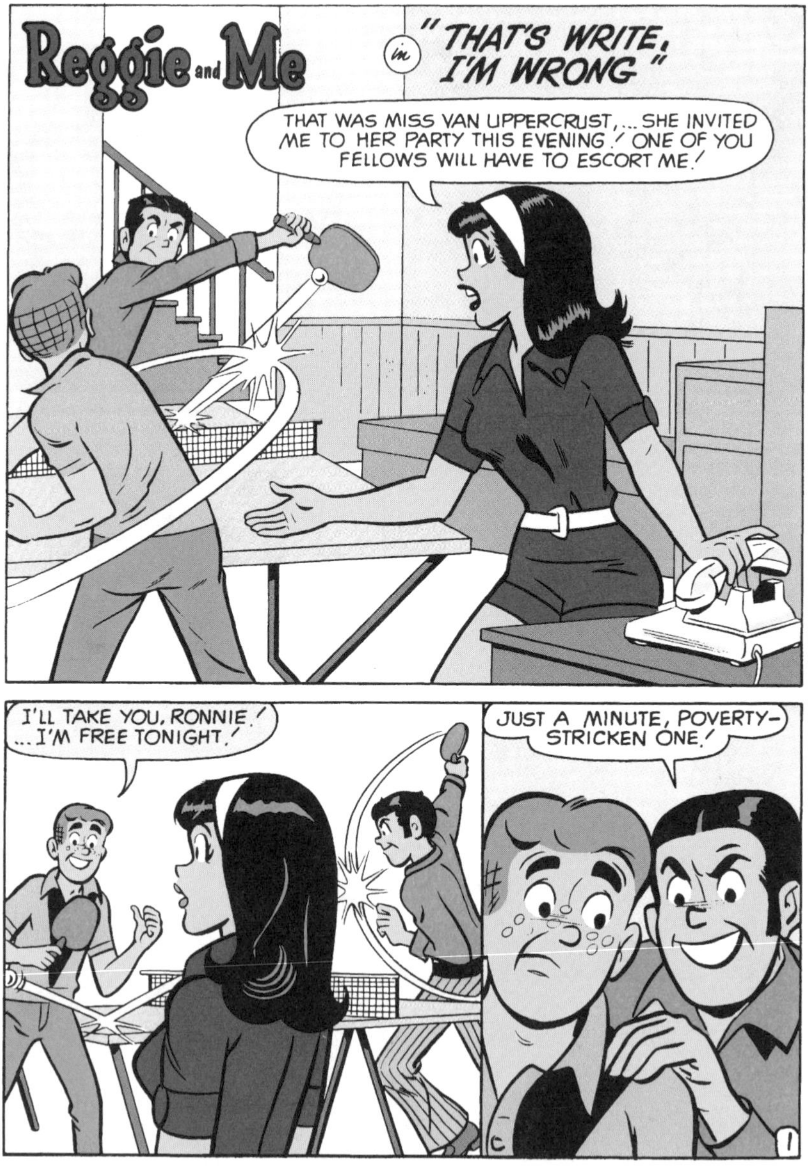
Reggie and Me
in
"THAT'S WRITE, I'M WRONG"
THAT WAS MISS VAN UPPERCRUST, ... SHE INVITED ME TO HER PARTY THIS EVENING! ONE OF YOU FELLOWS WILL HAVE TO ESCORT ME!
I'LL TAKE YOU, RONNIE! ... I'M FREE TONIGHT!
JUST A MINUTE, POVERTY-STRICKEN ONE!
1

Story & Pencils: Bob Bolling

Inks: Bob Smith Letters: Bill Yoshida Colors: Barry Grossman

Originally printed in REGGIE AND ME #43, SEPTEMBER 1970

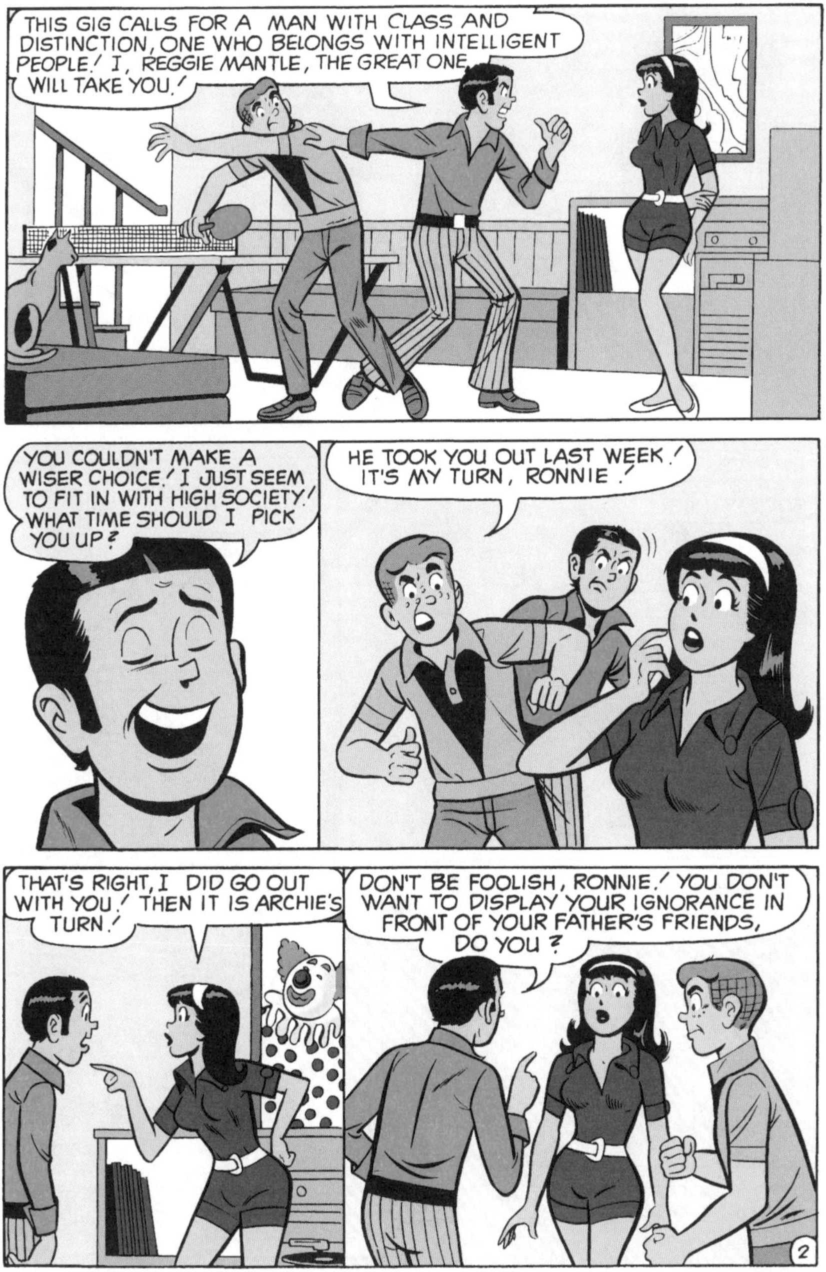
THIS GIG CALLS FOR A MAN WITH CLASS AND DISTINCTION, ONE WHO BELONGS WITH INTELLIGENT PEOPLE! I, REGGIE MANTLE, THE GREAT ONE, WILL TAKE YOU!
YOU COULDN'T MAKE A WISER CHOICE! I JUST SEEM TO FIT IN WITH HIGH SOCIETY! WHAT TIME SHOULD I PICK YOU UP?
HE TOOK YOU OUT LAST WEEK! IT'S MY TURN, RONNIE!
THAT'S RIGHT, I DID GO OUT WITH YOU! THEN IT IS ARCHIE'S TURN!
DON'T BE FOOLISH, RONNIE! YOU DON'T WANT TO DISPLAY YOUR IGNORANCE IN FRONT OF YOUR FATHER'S FRIENDS, DO YOU?
2

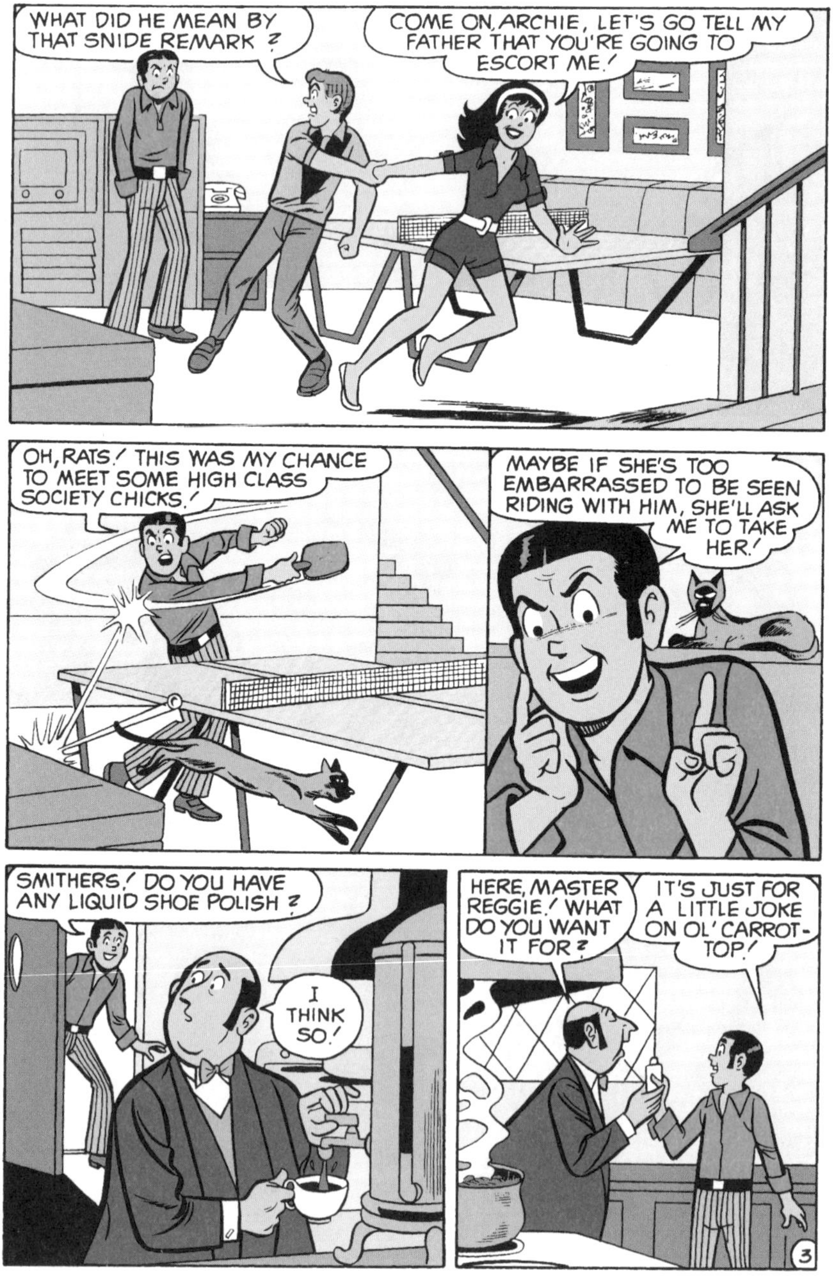
WHAT DID HE MEAN BY THAT SNIDE REMARK ?
COME ON, ARCHIE, LET'S GO TELL MY FATHER THAT YOU'RE GOING TO ESCORT ME!
OH, RATS! THIS WAS MY CHANCE TO MEET SOME HIGH CLASS SOCIETY CHICKS!
MAYBE IF SHE'S TOO EMBARRASSED TO BE SEEN RIDING WITH HIM, SHE'LL ASK ME TO TAKE HER!
SMITHERS! DO YOU HAVE ANY LIQUID SHOE POLISH ?
I THINK SO!
HERE, MASTER REGGIE! WHAT DO YOU WANT IT FOR ?
IT'S JUST FOR A LITTLE JOKE ON OL' CARROT-TOP!
3

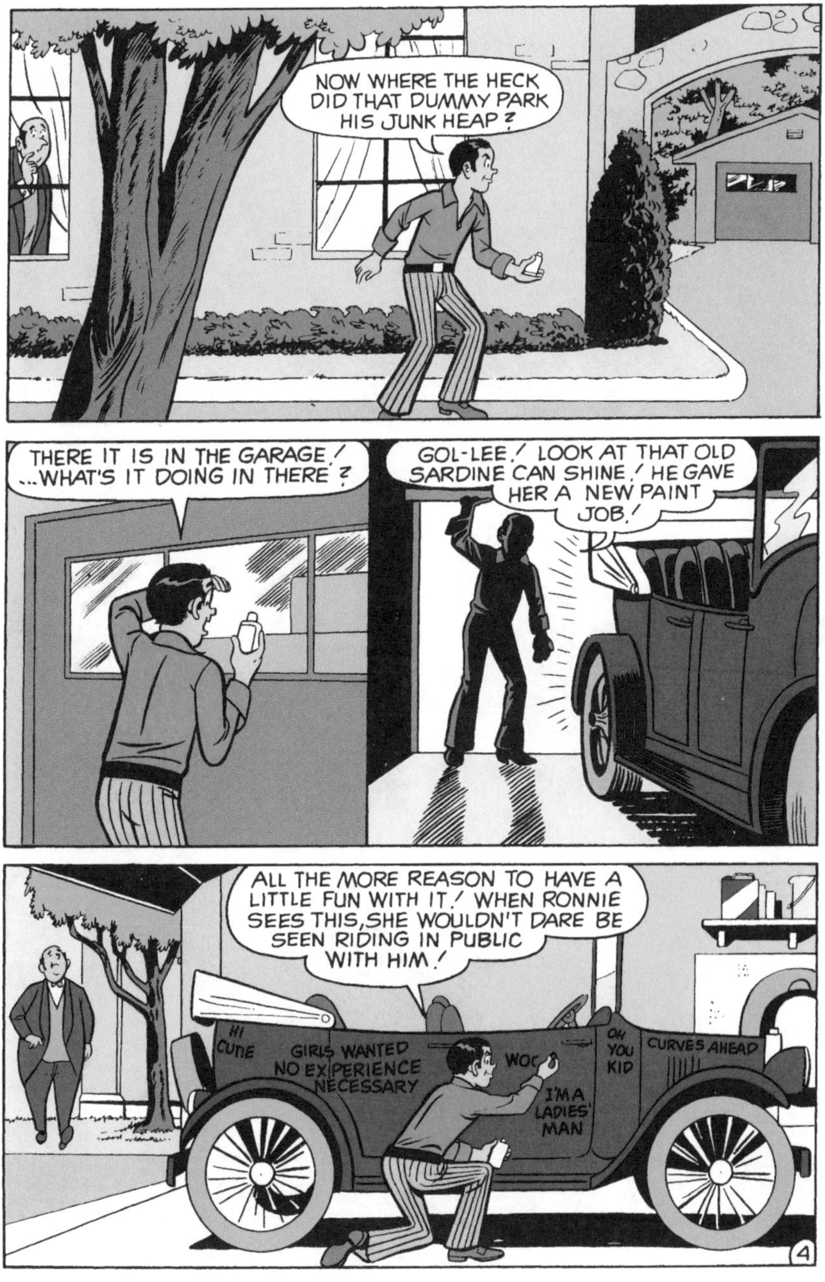
NOW WHERE THE HECK DID THAT DUMMY PARK HIS JUNK HEAP?
THERE IT IS IN THE GARAGE! ...WHAT'S IT DOING IN THERE?
GOL-LEE! LOOK AT THAT OLD SARDINE CAN SHINE! HE GAVE HER A NEW PAINT JOB!
ALL THE MORE REASON TO HAVE A LITTLE FUN WITH IT! WHEN RONNIE SEES THIS, SHE WOULDN'T DARE BE SEEN RIDING IN PUBLIC WITH HIM!
HI CUTIE
GIRLS WANTED NO EXPERIENCE NECESSARY
OH YOU KID
CURVES AHEAD
I'M A LADIES' MAN
4

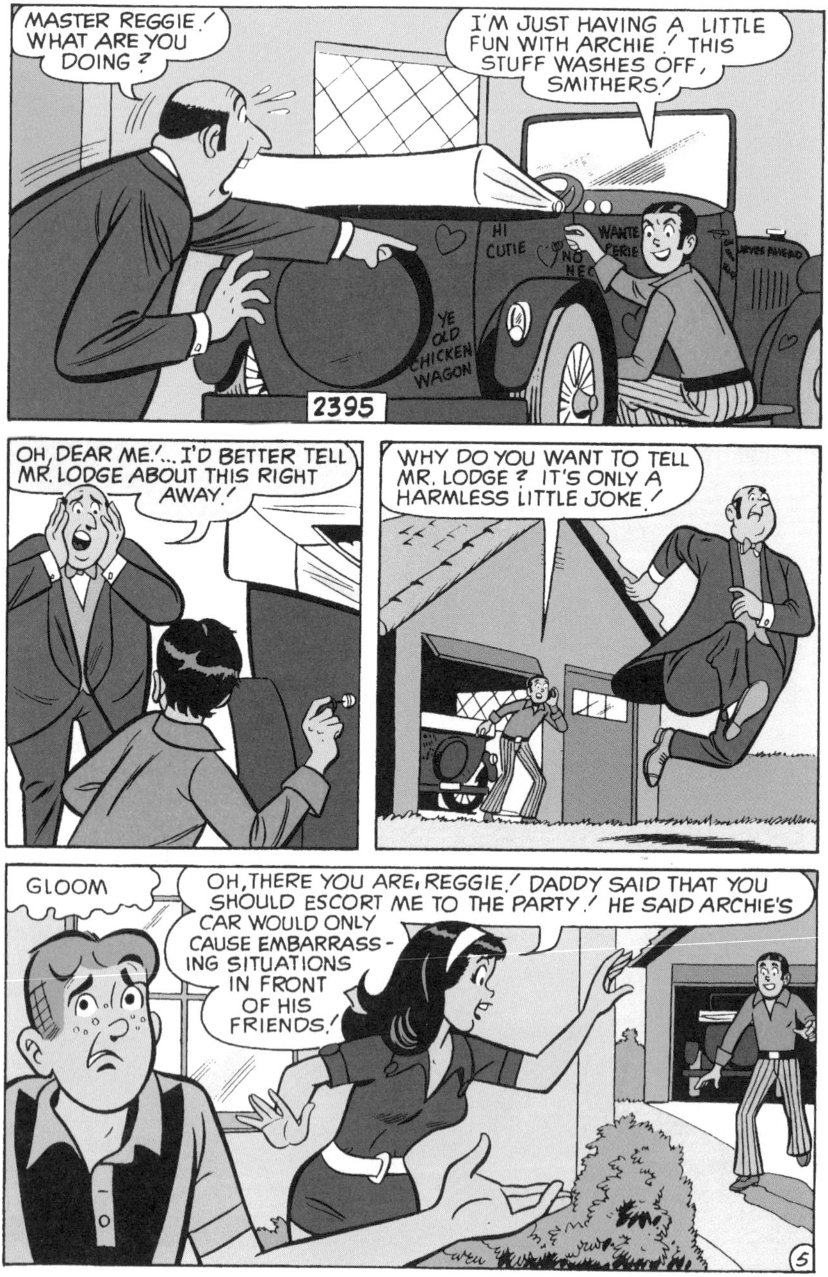
MASTER REGGIE! WHAT ARE YOU DOING?
I'M JUST HAVING A LITTLE FUN WITH ARCHIE! THIS STUFF WASHES OFF, SMITHERS!
HI CUTIE
YE OLD CHICKEN WAGON
2395
OH, DEAR ME!... I'D BETTER TELL MR. LODGE ABOUT THIS RIGHT AWAY!
WHY DO YOU WANT TO TELL MR. LODGE? IT'S ONLY A HARMLESS LITTLE JOKE!
GLOOM
OH, THERE YOU ARE, REGGIE! DADDY SAID THAT YOU SHOULD ESCORT ME TO THE PARTY! HE SAID ARCHIE'S CAR WOULD ONLY CAUSE EMBARRASSING SITUATIONS IN FRONT OF HIS FRIENDS!
5

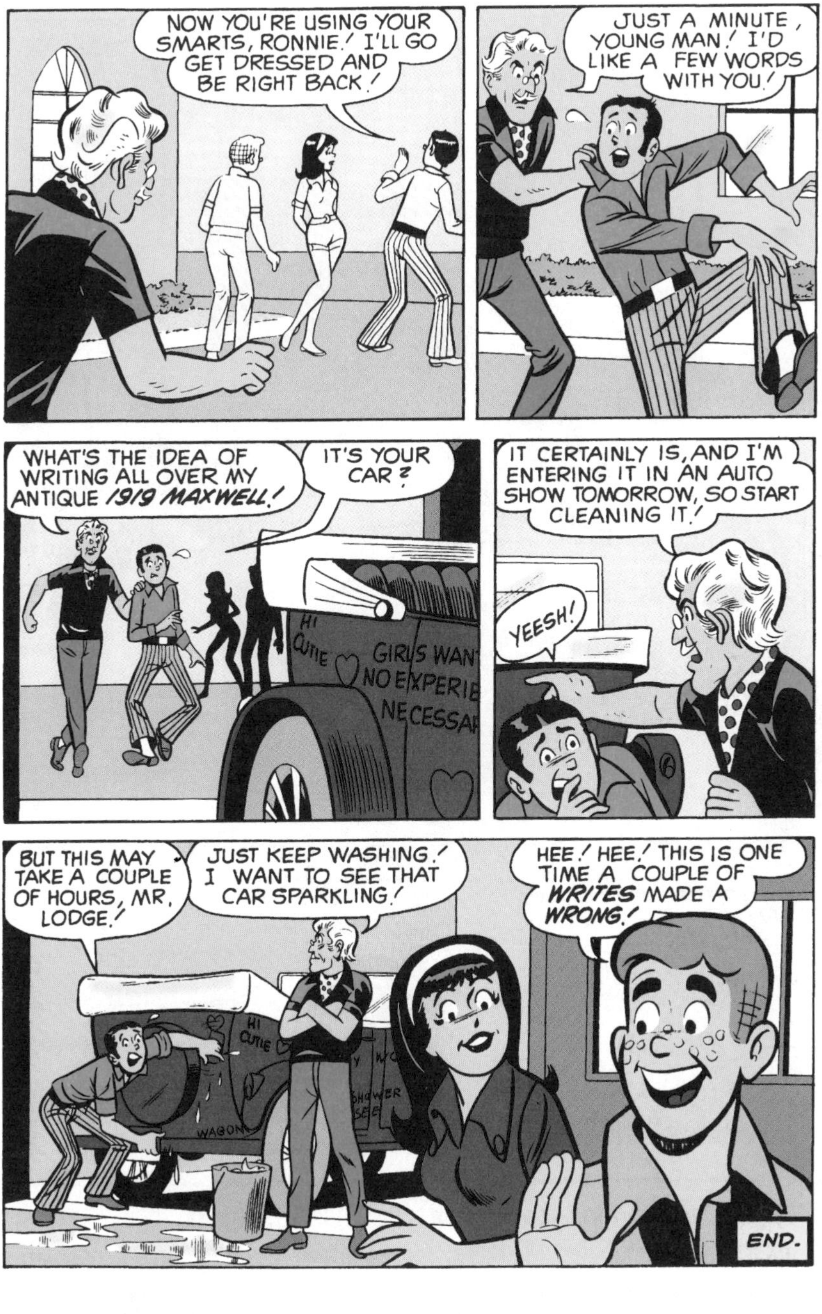
NOW YOU'RE USING YOUR SMARTS, RONNIE! I'LL GO GET DRESSED AND BE RIGHT BACK!
JUST A MINUTE, YOUNG MAN! I'D LIKE A FEW WORDS WITH YOU!
WHAT'S THE IDEA OF WRITING ALL OVER MY ANTIQUE 1919 MAXWELL!
IT'S YOUR CAR?
HI CUTIE
GIRLS WANT
NO EXPERIE
NECESSA
IT CERTAINLY IS, AND I'M ENTERING IT IN AN AUTO SHOW TOMORROW, SO START CLEANING IT!
YEESH!
BUT THIS MAY TAKE A COUPLE OF HOURS, MR. LODGE!
JUST KEEP WASHING! I WANT TO SEE THAT CAR SPARKLING!
HEE! HEE! THIS IS ONE TIME A COUPLE OF WRITES MADE A WRONG!
END.

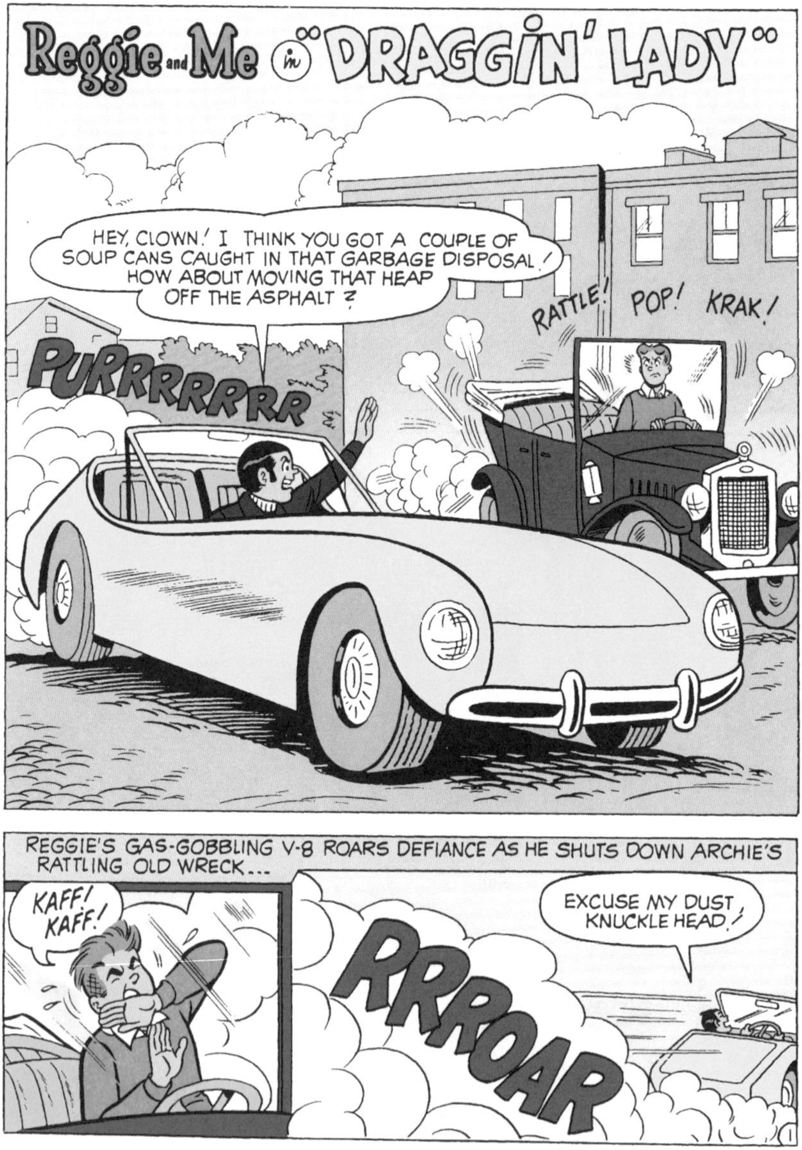
Reggie and Me in "DRAGGIN' LADY"
HEY, CLOWN! I THINK YOU GOT A COUPLE OF SOUP CANS CAUGHT IN THAT GARBAGE DISPOSAL! HOW ABOUT MOVING THAT HEAP OFF THE ASPHALT ?
RATTLE! POP! KRAK!
PURRRRRRRR
REGGIE'S GAS-GOBBLING V-8 ROARS DEFIANCE AS HE SHUTS DOWN ARCHIE'S RATTLING OLD WRECK...
KAFF! KAFF!
EXCUSE MY DUST, KNUCKLE HEAD!
RRROAR

Story: Frank Doyle Pencils: Bill Vigoda
Inks: Mario Acquaviva Letters: Bill Yoshida Colors: Barry Grossman

Originally printed in REGGIE AND ME #44, OCTOBER 1970

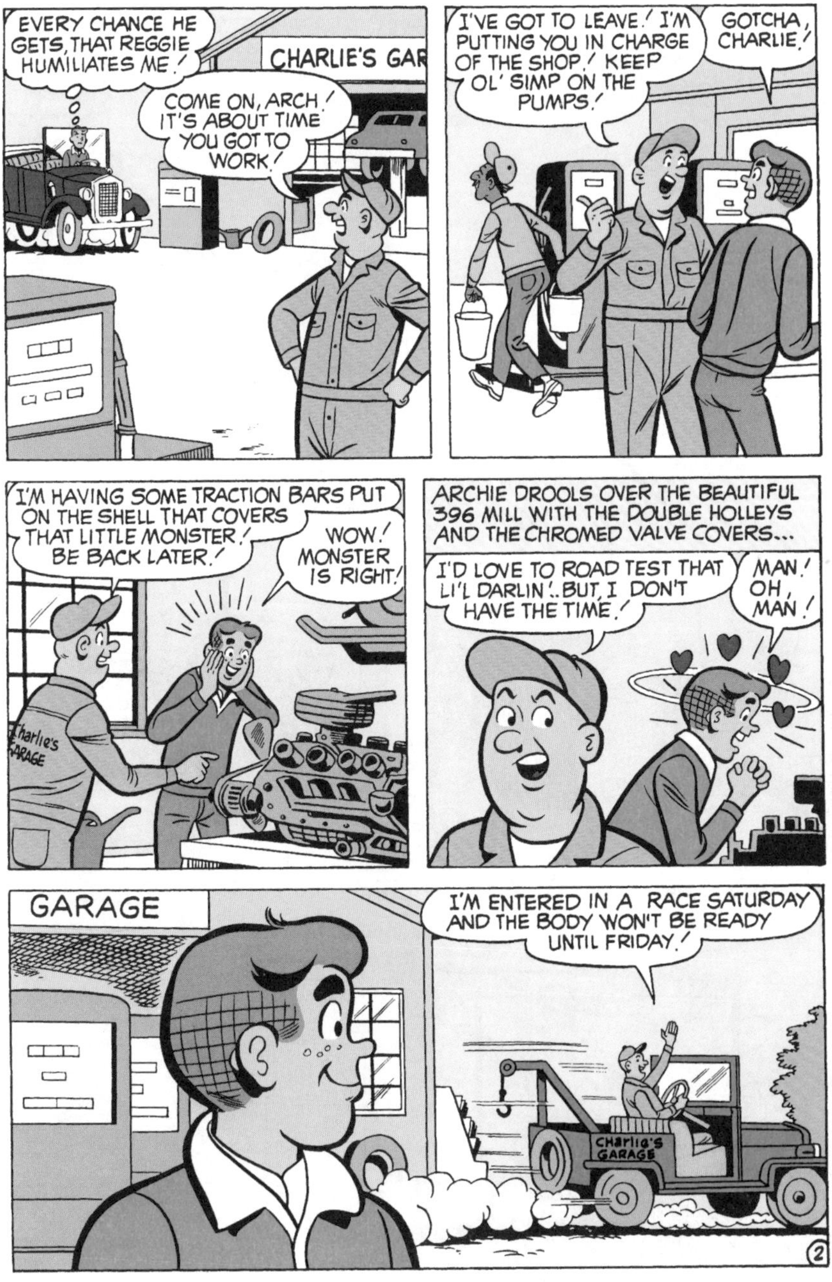
EVERY CHANCE HE GETS, THAT REGGIE HUMILIATES ME!
CHARLIE'S GAR
COME ON, ARCH! IT'S ABOUT TIME YOU GOT TO WORK!
I'VE GOT TO LEAVE! I'M PUTTING YOU IN CHARGE OF THE SHOP! KEEP OL' SIMP ON THE PUMPS!
GOTCHA, CHARLIE!
I'M HAVING SOME TRACTION BARS PUT ON THE SHELL THAT COVERS THAT LITTLE MONSTER! BE BACK LATER!
WOW! MONSTER IS RIGHT!
Charlie's GARAGE
ARCHIE DROOLS OVER THE BEAUTIFUL 396 MILL WITH THE DOUBLE HOLLEYS AND THE CHROMED VALVE COVERS...
I'D LOVE TO ROAD TEST THAT LI'L DARLIN'.. BUT, I DON'T HAVE THE TIME!
MAN! OH, MAN!
GARAGE
I'M ENTERED IN A RACE SATURDAY AND THE BODY WON'T BE READY UNTIL FRIDAY!
Charlie's GARAGE
2

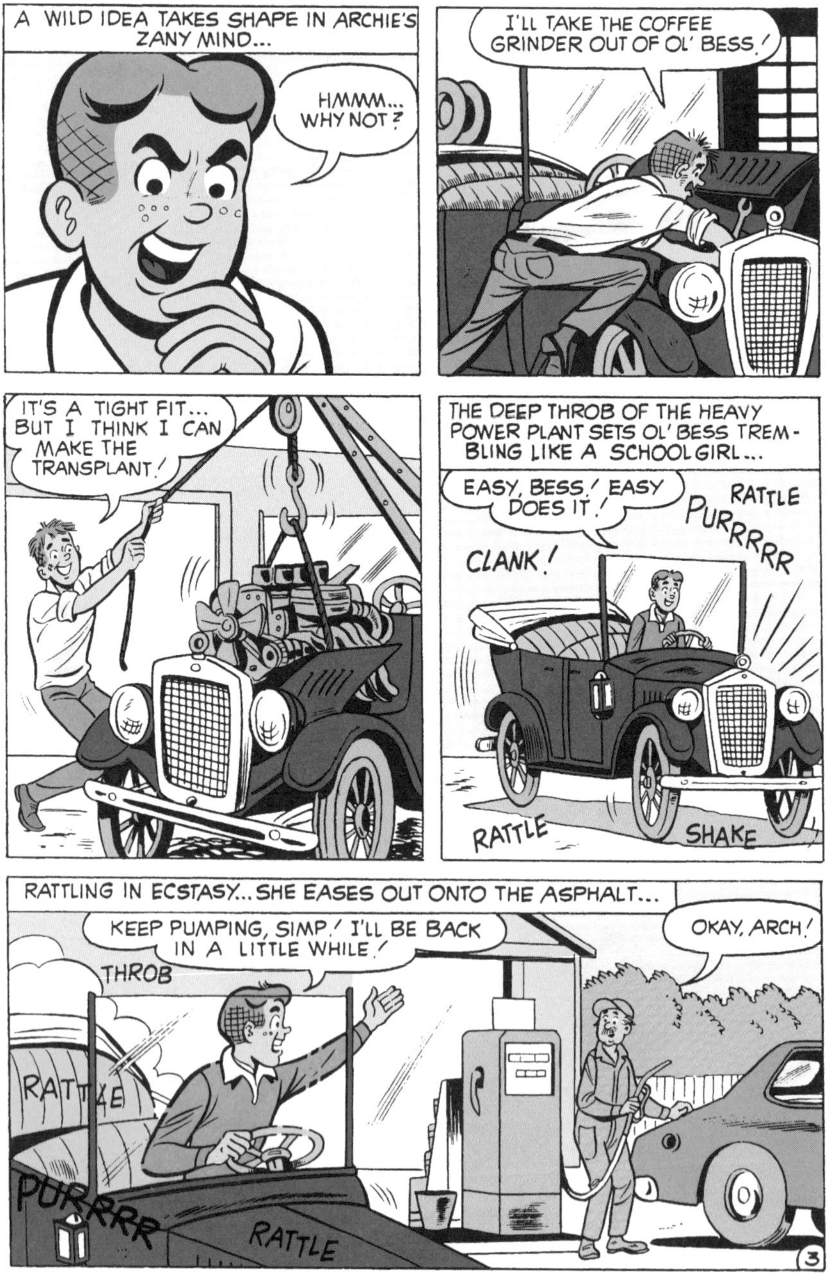
A WILD IDEA TAKES SHAPE IN ARCHIE'S ZANY MIND...
HMMM... WHY NOT?
I'LL TAKE THE COFFEE GRINDER OUT OF OL' BESS!
IT'S A TIGHT FIT... BUT I THINK I CAN MAKE THE TRANSPLANT!
THE DEEP THROB OF THE HEAVY POWER PLANT SETS OL' BESS TREM-BLING LIKE A SCHOOL GIRL...
EASY, BESS! EASY DOES IT!
RATTLE
PURRRRRR
CLANK!
RATTLE
SHAKE
RATTLING IN ECSTASY... SHE EASES OUT ONTO THE ASPHALT...
KEEP PUMPING, SIMP! I'LL BE BACK IN A LITTLE WHILE!
OKAY, ARCH!
THROB
RATTLE
PURRRRR
RATTLE
3

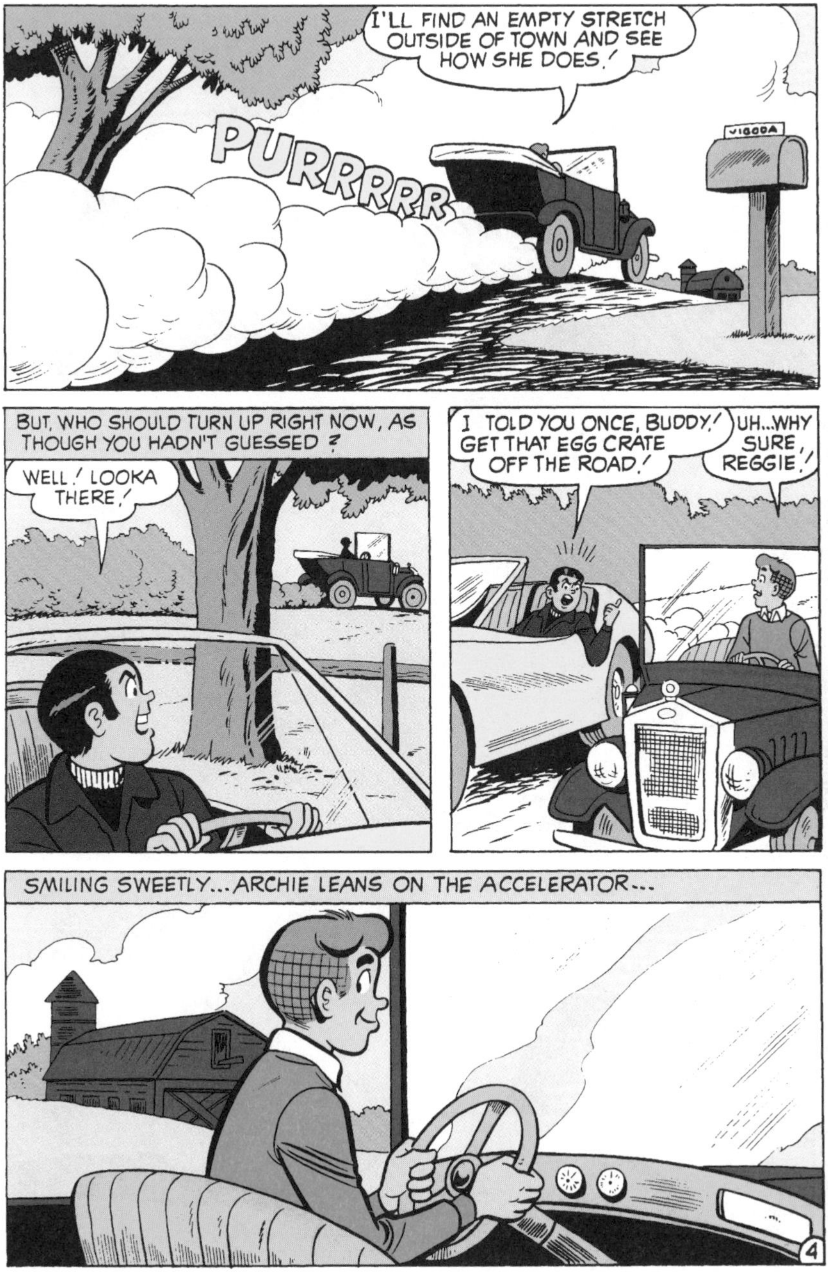
I'LL FIND AN EMPTY STRETCH OUTSIDE OF TOWN AND SEE HOW SHE DOES!
PURRRRRR
VIGODA
BUT, WHO SHOULD TURN UP RIGHT NOW, AS THOUGH YOU HADN'T GUESSED?
WELL! LOOKA THERE!
I TOLD YOU ONCE, BUDDY! GET THAT EGG CRATE OFF THE ROAD!
UH...WHY SURE, REGGIE!
SMILING SWEETLY... ARCHIE LEANS ON THE ACCELERATOR...
4

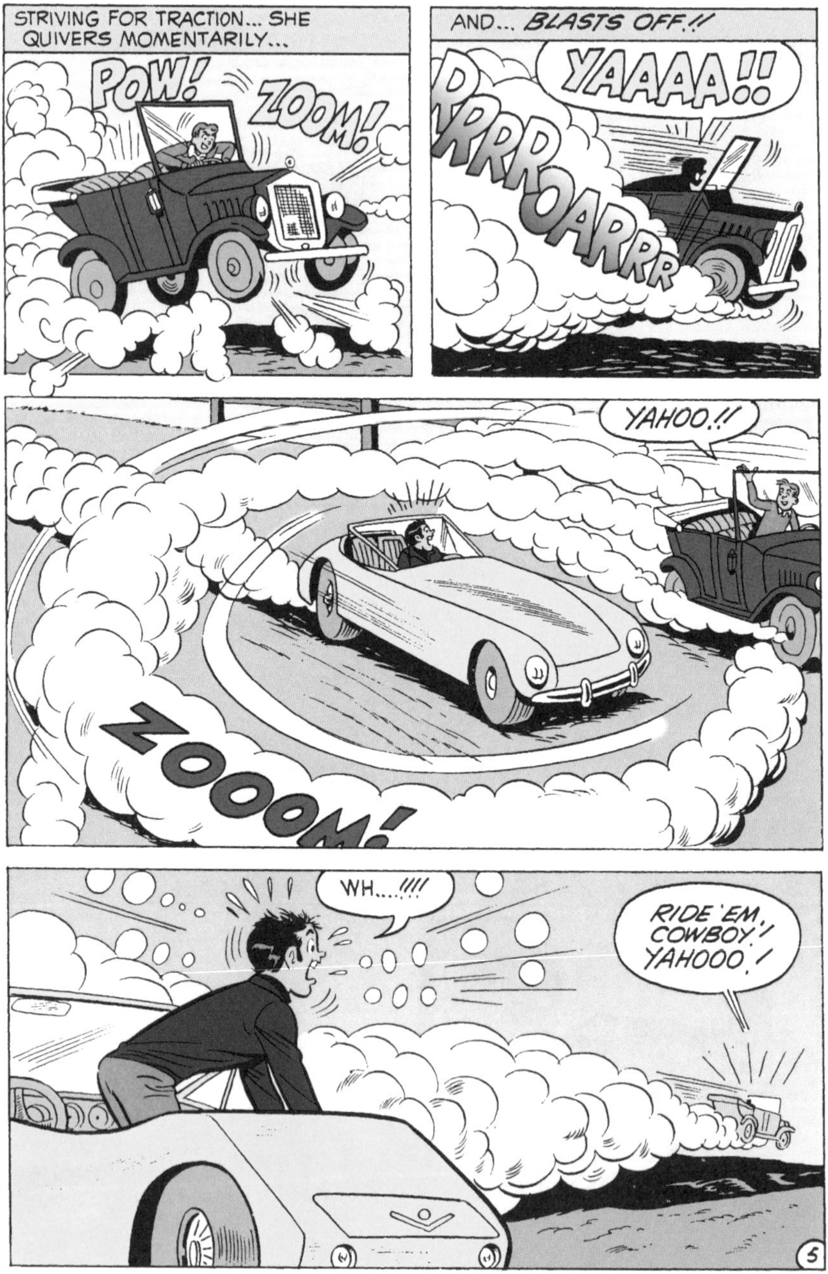

STRIVING FOR TRACTION... SHE QUIVERS MOMENTARILY...
POW!
ZOOM!
AND... BLASTS OFF.!!
YAAAA!!
RRRROARRRR
YAHOO.!!
ZOOOM!
WH....!!!!
RIDE 'EM, COWBOY.! YAHOOO.!
5

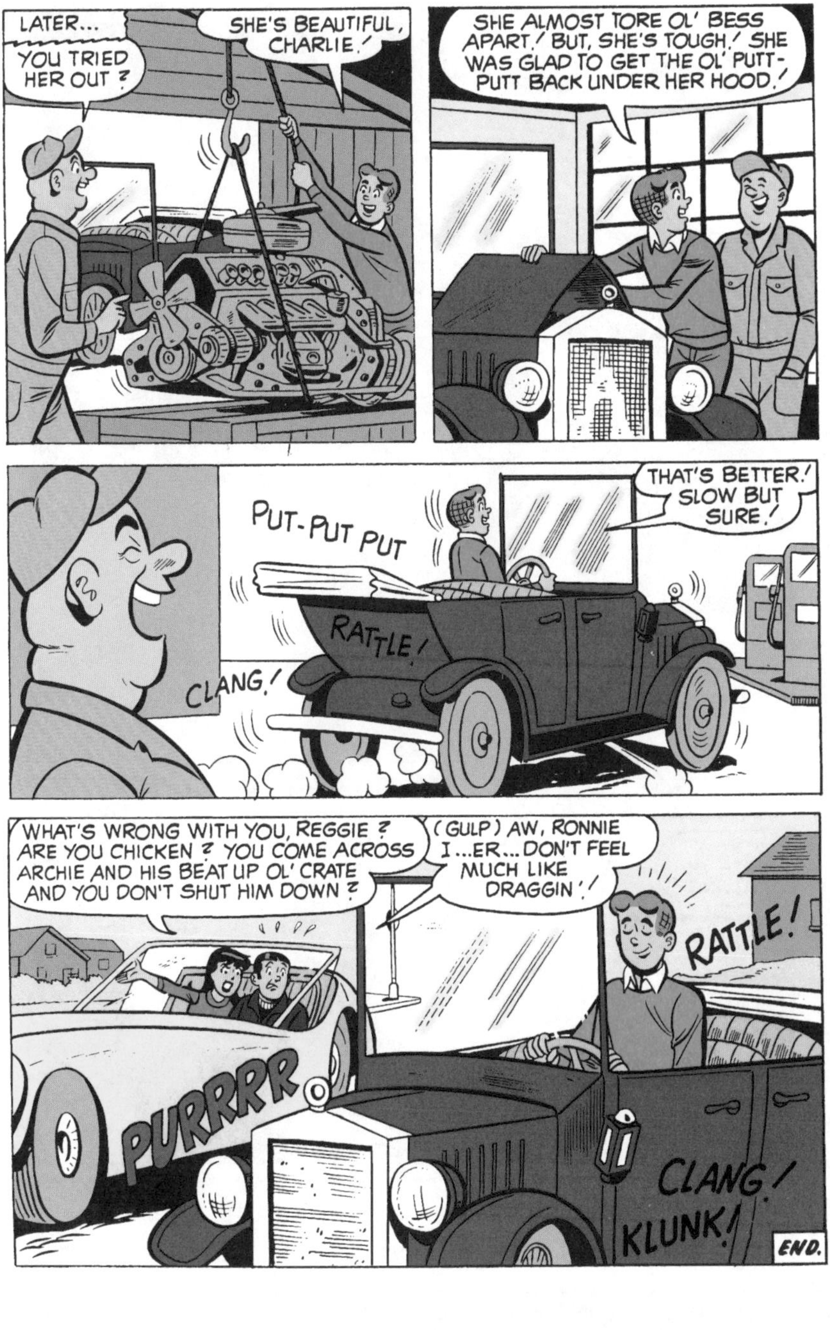
LATER...
YOU TRIED HER OUT ?
SHE'S BEAUTIFUL, CHARLIE!
SHE ALMOST TORE OL' BESS APART! BUT, SHE'S TOUGH! SHE WAS GLAD TO GET THE OL' PUTT-PUTT BACK UNDER HER HOOD!
PUT-PUT PUT
THAT'S BETTER! SLOW BUT SURE!
RATTLE!
CLANG!
WHAT'S WRONG WITH YOU, REGGIE ? ARE YOU CHICKEN ? YOU COME ACROSS ARCHIE AND HIS BEAT UP OL' CRATE AND YOU DON'T SHUT HIM DOWN ?
(GULP) AW, RONNIE I...ER...DON'T FEEL MUCH LIKE DRAGGIN'!
RATTLE!
PURRRR
CLANG!
KLUNK!
END.

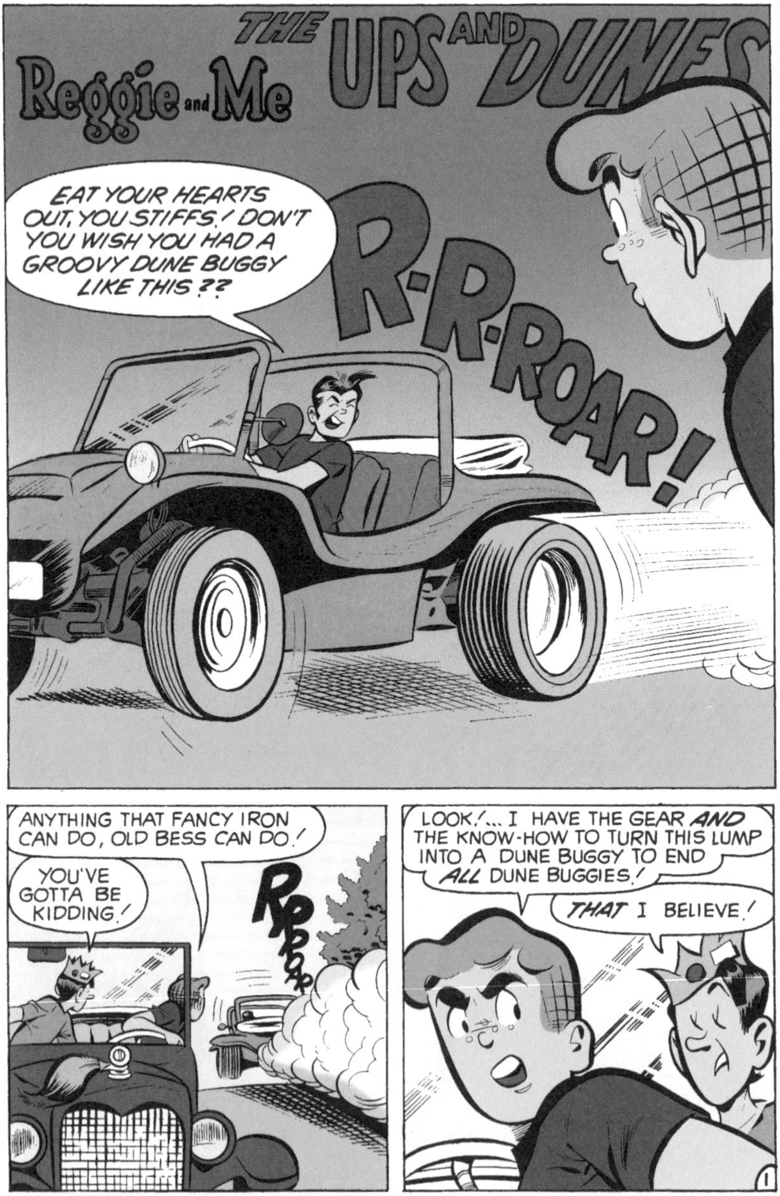
Reggie and Me
THE UPS AND DUNES
EAT YOUR HEARTS OUT, YOU STIFFS! DON'T YOU WISH YOU HAD A GROOVY DUNE BUGGY LIKE THIS??
R-R-ROAR!
ANYTHING THAT FANCY IRON CAN DO, OLD BESS CAN DO!
YOU'VE GOTTA BE KIDDING!
LOOK!... I HAVE THE GEAR AND THE KNOW-HOW TO TURN THIS LUMP INTO A DUNE BUGGY TO END ALL DUNE BUGGIES!
THAT I BELIEVE!

Story: Frank Doyle Pencils: Harry Lucey
Inks: Marty Epp Letters: Bill Yoshida Colors: Barry Grossman

Originally printed in REGGIE AND ME #44, OCTOBER 1970

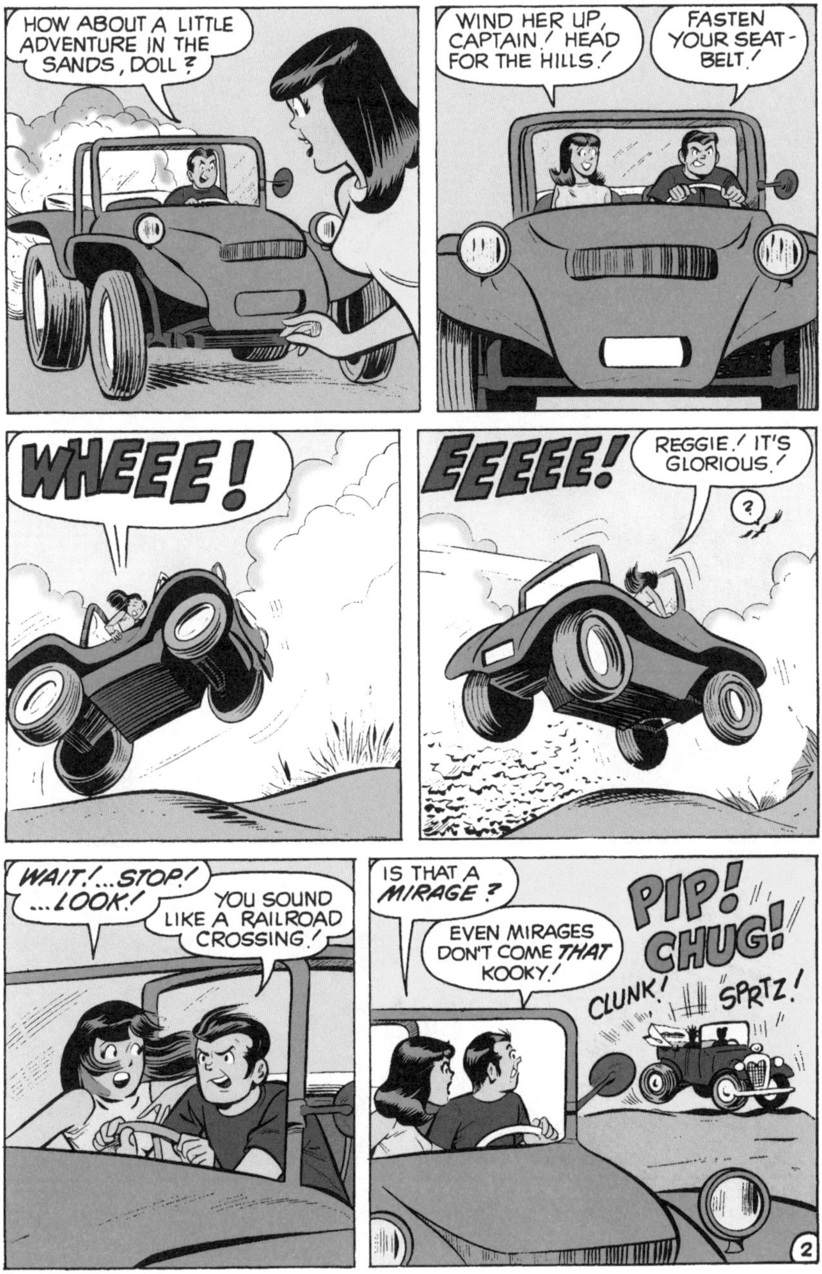
HOW ABOUT A LITTLE ADVENTURE IN THE SANDS, DOLL?
WIND HER UP, CAPTAIN! HEAD FOR THE HILLS!
FASTEN YOUR SEAT-BELT!
WHEEE!
EEEEE!
REGGIE! IT'S GLORIOUS!
?
WAIT!...STOP! ...LOOK!
YOU SOUND LIKE A RAILROAD CROSSING!
IS THAT A MIRAGE?
EVEN MIRAGES DON'T COME THAT KOOKY!
PIP! CHUG!
CLUNK!
SPRTZ!
2

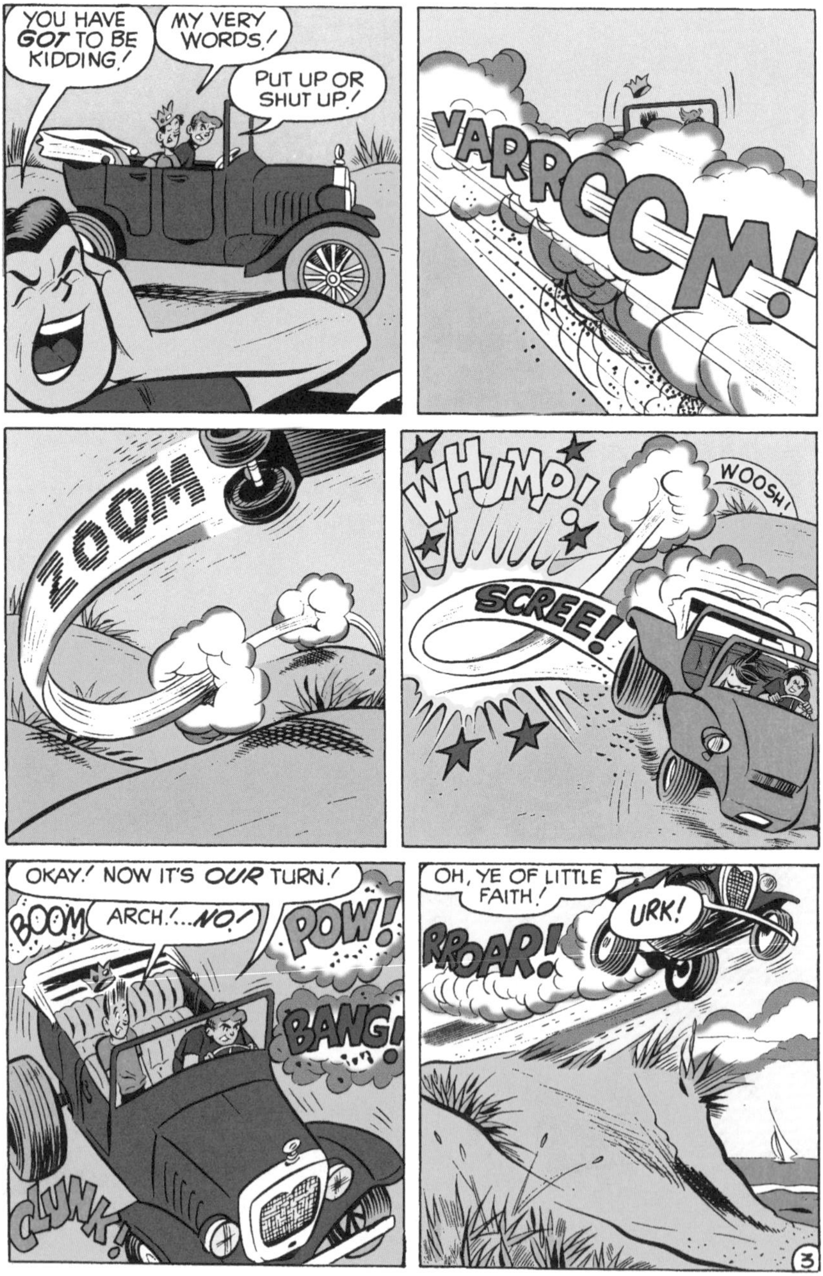
YOU HAVE GOT TO BE KIDDING!
MY VERY WORDS!
PUT UP OR SHUT UP!
VARROOM!
ZOOM
WHUMP!
WOOSH!
SCREE!
OKAY! NOW IT'S OUR TURN!
BOOM
ARCH!...NO!
POW!
BANG!
CLUNK!
OH, YE OF LITTLE FAITH!
URK!
RROAR!
3

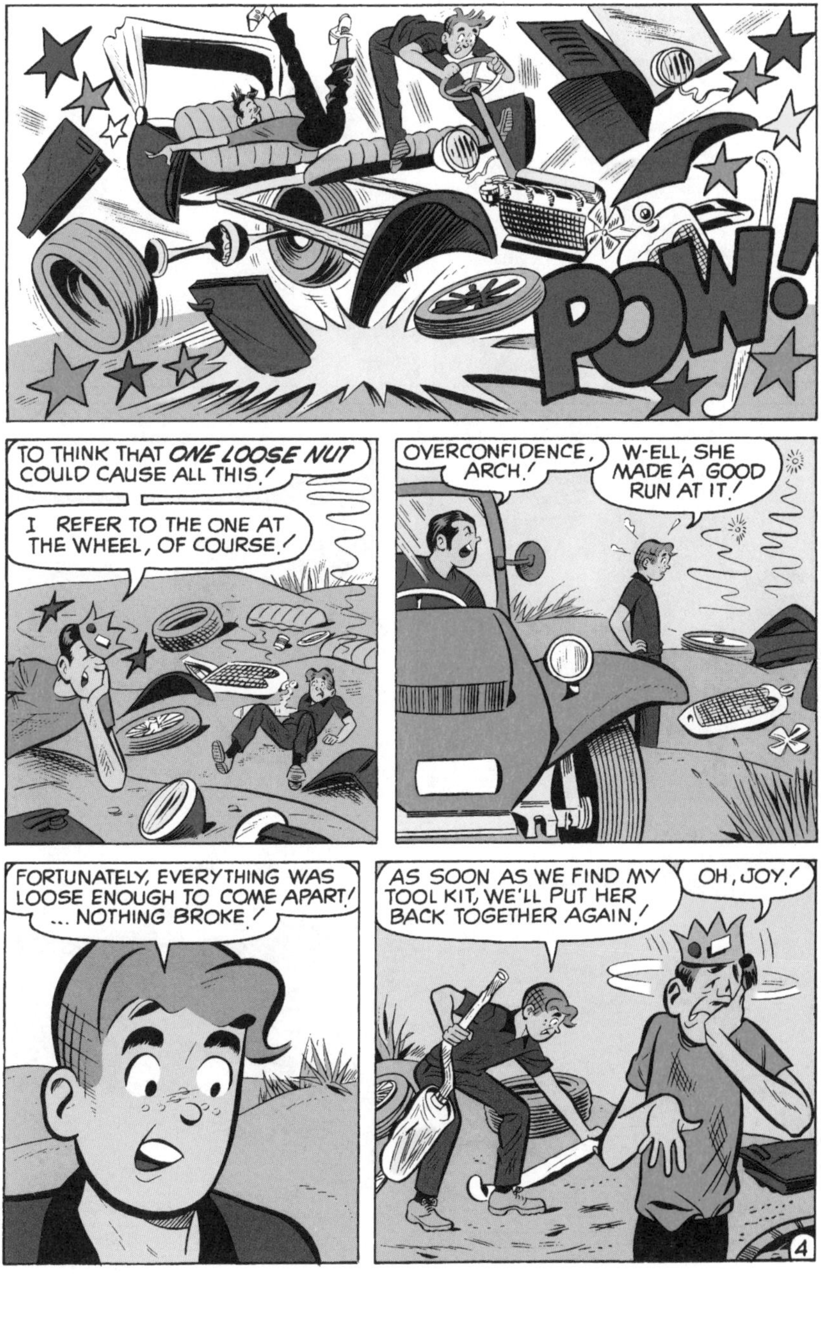
POW!
TO THINK THAT ONE LOOSE NUT COULD CAUSE ALL THIS!
I REFER TO THE ONE AT THE WHEEL, OF COURSE!
OVERCONFIDENCE, ARCH!
W-ELL, SHE MADE A GOOD RUN AT IT!
FORTUNATELY, EVERYTHING WAS LOOSE ENOUGH TO COME APART! ... NOTHING BROKE!
AS SOON AS WE FIND MY TOOL KIT, WE'LL PUT HER BACK TOGETHER AGAIN!
OH, JOY!
4

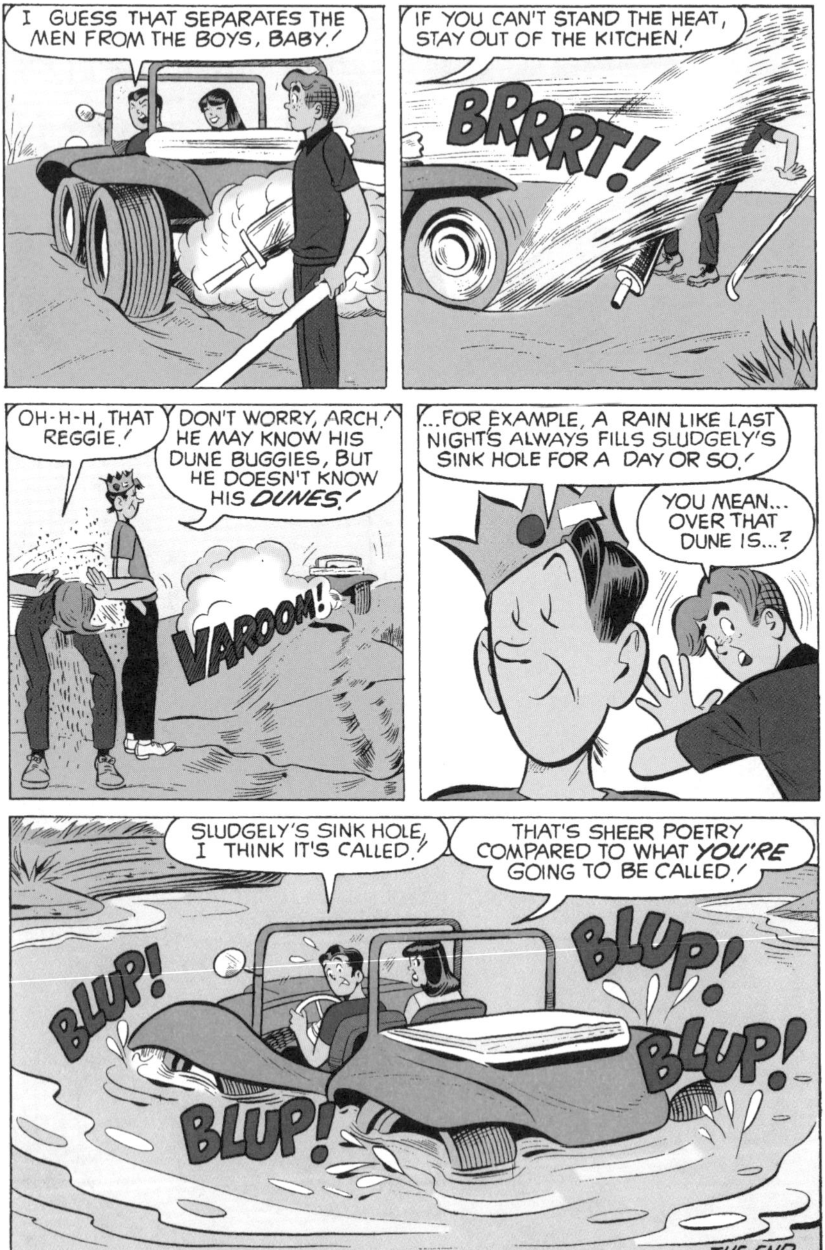
I GUESS THAT SEPARATES THE MEN FROM THE BOYS, BABY!
IF YOU CAN'T STAND THE HEAT, STAY OUT OF THE KITCHEN!
BRRRT!
OH-H-H, THAT REGGIE!
DON'T WORRY, ARCH! HE MAY KNOW HIS DUNE BUGGIES, BUT HE DOESN'T KNOW HIS DUNES!
VAROOM!
...FOR EXAMPLE, A RAIN LIKE LAST NIGHT'S ALWAYS FILLS SLUDGELY'S SINK HOLE FOR A DAY OR SO!
YOU MEAN... OVER THAT DUNE IS...?
SLUDGELY'S SINK HOLE, I THINK IT'S CALLED!
THAT'S SHEER POETRY COMPARED TO WHAT YOU'RE GOING TO BE CALLED!
BLUP!
BLUP!
BLUP!
BLUP!
THE END

Reggie and Me: RING MY CHIMES

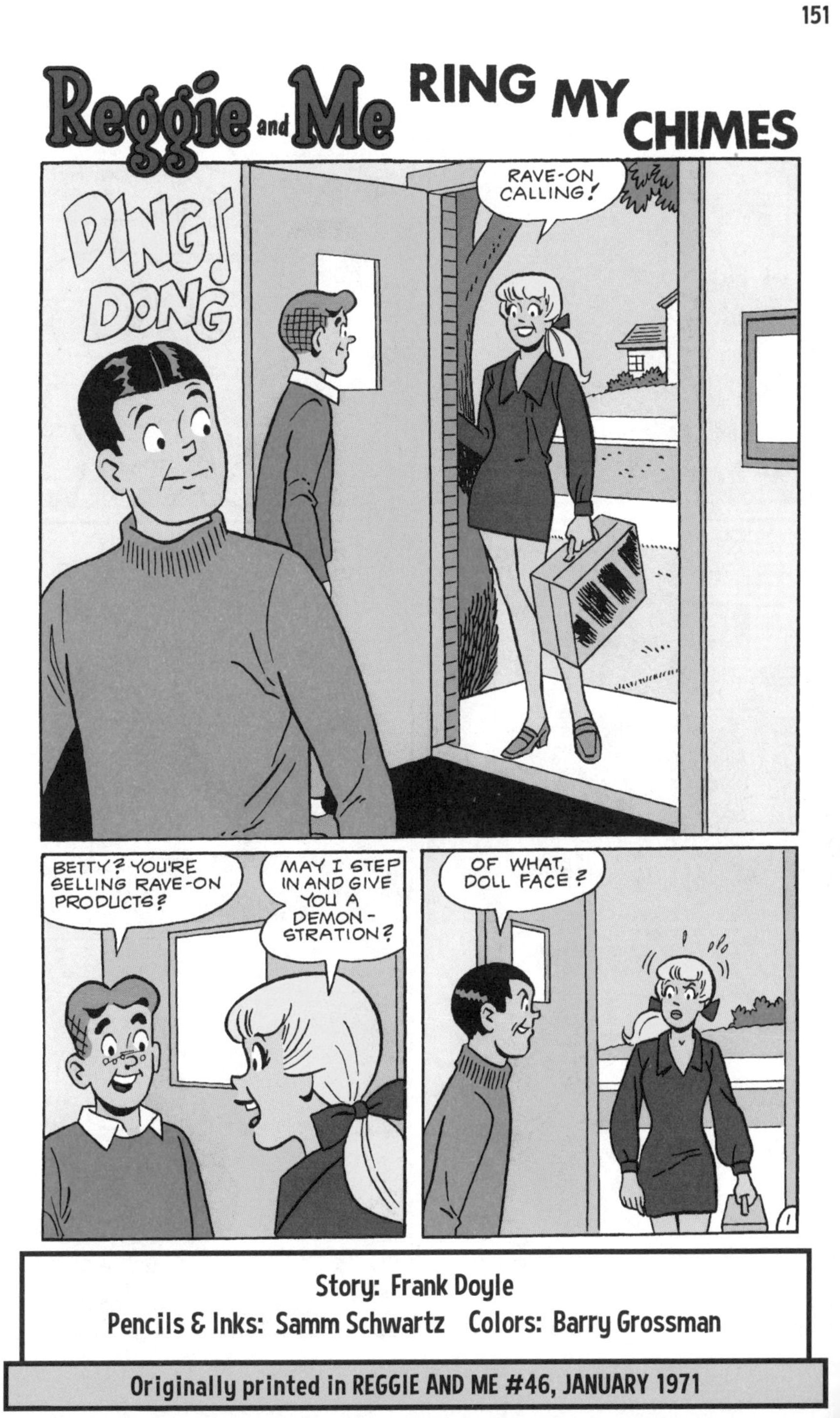
DING DONG
RAVE-ON CALLING!
BETTY? YOU'RE SELLING RAVE-ON PRODUCTS?
MAY I STEP IN AND GIVE YOU A DEMON-STRATION?
OF WHAT, DOLL FACE?

Story: Frank Doyle

Pencils & Inks: Samm Schwartz Colors: Barry Grossman

Originally printed in REGGIE AND ME #46, JANUARY 1971

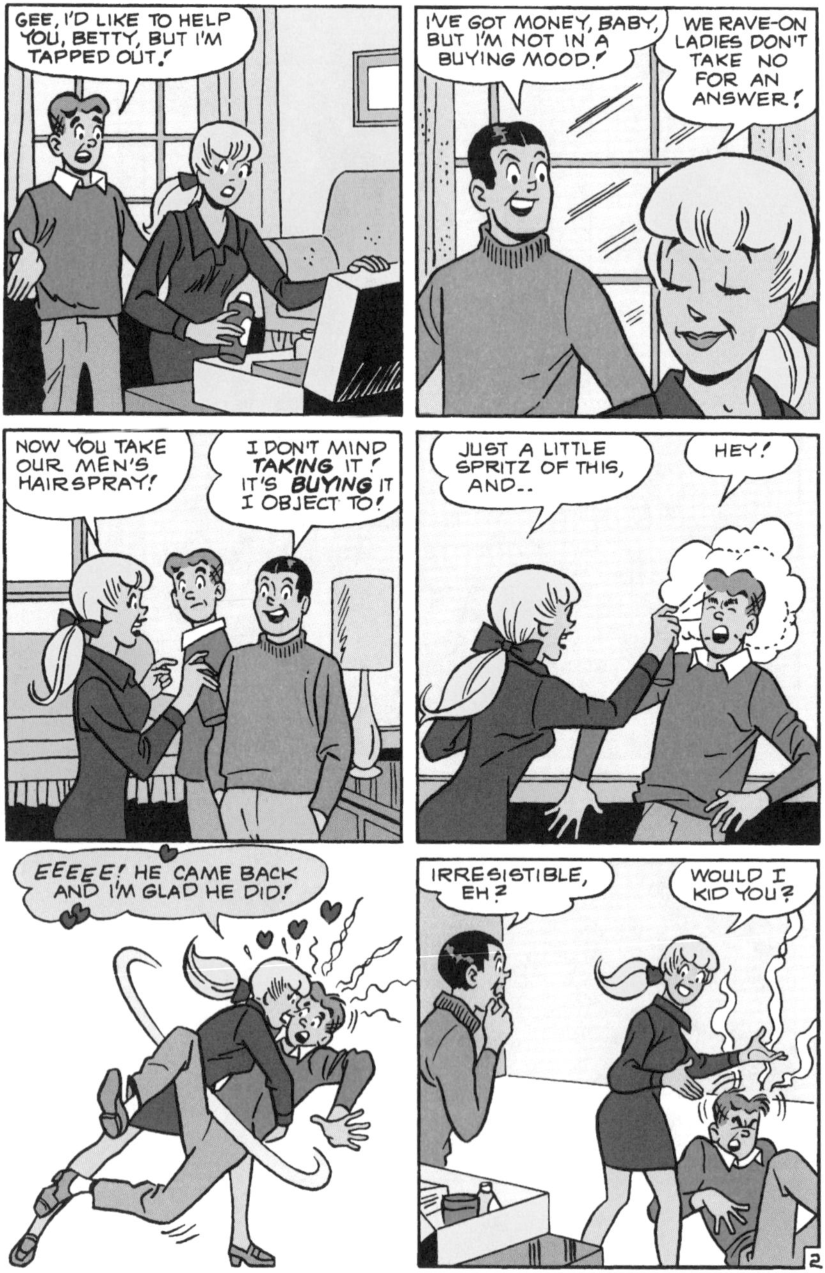
GEE, I'D LIKE TO HELP YOU, BETTY, BUT I'M TAPPED OUT!
I'VE GOT MONEY, BABY, BUT I'M NOT IN A BUYING MOOD!
WE RAVE-ON LADIES DON'T TAKE NO FOR AN ANSWER!
NOW YOU TAKE OUR MEN'S HAIRSPRAY!
I DON'T MIND TAKING IT! IT'S BUYING IT I OBJECT TO!
JUST A LITTLE SPRITZ OF THIS, AND..
HEY!
EEEEE! HE CAME BACK AND I'M GLAD HE DID!
IRRESISTIBLE, EH?
WOULD I KID YOU?
2

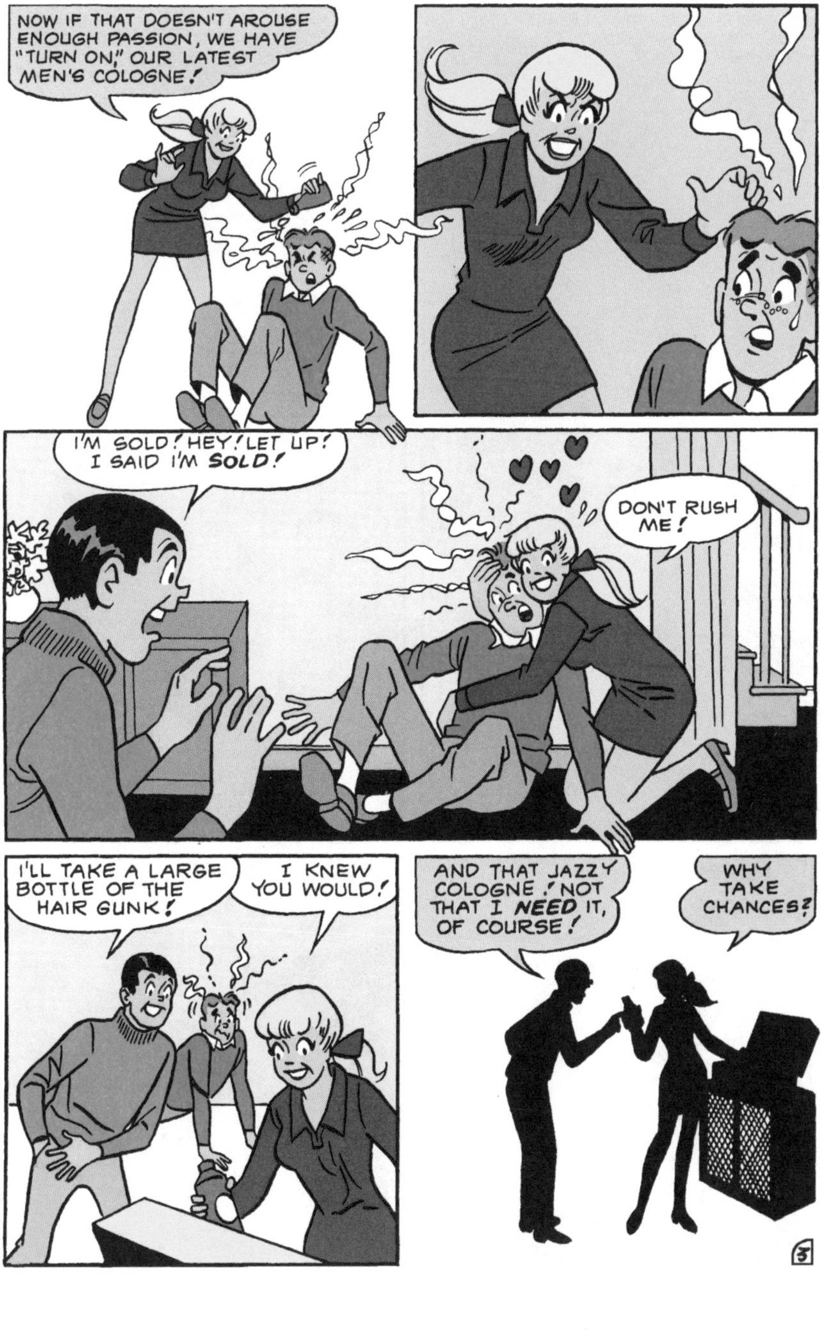
NOW IF THAT DOESN'T AROUSE ENOUGH PASSION, WE HAVE "TURN ON," OUR LATEST MEN'S COLOGNE!
I'M SOLD! HEY! LET UP! I SAID I'M **SOLD**!
DON'T RUSH ME!
I'LL TAKE A LARGE BOTTLE OF THE HAIR GUNK!
I KNEW YOU WOULD!
AND THAT JAZZY COLOGNE! NOT THAT I **NEED** IT, OF COURSE!
WHY TAKE CHANCES?
3

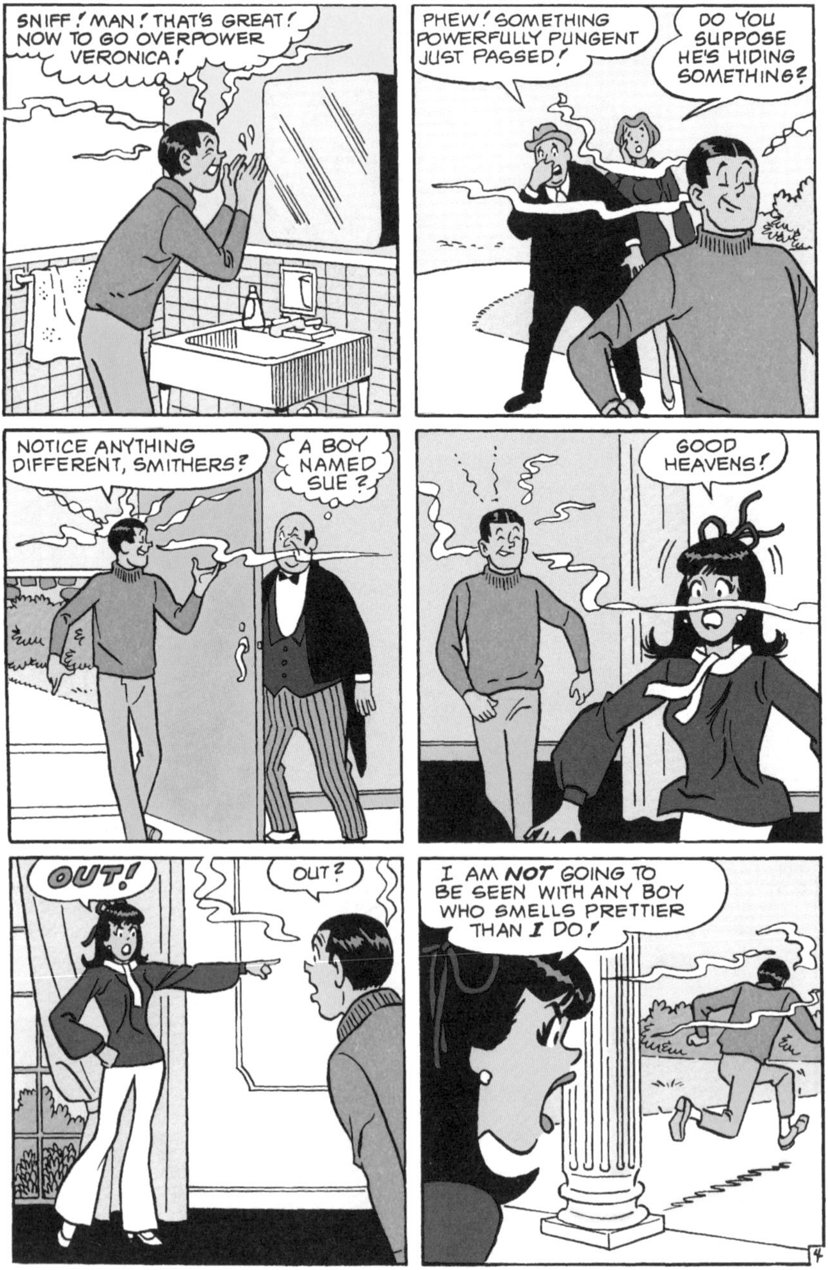
SNIFF! MAN! THAT'S GREAT! NOW TO GO OVERPOWER VERONICA!
PHEW! SOMETHING POWERFULLY PUNGENT JUST PASSED!
DO YOU SUPPOSE HE'S HIDING SOMETHING?
NOTICE ANYTHING DIFFERENT, SMITHERS?
A BOY NAMED SUE?
GOOD HEAVENS!
OUT!
OUT?
I AM NOT GOING TO BE SEEN WITH ANY BOY WHO SMELLS PRETTIER THAN I DO!
4

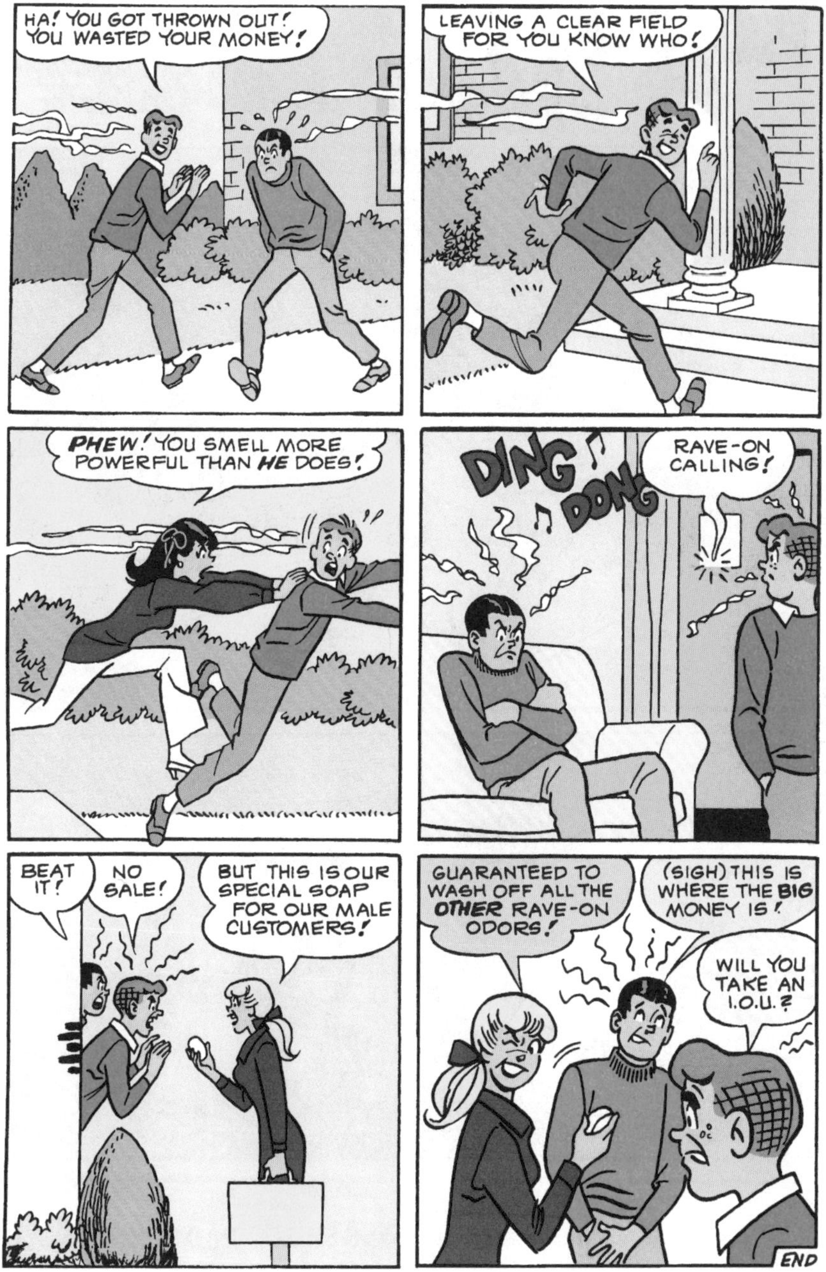
HA! YOU GOT THROWN OUT! YOU WASTED YOUR MONEY!
LEAVING A CLEAR FIELD FOR YOU KNOW WHO!
PHEW! YOU SMELL MORE POWERFUL THAN HE DOES!
DING DONG
RAVE-ON CALLING!
BEAT IT!
NO SALE!
BUT THIS IS OUR SPECIAL SOAP FOR OUR MALE CUSTOMERS!
GUARANTEED TO WASH OFF ALL THE OTHER RAVE-ON ODORS!
(SIGH) THIS IS WHERE THE BIG MONEY IS!
WILL YOU TAKE AN I.O.U.?
END

Reggie and Me in "A Sense of Balance"

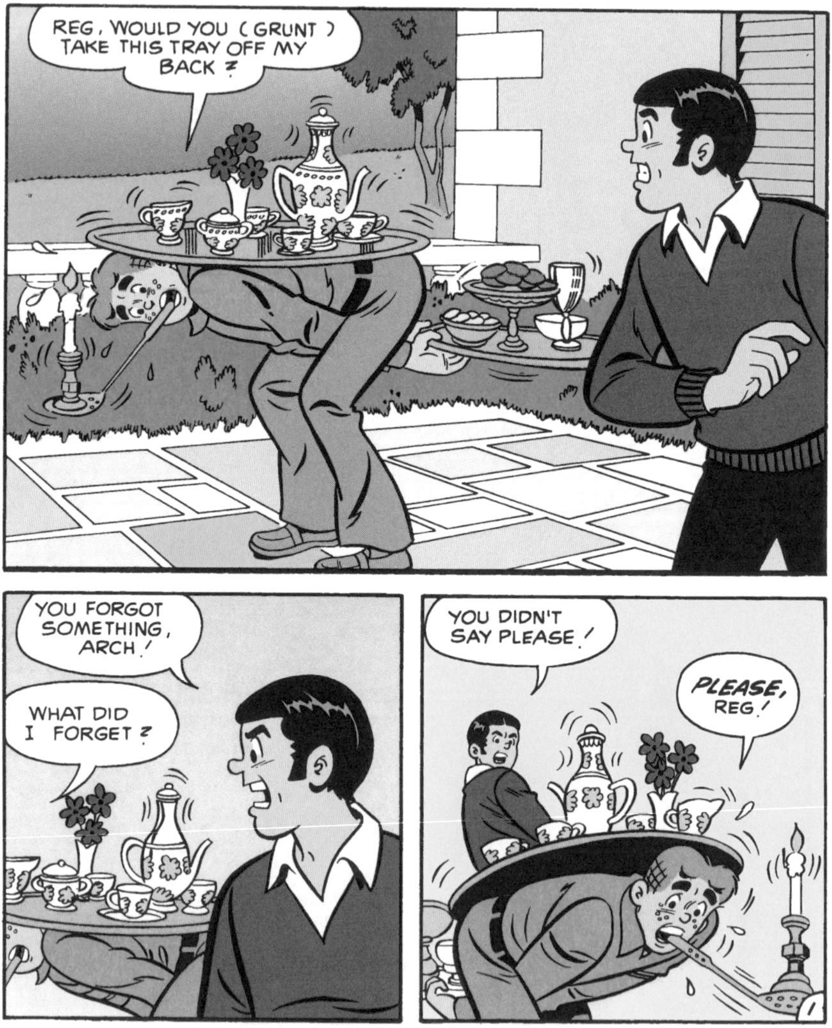
REG, WOULD YOU (GRUNT) TAKE THIS TRAY OFF MY BACK?
YOU FORGOT SOMETHING, ARCH!
WHAT DID I FORGET?
YOU DIDN'T SAY PLEASE!
PLEASE, REG!

Story & Pencils: Al Hartley Inks & Letters: Jon D'Agostino

Originally printed in REGGIE AND ME #51, OCTOBER 1971

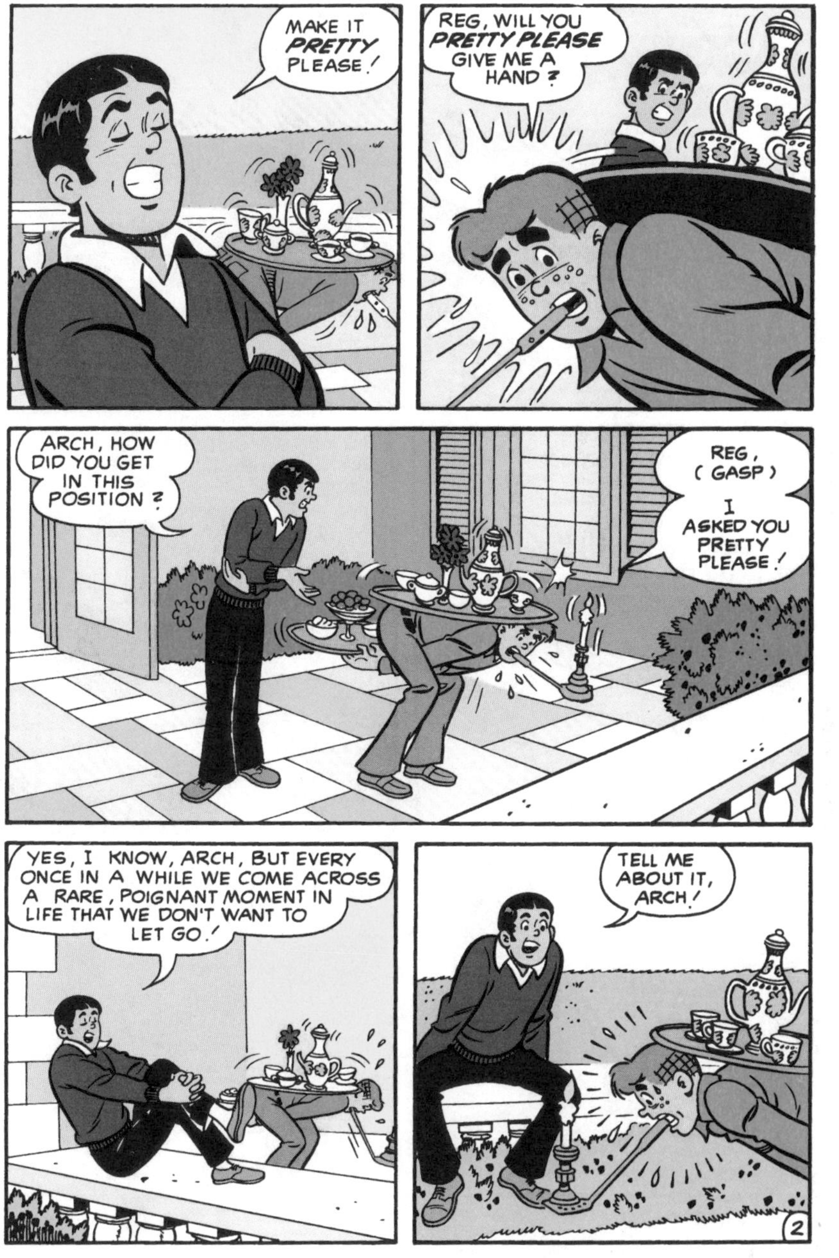
MAKE IT PRETTY PLEASE!
REG, WILL YOU PRETTY PLEASE GIVE ME A HAND?
ARCH, HOW DID YOU GET IN THIS POSITION?
REG, (GASP)
I ASKED YOU PRETTY PLEASE!
YES, I KNOW, ARCH, BUT EVERY ONCE IN A WHILE WE COME ACROSS A RARE, POIGNANT MOMENT IN LIFE THAT WE DON'T WANT TO LET GO!
TELL ME ABOUT IT, ARCH!
2

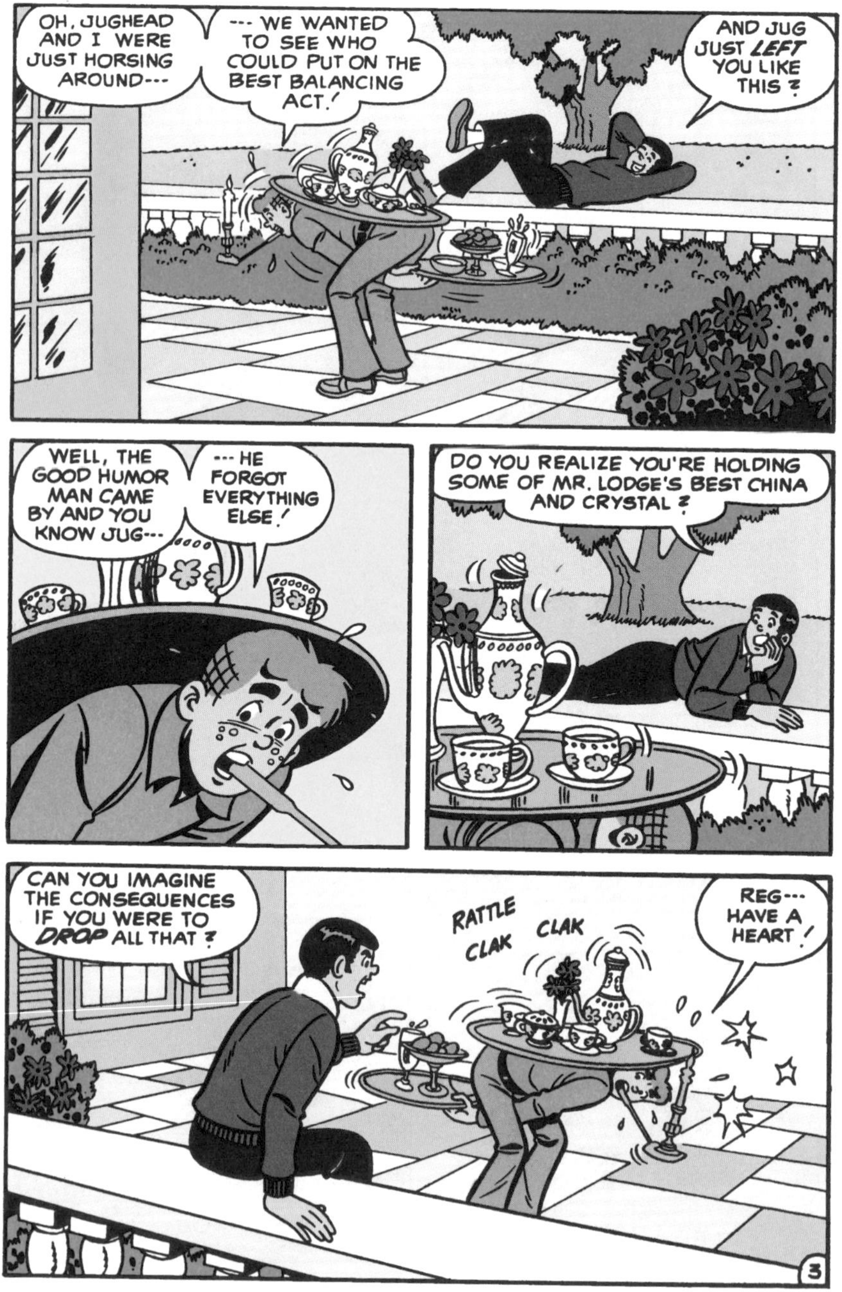
OH, JUGHEAD AND I WERE JUST HORSING AROUND---
--- WE WANTED TO SEE WHO COULD PUT ON THE BEST BALANCING ACT!
AND JUG JUST LEFT YOU LIKE THIS?
WELL, THE GOOD HUMOR MAN CAME BY AND YOU KNOW JUG---
--- HE FORGOT EVERYTHING ELSE!
DO YOU REALIZE YOU'RE HOLDING SOME OF MR. LODGE'S BEST CHINA AND CRYSTAL?
CAN YOU IMAGINE THE CONSEQUENCES IF YOU WERE TO DROP ALL THAT?
RATTLE
CLAK
CLAK
REG--- HAVE A HEART!
3

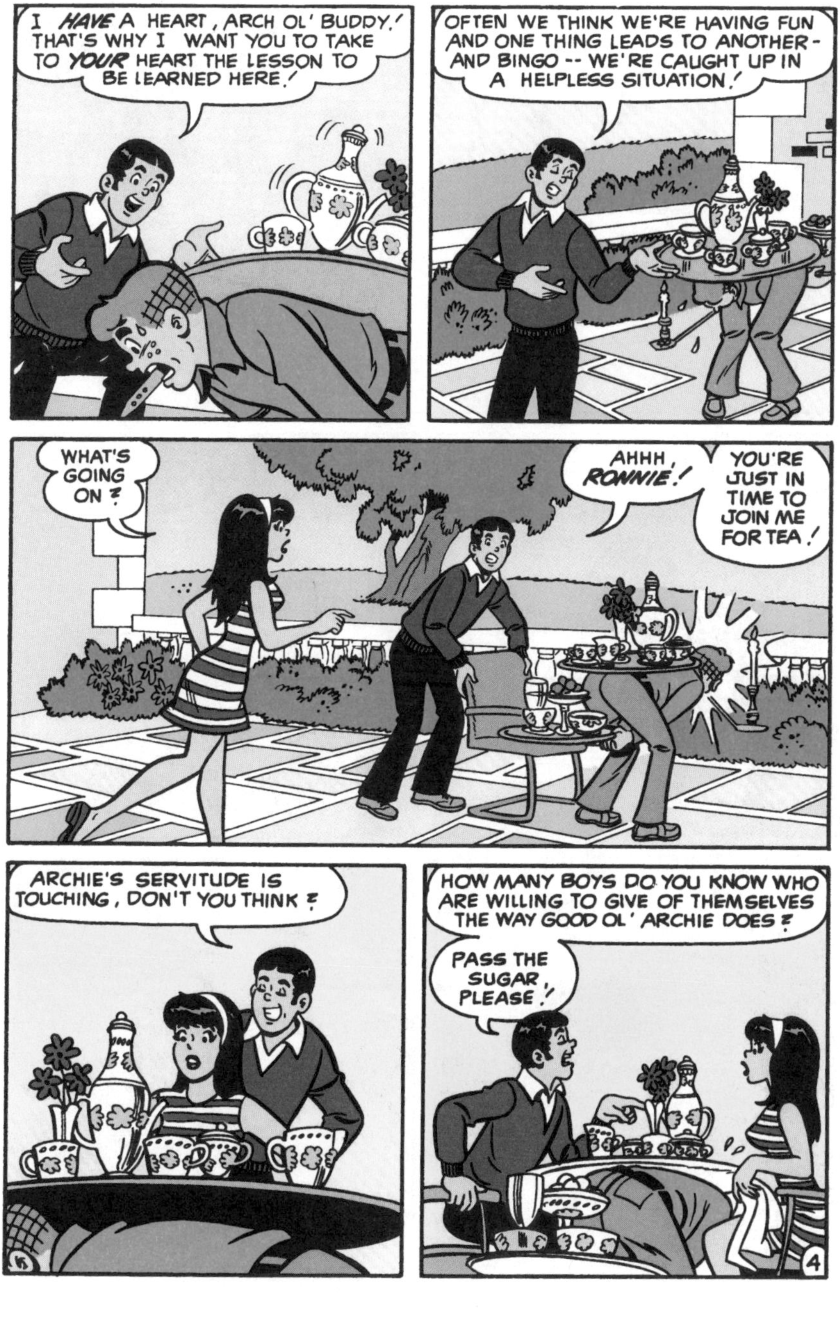
I HAVE A HEART, ARCH OL' BUDDY! THAT'S WHY I WANT YOU TO TAKE TO YOUR HEART THE LESSON TO BE LEARNED HERE!
OFTEN WE THINK WE'RE HAVING FUN AND ONE THING LEADS TO ANOTHER- AND BINGO -- WE'RE CAUGHT UP IN A HELPLESS SITUATION!
WHAT'S GOING ON ?
AHHH, RONNIE!
YOU'RE JUST IN TIME TO JOIN ME FOR TEA!
ARCHIE'S SERVITUDE IS TOUCHING, DON'T YOU THINK ?
HOW MANY BOYS DO YOU KNOW WHO ARE WILLING TO GIVE OF THEMSELVES THE WAY GOOD OL' ARCHIE DOES ?
PASS THE SUGAR, PLEASE!
5
4

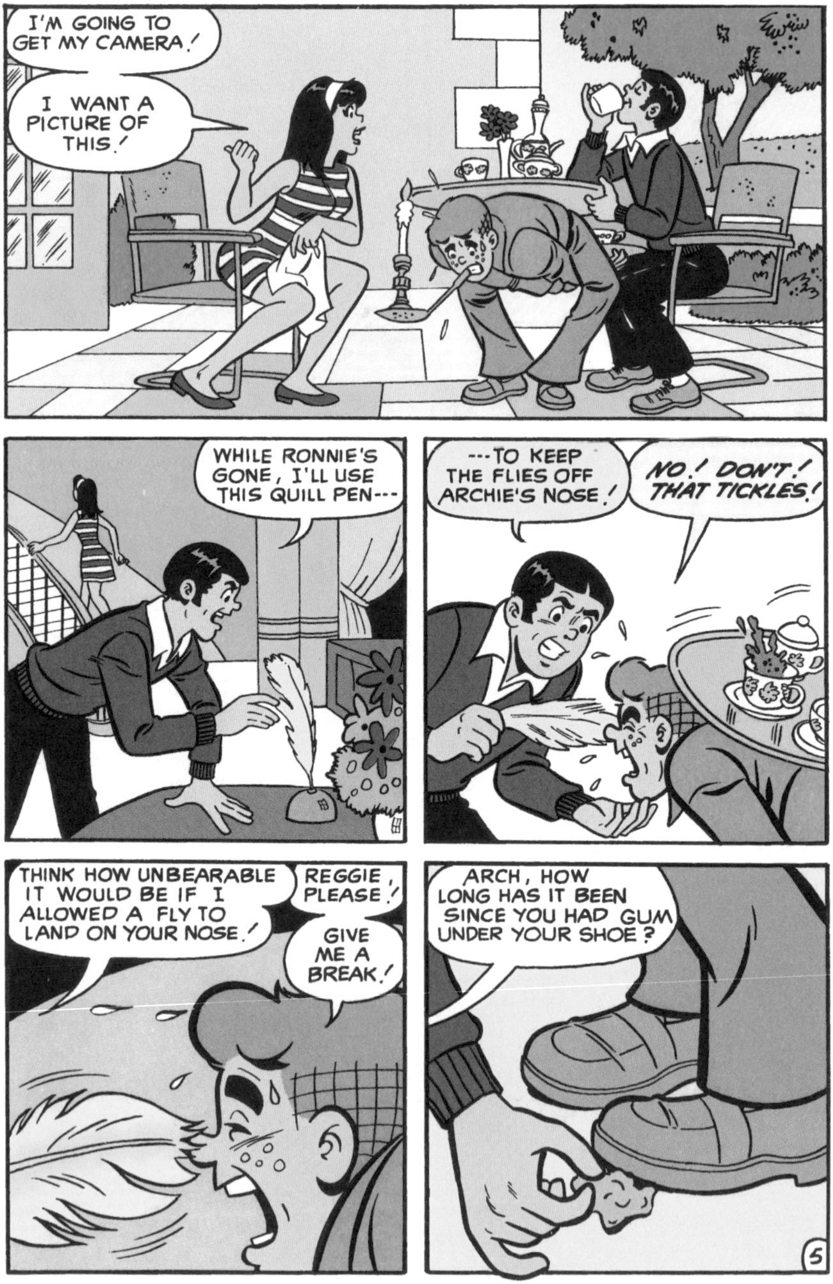
I'M GOING TO GET MY CAMERA!
I WANT A PICTURE OF THIS!
WHILE RONNIE'S GONE, I'LL USE THIS QUILL PEN---
---TO KEEP THE FLIES OFF ARCHIE'S NOSE!
NO! DON'T! THAT TICKLES!
THINK HOW UNBEARABLE IT WOULD BE IF I ALLOWED A FLY TO LAND ON YOUR NOSE!
REGGIE, PLEASE!
GIVE ME A BREAK!
ARCH, HOW LONG HAS IT BEEN SINCE YOU HAD GUM UNDER YOUR SHOE?
5

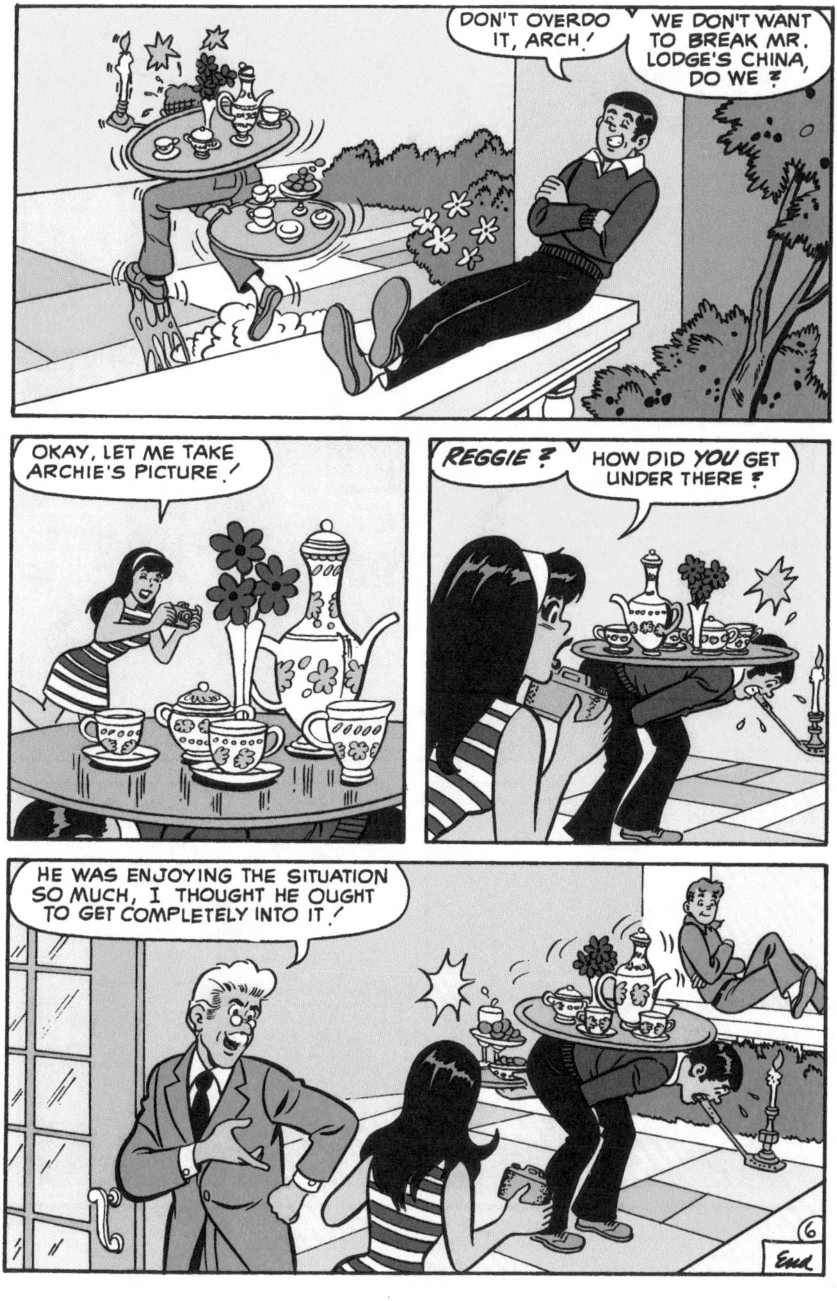
DON'T OVERDO IT, ARCH!
WE DON'T WANT TO BREAK MR. LODGE'S CHINA, DO WE?
OKAY, LET ME TAKE ARCHIE'S PICTURE!
REGGIE?
HOW DID YOU GET UNDER THERE?
HE WAS ENJOYING THE SITUATION SO MUCH, I THOUGHT HE OUGHT TO GET COMPLETELY INTO IT!
6
End

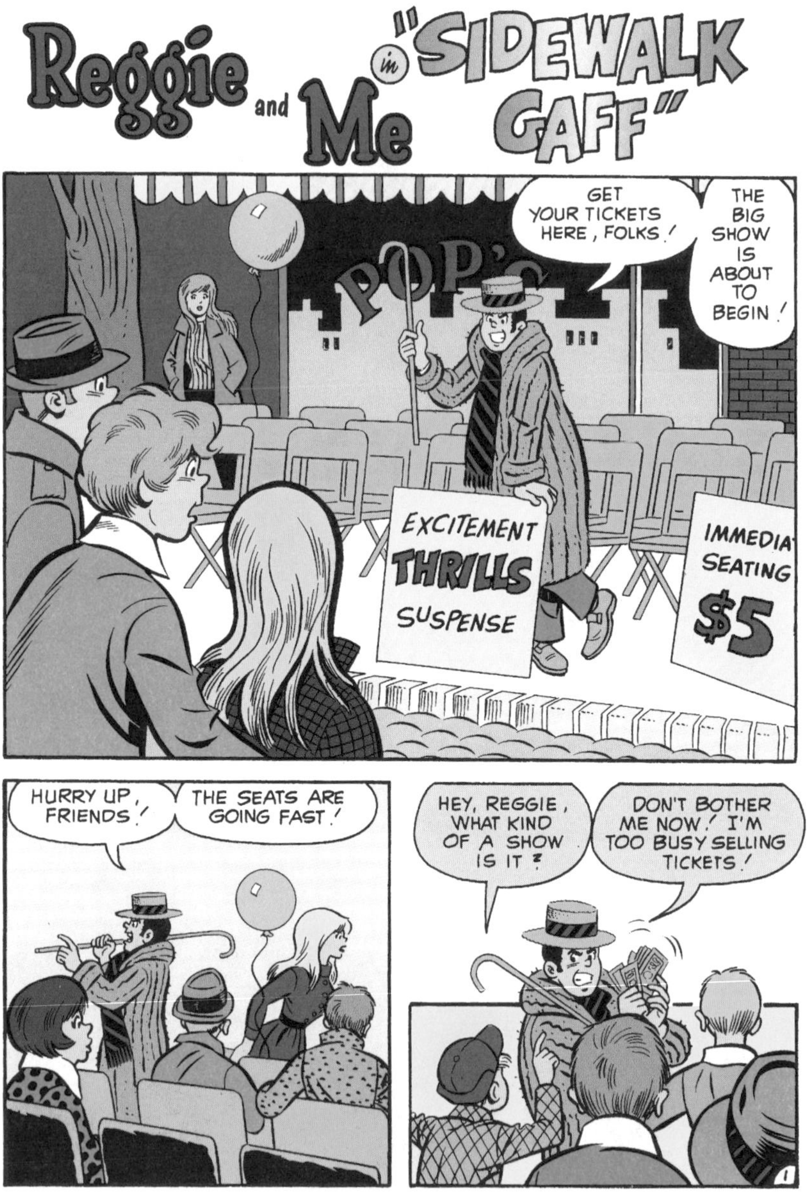

Reggie and Me in "SIDEWALK GAFF"
GET YOUR TICKETS HERE, FOLKS!
THE BIG SHOW IS ABOUT TO BEGIN!
POP'S
EXCITEMENT THRILLS SUSPENSE
IMMEDIA SEATING $5
HURRY UP, FRIENDS!
THE SEATS ARE GOING FAST!
HEY, REGGIE, WHAT KIND OF A SHOW IS IT?
DON'T BOTHER ME NOW! I'M TOO BUSY SELLING TICKETS!
1

Story & Pencils: Al Hartley

Inks: Jon D'Agostino Letters: Bill Yoshida Colors: Barry Grossman

Originally printed in REGGIE AND ME #53, JANUARY 1972

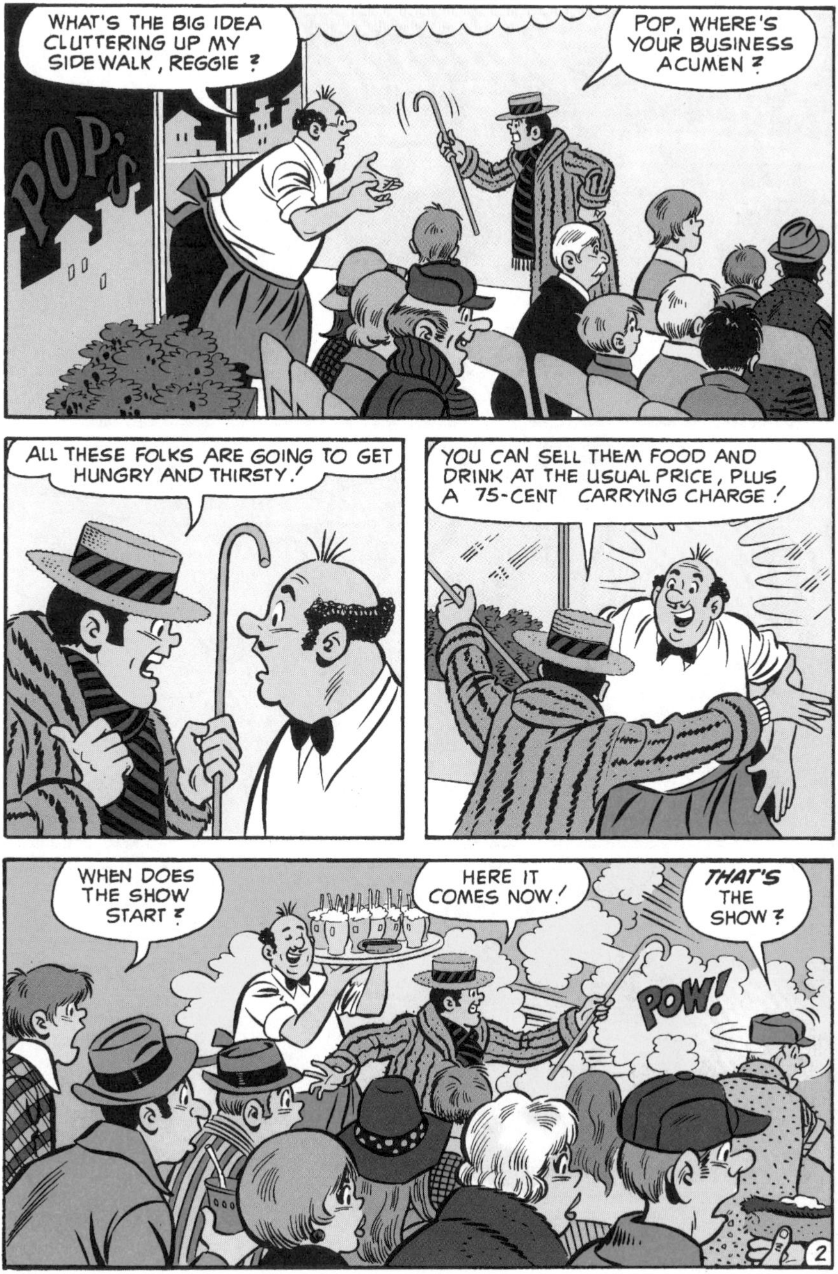
WHAT'S THE BIG IDEA CLUTTERING UP MY SIDEWALK, REGGIE ?
POP, WHERE'S YOUR BUSINESS ACUMEN ?
POP'S
ALL THESE FOLKS ARE GOING TO GET HUNGRY AND THIRSTY!
YOU CAN SELL THEM FOOD AND DRINK AT THE USUAL PRICE, PLUS A 75-CENT CARRYING CHARGE!
WHEN DOES THE SHOW START ?
HERE IT COMES NOW!
THAT'S THE SHOW ?
POW!
2

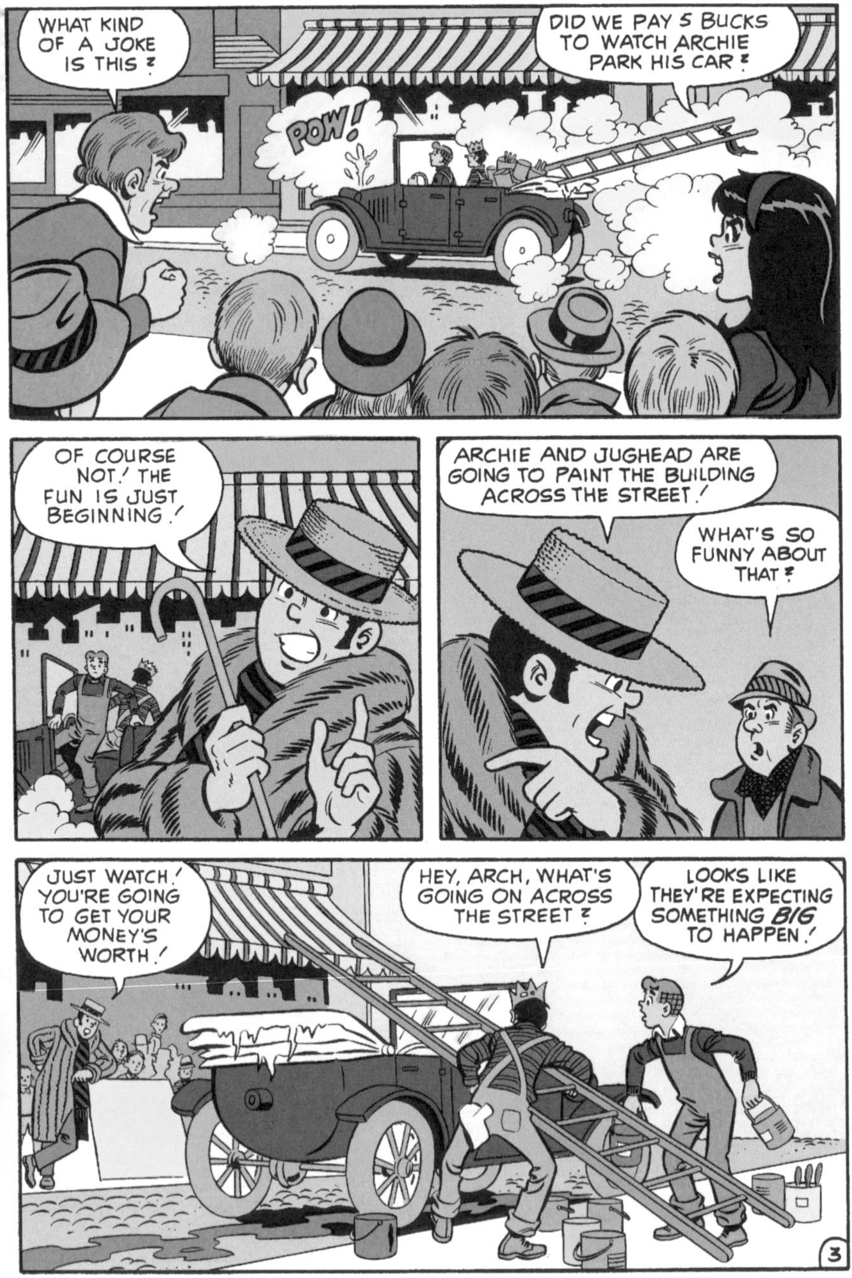
WHAT KIND OF A JOKE IS THIS ?
DID WE PAY 5 BUCKS TO WATCH ARCHIE PARK HIS CAR ?
POW!
OF COURSE NOT! THE FUN IS JUST BEGINNING!
ARCHIE AND JUGHEAD ARE GOING TO PAINT THE BUILDING ACROSS THE STREET!
WHAT'S SO FUNNY ABOUT THAT ?
JUST WATCH! YOU'RE GOING TO GET YOUR MONEY'S WORTH!
HEY, ARCH, WHAT'S GOING ON ACROSS THE STREET ?
LOOKS LIKE THEY'RE EXPECTING SOMETHING BIG TO HAPPEN!
3

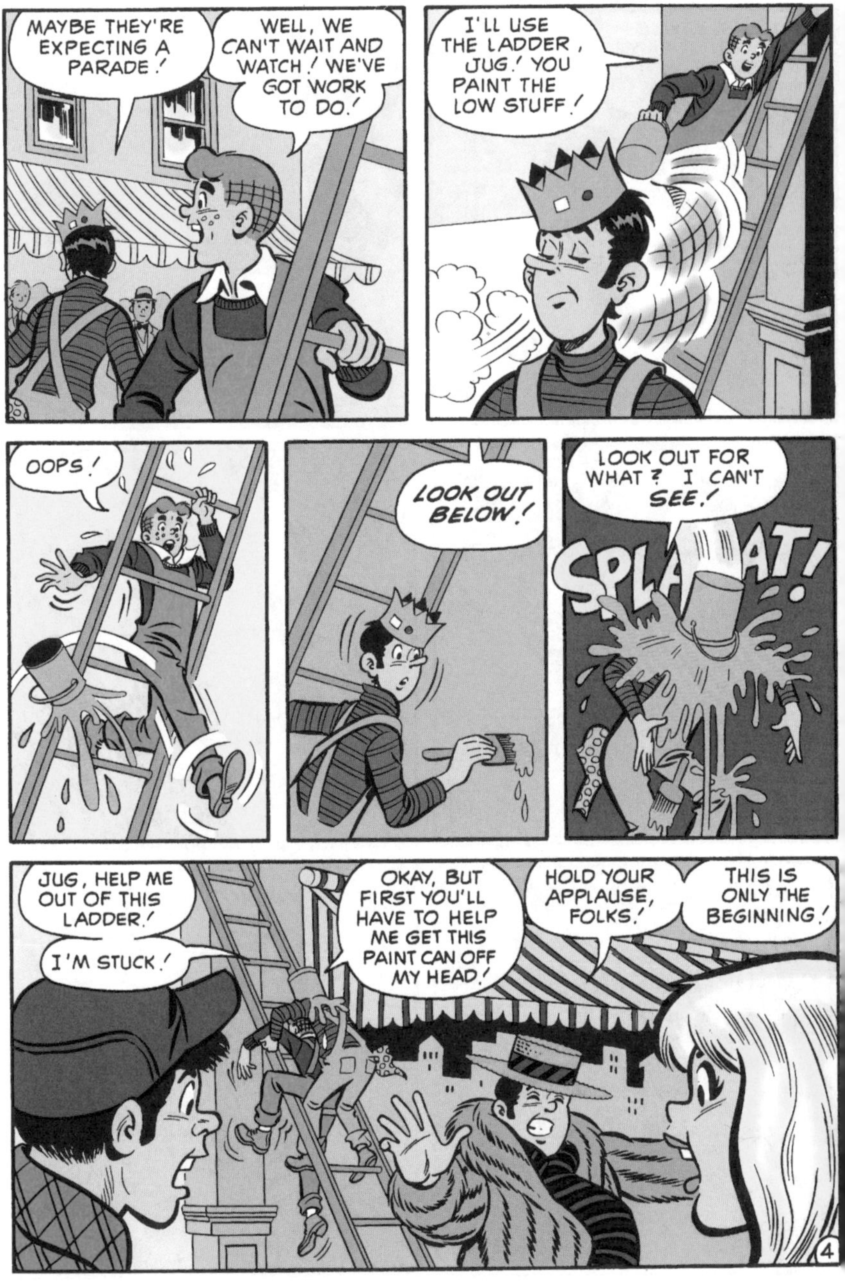
MAYBE THEY'RE EXPECTING A PARADE!
WELL, WE CAN'T WAIT AND WATCH! WE'VE GOT WORK TO DO!
I'LL USE THE LADDER, JUG! YOU PAINT THE LOW STUFF!
OOPS!
LOOK OUT BELOW!
LOOK OUT FOR WHAT? I CAN'T SEE!
SPLAT!
JUG, HELP ME OUT OF THIS LADDER!
I'M STUCK!
OKAY, BUT FIRST YOU'LL HAVE TO HELP ME GET THIS PAINT CAN OFF MY HEAD!
HOLD YOUR APPLAUSE, FOLKS!
THIS IS ONLY THE BEGINNING!
4

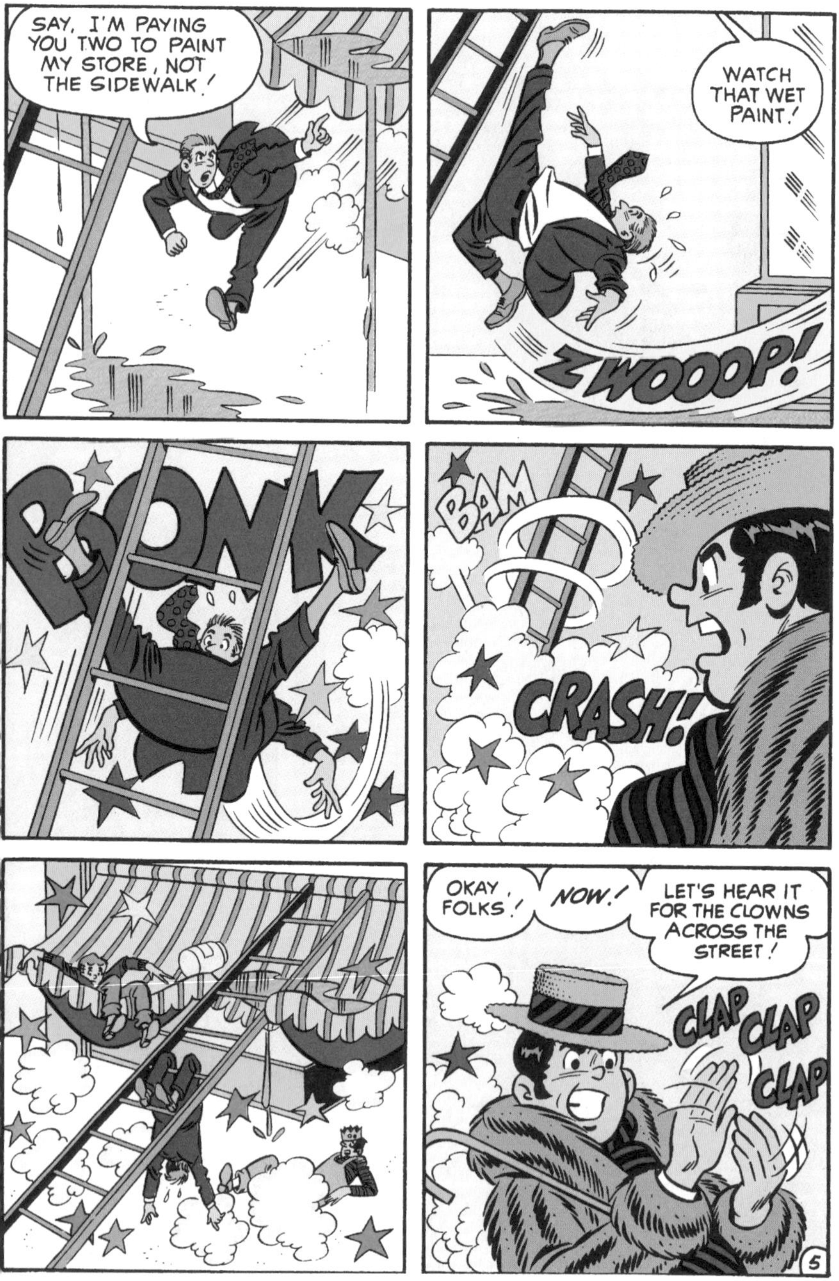
SAY, I'M PAYING YOU TWO TO PAINT MY STORE, NOT THE SIDEWALK!
WATCH THAT WET PAINT!
ZWOOOP!
BONK
BAM
CRASH!
OKAY, FOLKS!
NOW!
LET'S HEAR IT FOR THE CLOWNS ACROSS THE STREET!
CLAP CLAP CLAP
5

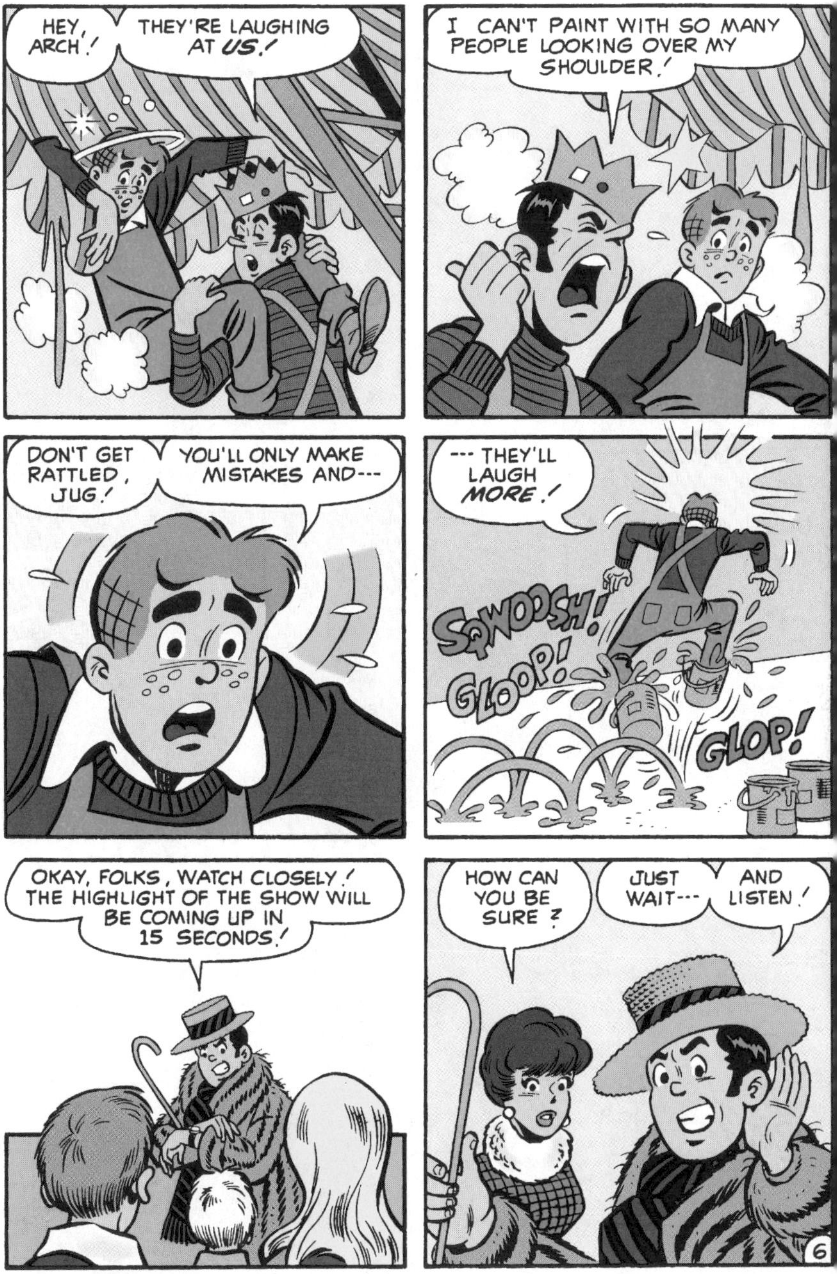
HEY, ARCH!
THEY'RE LAUGHING AT US!
I CAN'T PAINT WITH SO MANY PEOPLE LOOKING OVER MY SHOULDER!
DON'T GET RATTLED, JUG!
YOU'LL ONLY MAKE MISTAKES AND---
--- THEY'LL LAUGH MORE!
SQWOOSH!
GLOOP!
GLOP!
OKAY, FOLKS, WATCH CLOSELY! THE HIGHLIGHT OF THE SHOW WILL BE COMING UP IN 15 SECONDS!
HOW CAN YOU BE SURE?
JUST WAIT---
AND LISTEN!
6

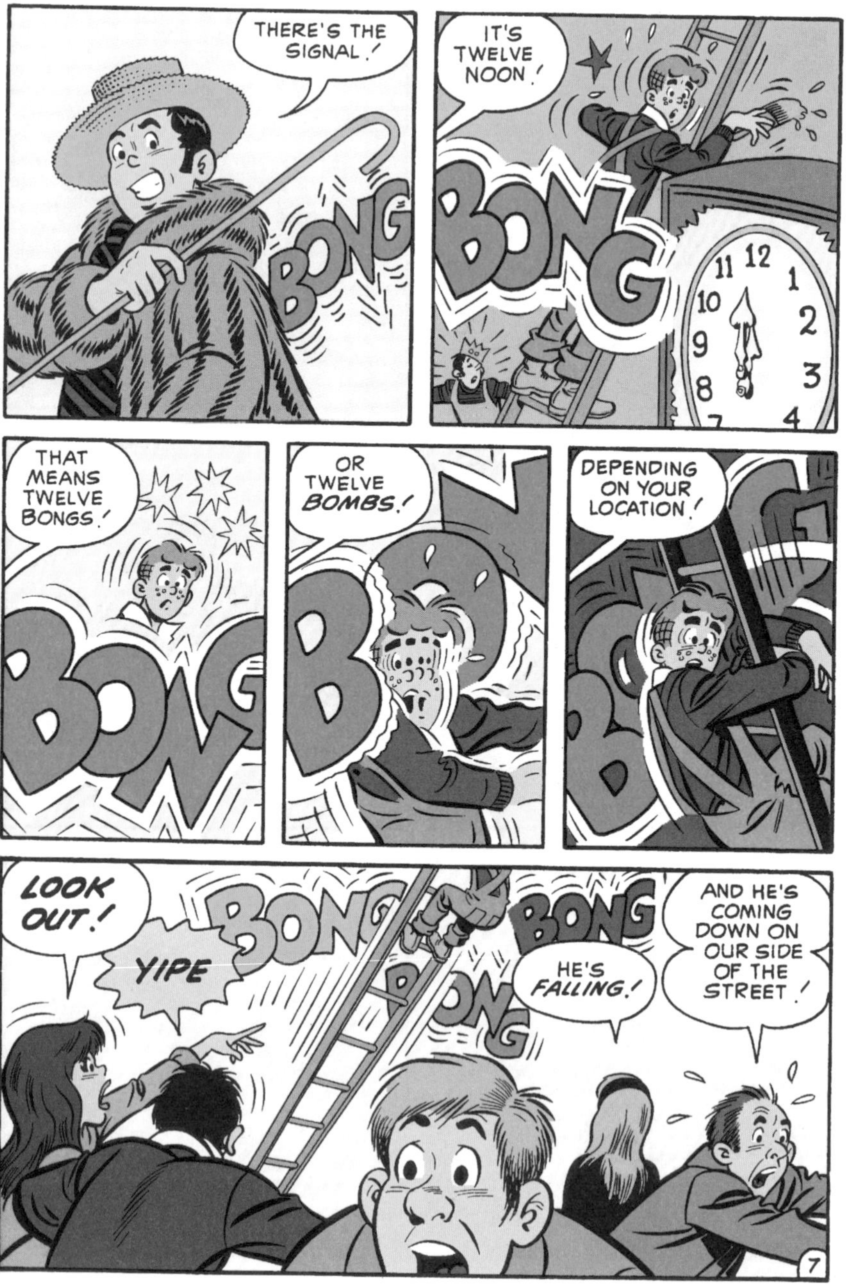
THERE'S THE SIGNAL!
BONG
IT'S TWELVE NOON!
BONG
THAT MEANS TWELVE BONGS!
BONG
OR TWELVE BOMBS!
DEPENDING ON YOUR LOCATION!
LOOK OUT!
YIPE
BONG
BONG
BONG
HE'S FALLING!
AND HE'S COMING DOWN ON OUR SIDE OF THE STREET!
7

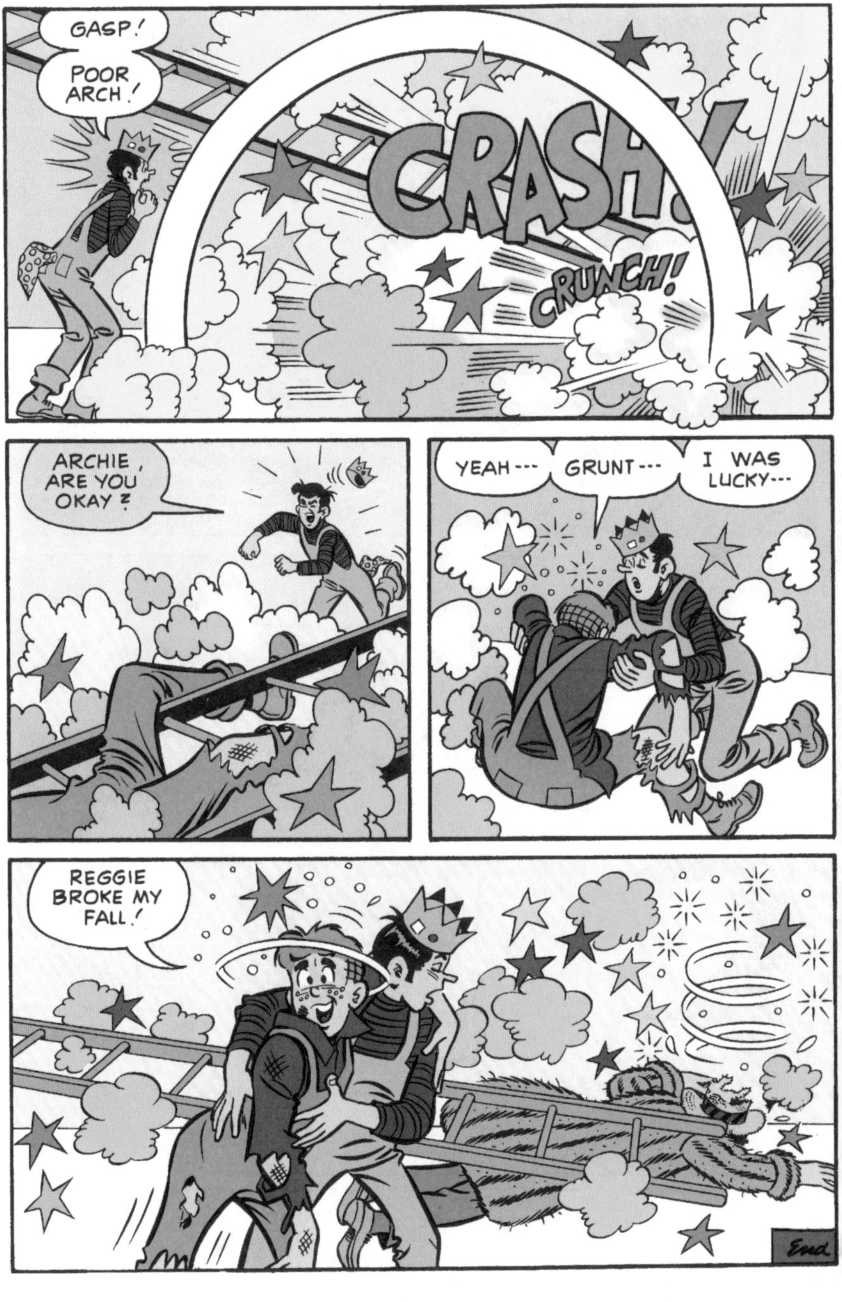
GASP!
POOR ARCH!
CRASH!
CRUNCH!
ARCHIE, ARE YOU OKAY?
YEAH ---
GRUNT ---
I WAS LUCKY---
REGGIE BROKE MY FALL!
End

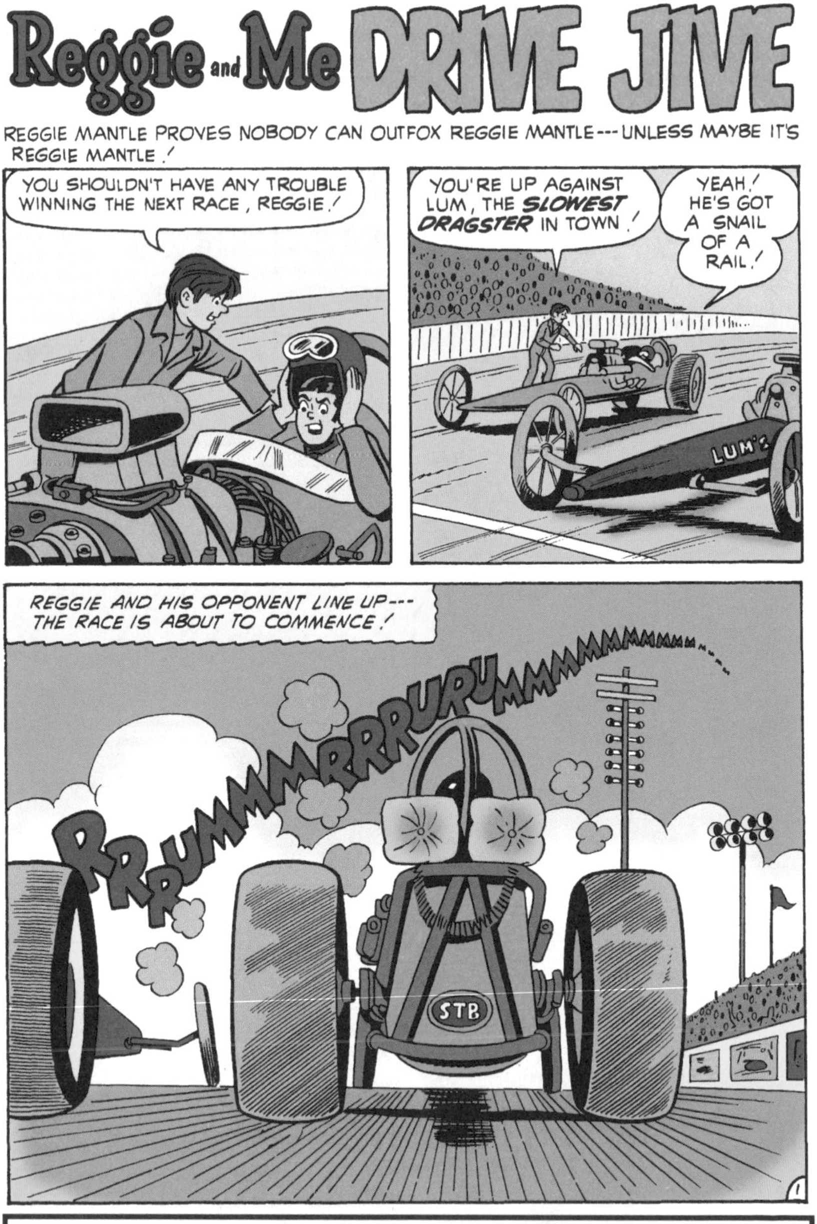

Reggie and Me DRIVE JIVE
REGGIE MANTLE PROVES NOBODY CAN OUTFOX REGGIE MANTLE---UNLESS MAYBE IT'S REGGIE MANTLE!
YOU SHOULDN'T HAVE ANY TROUBLE WINNING THE NEXT RACE, REGGIE!
YOU'RE UP AGAINST LUM, THE SLOWEST DRAGSTER IN TOWN!
YEAH! HE'S GOT A SNAIL OF A RAIL!
LUM'S
REGGIE AND HIS OPPONENT LINE UP--- THE RACE IS ABOUT TO COMMENCE!
RRRUMMMMRRRRURUMMMMMMMMMMMMM...
STB

Story: George Gladir Pencils: Al Hartley
Inks: Jon D'Agostino Letters: Bill Yoshida

Originally printed in REGGIE AND ME #56, JULY 1972

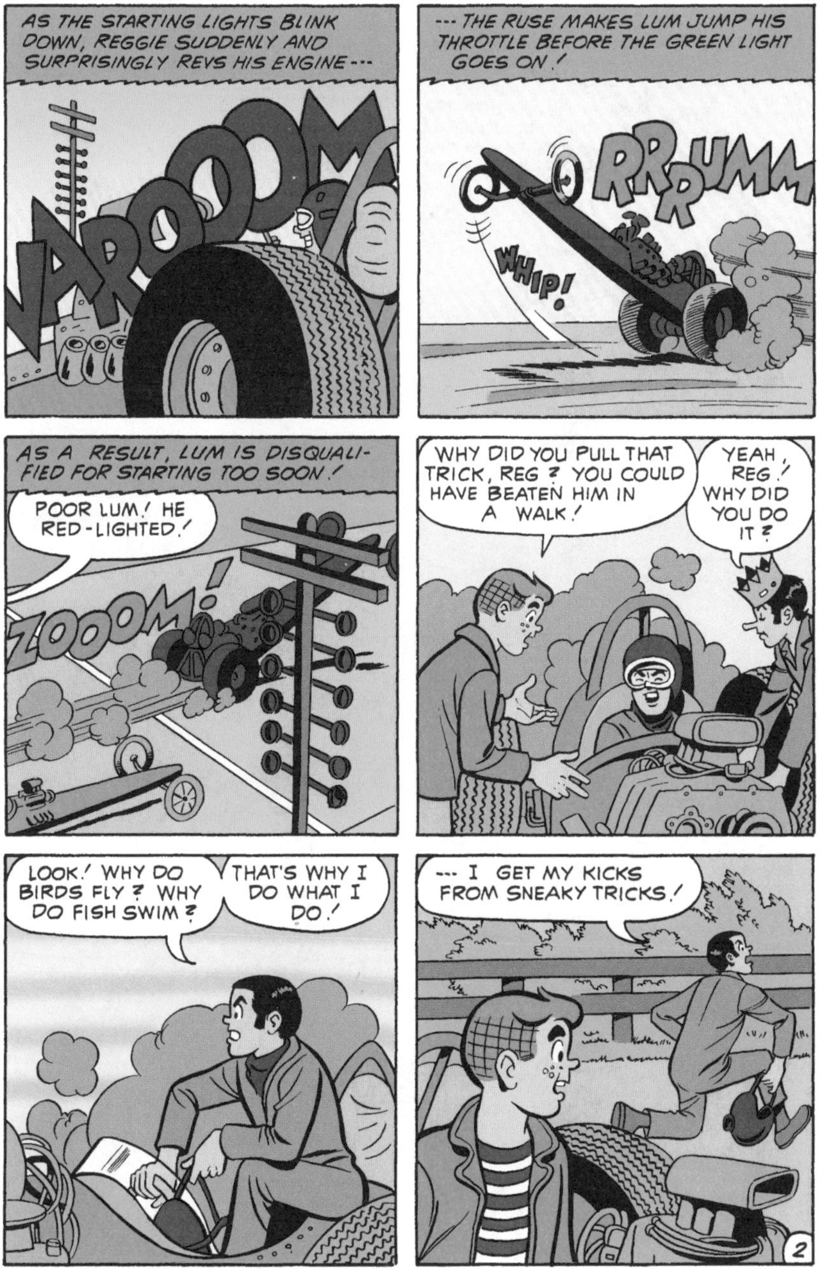
AS THE STARTING LIGHTS BLINK DOWN, REGGIE SUDDENLY AND SURPRISINGLY REVS HIS ENGINE---
VAROOOOM
--- THE RUSE MAKES LUM JUMP HIS THROTTLE BEFORE THE GREEN LIGHT GOES ON!
RRRUMM
WHIP!
AS A RESULT, LUM IS DISQUALIFIED FOR STARTING TOO SOON!
POOR LUM! HE RED-LIGHTED!
ZOOOM!
WHY DID YOU PULL THAT TRICK, REG? YOU COULD HAVE BEATEN HIM IN A WALK!
YEAH, REG! WHY DID YOU DO IT?
LOOK! WHY DO BIRDS FLY? WHY DO FISH SWIM?
THAT'S WHY I DO WHAT I DO!
--- I GET MY KICKS FROM SNEAKY TRICKS!
2

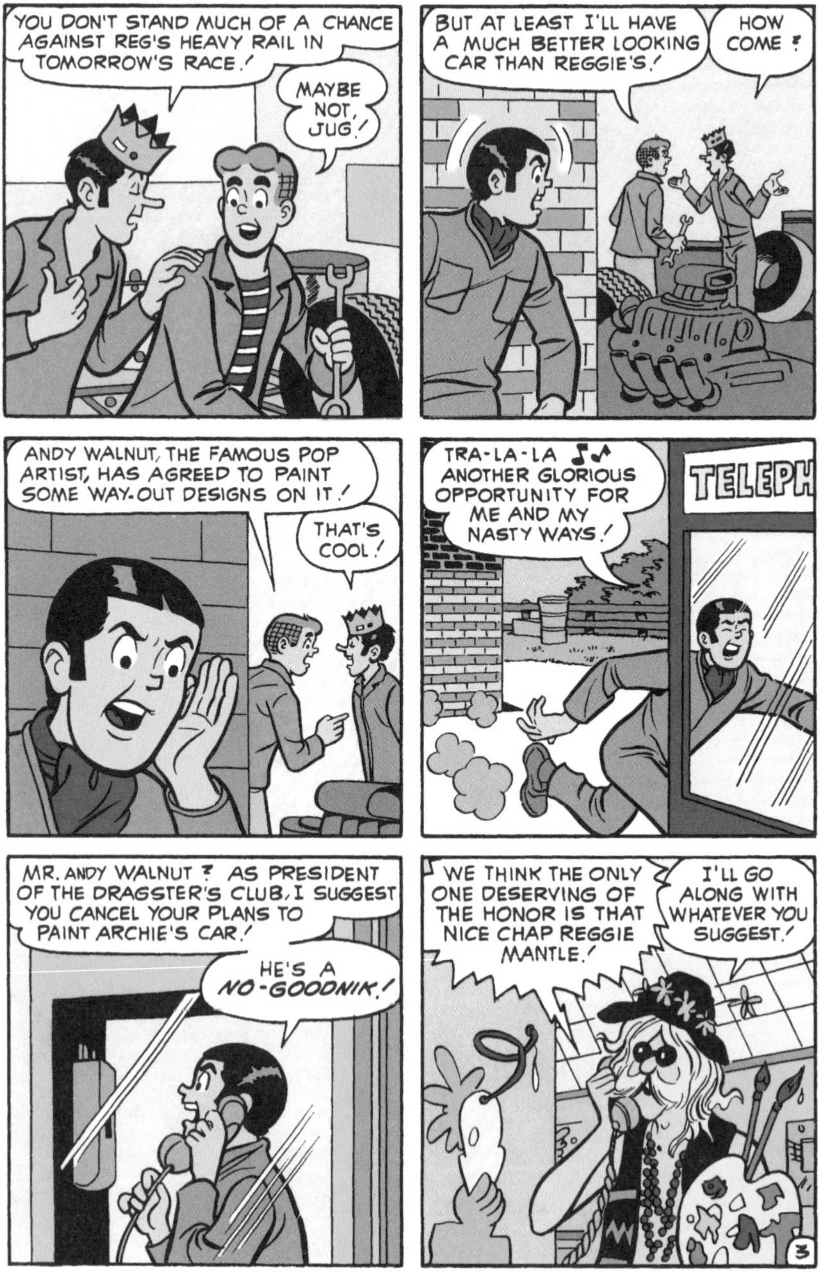

YOU DON'T STAND MUCH OF A CHANCE AGAINST REG'S HEAVY RAIL IN TOMORROW'S RACE!
MAYBE NOT, JUG!
BUT AT LEAST I'LL HAVE A MUCH BETTER LOOKING CAR THAN REGGIE'S!
HOW COME?
ANDY WALNUT, THE FAMOUS POP ARTIST, HAS AGREED TO PAINT SOME WAY-OUT DESIGNS ON IT!
THAT'S COOL!
TRA-LA-LA ANOTHER GLORIOUS OPPORTUNITY FOR ME AND MY NASTY WAYS!
TELEPH
MR. ANDY WALNUT? AS PRESIDENT OF THE DRAGSTER'S CLUB, I SUGGEST YOU CANCEL YOUR PLANS TO PAINT ARCHIE'S CAR!
HE'S A NO-GOODNIK!
WE THINK THE ONLY ONE DESERVING OF THE HONOR IS THAT NICE CHAP REGGIE MANTLE!
I'LL GO ALONG WITH WHATEVER YOU SUGGEST!
3

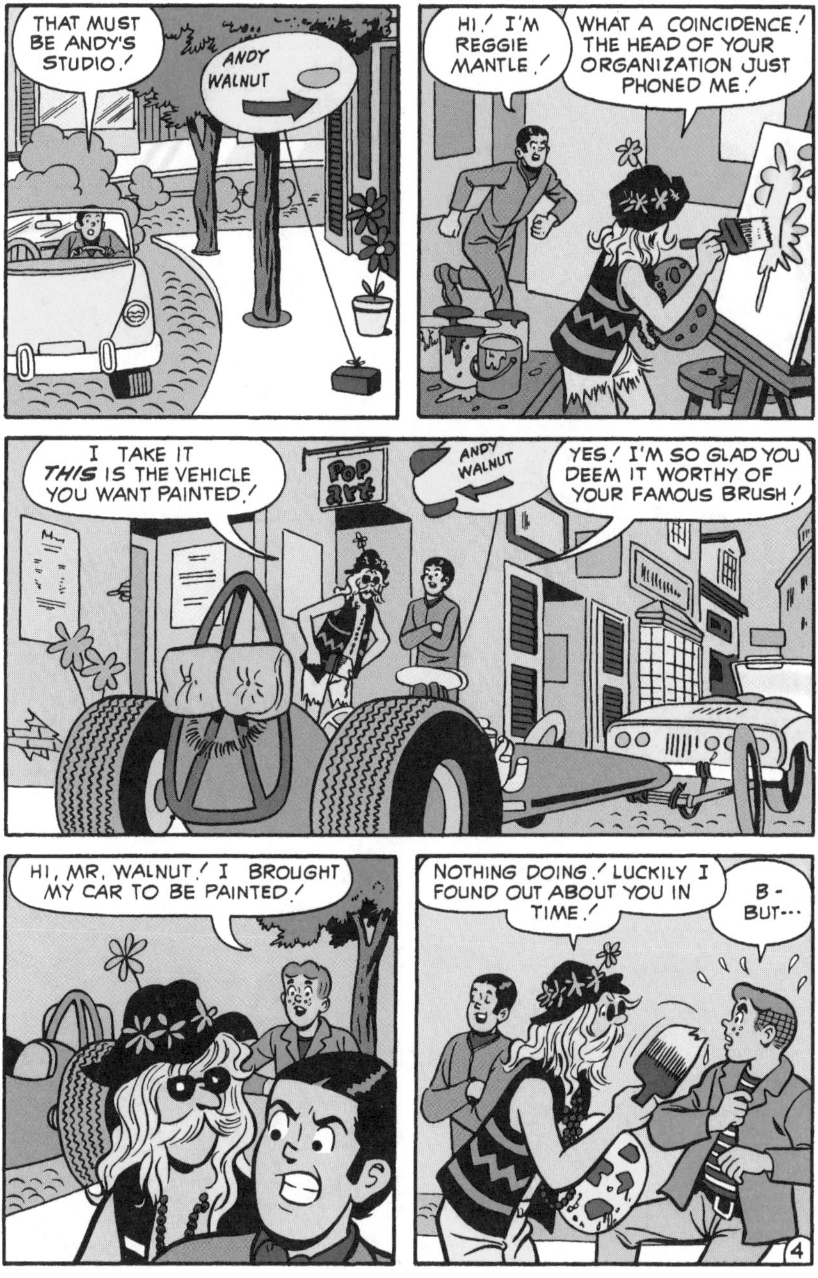
THAT MUST BE ANDY'S STUDIO.!
ANDY WALNUT
HI.! I'M REGGIE MANTLE.!
WHAT A COINCIDENCE.! THE HEAD OF YOUR ORGANIZATION JUST PHONED ME.!
I TAKE IT THIS IS THE VEHICLE YOU WANT PAINTED.!
POP ART
ANDY WALNUT
YES.! I'M SO GLAD YOU DEEM IT WORTHY OF YOUR FAMOUS BRUSH.!
HI, MR. WALNUT.! I BROUGHT MY CAR TO BE PAINTED.!
NOTHING DOING.! LUCKILY I FOUND OUT ABOUT YOU IN TIME.!
B-BUT...
4

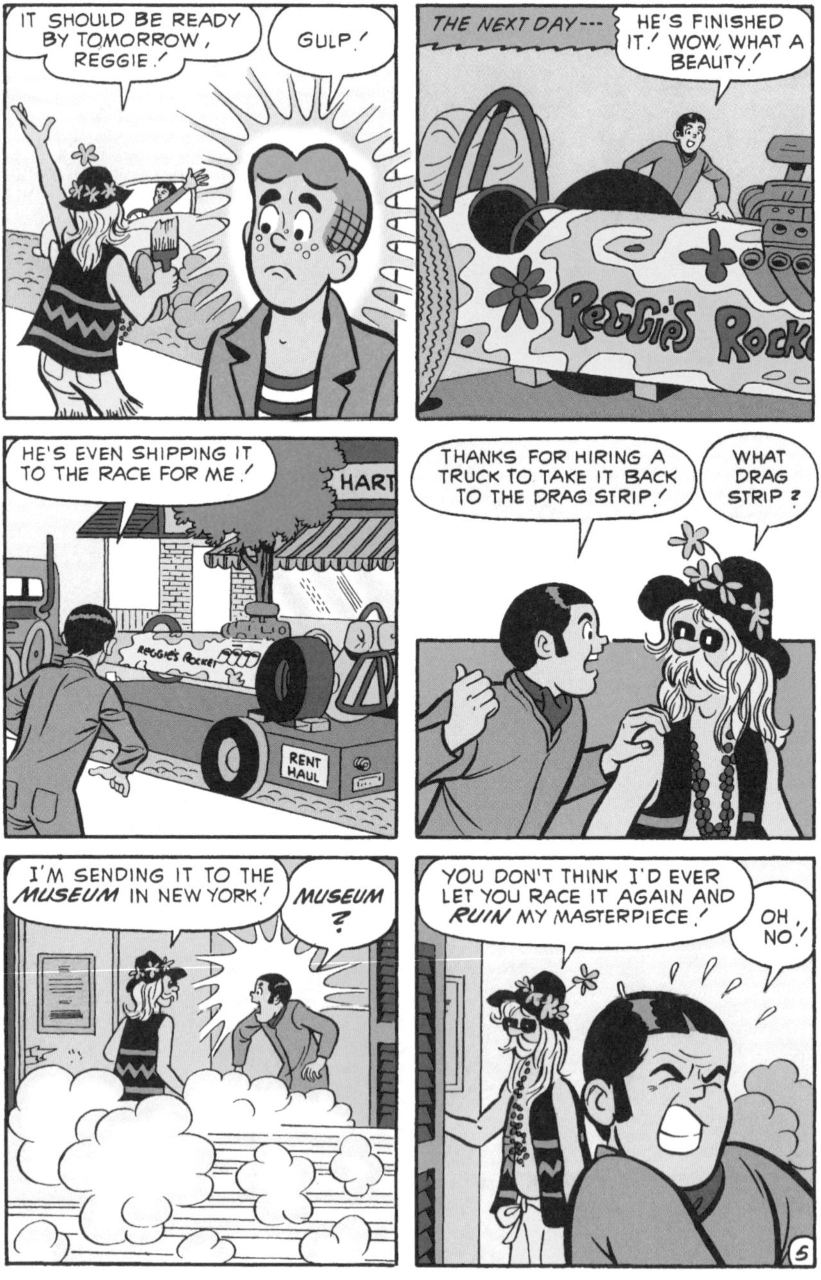
IT SHOULD BE READY BY TOMORROW, REGGIE!
GULP!
THE NEXT DAY---
HE'S FINISHED IT! WOW, WHAT A BEAUTY!
REGGIE'S ROCKET
HE'S EVEN SHIPPING IT TO THE RACE FOR ME!
HART
REGGIE'S ROCKET
RENT HAUL
THANKS FOR HIRING A TRUCK TO TAKE IT BACK TO THE DRAG STRIP!
WHAT DRAG STRIP?
I'M SENDING IT TO THE MUSEUM IN NEW YORK!
MUSEUM?
YOU DON'T THINK I'D EVER LET YOU RACE IT AGAIN AND RUIN MY MASTERPIECE!
OH NO!
5

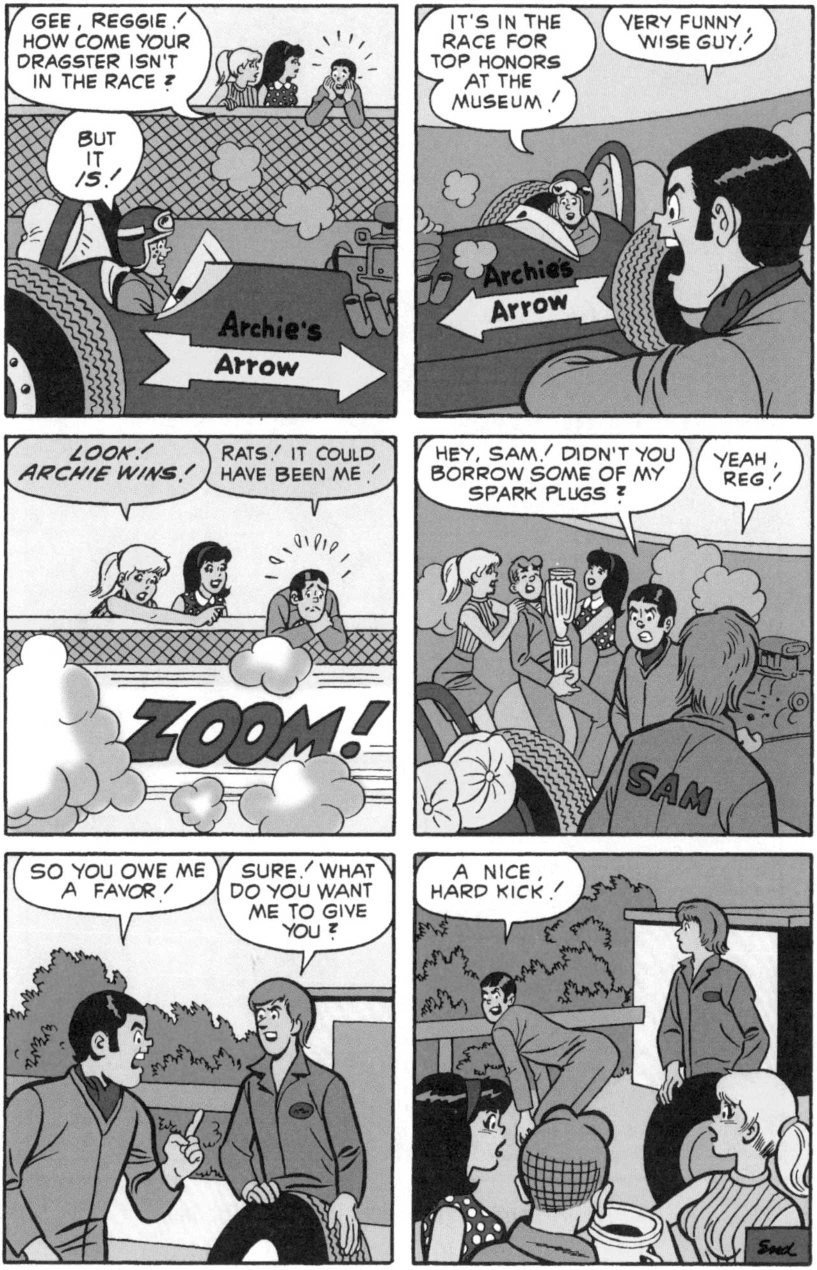
GEE, REGGIE! HOW COME YOUR DRAGSTER ISN'T IN THE RACE?
BUT IT IS!
Archie's Arrow
IT'S IN THE RACE FOR TOP HONORS AT THE MUSEUM!
VERY FUNNY, WISE GUY!
Archie's Arrow
LOOK! ARCHIE WINS!
RATS! IT COULD HAVE BEEN ME!
ZOOM!
HEY, SAM! DIDN'T YOU BORROW SOME OF MY SPARK PLUGS?
YEAH, REG!
SAM
SO YOU OWE ME A FAVOR!
SURE! WHAT DO YOU WANT ME TO GIVE YOU?
A NICE, HARD KICK!

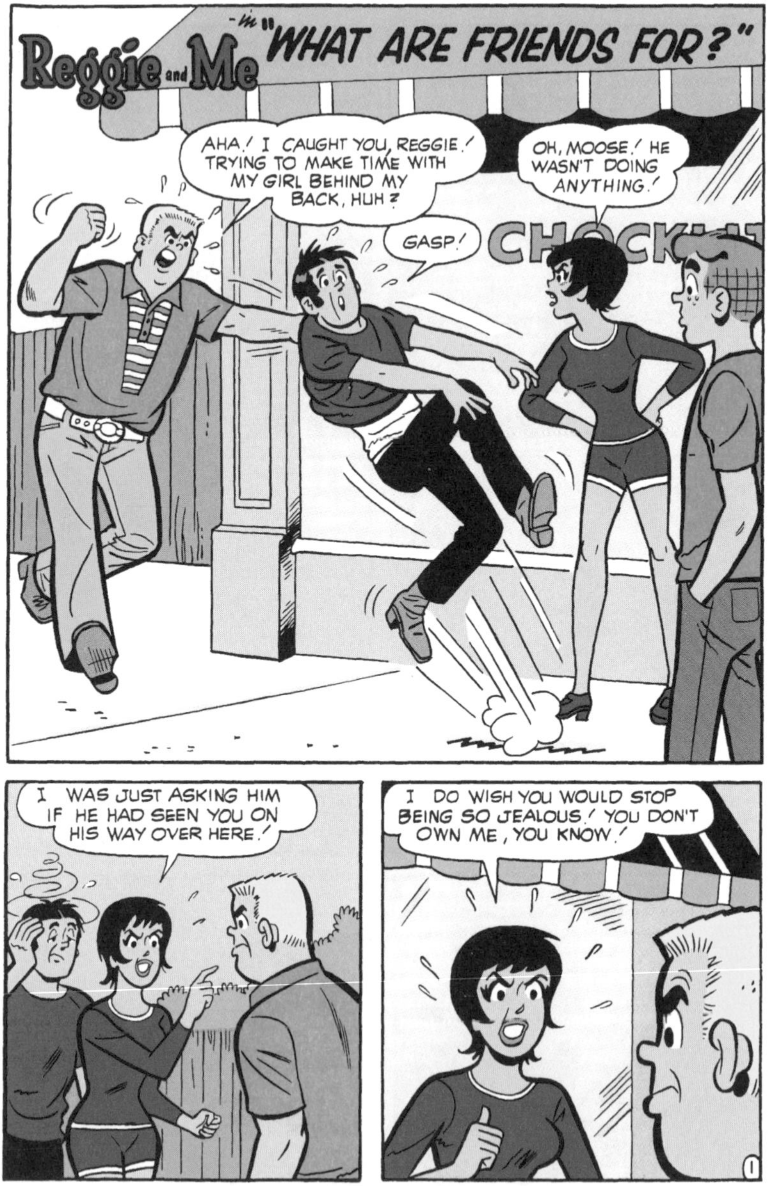
Reggie and Me
-in "WHAT ARE FRIENDS FOR?"
AHA! I CAUGHT YOU, REGGIE! TRYING TO MAKE TIME WITH MY GIRL BEHIND MY BACK, HUH?
OH, MOOSE! HE WASN'T DOING ANYTHING!
GASP!
CHOCK
I WAS JUST ASKING HIM IF HE HAD SEEN YOU ON HIS WAY OVER HERE!
I DO WISH YOU WOULD STOP BEING SO JEALOUS! YOU DON'T OWN ME, YOU KNOW!
1

Story: Frank Doyle Pencils: Bill Vigoda
Inks: Henry Scarpelli Letters: Bill Yoshida

Originally printed in REGGIE AND ME #56, JULY 1972

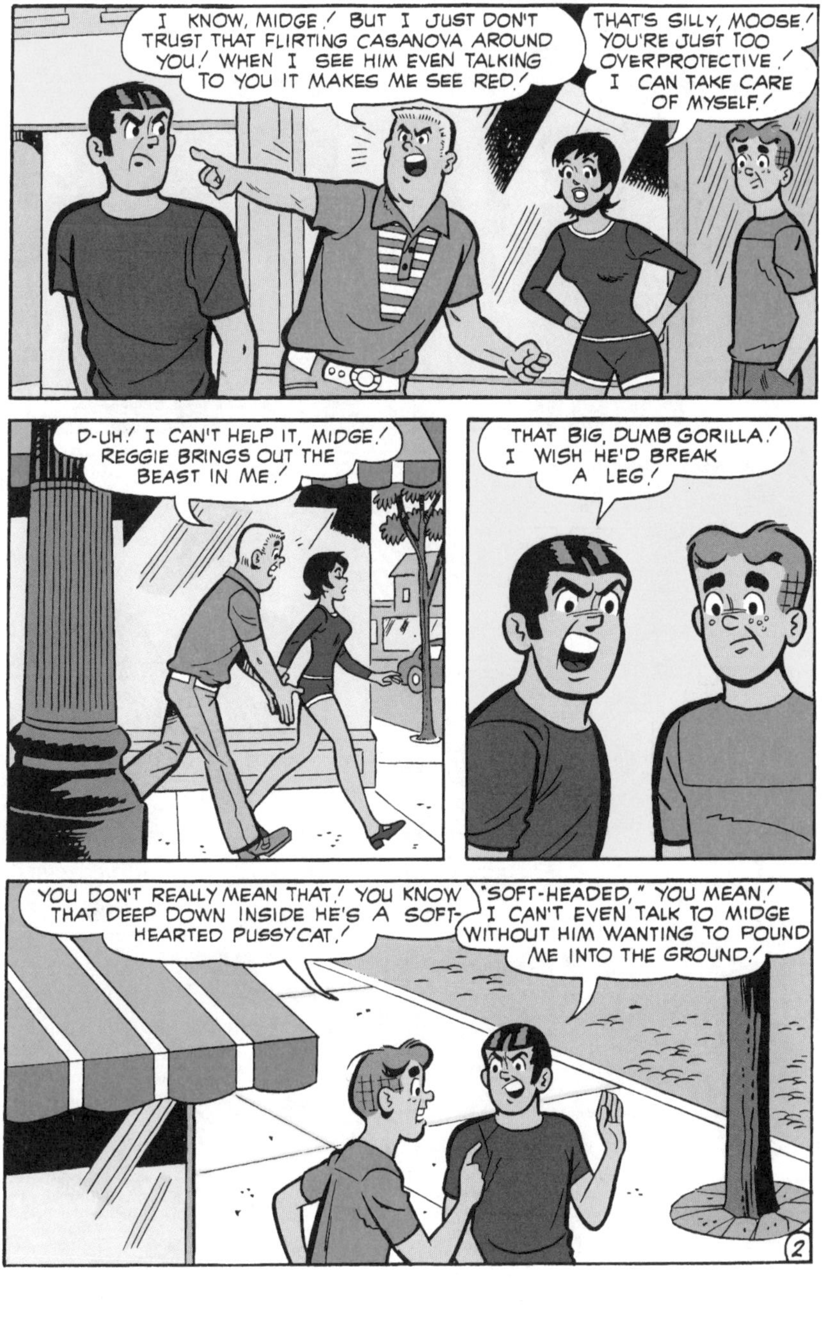
I KNOW, MIDGE! BUT I JUST DON'T TRUST THAT FLIRTING CASANOVA AROUND YOU! WHEN I SEE HIM EVEN TALKING TO YOU IT MAKES ME SEE RED!
THAT'S SILLY, MOOSE! YOU'RE JUST TOO OVERPROTECTIVE! I CAN TAKE CARE OF MYSELF!
D-UH! I CAN'T HELP IT, MIDGE! REGGIE BRINGS OUT THE BEAST IN ME!
THAT BIG, DUMB GORILLA! I WISH HE'D BREAK A LEG!
YOU DON'T REALLY MEAN THAT! YOU KNOW THAT DEEP DOWN INSIDE HE'S A SOFT-HEARTED PUSSYCAT!
"SOFT-HEADED," YOU MEAN! I CAN'T EVEN TALK TO MIDGE WITHOUT HIM WANTING TO POUND ME INTO THE GROUND!
2

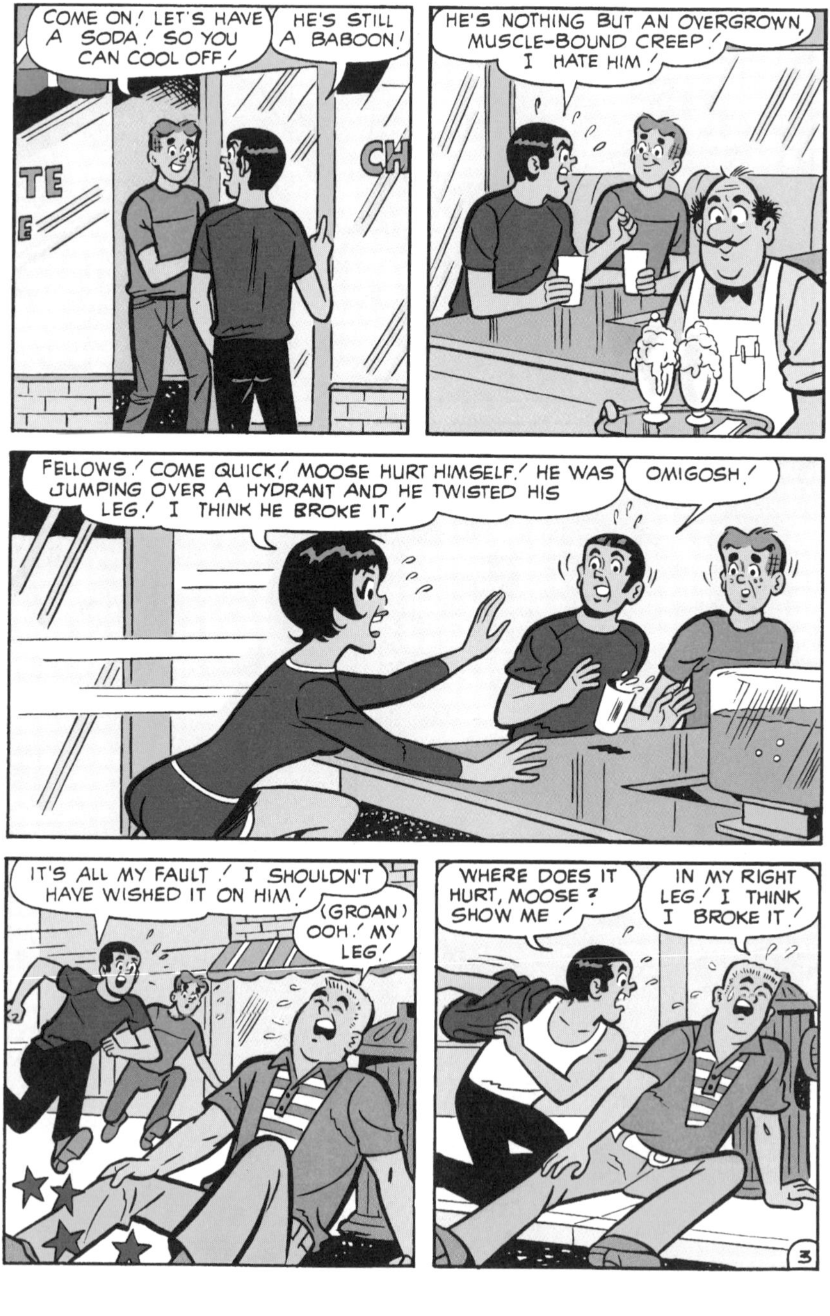
COME ON! LET'S HAVE A SODA! SO YOU CAN COOL OFF!
HE'S STILL A BABOON!
HE'S NOTHING BUT AN OVERGROWN, MUSCLE-BOUND CREEP! I HATE HIM!
FELLOWS! COME QUICK! MOOSE HURT HIMSELF! HE WAS JUMPING OVER A HYDRANT AND HE TWISTED HIS LEG! I THINK HE BROKE IT!
OMIGOSH!
IT'S ALL MY FAULT! I SHOULDN'T HAVE WISHED IT ON HIM!
(GROAN) OOH! MY LEG!
WHERE DOES IT HURT, MOOSE? SHOW ME!
IN MY RIGHT LEG! I THINK I BROKE IT!
3

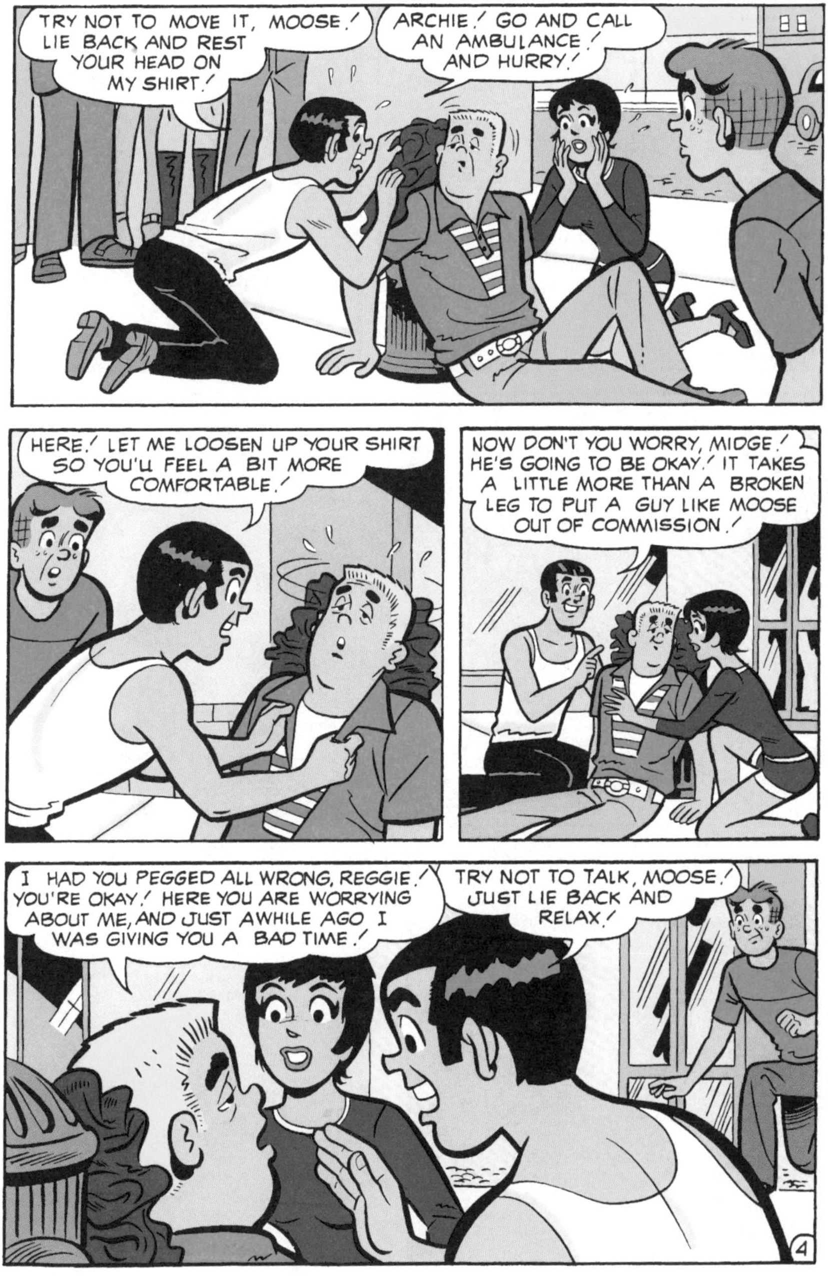
TRY NOT TO MOVE IT, MOOSE! LIE BACK AND REST YOUR HEAD ON MY SHIRT!
ARCHIE! GO AND CALL AN AMBULANCE! AND HURRY!
HERE! LET ME LOOSEN UP YOUR SHIRT SO YOU'LL FEEL A BIT MORE COMFORTABLE!
NOW DON'T YOU WORRY, MIDGE! HE'S GOING TO BE OKAY! IT TAKES A LITTLE MORE THAN A BROKEN LEG TO PUT A GUY LIKE MOOSE OUT OF COMMISSION!
I HAD YOU PEGGED ALL WRONG, REGGIE! YOU'RE OKAY! HERE YOU ARE WORRYING ABOUT ME, AND JUST AWHILE AGO I WAS GIVING YOU A BAD TIME!
TRY NOT TO TALK, MOOSE! JUST LIE BACK AND RELAX!
4

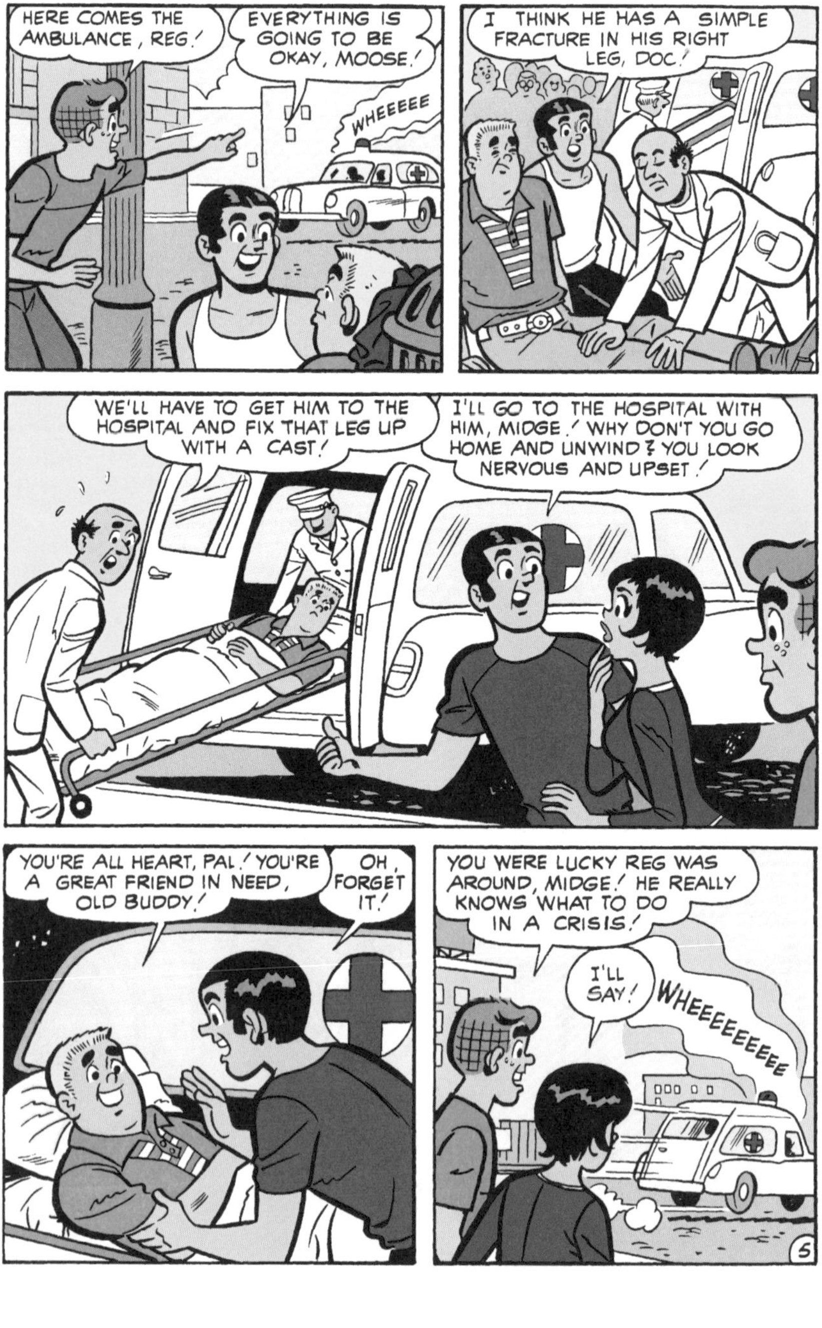
HERE COMES THE AMBULANCE, REG!
EVERYTHING IS GOING TO BE OKAY, MOOSE!
WHEEEEE
I THINK HE HAS A SIMPLE FRACTURE IN HIS RIGHT LEG, DOC!
WE'LL HAVE TO GET HIM TO THE HOSPITAL AND FIX THAT LEG UP WITH A CAST!
I'LL GO TO THE HOSPITAL WITH HIM, MIDGE! WHY DON'T YOU GO HOME AND UNWIND? YOU LOOK NERVOUS AND UPSET!
YOU'RE ALL HEART, PAL! YOU'RE A GREAT FRIEND IN NEED, OLD BUDDY!
OH, FORGET IT!
YOU WERE LUCKY REG WAS AROUND, MIDGE! HE REALLY KNOWS WHAT TO DO IN A CRISIS!
I'LL SAY!
WHEEEEEEEEEE
5

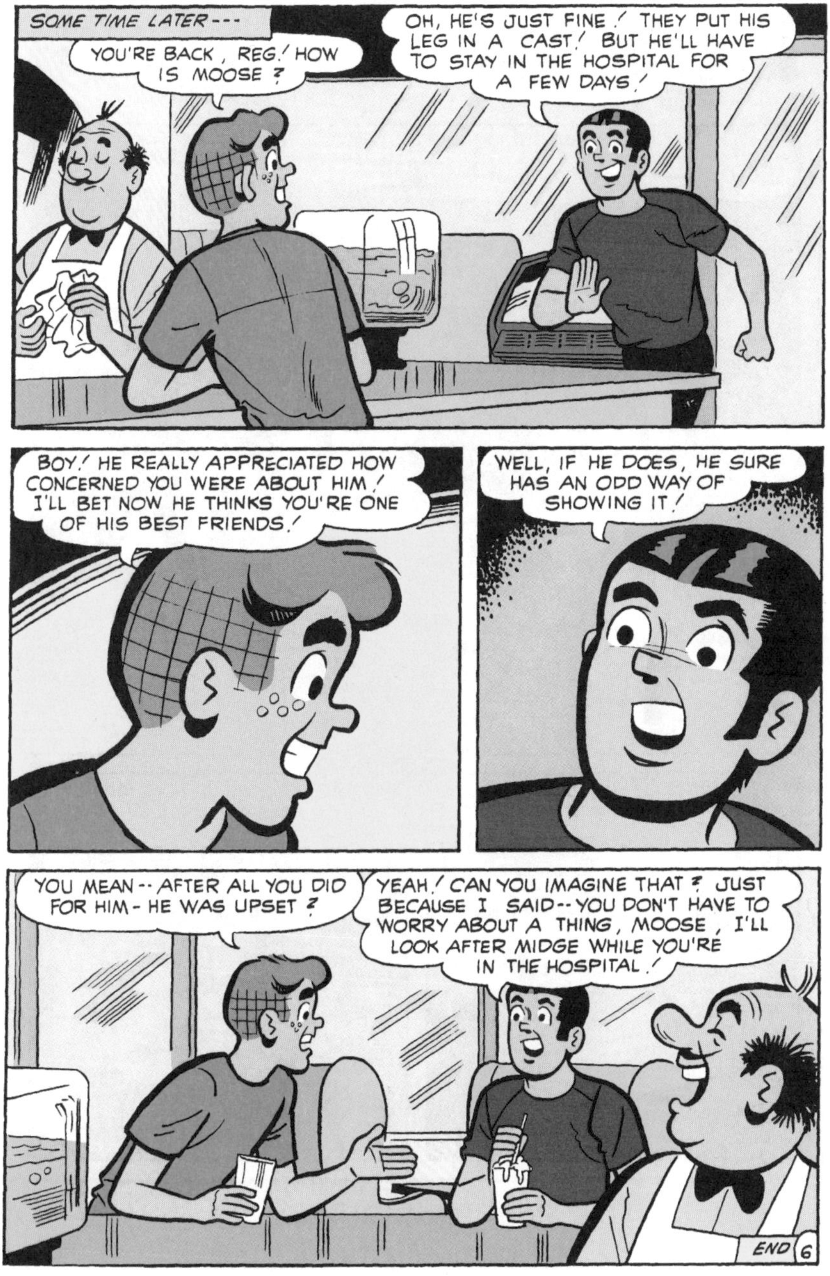
SOME TIME LATER---
YOU'RE BACK, REG.! HOW IS MOOSE?
OH, HE'S JUST FINE! THEY PUT HIS LEG IN A CAST! BUT HE'LL HAVE TO STAY IN THE HOSPITAL FOR A FEW DAYS!
BOY! HE REALLY APPRECIATED HOW CONCERNED YOU WERE ABOUT HIM! I'LL BET NOW HE THINKS YOU'RE ONE OF HIS BEST FRIENDS!
WELL, IF HE DOES, HE SURE HAS AN ODD WAY OF SHOWING IT!
YOU MEAN--AFTER ALL YOU DID FOR HIM-HE WAS UPSET?
YEAH! CAN YOU IMAGINE THAT? JUST BECAUSE I SAID--YOU DON'T HAVE TO WORRY ABOUT A THING, MOOSE, I'LL LOOK AFTER MIDGE WHILE YOU'RE IN THE HOSPITAL!
END 6

Reggie and Me in The Tingle Dingle Part One

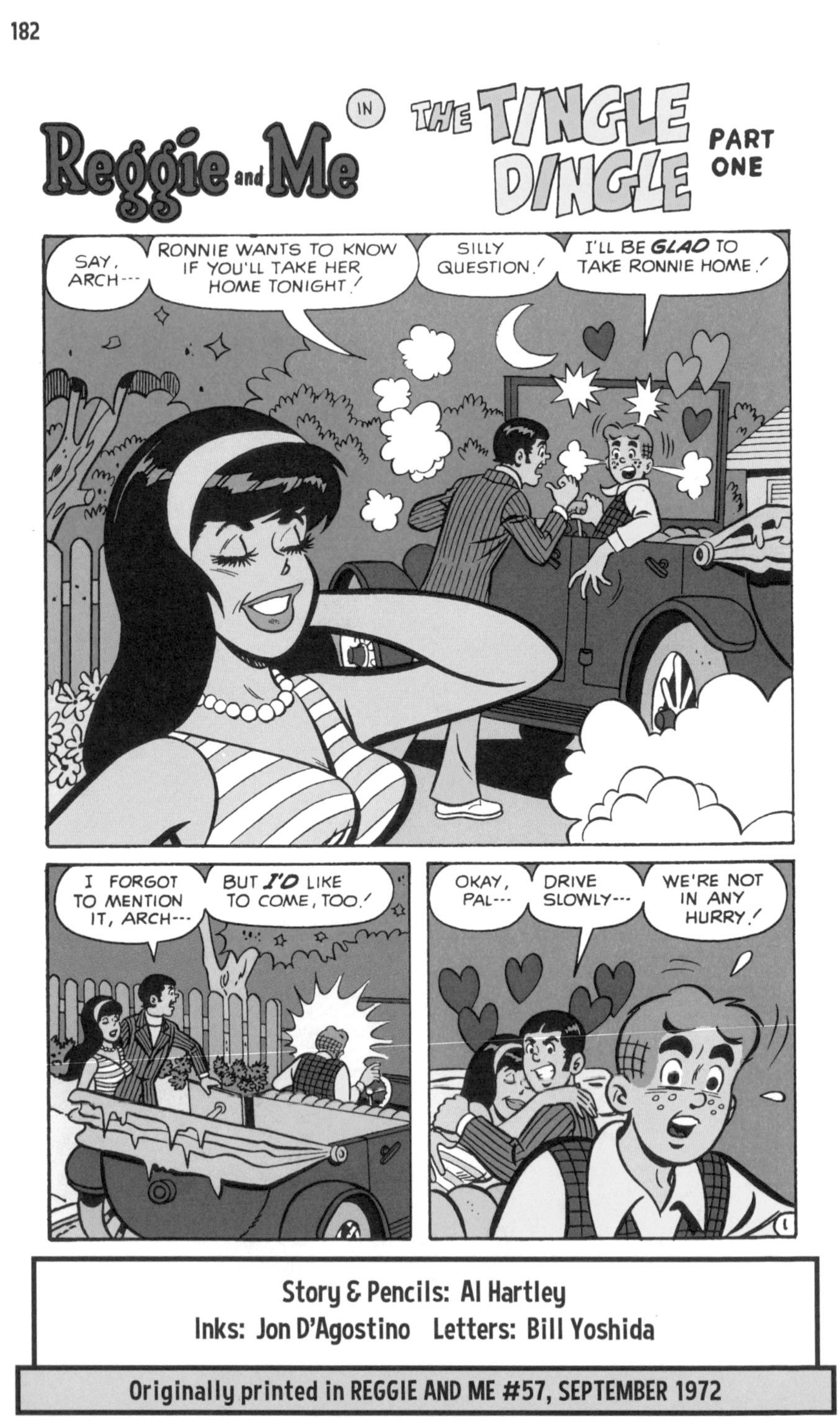
SAY, ARCH---
RONNIE WANTS TO KNOW IF YOU'LL TAKE HER HOME TONIGHT!
SILLY QUESTION!
I'LL BE GLAD TO TAKE RONNIE HOME!
I FORGOT TO MENTION IT, ARCH---
BUT I'D LIKE TO COME, TOO!
OKAY, PAL---
DRIVE SLOWLY---
WE'RE NOT IN ANY HURRY!

Story & Pencils: Al Hartley

Inks: Jon D'Agostino   Letters: Bill Yoshida

Originally printed in REGGIE AND ME #57, SEPTEMBER 1972

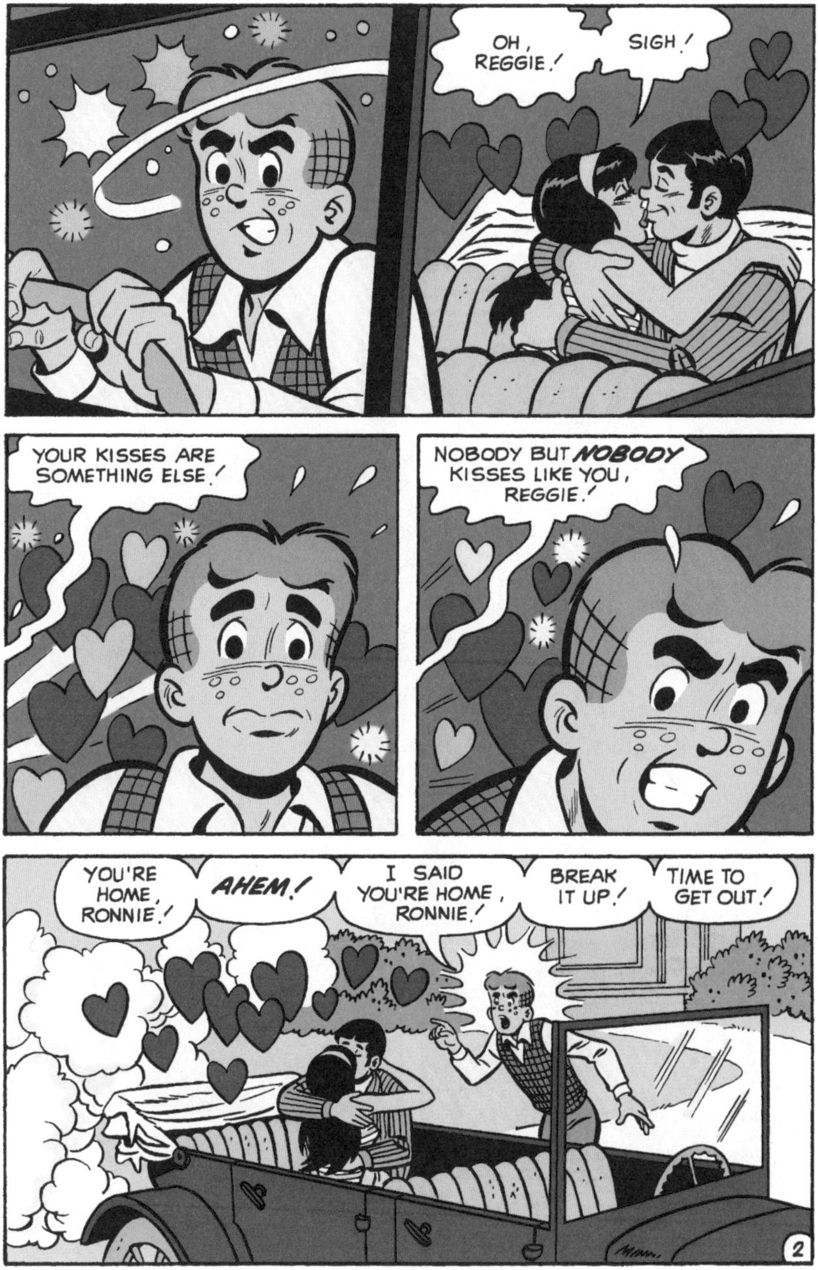

OH, REGGIE!
SIGH!
YOUR KISSES ARE SOMETHING ELSE!
NOBODY BUT NOBODY KISSES LIKE YOU, REGGIE!
YOU'RE HOME, RONNIE!
AHEM!
I SAID YOU'RE HOME, RONNIE!
BREAK IT UP!
TIME TO GET OUT!
2

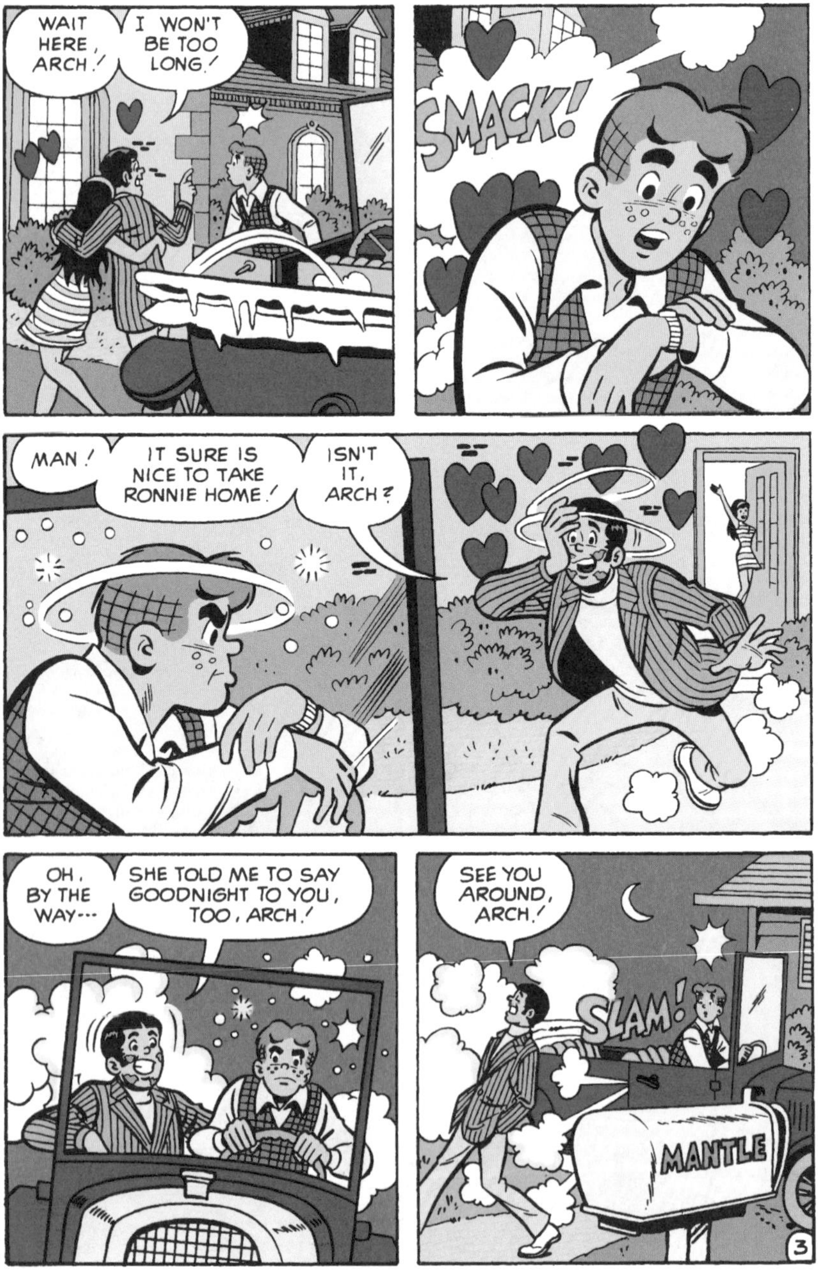
WAIT HERE, ARCH!
I WON'T BE TOO LONG!
SMACK!
MAN!
IT SURE IS NICE TO TAKE RONNIE HOME!
ISN'T IT, ARCH?
OH, BY THE WAY---
SHE TOLD ME TO SAY GOODNIGHT TO YOU, TOO, ARCH!
SEE YOU AROUND, ARCH!
SLAM!
MANTLE
3

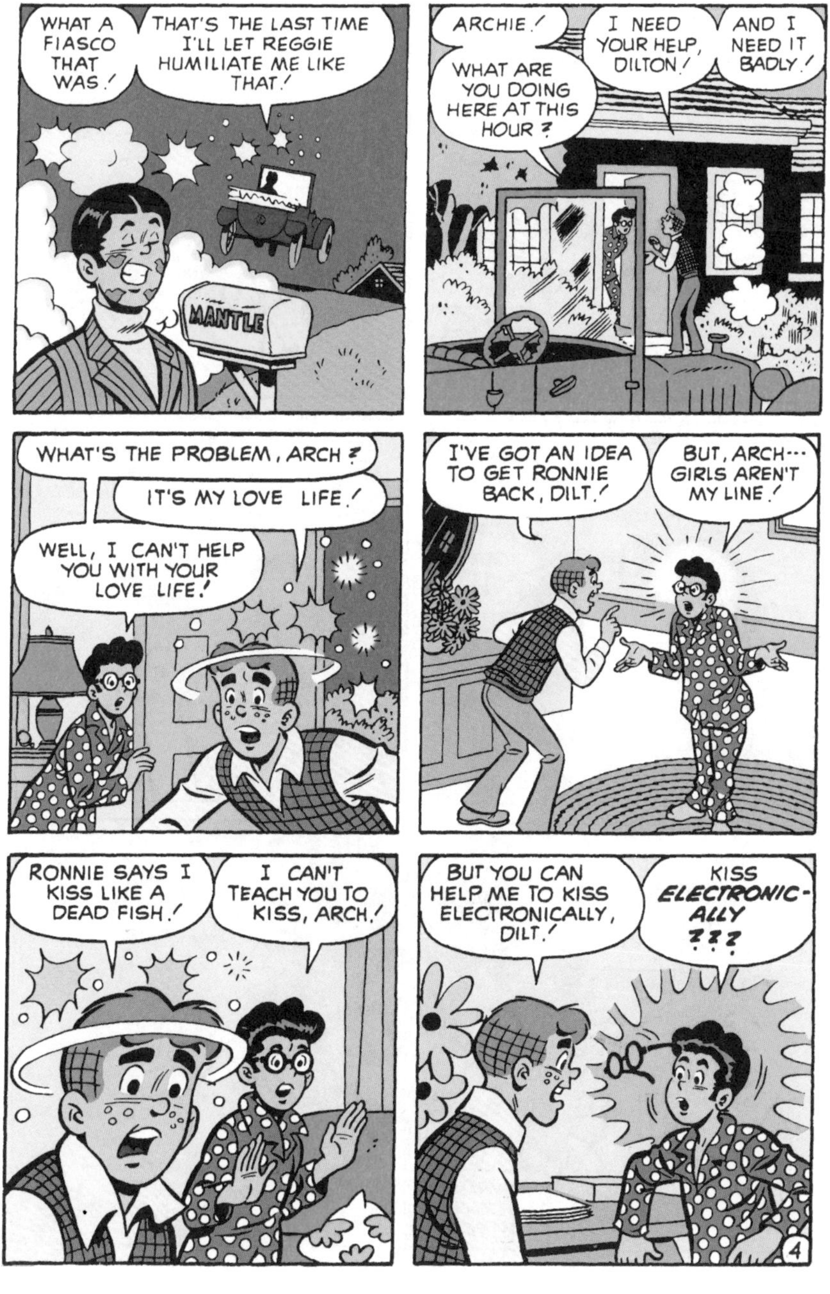
WHAT A FIASCO THAT WAS!
THAT'S THE LAST TIME I'LL LET REGGIE HUMILIATE ME LIKE THAT!
MANTLE
ARCHIE!
WHAT ARE YOU DOING HERE AT THIS HOUR?
I NEED YOUR HELP, DILTON!
AND I NEED IT BADLY!
WHAT'S THE PROBLEM, ARCH?
IT'S MY LOVE LIFE!
WELL, I CAN'T HELP YOU WITH YOUR LOVE LIFE!
I'VE GOT AN IDEA TO GET RONNIE BACK, DILT!
BUT, ARCH... GIRLS AREN'T MY LINE!
RONNIE SAYS I KISS LIKE A DEAD FISH!
I CAN'T TEACH YOU TO KISS, ARCH!
BUT YOU CAN HELP ME TO KISS ELECTRONICALLY, DILT!
KISS *ELECTRONIC-ALLY* ???
4

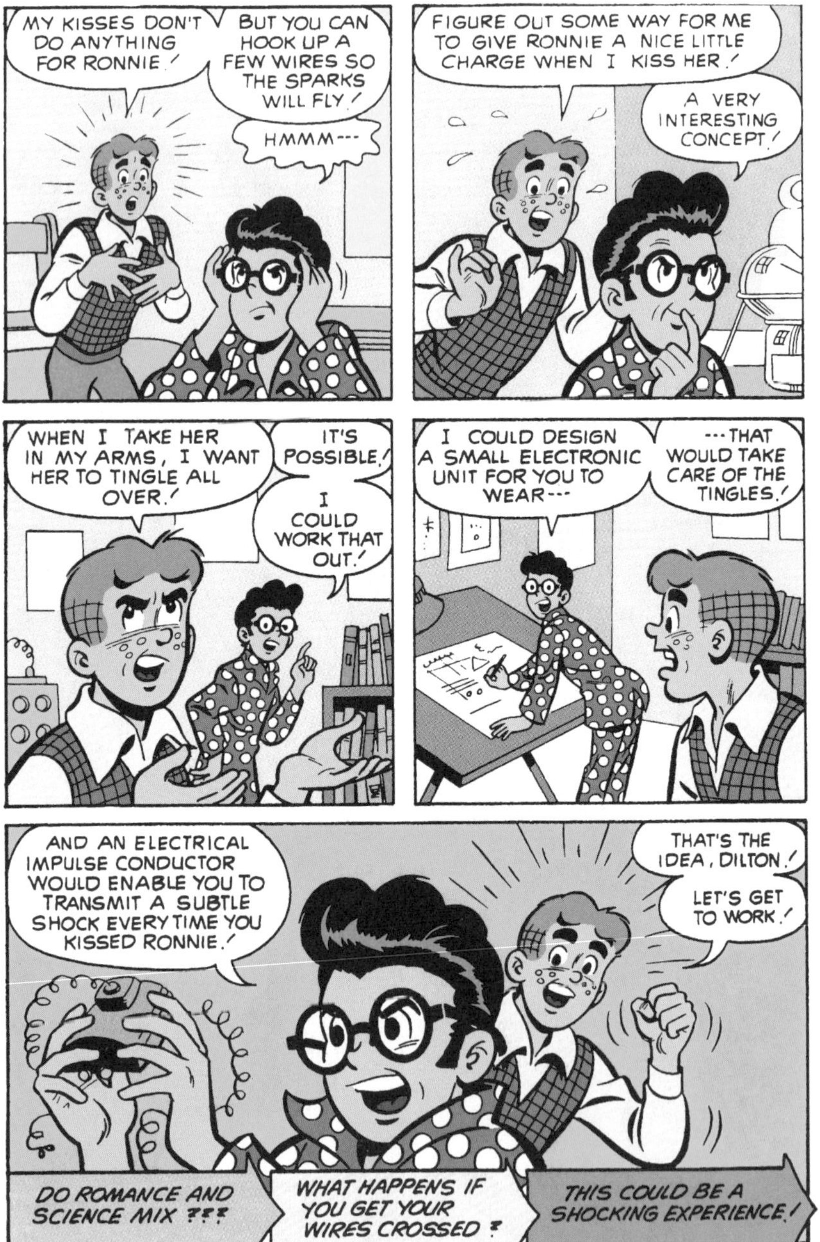
MY KISSES DON'T DO ANYTHING FOR RONNIE!
BUT YOU CAN HOOK UP A FEW WIRES SO THE SPARKS WILL FLY!
HMMM---
FIGURE OUT SOME WAY FOR ME TO GIVE RONNIE A NICE LITTLE CHARGE WHEN I KISS HER!
A VERY INTERESTING CONCEPT!
WHEN I TAKE HER IN MY ARMS, I WANT HER TO TINGLE ALL OVER!
IT'S POSSIBLE!
I COULD WORK THAT OUT!
I COULD DESIGN A SMALL ELECTRONIC UNIT FOR YOU TO WEAR---
---THAT WOULD TAKE CARE OF THE TINGLES!
AND AN ELECTRICAL IMPULSE CONDUCTOR WOULD ENABLE YOU TO TRANSMIT A SUBTLE SHOCK EVERY TIME YOU KISSED RONNIE!
THAT'S THE IDEA, DILTON!
LET'S GET TO WORK!
DO ROMANCE AND SCIENCE MIX ???
WHAT HAPPENS IF YOU GET YOUR WIRES CROSSED ?
THIS COULD BE A SHOCKING EXPERIENCE!

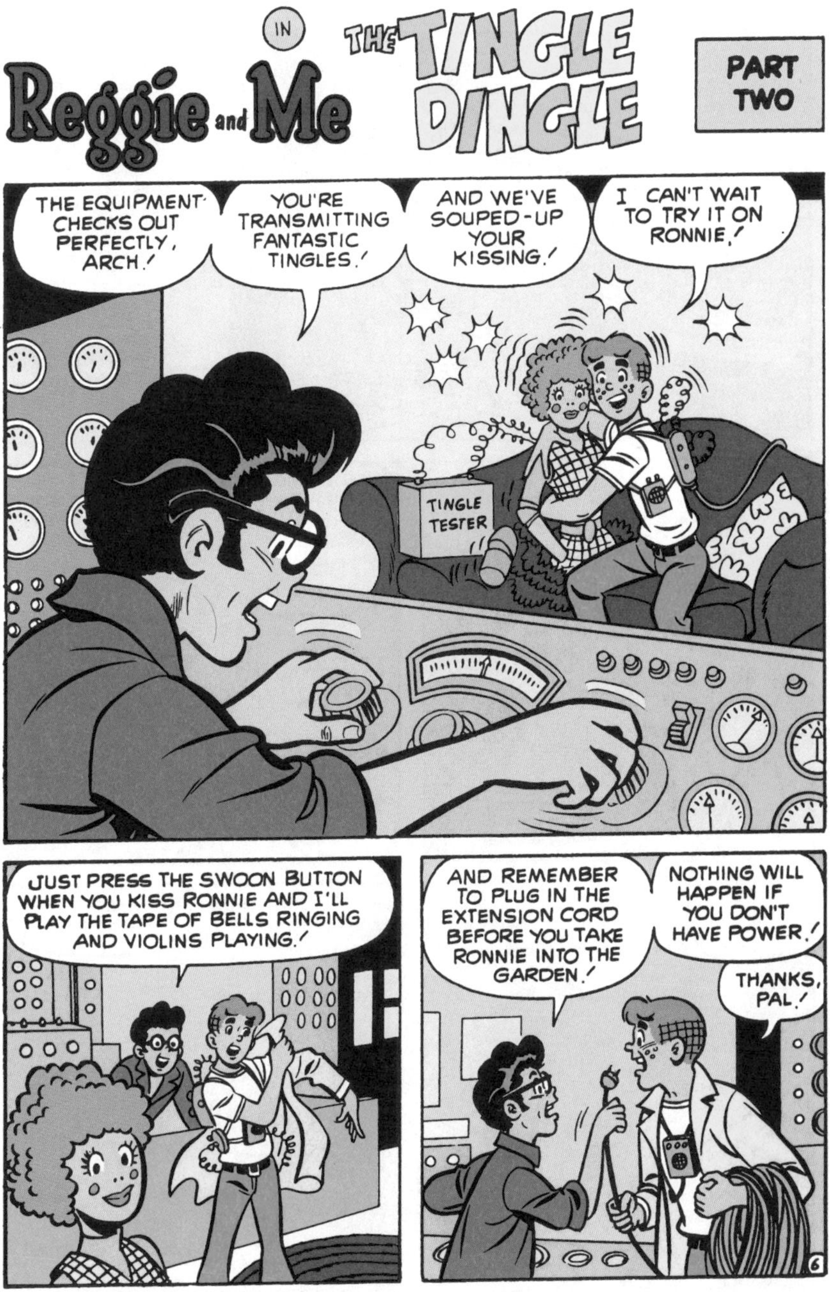
Reggie and Me
IN
THE TINGLE DINGLE
PART TWO
THE EQUIPMENT CHECKS OUT PERFECTLY, ARCH!
YOU'RE TRANSMITTING FANTASTIC TINGLES!
AND WE'VE SOUPED-UP YOUR KISSING!
I CAN'T WAIT TO TRY IT ON RONNIE!
TINGLE TESTER
JUST PRESS THE SWOON BUTTON WHEN YOU KISS RONNIE AND I'LL PLAY THE TAPE OF BELLS RINGING AND VIOLINS PLAYING!
AND REMEMBER TO PLUG IN THE EXTENSION CORD BEFORE YOU TAKE RONNIE INTO THE GARDEN!
NOTHING WILL HAPPEN IF YOU DON'T HAVE POWER!
THANKS, PAL!
6

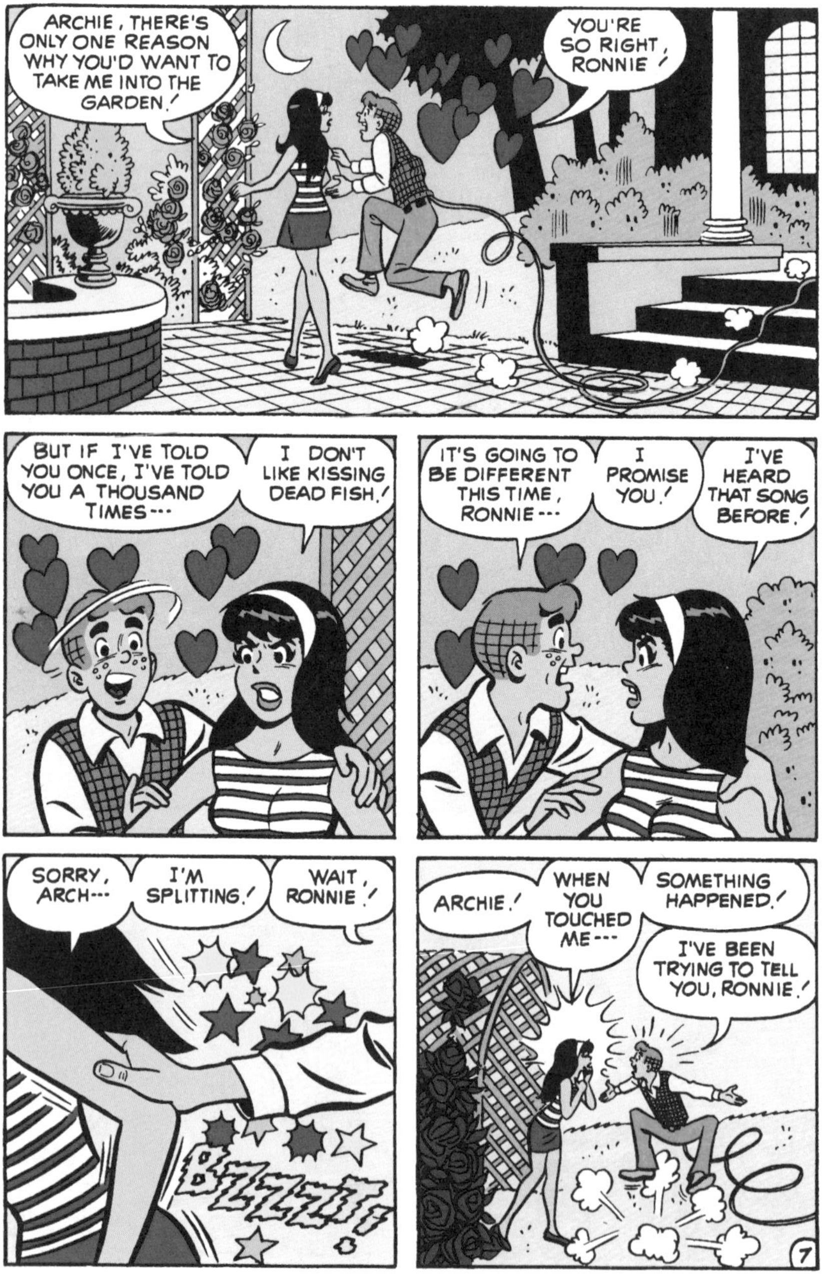
ARCHIE, THERE'S ONLY ONE REASON WHY YOU'D WANT TO TAKE ME INTO THE GARDEN!
YOU'RE SO RIGHT, RONNIE!
BUT IF I'VE TOLD YOU ONCE, I'VE TOLD YOU A THOUSAND TIMES---
I DON'T LIKE KISSING DEAD FISH!
IT'S GOING TO BE DIFFERENT THIS TIME, RONNIE---
I PROMISE YOU!
I'VE HEARD THAT SONG BEFORE!
SORRY, ARCH---
I'M SPLITTING!
WAIT, RONNIE!
ARCHIE!
WHEN YOU TOUCHED ME---
SOMETHING HAPPENED!
I'VE BEEN TRYING TO TELL YOU, RONNIE!
7

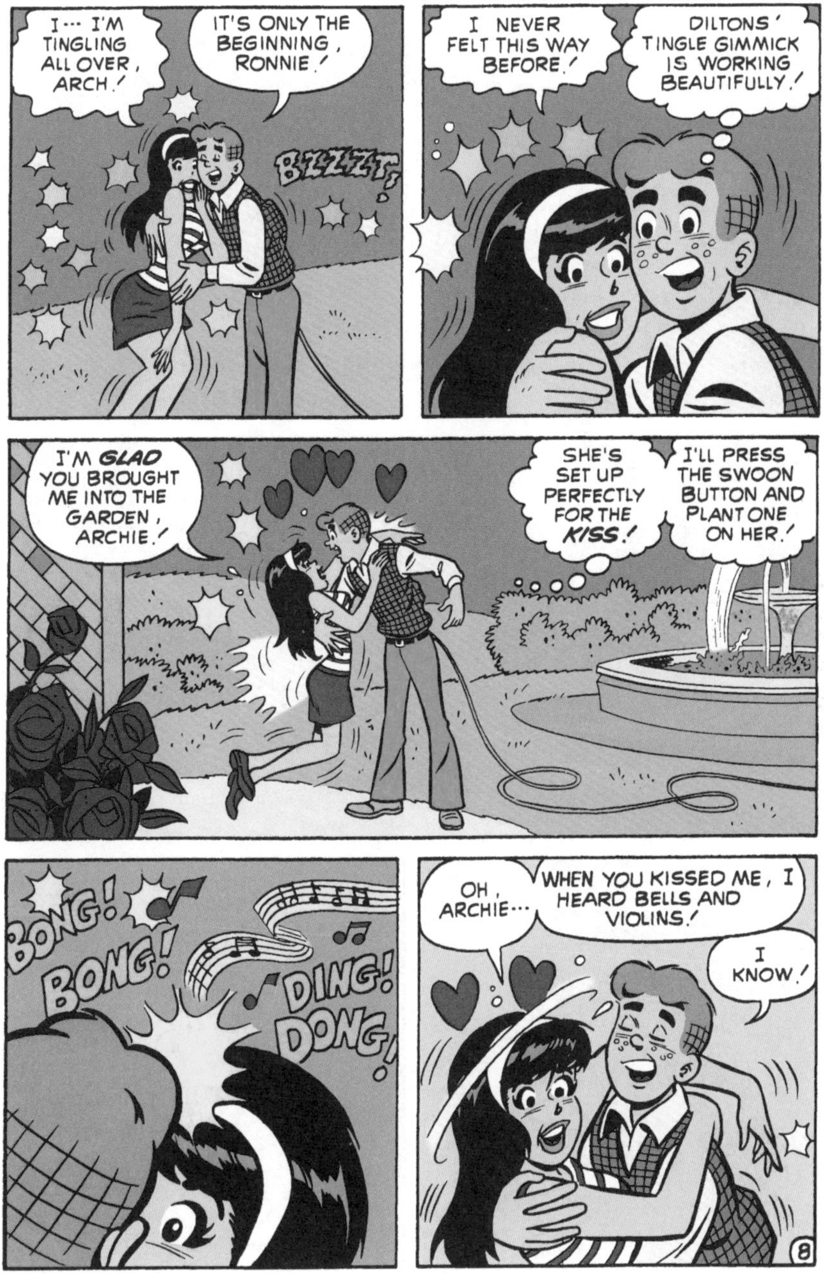
I··· I'M TINGLING ALL OVER, ARCH.!
IT'S ONLY THE BEGINNING, RONNIE.!
BZZZZT
I NEVER FELT THIS WAY BEFORE.!
DILTONS' TINGLE GIMMICK IS WORKING BEAUTIFULLY.!
I'M GLAD YOU BROUGHT ME INTO THE GARDEN, ARCHIE.!
SHE'S SET UP PERFECTLY FOR THE KISS.!
I'LL PRESS THE SWOON BUTTON AND PLANT ONE ON HER.!
BONG! BONG!
DING! DONG!
OH, ARCHIE···
WHEN YOU KISSED ME, I HEARD BELLS AND VIOLINS.!
I KNOW.!
8

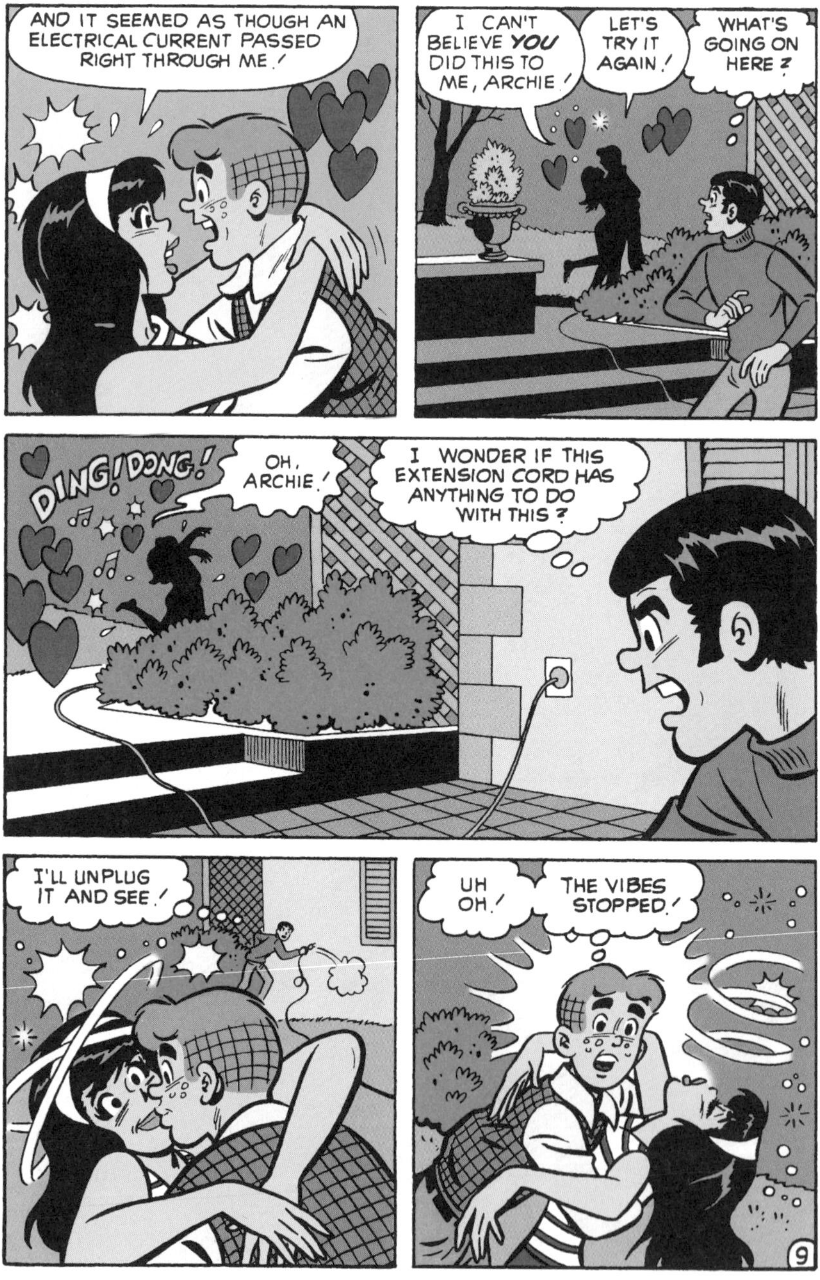
AND IT SEEMED AS THOUGH AN ELECTRICAL CURRENT PASSED RIGHT THROUGH ME!
I CAN'T BELIEVE YOU DID THIS TO ME, ARCHIE!
LET'S TRY IT AGAIN!
WHAT'S GOING ON HERE?
DING! DONG!
OH, ARCHIE!
I WONDER IF THIS EXTENSION CORD HAS ANYTHING TO DO WITH THIS?
I'LL UNPLUG IT AND SEE!
UH OH!
THE VIBES STOPPED!
9

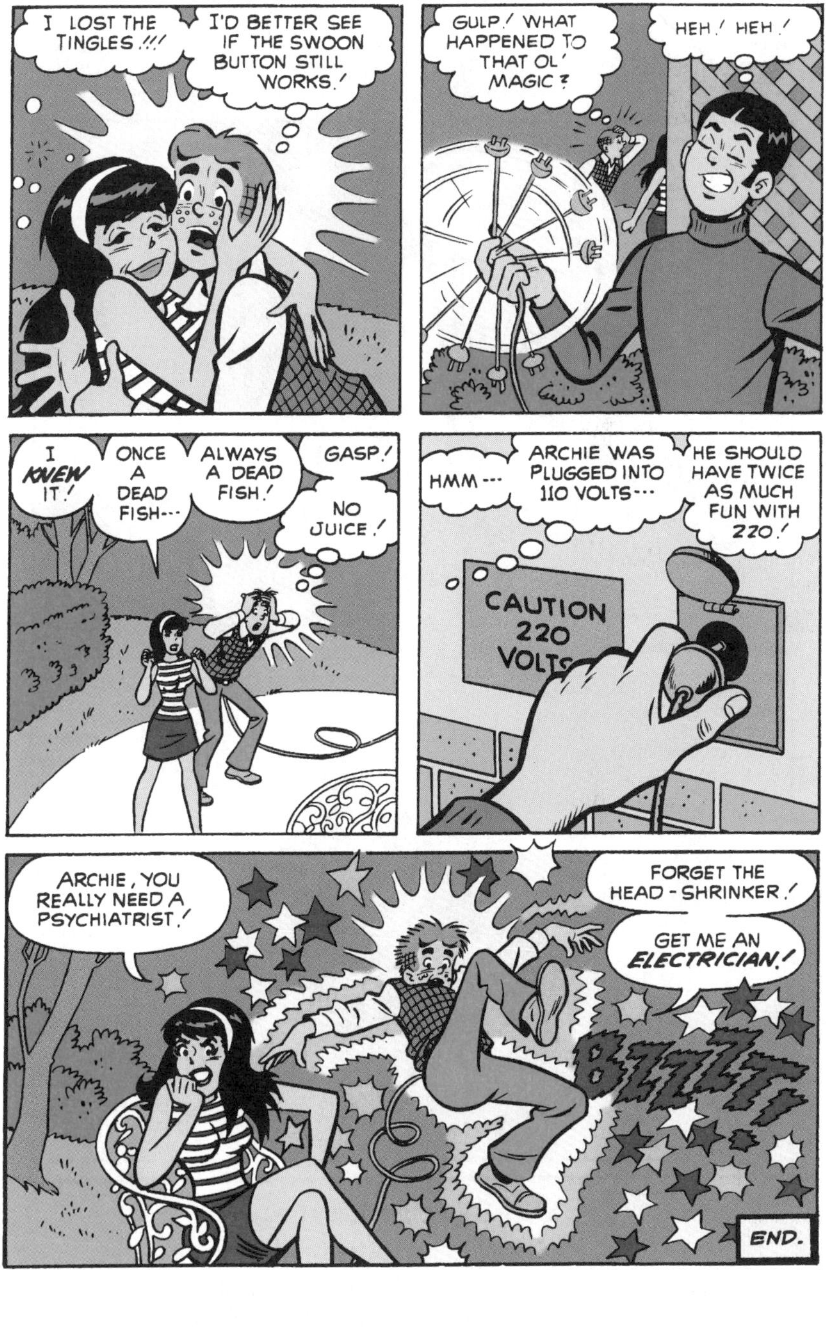
I LOST THE TINGLES!!!
I'D BETTER SEE IF THE SWOON BUTTON STILL WORKS!
GULP! WHAT HAPPENED TO THAT OL' MAGIC?
HEH! HEH!
I KNEW IT!
ONCE A DEAD FISH---
ALWAYS A DEAD FISH!
GASP!
NO JUICE!
HMM---
ARCHIE WAS PLUGGED INTO 110 VOLTS---
HE SHOULD HAVE TWICE AS MUCH FUN WITH 220!
CAUTION 220 VOLTS
ARCHIE, YOU REALLY NEED A PSYCHIATRIST!
FORGET THE HEAD-SHRINKER!
GET ME AN ELECTRICIAN!
BZZZT!
END.

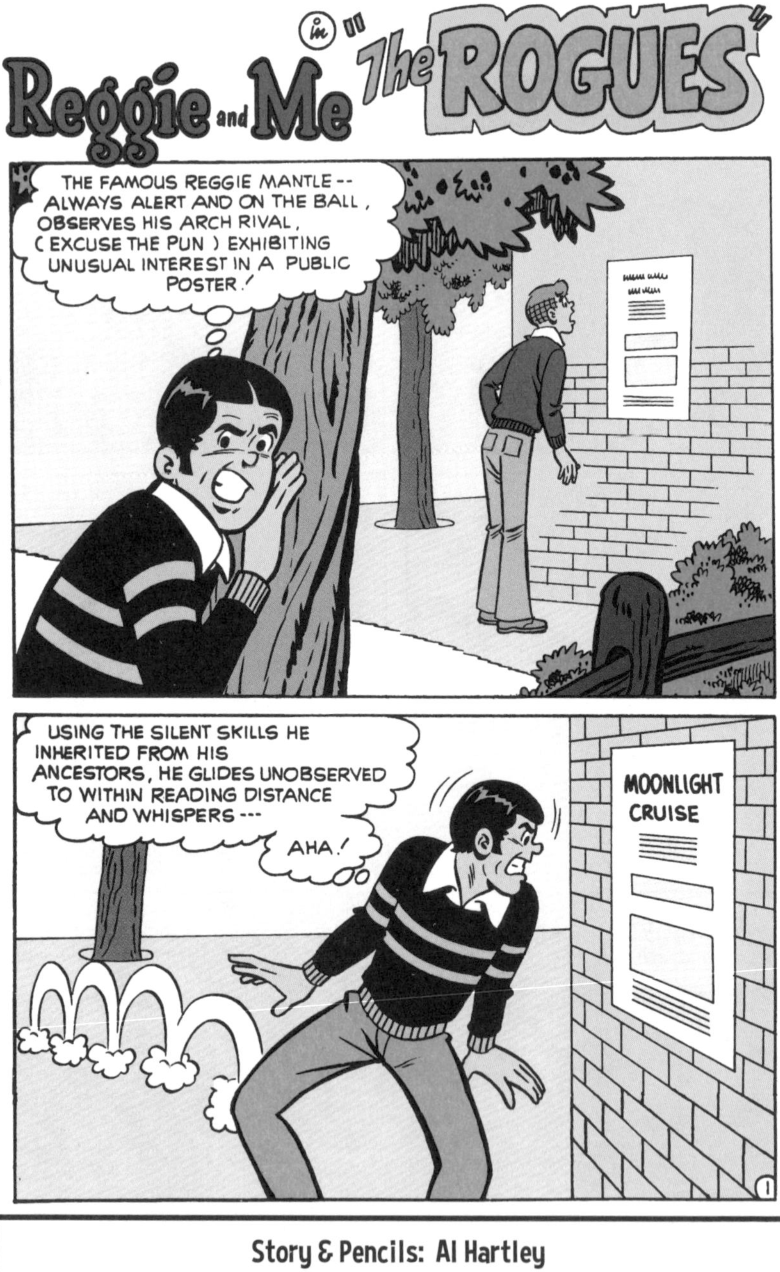
Reggie and Me in "The ROGUES"
THE FAMOUS REGGIE MANTLE -- ALWAYS ALERT AND ON THE BALL, OBSERVES HIS ARCH RIVAL, (EXCUSE THE PUN) EXHIBITING UNUSUAL INTEREST IN A PUBLIC POSTER!
USING THE SILENT SKILLS HE INHERITED FROM HIS ANCESTORS, HE GLIDES UNOBSERVED TO WITHIN READING DISTANCE AND WHISPERS ---
AHA!
MOONLIGHT CRUISE

Story & Pencils: Al Hartley

Inks: Jon D'Agostino Letters: Bill Yoshida

Originally printed in REGGIE AND ME #59, NOVEMBER 1972

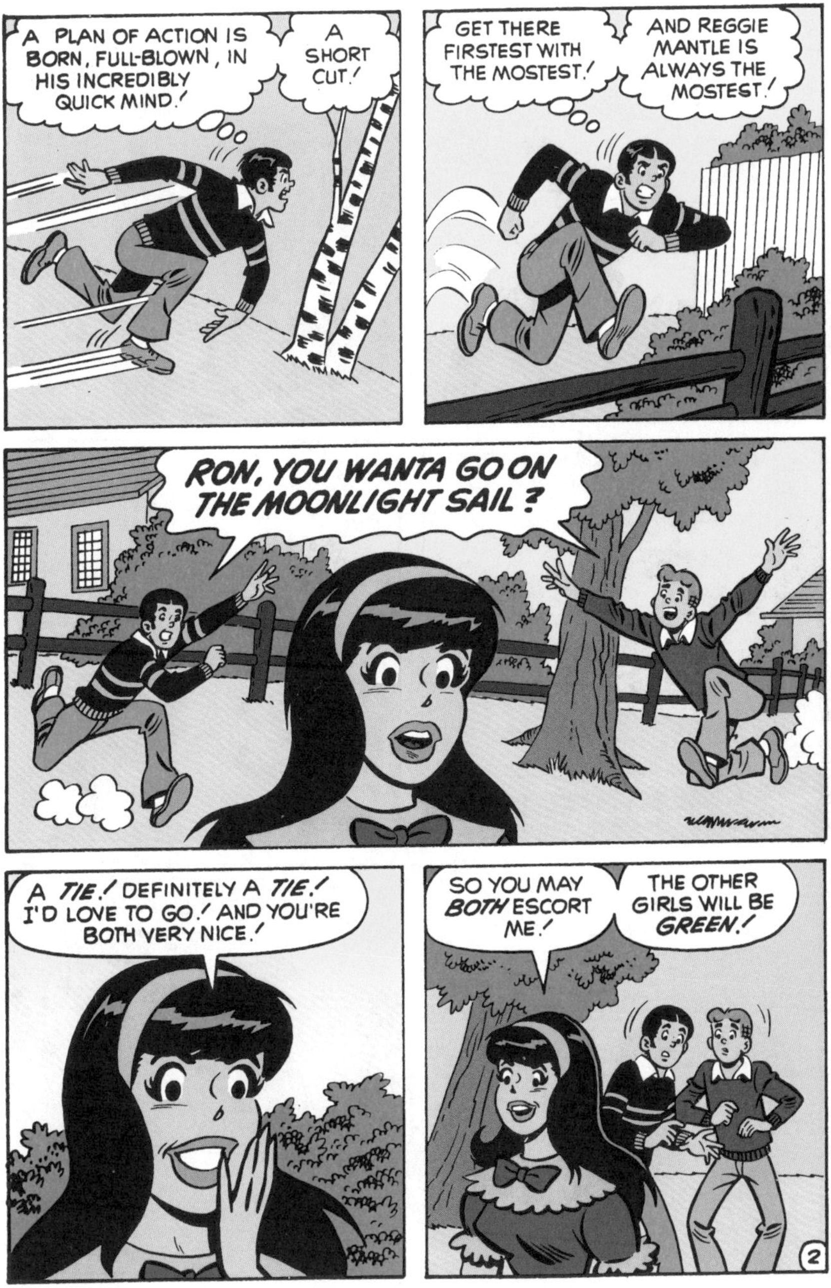
A PLAN OF ACTION IS BORN, FULL-BLOWN, IN HIS INCREDIBLY QUICK MIND!
A SHORT CUT!
GET THERE FIRSTEST WITH THE MOSTEST!
AND REGGIE MANTLE IS ALWAYS THE MOSTEST!
RON, YOU WANTA GO ON THE MOONLIGHT SAIL?
A TIE! DEFINITELY A TIE! I'D LOVE TO GO! AND YOU'RE BOTH VERY NICE!
SO YOU MAY BOTH ESCORT ME!
THE OTHER GIRLS WILL BE GREEN!
2

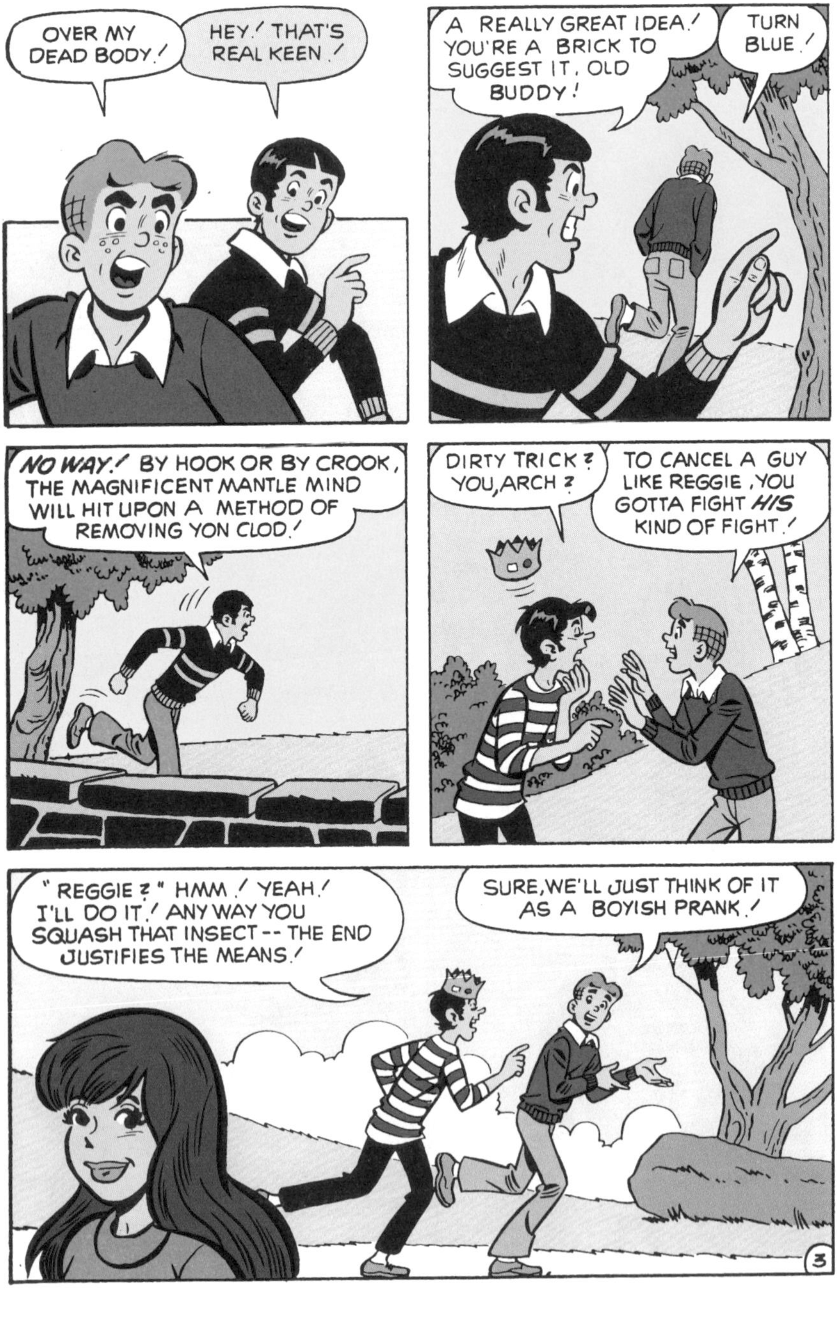
OVER MY DEAD BODY!
HEY! THAT'S REAL KEEN!
A REALLY GREAT IDEA! YOU'RE A BRICK TO SUGGEST IT, OLD BUDDY!
TURN BLUE!
NO WAY! BY HOOK OR BY CROOK, THE MAGNIFICENT MANTLE MIND WILL HIT UPON A METHOD OF REMOVING YON CLOD!
DIRTY TRICK? YOU, ARCH?
TO CANCEL A GUY LIKE REGGIE, YOU GOTTA FIGHT HIS KIND OF FIGHT!
"REGGIE?" HMM! YEAH! I'LL DO IT! ANY WAY YOU SQUASH THAT INSECT -- THE END JUSTIFIES THE MEANS!
SURE, WE'LL JUST THINK OF IT AS A BOYISH PRANK!
3

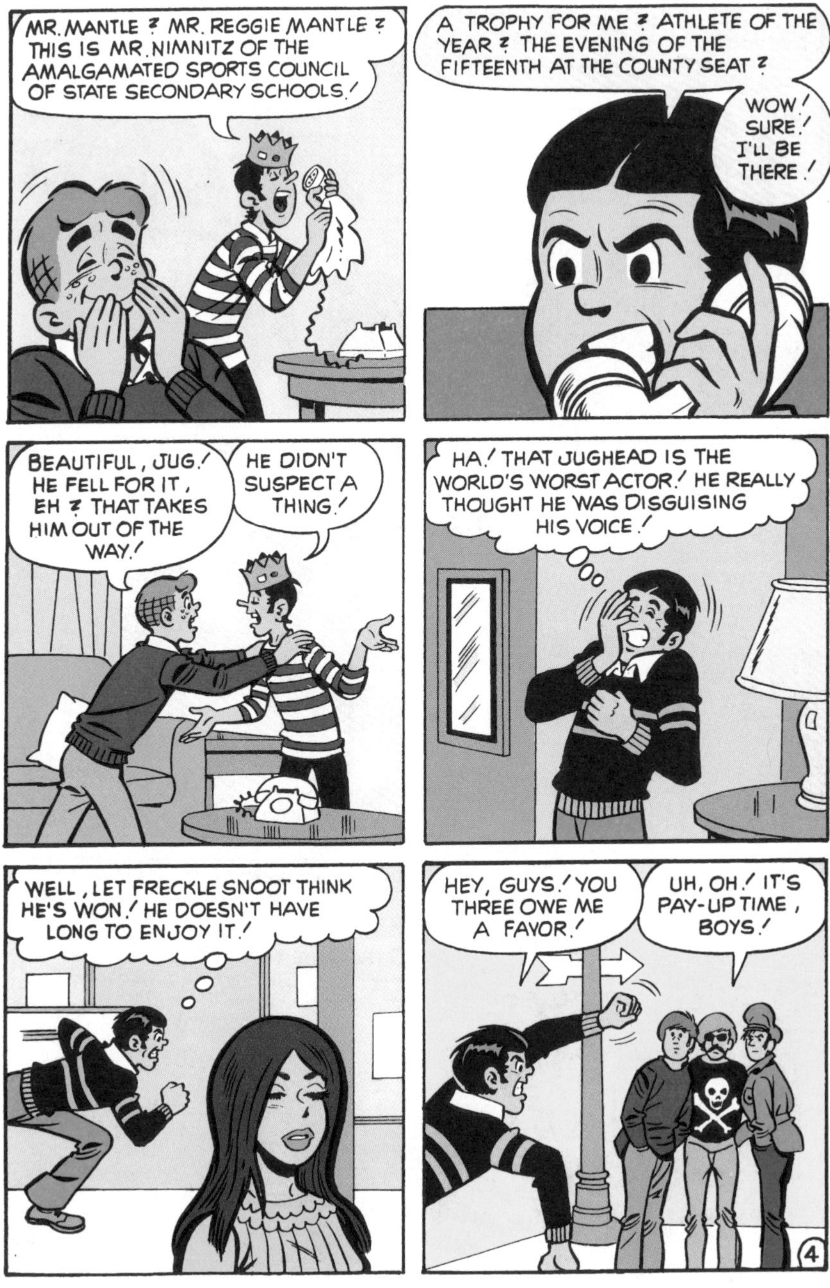
MR. MANTLE ? MR. REGGIE MANTLE ? THIS IS MR. NIMNITZ OF THE AMALGAMATED SPORTS COUNCIL OF STATE SECONDARY SCHOOLS!
A TROPHY FOR ME ? ATHLETE OF THE YEAR ? THE EVENING OF THE FIFTEENTH AT THE COUNTY SEAT ?
WOW! SURE! I'LL BE THERE!
BEAUTIFUL, JUG! HE FELL FOR IT, EH ? THAT TAKES HIM OUT OF THE WAY!
HE DIDN'T SUSPECT A THING!
HA! THAT JUGHEAD IS THE WORLD'S WORST ACTOR! HE REALLY THOUGHT HE WAS DISGUISING HIS VOICE!
WELL, LET FRECKLE SNOOT THINK HE'S WON! HE DOESN'T HAVE LONG TO ENJOY IT!
HEY, GUYS! YOU THREE OWE ME A FAVOR!
UH, OH! IT'S PAY-UP TIME, BOYS!
4

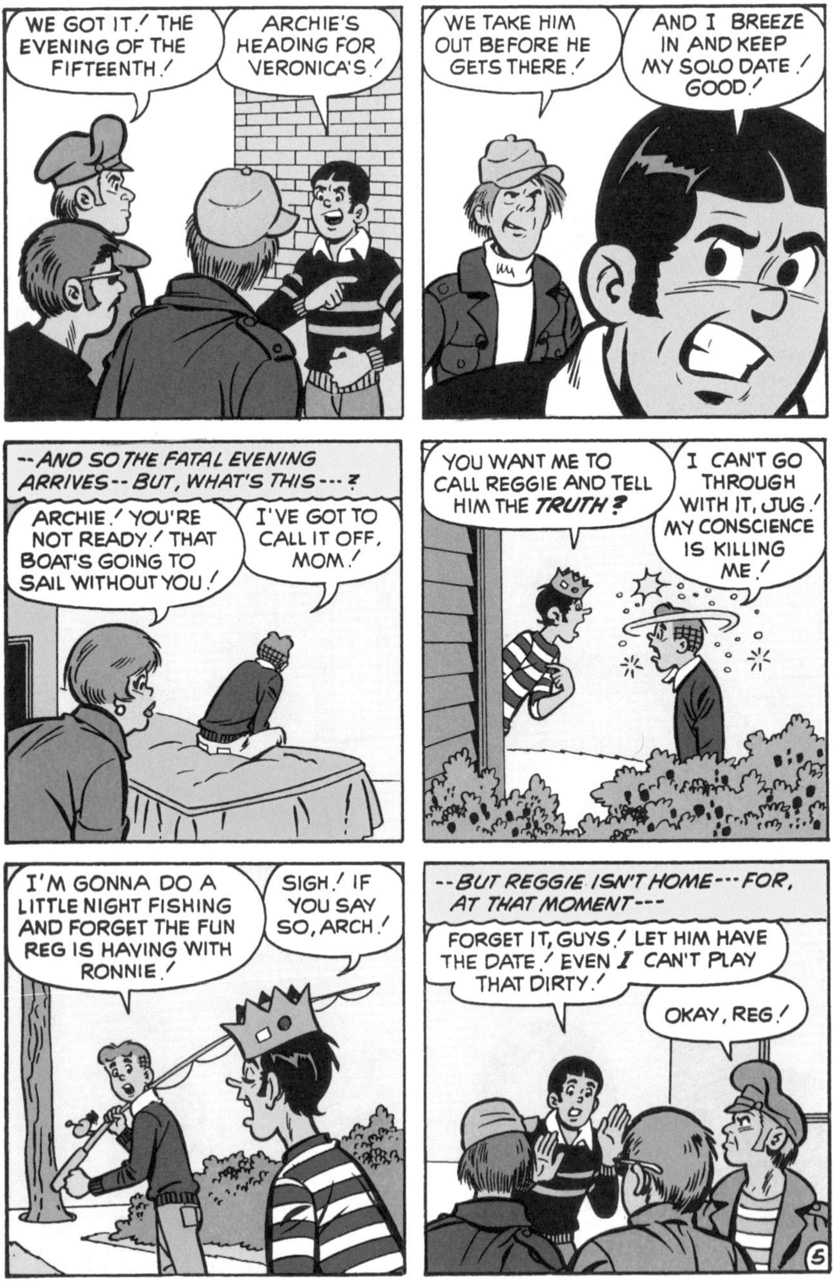
WE GOT IT! THE EVENING OF THE FIFTEENTH!
ARCHIE'S HEADING FOR VERONICA'S!
WE TAKE HIM OUT BEFORE HE GETS THERE!
AND I BREEZE IN AND KEEP MY SOLO DATE! GOOD!
--AND SO THE FATAL EVENING ARRIVES--BUT, WHAT'S THIS---?
ARCHIE! YOU'RE NOT READY! THAT BOAT'S GOING TO SAIL WITHOUT YOU!
I'VE GOT TO CALL IT OFF, MOM!
YOU WANT ME TO CALL REGGIE AND TELL HIM THE TRUTH?
I CAN'T GO THROUGH WITH IT, JUG! MY CONSCIENCE IS KILLING ME!
I'M GONNA DO A LITTLE NIGHT FISHING AND FORGET THE FUN REG IS HAVING WITH RONNIE!
SIGH! IF YOU SAY SO, ARCH!
--BUT REGGIE ISN'T HOME---FOR, AT THAT MOMENT---
FORGET IT, GUYS! LET HIM HAVE THE DATE! EVEN I CAN'T PLAY THAT DIRTY!
OKAY, REG!
5

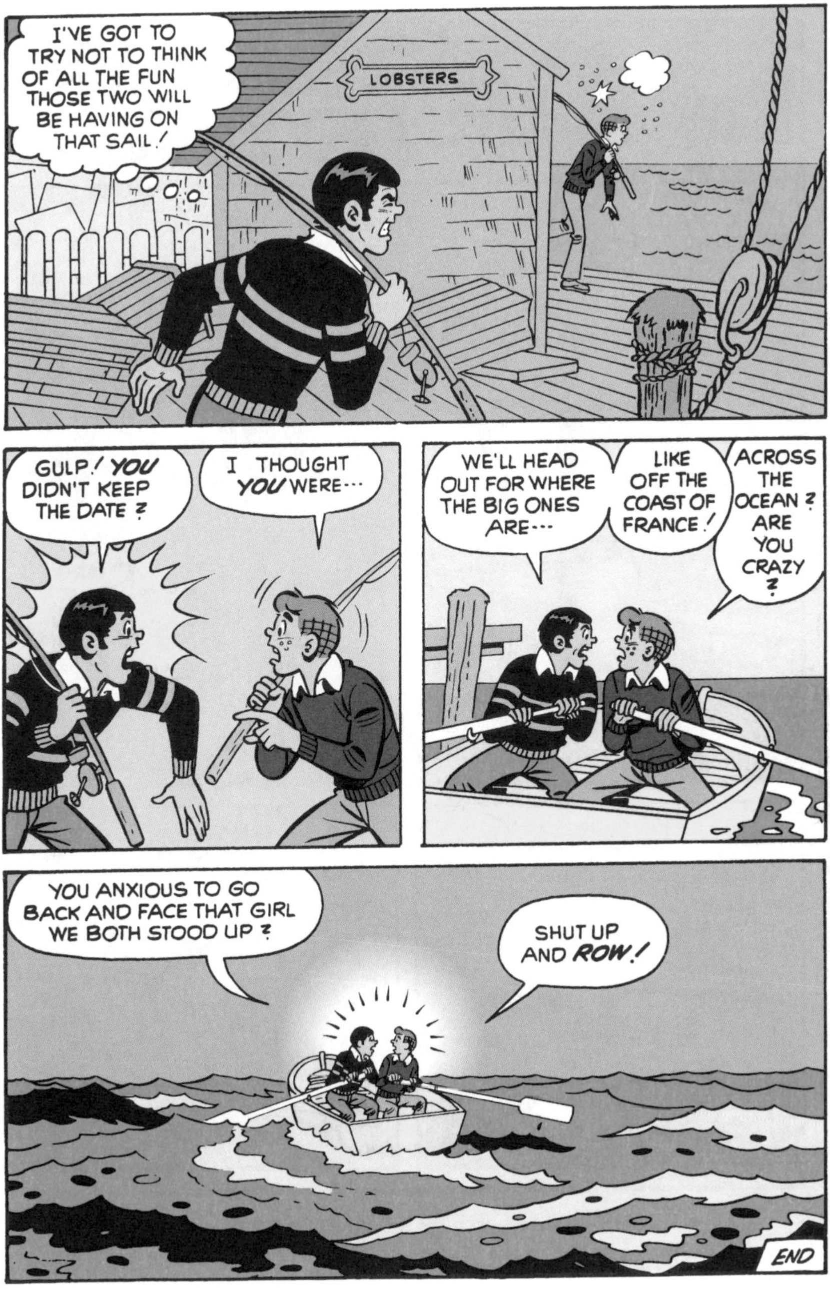
I'VE GOT TO TRY NOT TO THINK OF ALL THE FUN THOSE TWO WILL BE HAVING ON THAT SAIL!
LOBSTERS
GULP! YOU DIDN'T KEEP THE DATE?
I THOUGHT YOU WERE...
WE'LL HEAD OUT FOR WHERE THE BIG ONES ARE...
LIKE OFF THE COAST OF FRANCE!
ACROSS THE OCEAN? ARE YOU CRAZY?
YOU ANXIOUS TO GO BACK AND FACE THAT GIRL WE BOTH STOOD UP?
SHUT UP AND ROW!
END

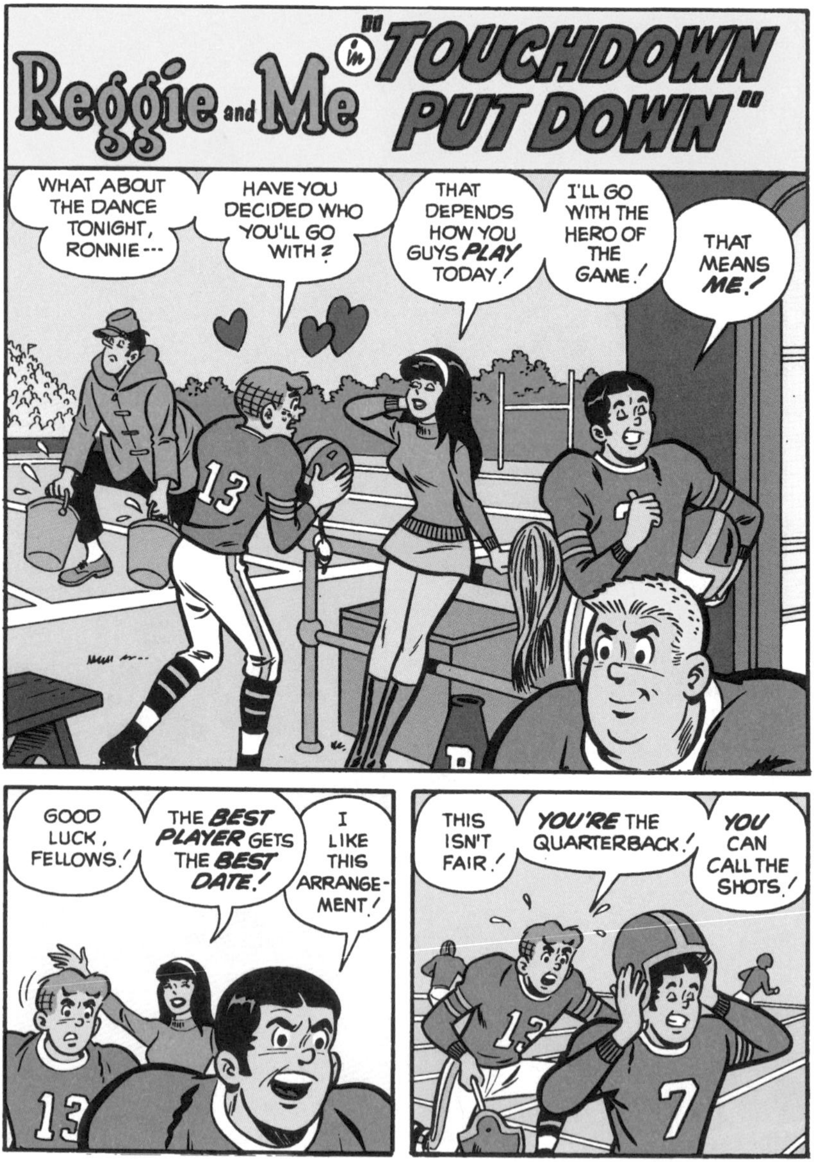
Reggie and Me in "TOUCHDOWN PUT DOWN"
WHAT ABOUT THE DANCE TONIGHT, RONNIE---
HAVE YOU DECIDED WHO YOU'LL GO WITH?
THAT DEPENDS HOW YOU GUYS PLAY TODAY!
I'LL GO WITH THE HERO OF THE GAME!
THAT MEANS ME!
GOOD LUCK, FELLOWS!
THE BEST PLAYER GETS THE BEST DATE!
I LIKE THIS ARRANGE-MENT!
THIS ISN'T FAIR!
YOU'RE THE QUARTERBACK!
YOU CAN CALL THE SHOTS!

Story & Pencils: Al Hartley

Inks: Jon D'Agostino Letters: Bill Yoshida Colors: Barry Grossman

Originally printed in REGGIE AND ME #61, APRIL 1973

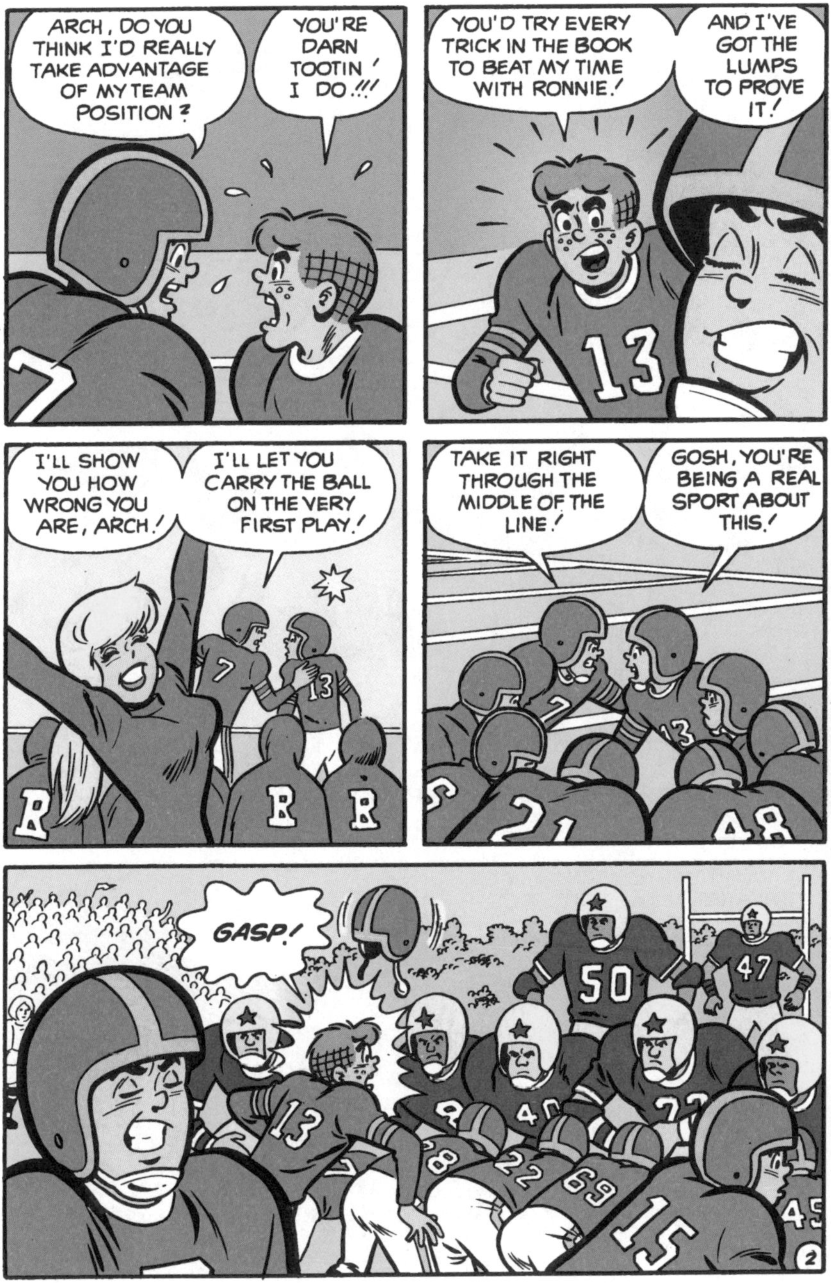
ARCH, DO YOU THINK I'D REALLY TAKE ADVANTAGE OF MY TEAM POSITION?
YOU'RE DARN TOOTIN' I DO!!!
YOU'D TRY EVERY TRICK IN THE BOOK TO BEAT MY TIME WITH RONNIE!
AND I'VE GOT THE LUMPS TO PROVE IT!
I'LL SHOW YOU HOW WRONG YOU ARE, ARCH!
I'LL LET YOU CARRY THE BALL ON THE VERY FIRST PLAY!
TAKE IT RIGHT THROUGH THE MIDDLE OF THE LINE!
GOSH, YOU'RE BEING A REAL SPORT ABOUT THIS!
GASP!
2

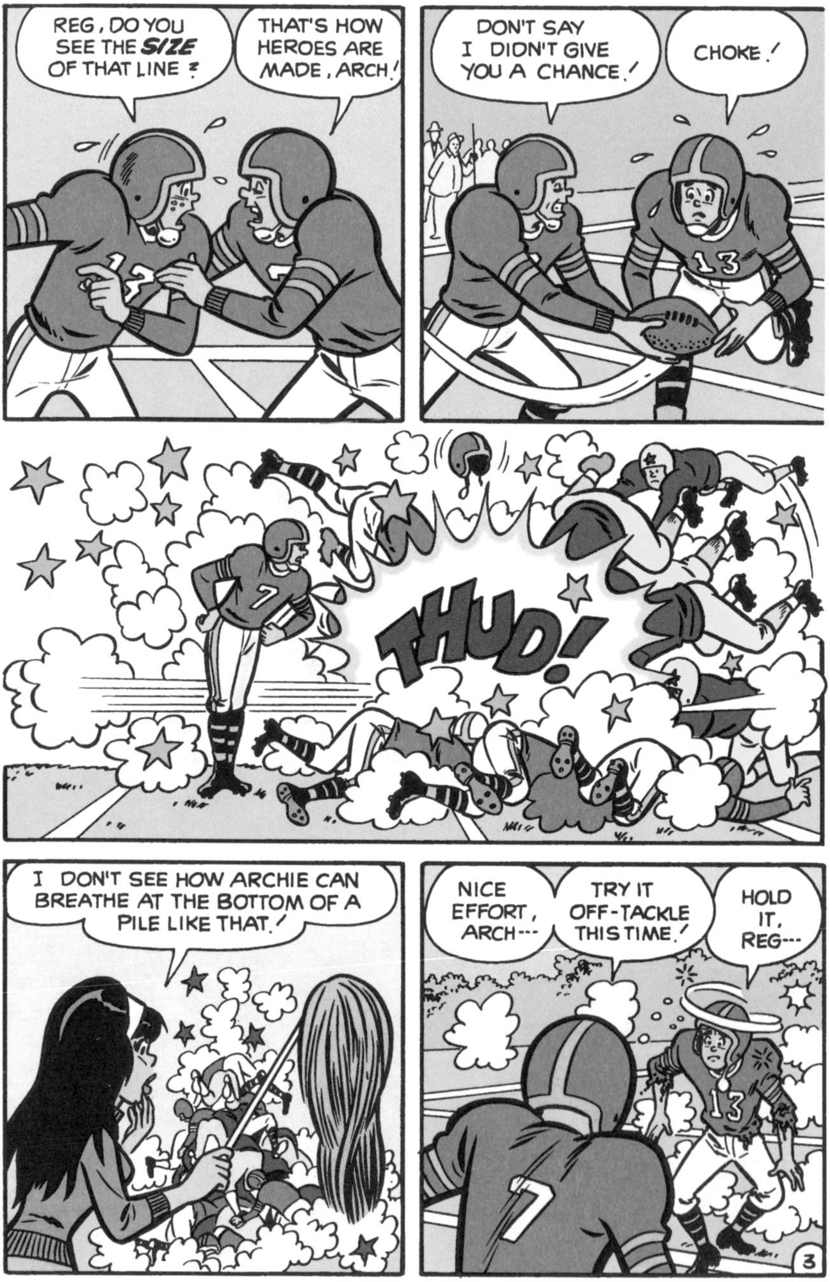
REG, DO YOU SEE THE SIZE OF THAT LINE?
THAT'S HOW HEROES ARE MADE, ARCH!
DON'T SAY I DIDN'T GIVE YOU A CHANCE!
CHOKE!
THUD!
I DON'T SEE HOW ARCHIE CAN BREATHE AT THE BOTTOM OF A PILE LIKE THAT!
NICE EFFORT, ARCH---
TRY IT OFF-TACKLE THIS TIME!
HOLD IT, REG---
3

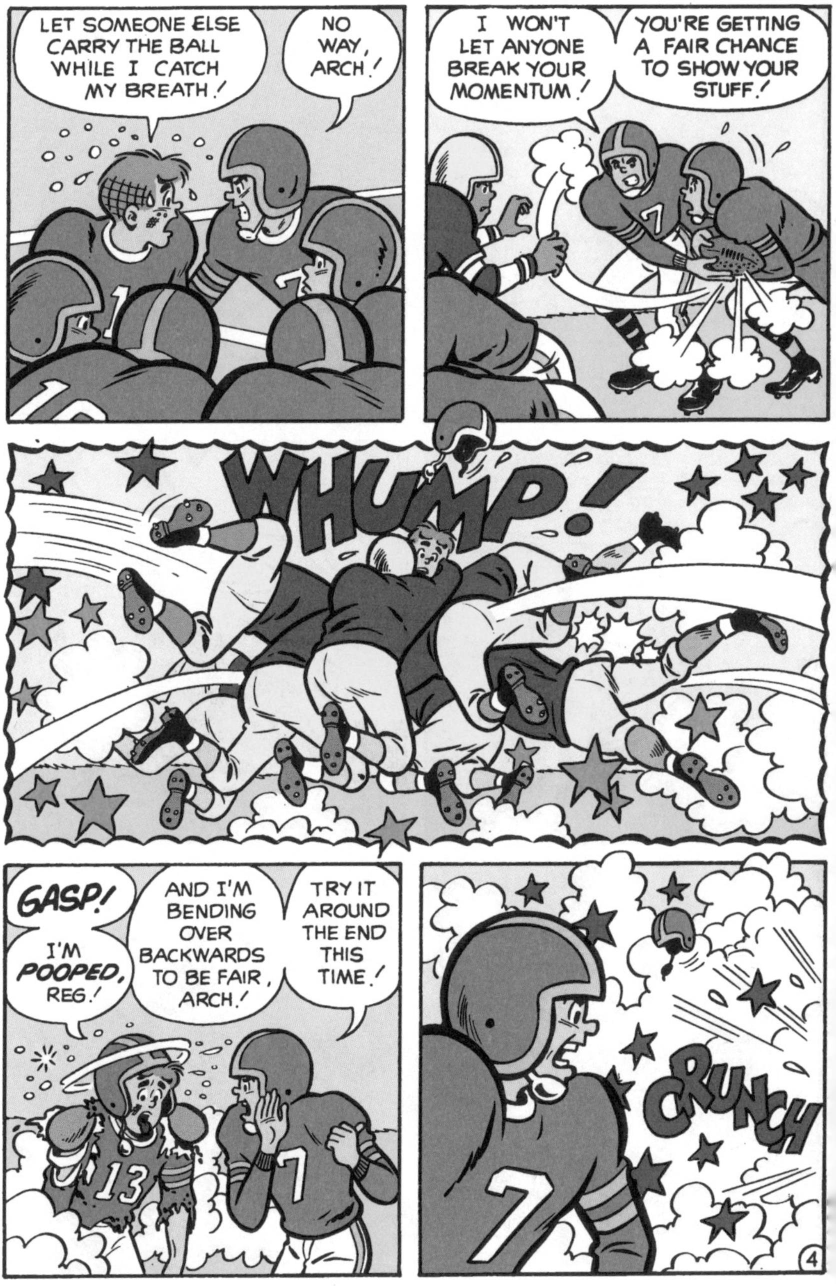
LET SOMEONE ELSE CARRY THE BALL WHILE I CATCH MY BREATH!
NO WAY, ARCH!
I WON'T LET ANYONE BREAK YOUR MOMENTUM!
YOU'RE GETTING A FAIR CHANCE TO SHOW YOUR STUFF!
WHUMP!
GASP!
I'M POOPED, REG.!
AND I'M BENDING OVER BACKWARDS TO BE FAIR, ARCH!
TRY IT AROUND THE END THIS TIME!
CRUNCH
4

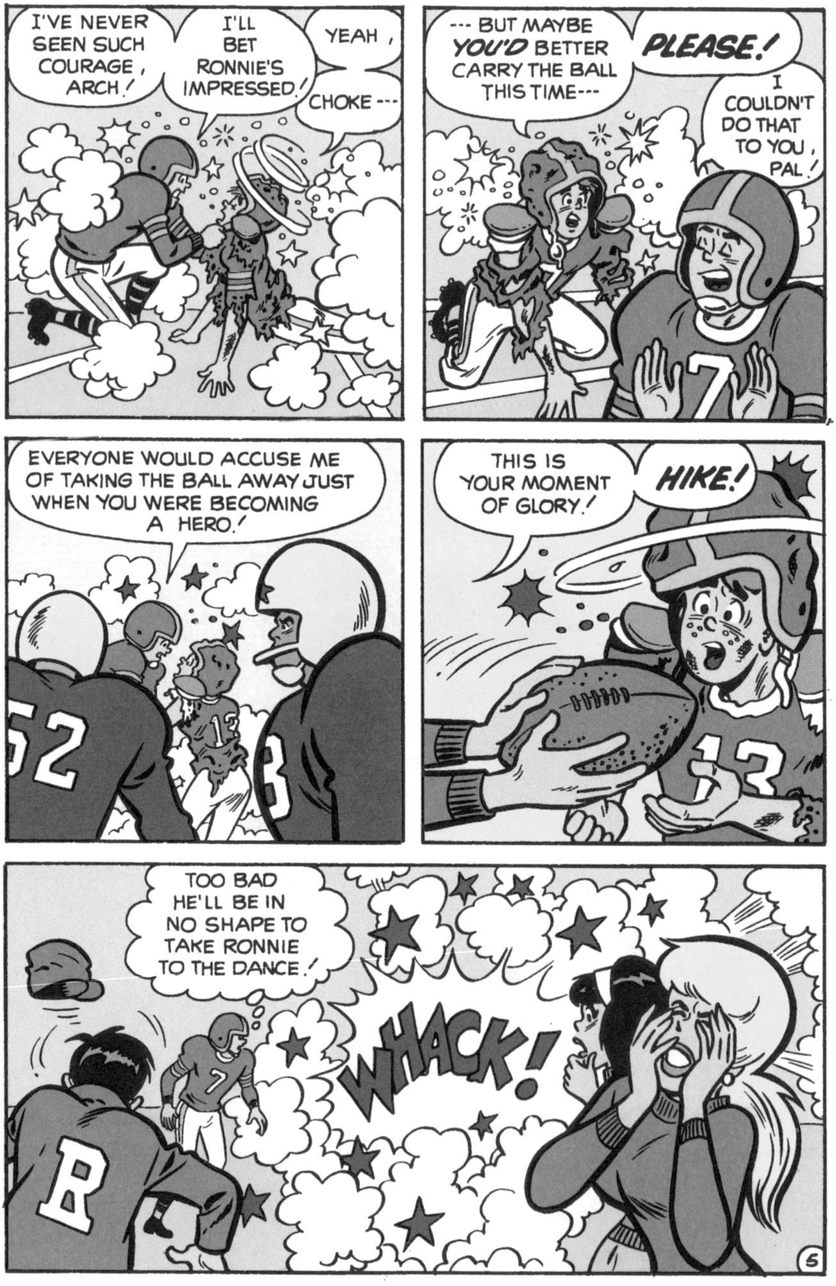
I'VE NEVER SEEN SUCH COURAGE, ARCH!
I'LL BET RONNIE'S IMPRESSED!
YEAH,
CHOKE ---
--- BUT MAYBE YOU'D BETTER CARRY THE BALL THIS TIME---
PLEASE!
I COULDN'T DO THAT TO YOU, PAL!
EVERYONE WOULD ACCUSE ME OF TAKING THE BALL AWAY JUST WHEN YOU WERE BECOMING A HERO!
THIS IS YOUR MOMENT OF GLORY!
HIKE!
TOO BAD HE'LL BE IN NO SHAPE TO TAKE RONNIE TO THE DANCE!
WHACK!
5

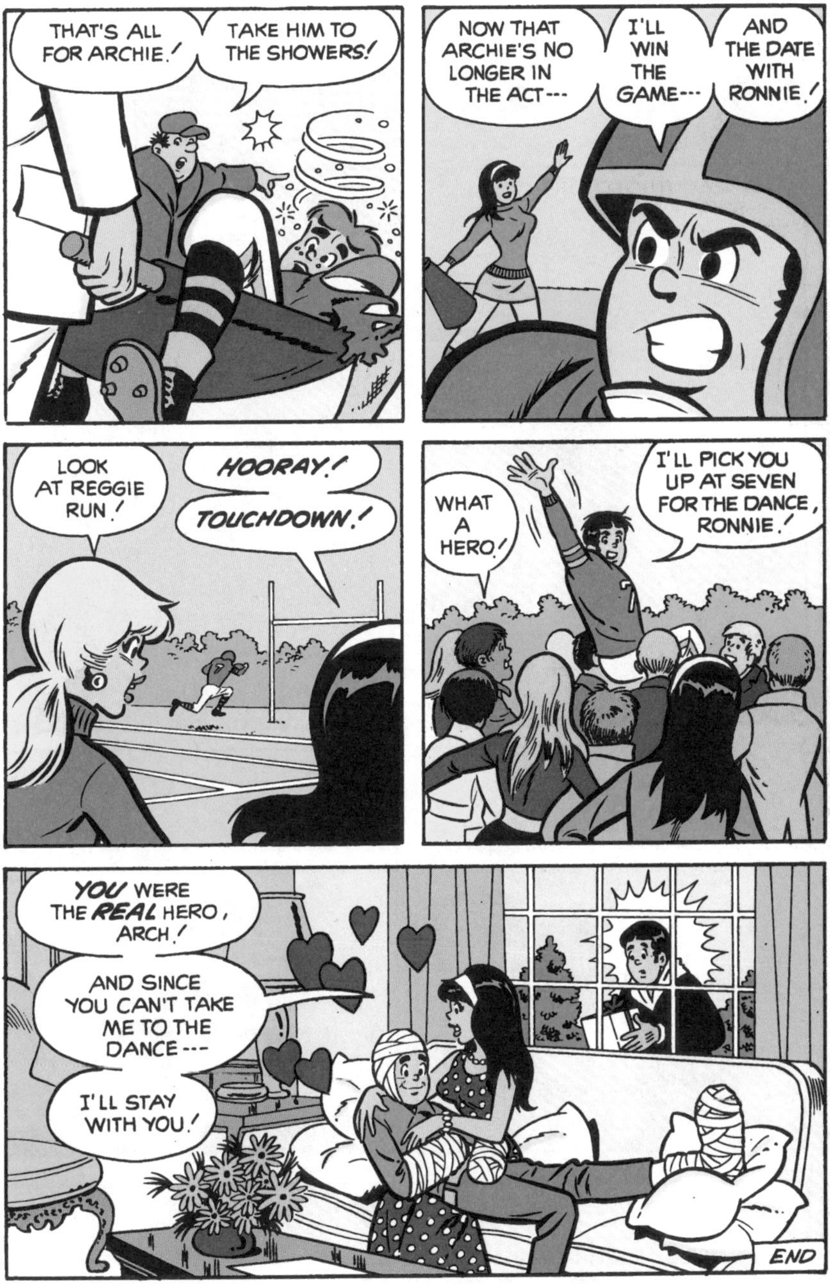
THAT'S ALL FOR ARCHIE.!
TAKE HIM TO THE SHOWERS!
NOW THAT ARCHIE'S NO LONGER IN THE ACT---
I'LL WIN THE GAME---
AND THE DATE WITH RONNIE.!
LOOK AT REGGIE RUN.!
HOORAY.!
TOUCHDOWN.!
WHAT A HERO!
I'LL PICK YOU UP AT SEVEN FOR THE DANCE, RONNIE.!
YOU WERE THE REAL HERO, ARCH.!
AND SINCE YOU CAN'T TAKE ME TO THE DANCE---
I'LL STAY WITH YOU.!
END

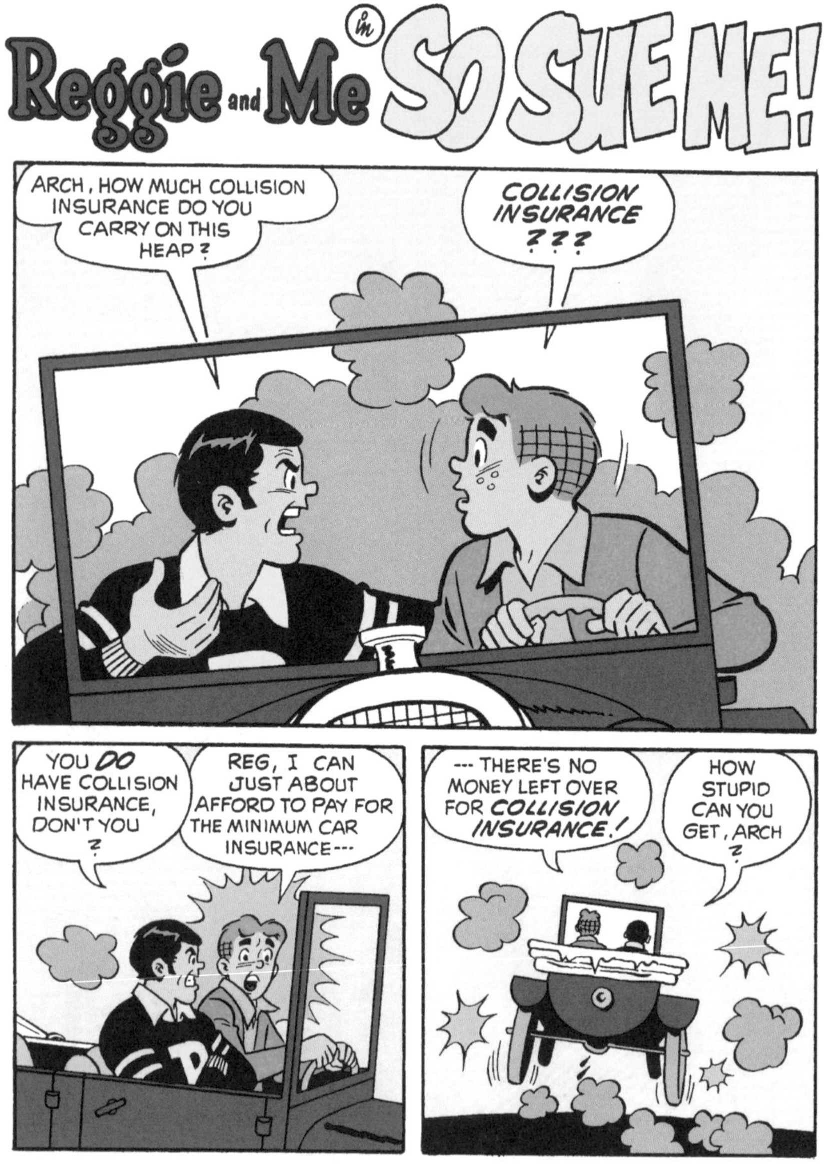
Reggie and Me in
SO SUE ME!
ARCH, HOW MUCH COLLISION INSURANCE DO YOU CARRY ON THIS HEAP?
COLLISION INSURANCE???
YOU DO HAVE COLLISION INSURANCE, DON'T YOU?
REG, I CAN JUST ABOUT AFFORD TO PAY FOR THE MINIMUM CAR INSURANCE---
--- THERE'S NO MONEY LEFT OVER FOR COLLISION INSURANCE!
HOW STUPID CAN YOU GET, ARCH?

Story & Pencils: Al Hartley

Inks: Jon D'Agostino Letters: Bill Yoshida Colors: Barry Grossman

Originally printed in REGGIE AND ME #65, SEPTEMBER 1973

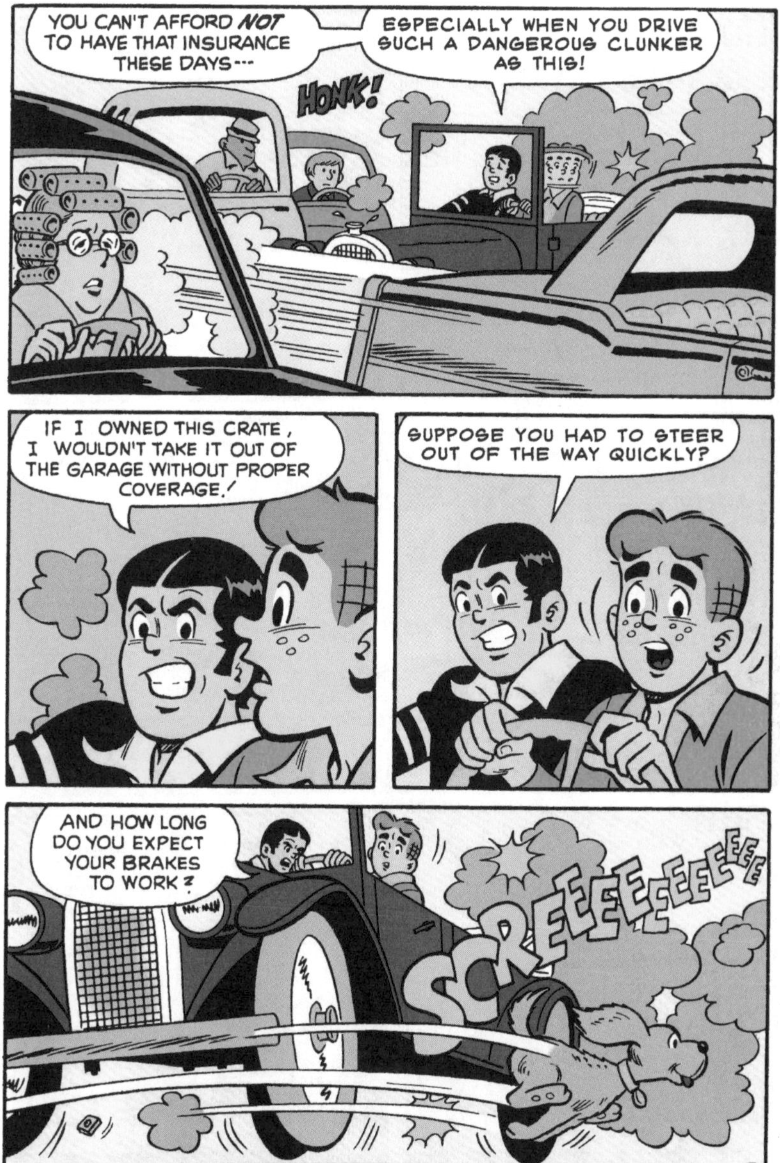
YOU CAN'T AFFORD *NOT* TO HAVE THAT INSURANCE THESE DAYS---
ESPECIALLY WHEN YOU DRIVE SUCH A DANGEROUS CLUNKER AS THIS!
HONK!
IF I OWNED THIS CRATE, I WOULDN'T TAKE IT OUT OF THE GARAGE WITHOUT PROPER COVERAGE!
SUPPOSE YOU HAD TO STEER OUT OF THE WAY QUICKLY?
AND HOW LONG DO YOU EXPECT YOUR BRAKES TO WORK?
SCREEEEEEEEEEE
2

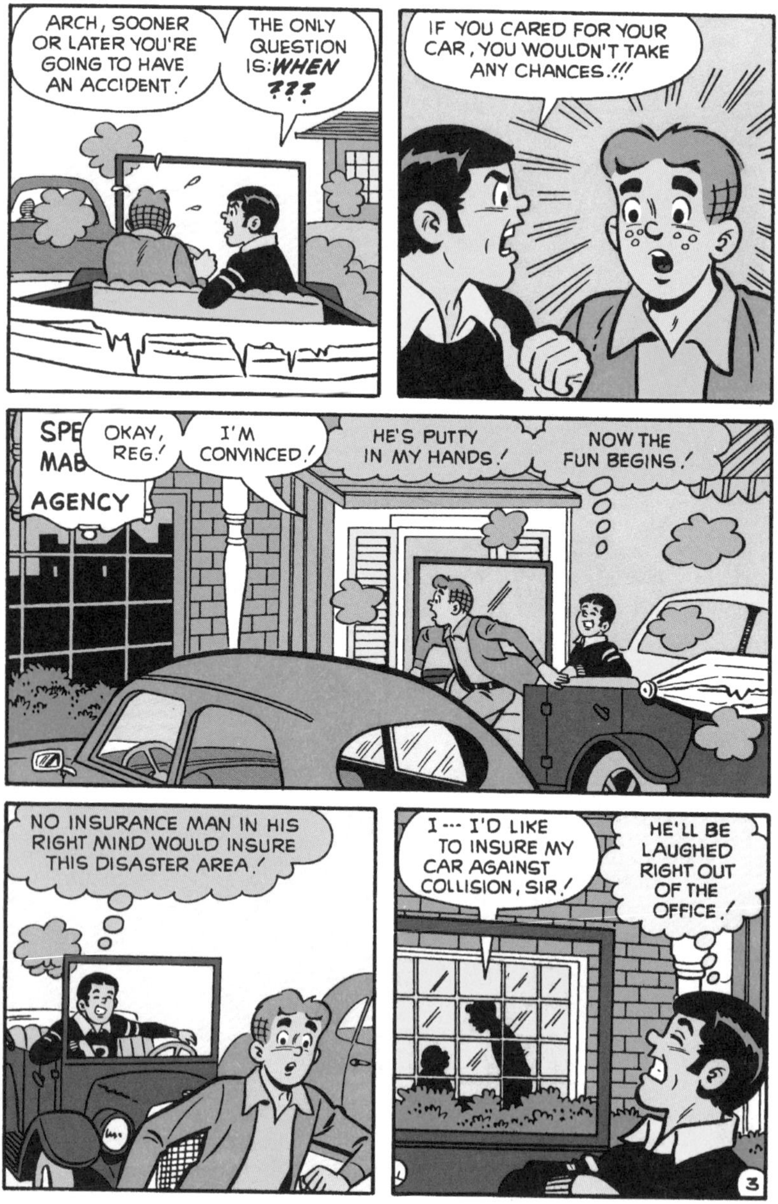
ARCH, SOONER OR LATER YOU'RE GOING TO HAVE AN ACCIDENT!
THE ONLY QUESTION IS: WHEN ???
IF YOU CARED FOR YOUR CAR, YOU WOULDN'T TAKE ANY CHANCES!!!
AGENCY
OKAY, REG.!
I'M CONVINCED!
HE'S PUTTY IN MY HANDS!
NOW THE FUN BEGINS!
NO INSURANCE MAN IN HIS RIGHT MIND WOULD INSURE THIS DISASTER AREA!
I--- I'D LIKE TO INSURE MY CAR AGAINST COLLISION, SIR!
HE'LL BE LAUGHED RIGHT OUT OF THE OFFICE!
3

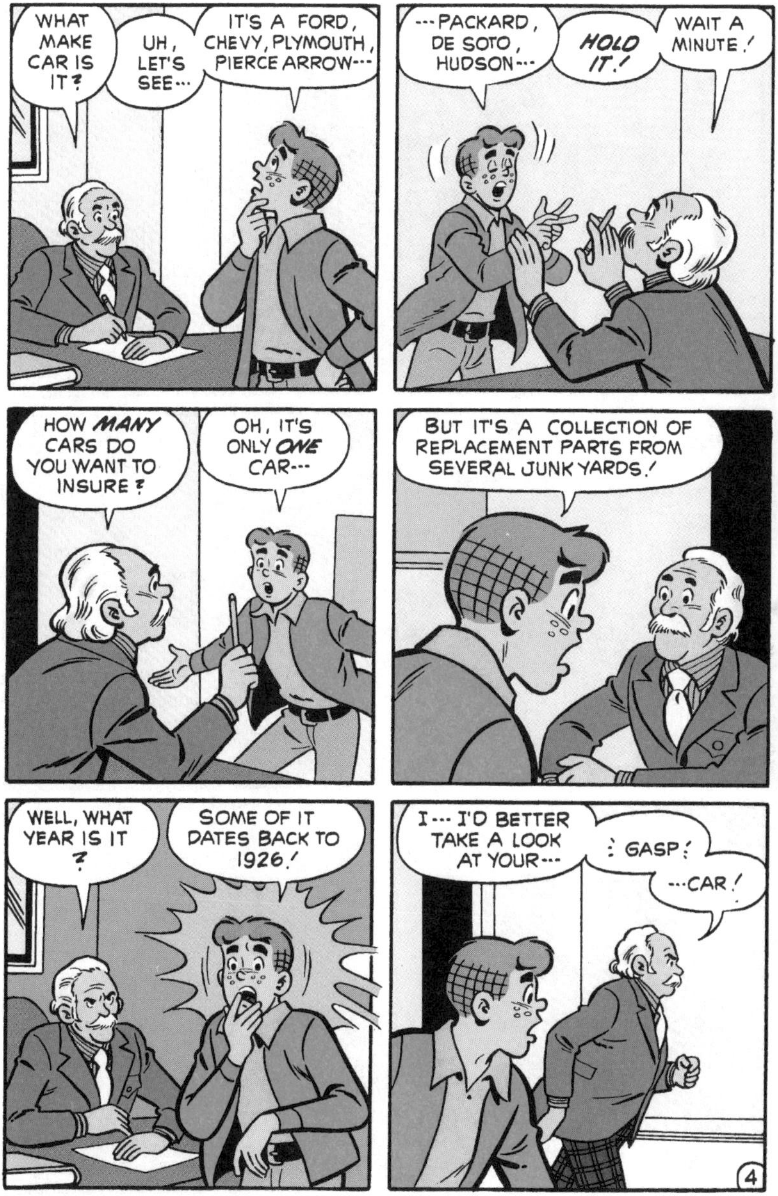
WHAT MAKE CAR IS IT?
UH, LET'S SEE...
IT'S A FORD, CHEVY, PLYMOUTH, PIERCE ARROW...
...PACKARD, DE SOTO, HUDSON...
HOLD IT!
WAIT A MINUTE!
HOW MANY CARS DO YOU WANT TO INSURE?
OH, IT'S ONLY ONE CAR...
BUT IT'S A COLLECTION OF REPLACEMENT PARTS FROM SEVERAL JUNK YARDS!
WELL, WHAT YEAR IS IT?
SOME OF IT DATES BACK TO 1926!
I... I'D BETTER TAKE A LOOK AT YOUR...
GASP!
...CAR!
4

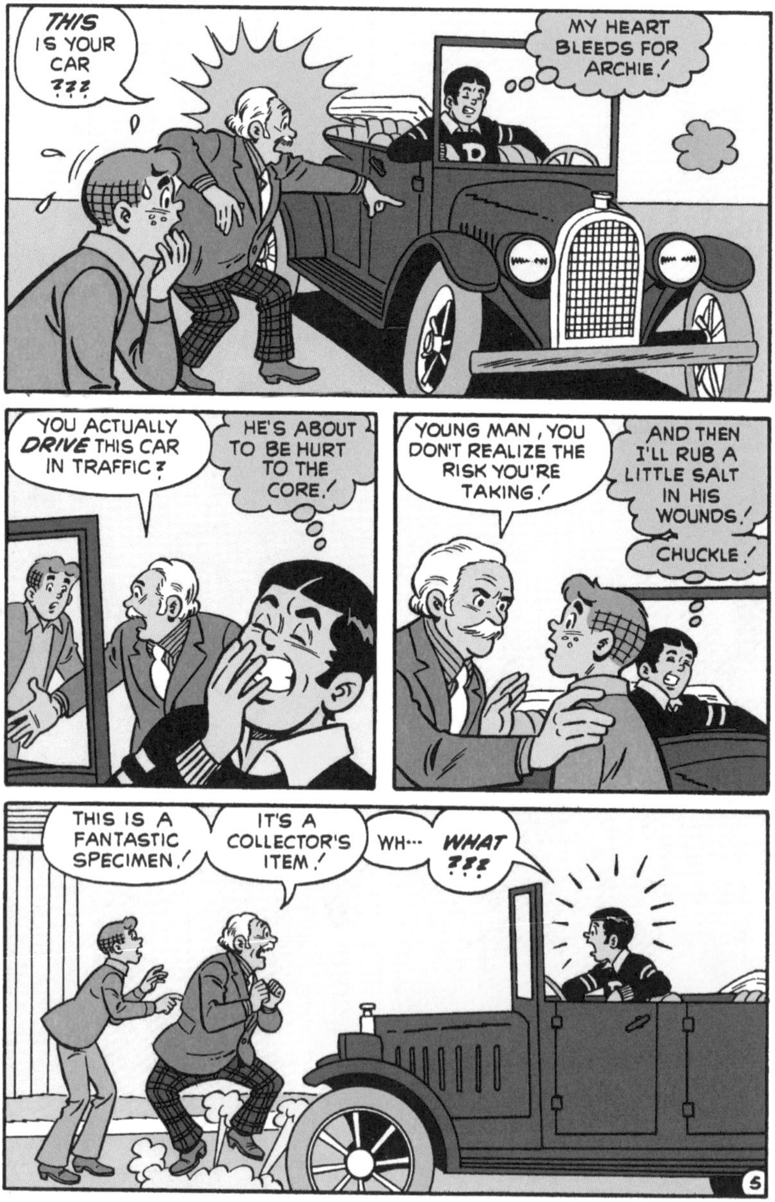
THIS IS YOUR CAR ???
MY HEART BLEEDS FOR ARCHIE!
YOU ACTUALLY DRIVE THIS CAR IN TRAFFIC?
HE'S ABOUT TO BE HURT TO THE CORE!
YOUNG MAN, YOU DON'T REALIZE THE RISK YOU'RE TAKING!
AND THEN I'LL RUB A LITTLE SALT IN HIS WOUNDS!
CHUCKLE!
THIS IS A FANTASTIC SPECIMEN!
IT'S A COLLECTOR'S ITEM!
WH···
WHAT ???
5

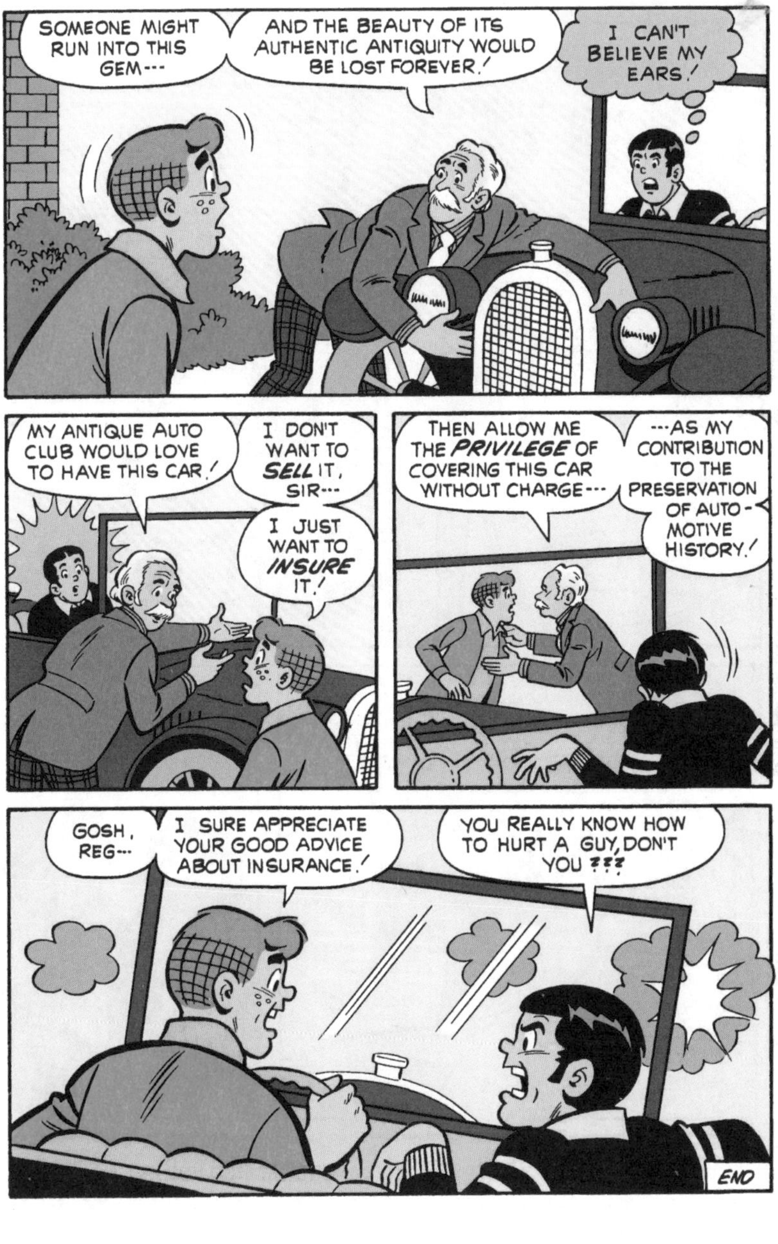

SOMEONE MIGHT RUN INTO THIS GEM---
AND THE BEAUTY OF ITS AUTHENTIC ANTIQUITY WOULD BE LOST FOREVER!
I CAN'T BELIEVE MY EARS!
MY ANTIQUE AUTO CLUB WOULD LOVE TO HAVE THIS CAR!
I DON'T WANT TO SELL IT, SIR---
I JUST WANT TO INSURE IT!
THEN ALLOW ME THE PRIVILEGE OF COVERING THIS CAR WITHOUT CHARGE---
---AS MY CONTRIBUTION TO THE PRESERVATION OF AUTO-MOTIVE HISTORY!
GOSH, REG---
I SURE APPRECIATE YOUR GOOD ADVICE ABOUT INSURANCE!
YOU REALLY KNOW HOW TO HURT A GUY, DON'T YOU ???
END

Reggie & Me in "model muddle"

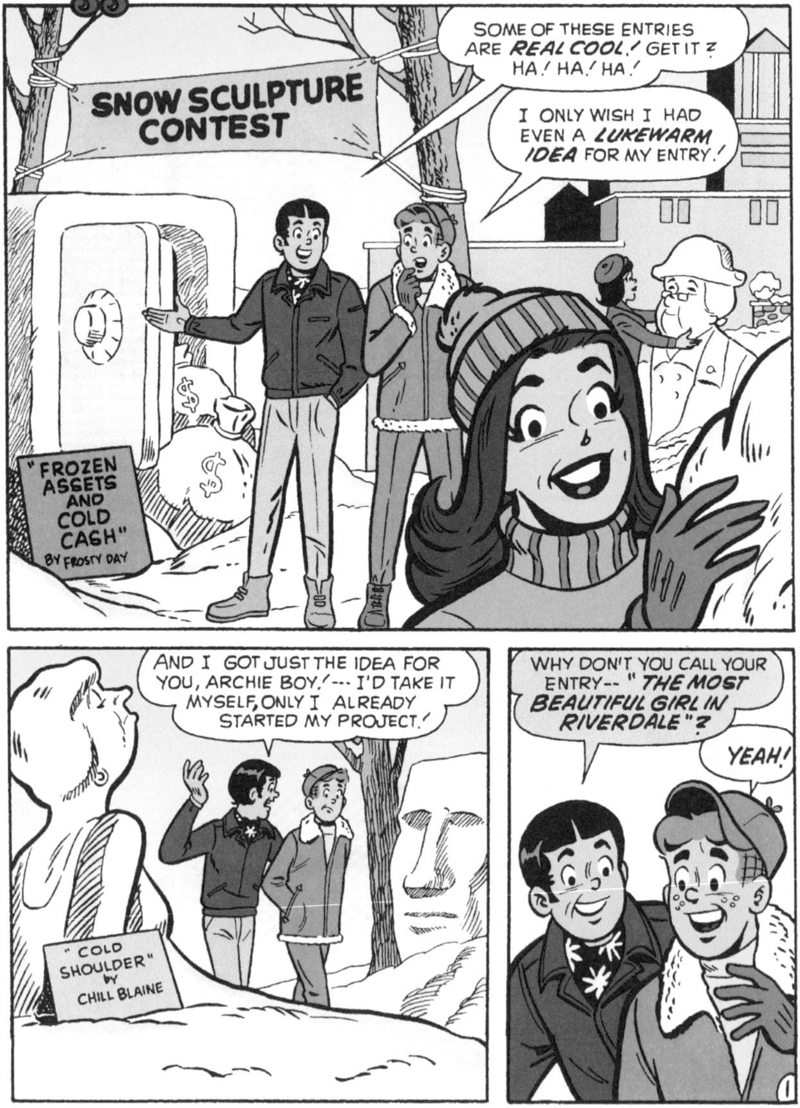
SNOW SCULPTURE CONTEST
SOME OF THESE ENTRIES ARE REAL COOL! GET IT? HA! HA! HA!
I ONLY WISH I HAD EVEN A LUKEWARM IDEA FOR MY ENTRY!
"FROZEN ASSETS AND COLD CASH" BY FROSTY DAY
AND I GOT JUST THE IDEA FOR YOU, ARCHIE BOY! --- I'D TAKE IT MYSELF, ONLY I ALREADY STARTED MY PROJECT!
"COLD SHOULDER" by CHILL BLAINE
WHY DON'T YOU CALL YOUR ENTRY-- "THE MOST BEAUTIFUL GIRL IN RIVERDALE"?
YEAH!
1

Story: George Gladir Pencils: Bob Bolling
Inks: Jon D'Agostino Letters: Bill Yoshida Colors: Barry Grossman

Originally printed in REGGIE AND ME #69, APRIL 1974

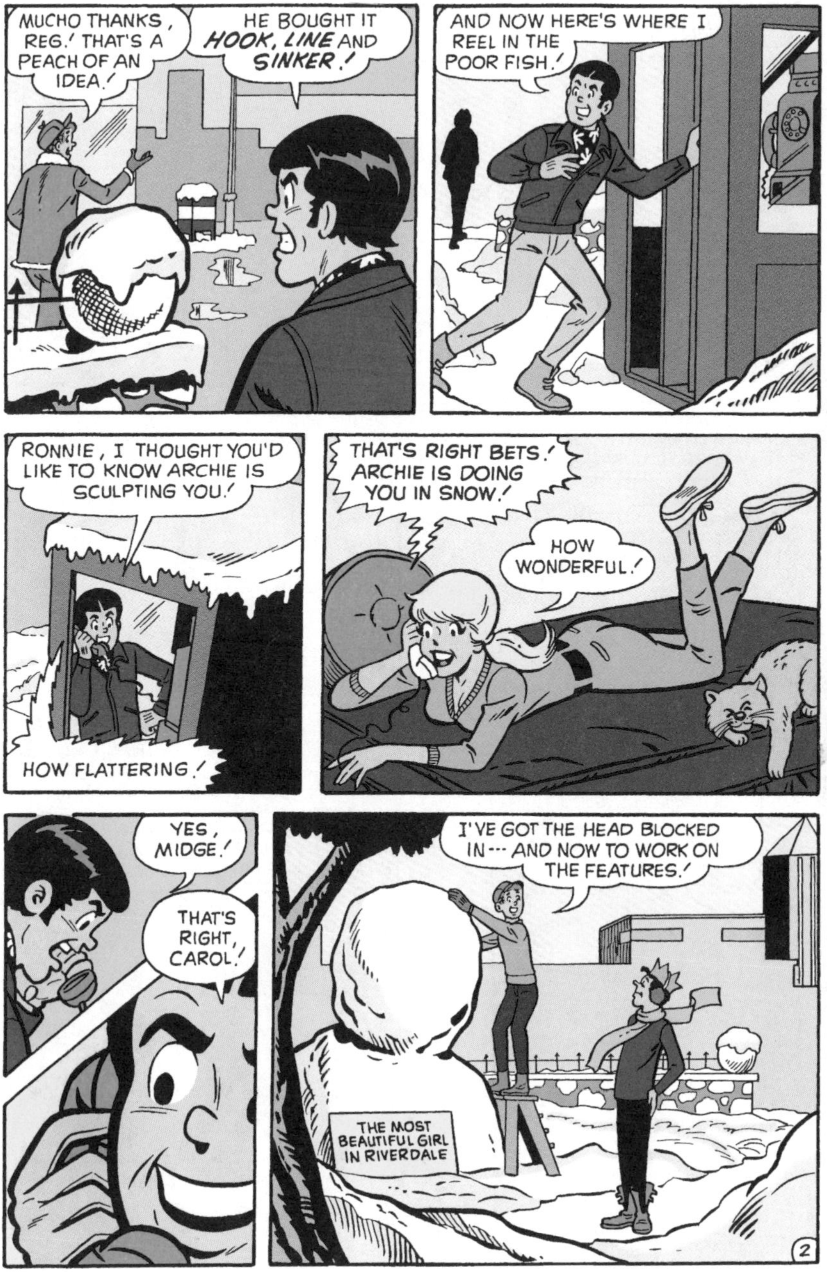
MUCHO THANKS, REG.! THAT'S A PEACH OF AN IDEA.!
HE BOUGHT IT HOOK, LINE AND SINKER.!
AND NOW HERE'S WHERE I REEL IN THE POOR FISH.!
RONNIE, I THOUGHT YOU'D LIKE TO KNOW ARCHIE IS SCULPTING YOU.!
HOW FLATTERING.!
THAT'S RIGHT BETS.! ARCHIE IS DOING YOU IN SNOW.!
HOW WONDERFUL.!
YES, MIDGE.!
THAT'S RIGHT, CAROL.!
I'VE GOT THE HEAD BLOCKED IN --- AND NOW TO WORK ON THE FEATURES.!
THE MOST BEAUTIFUL GIRL IN RIVERDALE
2

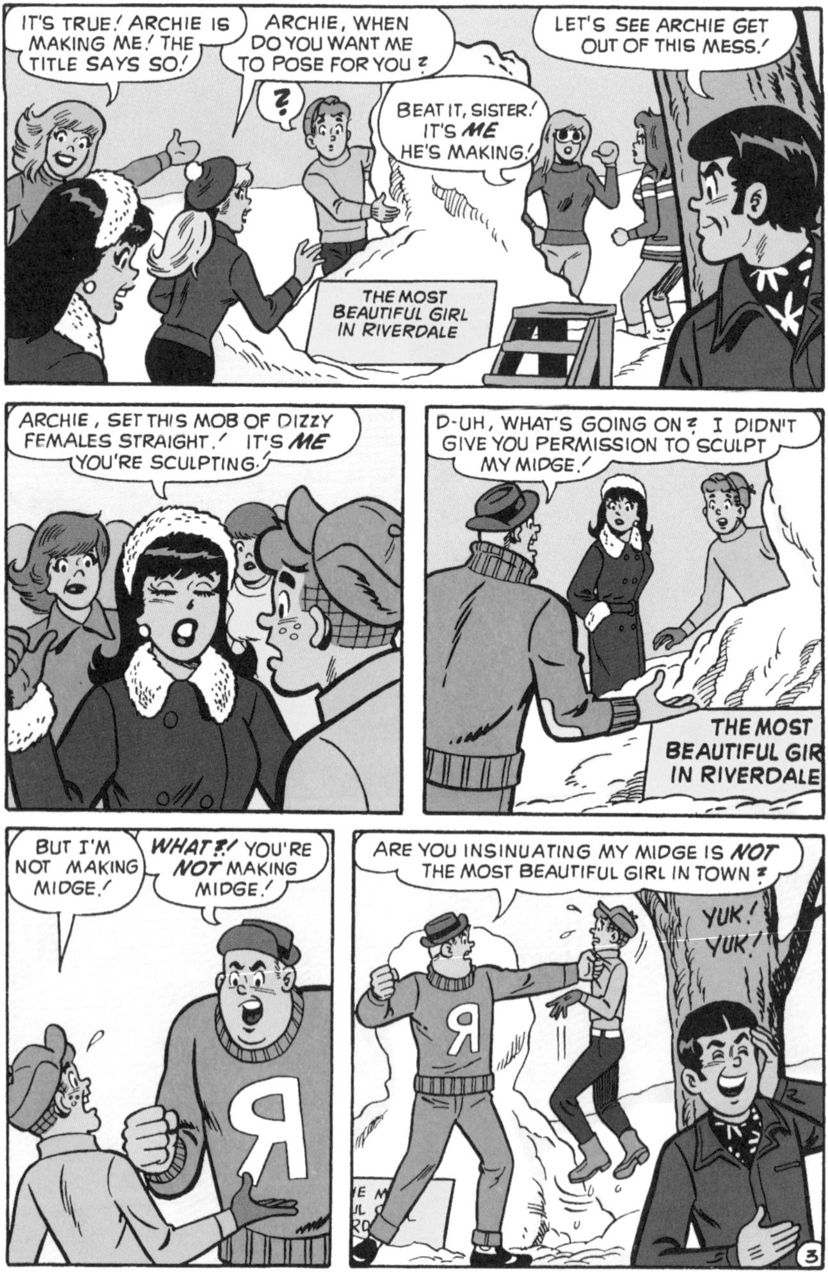
IT'S TRUE! ARCHIE IS MAKING ME! THE TITLE SAYS SO!
ARCHIE, WHEN DO YOU WANT ME TO POSE FOR YOU?
?
BEAT IT, SISTER! IT'S ME HE'S MAKING!
LET'S SEE ARCHIE GET OUT OF THIS MESS!
THE MOST BEAUTIFUL GIRL IN RIVERDALE
ARCHIE, SET THIS MOB OF DIZZY FEMALES STRAIGHT! IT'S ME YOU'RE SCULPTING!
D-UH, WHAT'S GOING ON? I DIDN'T GIVE YOU PERMISSION TO SCULPT MY MIDGE!
THE MOST BEAUTIFUL GIR IN RIVERDALE
BUT I'M NOT MAKING MIDGE!
WHAT?! YOU'RE NOT MAKING MIDGE!
ARE YOU INSINUATING MY MIDGE IS NOT THE MOST BEAUTIFUL GIRL IN TOWN?
YUK! YUK!
3

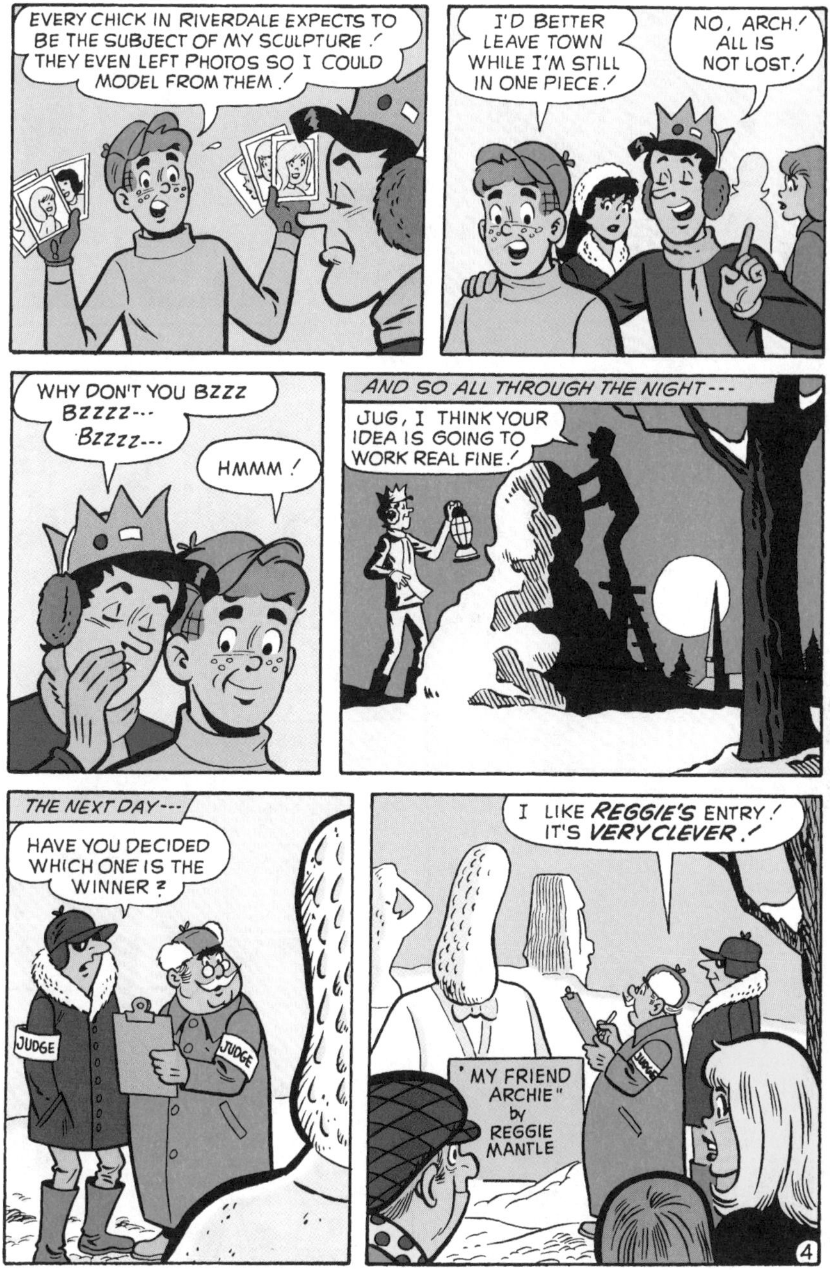
EVERY CHICK IN RIVERDALE EXPECTS TO BE THE SUBJECT OF MY SCULPTURE! THEY EVEN LEFT PHOTOS SO I COULD MODEL FROM THEM!
I'D BETTER LEAVE TOWN WHILE I'M STILL IN ONE PIECE!
NO, ARCH! ALL IS NOT LOST!
WHY DON'T YOU BZZZ BZZZZ--- BZZZZ---
HMMM!
AND SO ALL THROUGH THE NIGHT---
JUG, I THINK YOUR IDEA IS GOING TO WORK REAL FINE!
THE NEXT DAY---
HAVE YOU DECIDED WHICH ONE IS THE WINNER?
JUDGE
JUDGE
I LIKE REGGIE'S ENTRY! IT'S VERY CLEVER!
"MY FRIEND ARCHIE" by REGGIE MANTLE
JUDGE
4

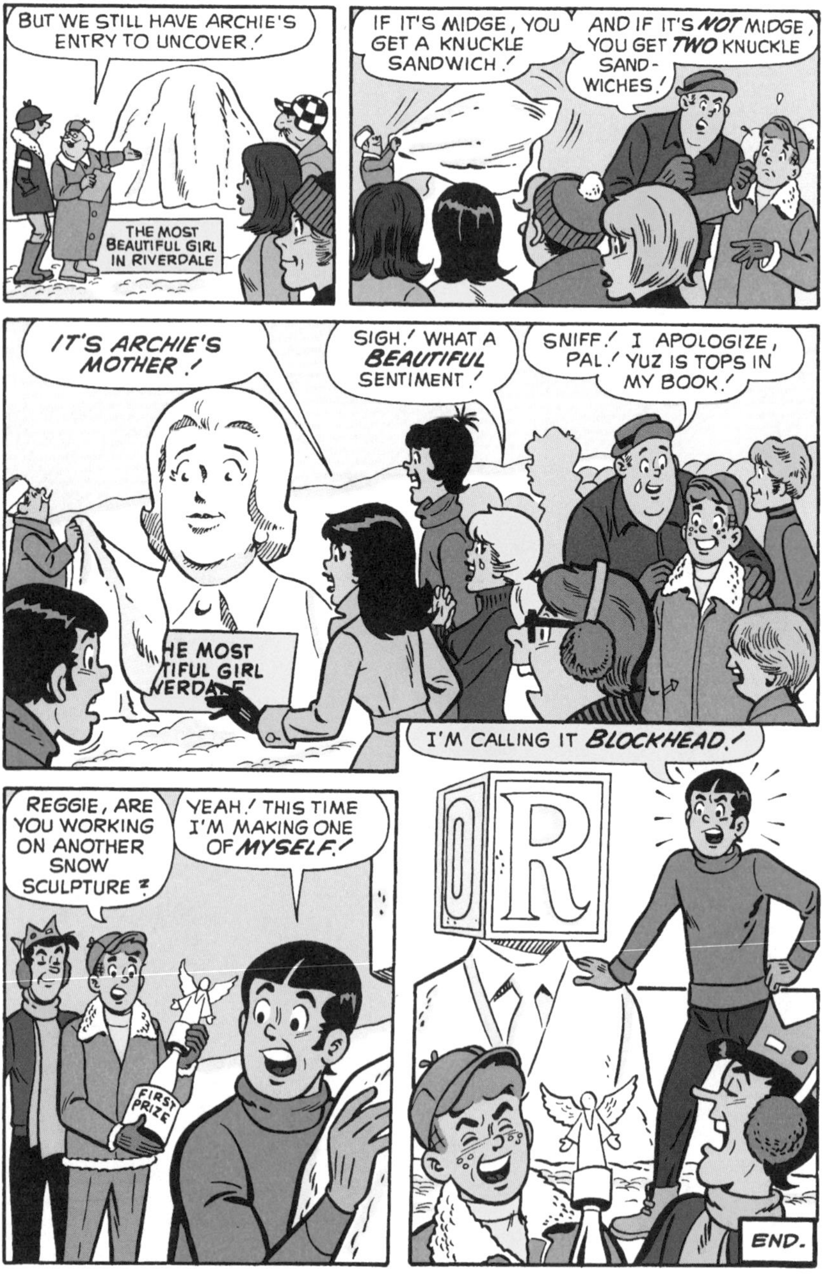
BUT WE STILL HAVE ARCHIE'S ENTRY TO UNCOVER!
THE MOST BEAUTIFUL GIRL IN RIVERDALE
IF IT'S MIDGE, YOU GET A KNUCKLE SANDWICH!
AND IF IT'S NOT MIDGE, YOU GET TWO KNUCKLE SAND-WICHES!
IT'S ARCHIE'S MOTHER!
SIGH! WHAT A BEAUTIFUL SENTIMENT!
SNIFF! I APOLOGIZE, PAL! YUZ IS TOPS IN MY BOOK!
HE MOST TIFUL GIRL VERDALE
REGGIE, ARE YOU WORKING ON ANOTHER SNOW SCULPTURE?
YEAH! THIS TIME I'M MAKING ONE OF MYSELF!
FIRST PRIZE
I'M CALLING IT BLOCKHEAD!
R
END.

Reggie and Me in "The DUDES"

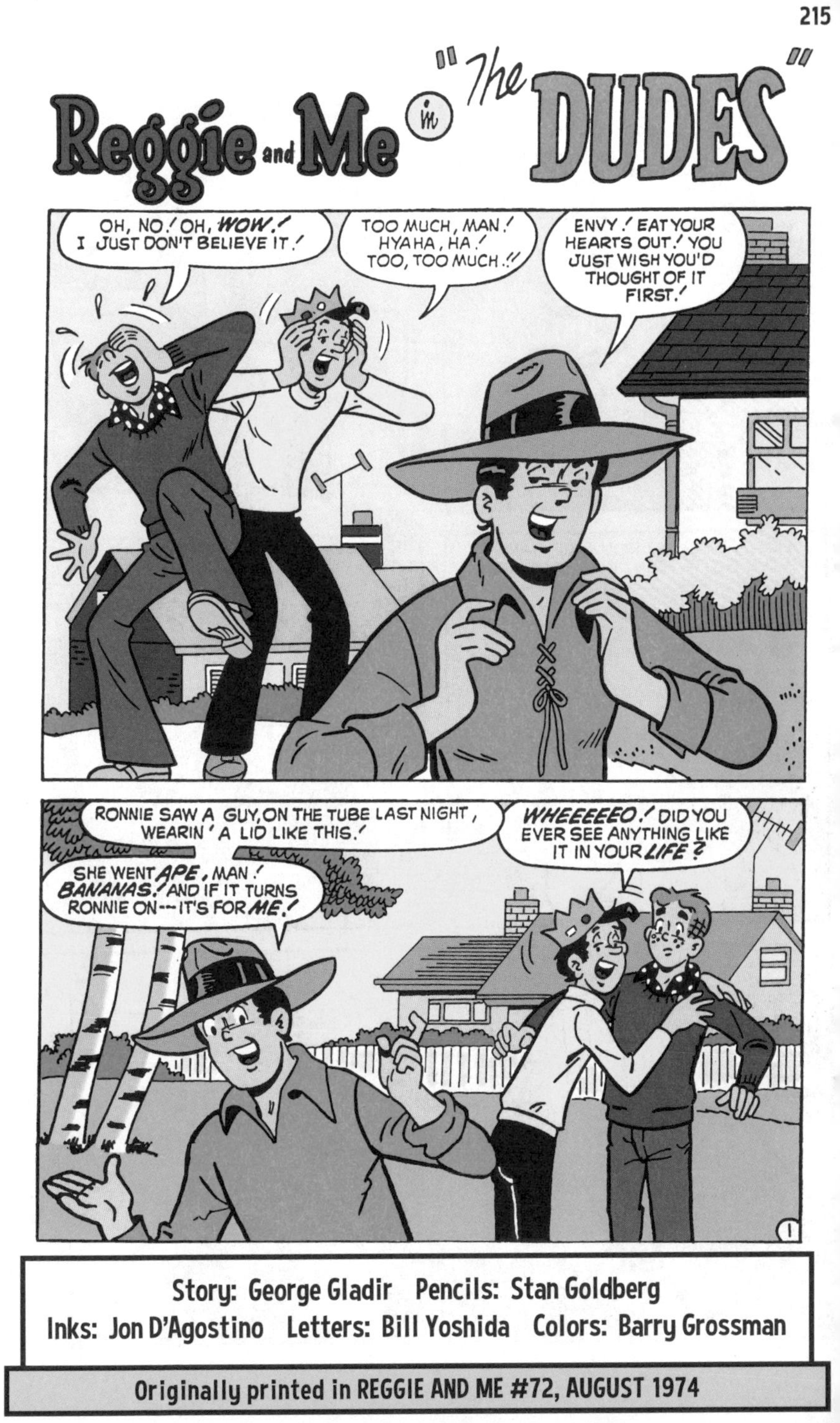
OH, NO! OH, WOW! I JUST DON'T BELIEVE IT!
TOO MUCH, MAN! HYAHA, HA! TOO, TOO MUCH!!
ENVY! EAT YOUR HEARTS OUT! YOU JUST WISH YOU'D THOUGHT OF IT FIRST!
RONNIE SAW A GUY, ON THE TUBE LAST NIGHT, WEARIN' A LID LIKE THIS!
SHE WENT APE, MAN! BANANAS! AND IF IT TURNS RONNIE ON-- IT'S FOR ME!
WHEEEEEEO! DID YOU EVER SEE ANYTHING LIKE IT IN YOUR LIFE?

Story: George Gladir Pencils: Stan Goldberg
Inks: Jon D'Agostino Letters: Bill Yoshida Colors: Barry Grossman

Originally printed in REGGIE AND ME #72, AUGUST 1974

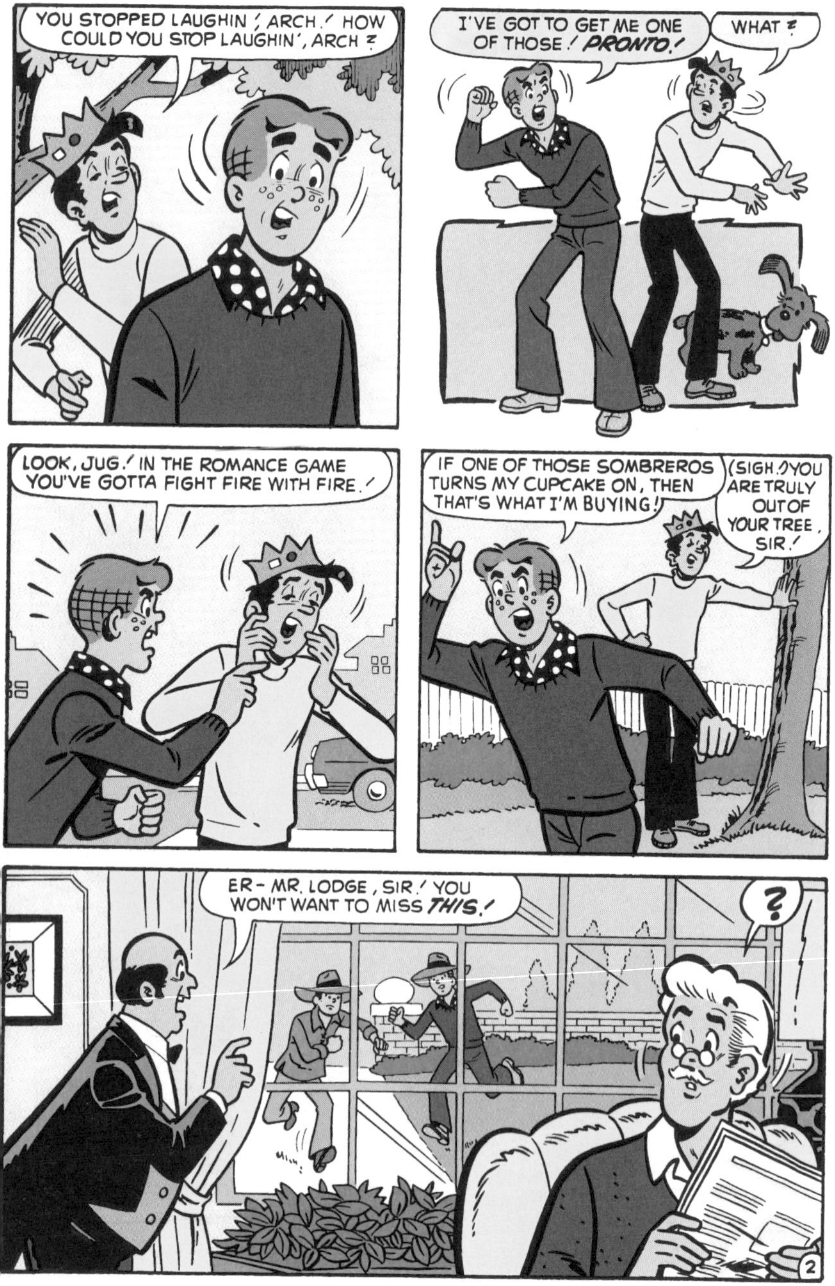

YOU STOPPED LAUGHIN', ARCH.! HOW COULD YOU STOP LAUGHIN', ARCH?
I'VE GOT TO GET ME ONE OF THOSE! PRONTO!
WHAT?
LOOK, JUG.! IN THE ROMANCE GAME YOU'VE GOTTA FIGHT FIRE WITH FIRE.!
IF ONE OF THOSE SOMBREROS TURNS MY CUPCAKE ON, THEN THAT'S WHAT I'M BUYING!
(SIGH.!) YOU ARE TRULY OUT OF YOUR TREE, SIR.!
ER- MR. LODGE, SIR.! YOU WON'T WANT TO MISS THIS.!
?
2

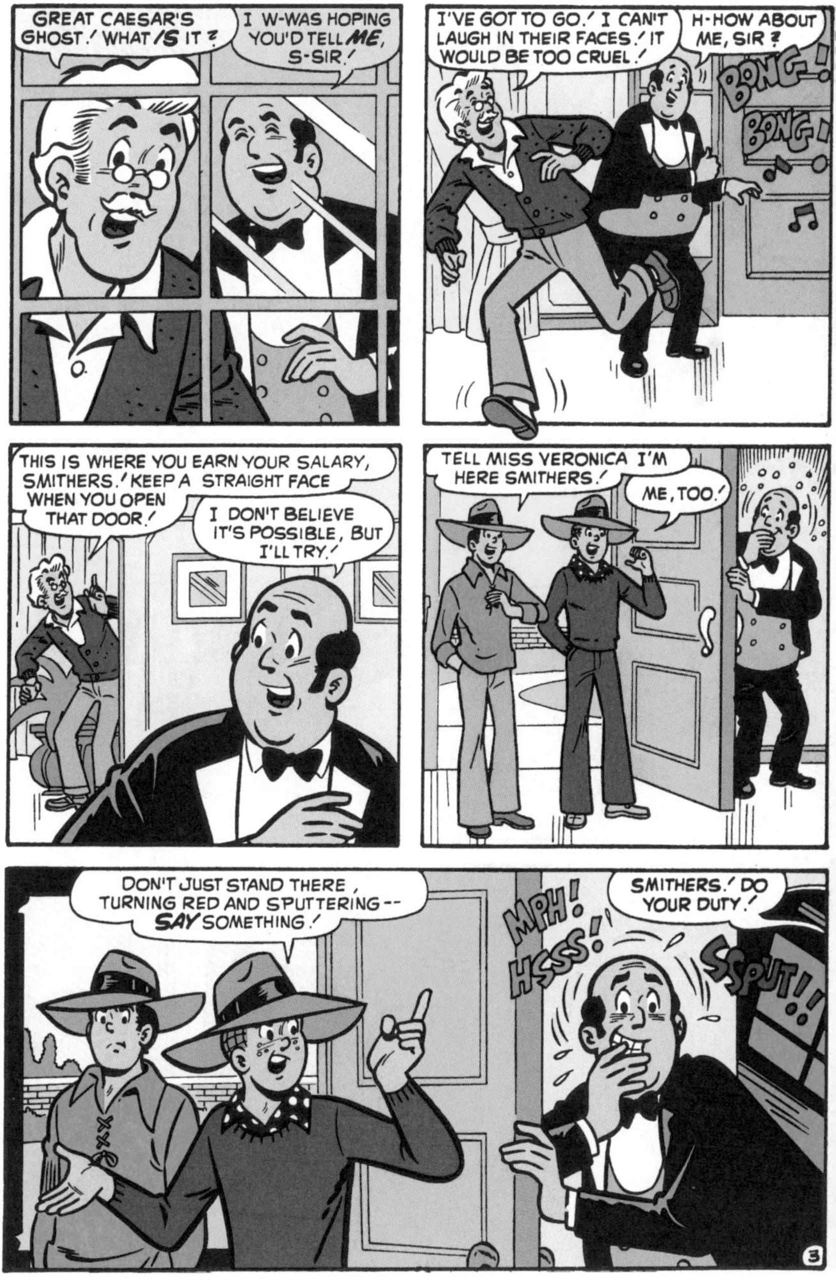
GREAT CAESAR'S GHOST! WHAT IS IT?
I W-WAS HOPING YOU'D TELL ME, S-SIR!
I'VE GOT TO GO! I CAN'T LAUGH IN THEIR FACES! IT WOULD BE TOO CRUEL!
H-HOW ABOUT ME, SIR?
BONG!
BONG!
THIS IS WHERE YOU EARN YOUR SALARY, SMITHERS! KEEP A STRAIGHT FACE WHEN YOU OPEN THAT DOOR!
I DON'T BELIEVE IT'S POSSIBLE, BUT I'LL TRY!
TELL MISS VERONICA I'M HERE SMITHERS!
ME, TOO!
DON'T JUST STAND THERE, TURNING RED AND SPUTTERING -- SAY SOMETHING!
MPH!
HSSS!
SMITHERS! DO YOUR DUTY!
SSPUT!!
3

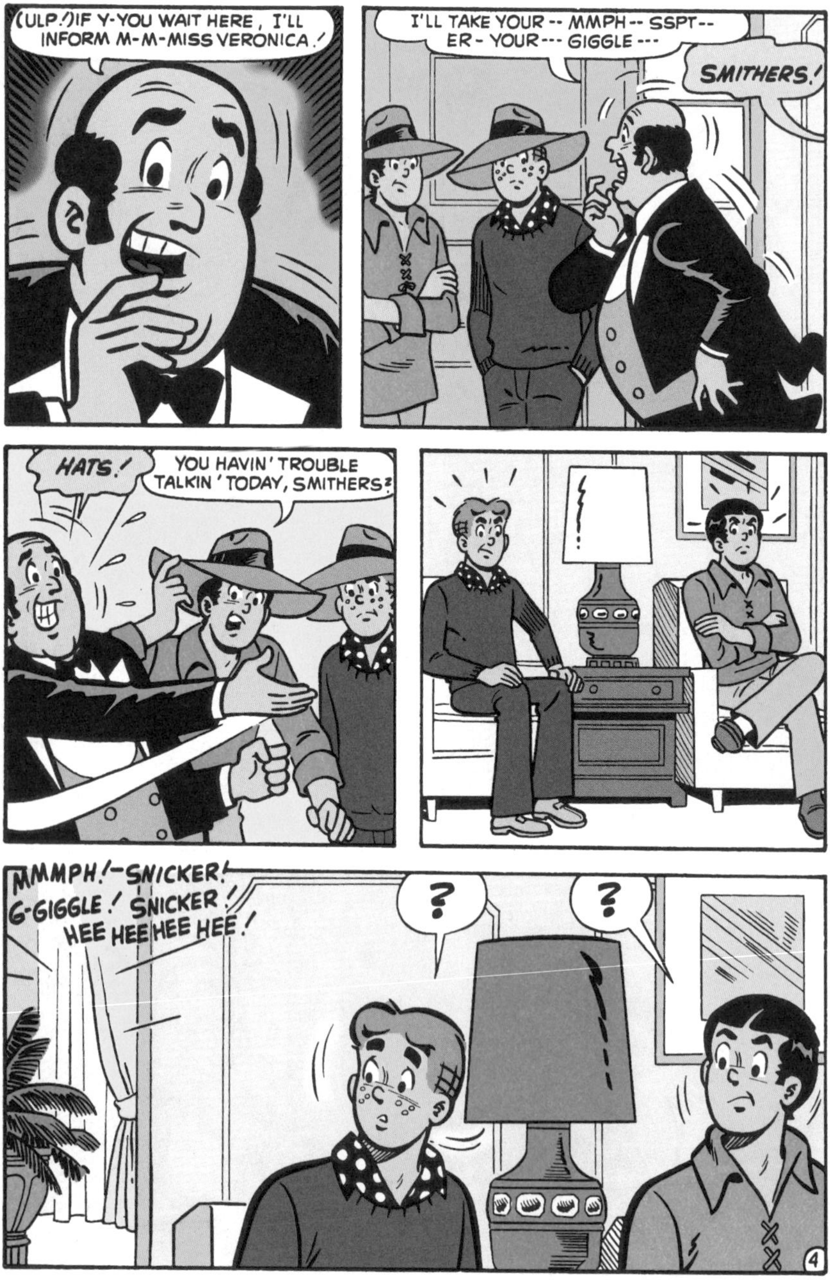
(ULP.!) IF Y-YOU WAIT HERE, I'LL INFORM M-M-MISS VERONICA.!
I'LL TAKE YOUR -- MMPH -- SSPT -- ER - YOUR --- GIGGLE ---
SMITHERS!
HATS!
YOU HAVIN' TROUBLE TALKIN' TODAY, SMITHERS?
MMMPH!-SNICKER! G-GIGGLE! SNICKER! HEE HEE HEE HEE!
?
?
4

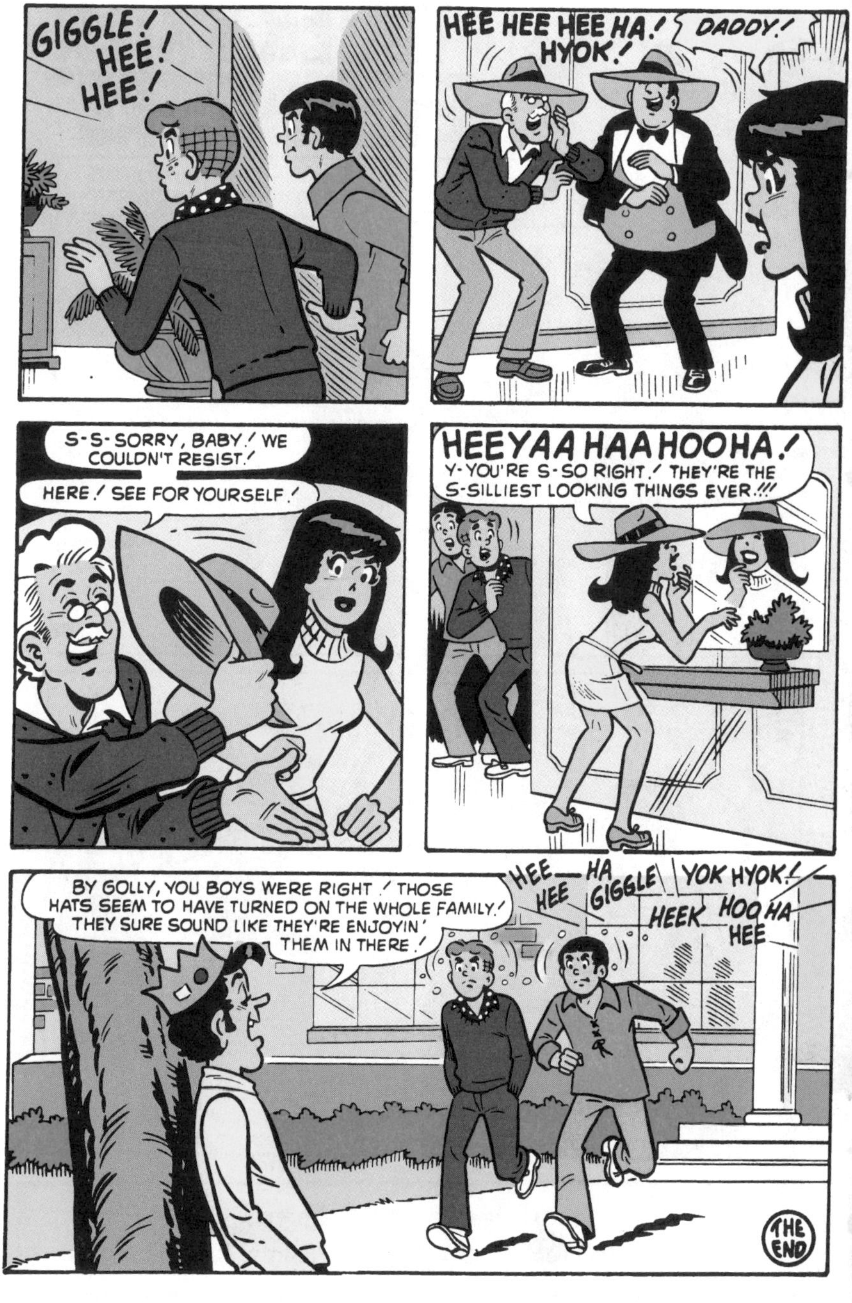
GIGGLE! HEE! HEE!
HEE HEE HEE HA! HYOK!
DADDY!
S-S-SORRY, BABY! WE COULDN'T RESIST!
HERE! SEE FOR YOURSELF!
HEEYAA HAA HOOHA!
Y-YOU'RE S-SO RIGHT! THEY'RE THE S-SILLIEST LOOKING THINGS EVER!!!
BY GOLLY, YOU BOYS WERE RIGHT! THOSE HATS SEEM TO HAVE TURNED ON THE WHOLE FAMILY! THEY SURE SOUND LIKE THEY'RE ENJOYIN' THEM IN THERE!
HEE HA HEE GIGGLE
YOK HYOK!
HEEK HOO HA HEE
THE END

Reggie and Me "WATER WATER EVERYWHERE"

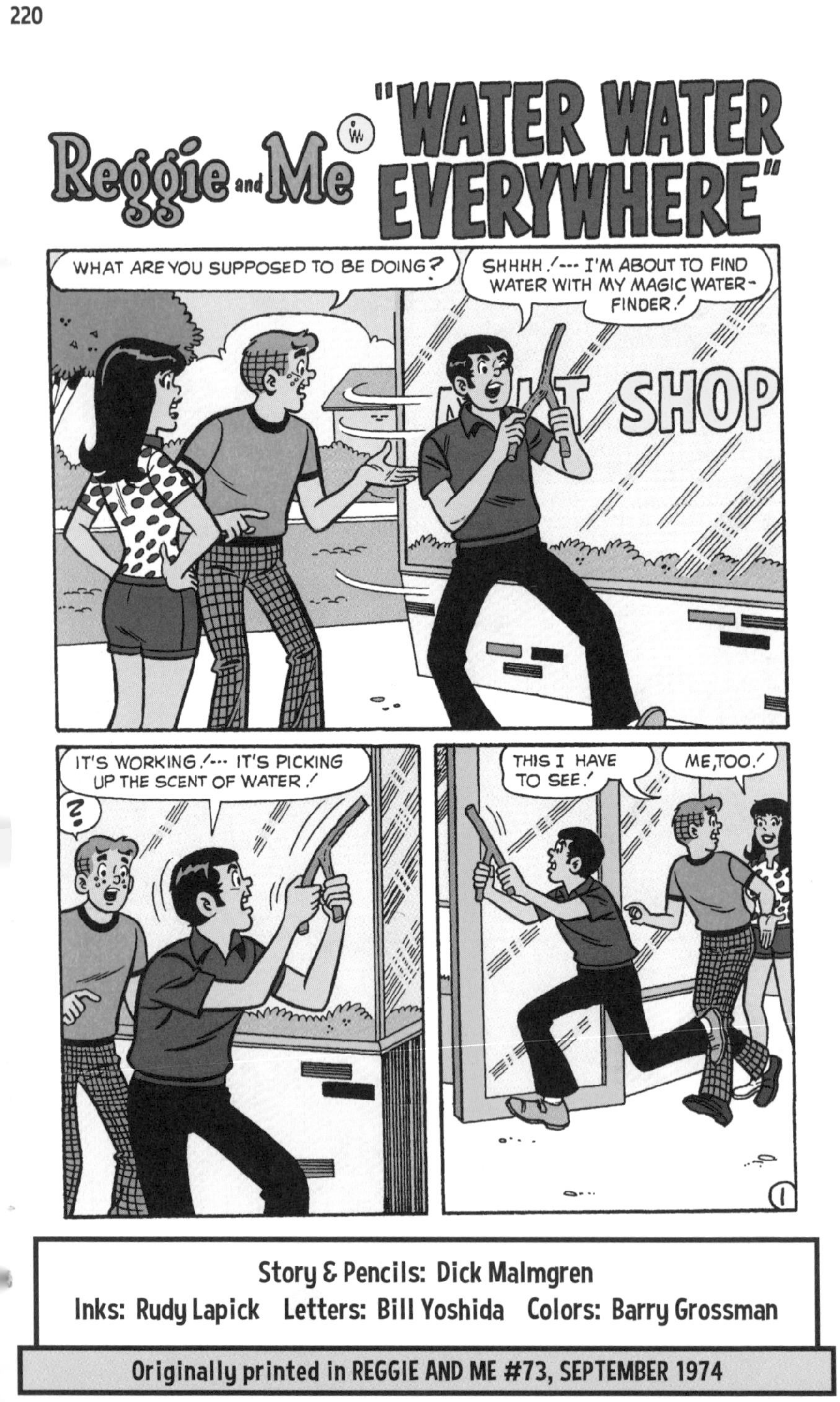
WHAT ARE YOU SUPPOSED TO BE DOING?
SHHHH!--- I'M ABOUT TO FIND WATER WITH MY MAGIC WATER-FINDER!
SHOP
IT'S WORKING!--- IT'S PICKING UP THE SCENT OF WATER!
?
THIS I HAVE TO SEE!
ME, TOO!
1

Story & Pencils: Dick Malmgren
Inks: Rudy Lapick Letters: Bill Yoshida Colors: Barry Grossman

Originally printed in REGGIE AND ME #73, SEPTEMBER 1974

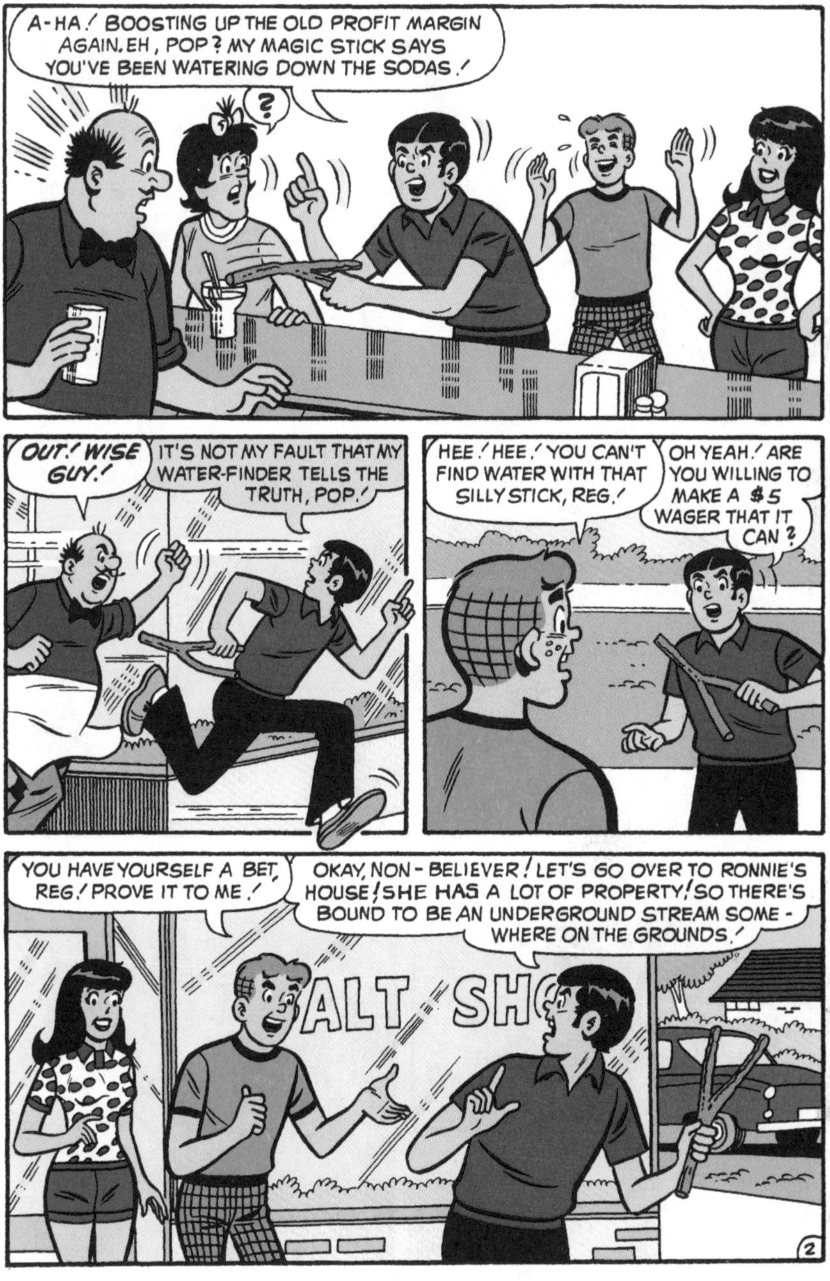
A-HA! BOOSTING UP THE OLD PROFIT MARGIN AGAIN, EH, POP? MY MAGIC STICK SAYS YOU'VE BEEN WATERING DOWN THE SODAS!
?
OUT! WISE GUY!
IT'S NOT MY FAULT THAT MY WATER-FINDER TELLS THE TRUTH, POP!
HEE! HEE! YOU CAN'T FIND WATER WITH THAT SILLY STICK, REG!
OH YEAH! ARE YOU WILLING TO MAKE A $5 WAGER THAT IT CAN?
YOU HAVE YOURSELF A BET, REG! PROVE IT TO ME!
OKAY, NON-BELIEVER! LET'S GO OVER TO RONNIE'S HOUSE! SHE HAS A LOT OF PROPERTY! SO THERE'S BOUND TO BE AN UNDERGROUND STREAM SOMEWHERE ON THE GROUNDS!
ALT SH
2

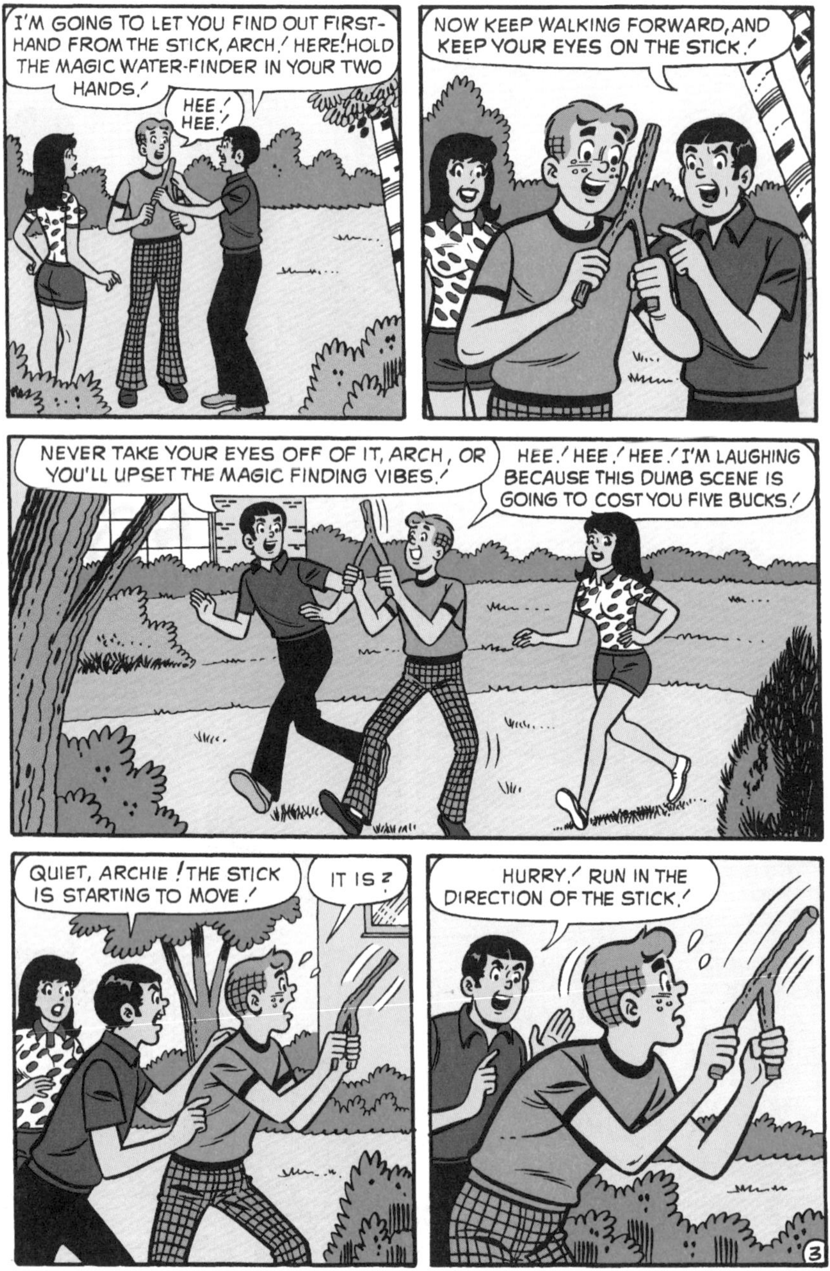

I'M GOING TO LET YOU FIND OUT FIRST-HAND FROM THE STICK, ARCH! HERE! HOLD THE MAGIC WATER-FINDER IN YOUR TWO HANDS!
HEE! HEE!
NOW KEEP WALKING FORWARD, AND KEEP YOUR EYES ON THE STICK!
NEVER TAKE YOUR EYES OFF OF IT, ARCH, OR YOU'LL UPSET THE MAGIC FINDING VIBES!
HEE! HEE! HEE! I'M LAUGHING BECAUSE THIS DUMB SCENE IS GOING TO COST YOU FIVE BUCKS!
QUIET, ARCHIE! THE STICK IS STARTING TO MOVE!
IT IS?
HURRY! RUN IN THE DIRECTION OF THE STICK!
3